POWER PLAY

SILICON BILLIONAIRES

ALEXIS KNIGHTLY

Power Play

Editor: Mackenzie at Nice Girl, Naughty Edits

Proofreaders: Catherine P., Jasmine Jauregui

Cover Designer: Ashley at Book Cover Couture

Photographer: Wander Aguiar

Model: Cooper

To Mom,

For showing me there's never a wrong time to start a business.

CONTENT WARNINGS

This book contains a possessive and very morally grey hero, sexually explicit content, profanity, and topics that may be sensitive to some readers.

Including but not limited to…

Hacking
Spying
Digital Voyeurism

Please read at your own discretion.

For a larger and more specific list of content warnings, please visit:
alexisknightly.com/content-warnings

The Playlist

RUNRUNRUN - Dutch Melrose

Glitch In Matrix - Pesukone

Lethal Woman - Dove Cameron

Worship - Ari Abdul

Make Me Feel - Elvis Drew

DO IT - Beneld, BURY

Crazy in Love - Sofia Karlberg

One of the Girls - The Weeknd

Twisted - Two Feet

Seven Devils - Florence + The Machine

Toxic - Sofia Karlberg

Karma - Taylor Swift

PROLOGUE

8 MONTHS AGO

I make it a habit not to hack the innocent.

But with her, I can't stop myself.

Driving back again, she impales herself onto the pink dildo suctioned to the shower's glass. Her phone lies on the counter where it always is—at a convenient angle next to the mirror facing the shower, granting me a full view of the delicious scene. Even over the thrashing of water, the mic picks up every one of her lustful moans.

As she sways forward ever-so slowly, her pussy lips grip along the shaft, until the tip kisses her entrance.

Fucking hell...

I mimic the motion along my cock, veins flaring atop my muscled, tatted forearm, imagining she's wrapped around my skin instead of my hand. With eyes glued to the monitor in front of me, nothing could break my trance as she slams back once more. Nearby, the shower door rattles on its hinges, doing little to drown out her desperate cry. Then she slows her movements again, pulling out, inch-by-inch, teasing herself.

Gritting my teeth, I loosen up some pressure, slowing my pace. *She's such an insatiable little thing...*

My obsession with Lauren started out as simple curiosity, hungering to know her before our paths are destined to cross. And while I realized it may be unfair when our time comes—as she's unaware of my existence—I'll know *everything* there is to know about her.

Initially, I was interested in her routine. Who she hung out with, her mannerisms, habits, and personality. That kind of stuff. Until my curiosity grew into something more, something I couldn't hold the reins on.

The line between interest and obsession was first crossed the night I hacked into this exact predicament by chance. Catching the rising steam and spouts of water, I immediately went to kill the established connection, until I heard her inviting sounds, which were music to my ears.

And from then on...

I've been hooked.

Because this type-A, rich, smart-mouthed, preppy girl has quite the appetite, one that tells me her play toys aren't enough to tame. So, I've taken a personal vow to learn her every tick, her every kink, even gone as far as hacking her porn accounts, only to fulfill her fantasies.

To hear *my name* on her lips.

Abandoning the dildo, soapy suds ooze from her loofah, traveling sinfully slow down the length of her arms... between the grooves of her breasts... across her belly, and... between her thighs. Water cascades from the showerhead onto her tight body like scorching rain, and steam rises along her wet auburn locks as she grinds her clit against the sponge.

Fuck, yes... I thrust into my fist. *Show me how needy you get.*

Picking up speed, she scrapes the loofah across her sex, back and forth, angling a parted mouth to the sky. In a mere minute, I spot her legs quiver, signaling her climax is near—but she never stops there. Her free hand clasps against the marbled wall as she bends herself over again and aligns up to the dildo, offering a mouthwatering view of her soapy pussy.

For a fleeting moment, before she makes her move, I imagine all the heinous acts I would inflict upon every one of her tight holes, if only I were in that bathroom...

A vivid scene unfolds in my mind, one where I lose control, taking her against the glass from behind. My name is on her lips, but it's not enough. *It's never enough,* not until her throat is raw and pussy is spent. Because that's how she needs it. Only then would she know what it truly means to be filled to the brim, to be so full she'll never want to come back up for air.

She impales herself once more, yanking me from my dream. And this time, she doesn't tease or slow, but rides the silicone with full force, ass cheeks clapping and imprinting circular, wet suds against the foggy glass.

With a groan, I match her savage speed, using all my mental strength to wait for her arrival. I study the steam thickening around her body, painting a hazy silhouette through the glass. Panting in a wild craze, when her cries move up a subtle octave, I know she's there.

Anticipation coils around me like a fiery band, rotating my grip as I pump harder, preparing to come with her. Then her head flies back, a sound emanating from her that can only be described as pure, heavenly ecstasy. Unrelenting, she drives hard against the glass, riding out the waves of euphoria.

When her movements slow, I keep my fist tight around my cock, not allowing myself to retreat while she's still mounted. I shadow her movements across my now sensitive shaft, even as she rocks back and forth at a leisurely tempo. All the while, a single thought burns its way through the center of my consciousness.

Lauren Astor is mine.

~

By midday, I admire her at work through the camera of her desktop. Her fiery hair loops into an intricate low bun, as she buries her head amongst the thick law textbooks sprawled open on her desk.

Behind her, I recognize the skyscraper shining through the window as one of the beacons on Silicon Avenue—Astor Security. Although, I wouldn't need that little fact to know exactly what firm she works at, what type of law she specializes in, among many other details regarding the youngest of the prominent Astor family.

She's such an intriguing creature, with all the characteristics of an undeniable spitfire—driven and intelligent, headstrong and confident. Yet... *damaged,* in a subtle way that's captivating, but a complete mystery to me. Maybe it's because the answers she doesn't know she should look for are right under her nose, weaved in the shadows of the monumental trial she's spearheading.

Too bad she'll never find them.

Or maybe that's not the reason. One way or another, I'll extract the source of the glimmering sadness and anger in her otherwise sharp gaze, as it's my sole intention to understand her on a deeper level.

And what's wrong with that?

No secrets should exist between a man and his cunning bride-to-be.

ONE

LAUREN

"MISS ASTOR—*MISS Astor!* Has there been any communication between you and your uncle?"

Cameras flash around me like a flurry of snow as news media personnel shoulder one another, fighting for the better shot. The butt-end of a microphone shoots closer than the others, nearly smudging my lipstick.

I keep a languid pace through the courthouse, the aggressive hollering of questions drowning out the clacking of my Prada pumps. But it's quite hard to focus on the reporters, when the only thing running a feedback loop in my head is the judge's final words—solidifying my team's victory.

In the matter of New York v. Bass Mobile, the court orders the defendants to pay a sum of one-point-five billion in restitution.

"Of course not." Swinging a left, the exit doors come into sight over the tops of their heads, where there are, without a doubt, even more news anchors waiting out on the streets. "That would be a conflict of interest."

And that's not a lie. I don't know who got it in the public's minds that all lawyers do is lie. But I don't. At least, not in court. *Especially* not while representing the prosecution of the state of New York against none-other-than my own uncle, Oscar Bass, executive owner and founder of Bass Mobile.

Normally, a private firm lawyer like me would never represent the state, certainly not with familial ties to the opposing side, but they needed me. It's no mystery why the state chose me, a junior partner at Astor Associates, to join the team—aside from my flawless track record, specialization in data privacy, and litigation portfolio that would make a senior partner think twice about going toe-to-toe with me in a courtroom.

The state wanted publicity. Tabloids, national headlines, to have as many eyes as possible on this trial. *And that's exactly what they got.*

"What about the final verdict? Do you think it was fair?" another asks. "Never in history has New York imposed a restitution so high."

One-point-five billion. I soak the number in one last time, before descending the marbled stairs. When I'm halfway down, I catch the buzzing mob of people out on the streets, waiting to ambush me as soon as I exit the double doors.

"It was more than fair. Judge Palmer acted in the best interest of the state," I say, reaching the bottom step as both doors swing open by security on the other side. When my heels make contact with the sidewalk, I'm barraged by the bright summer sun and hundreds of camera flashes. "Although high, the restitution will serve as a deterrent for future misconduct and compensate those who fell victim to Bass Mobile's prying eyes."

Plunging my hand into my Birkin, I aim for the cars parked along the sidewalk, while the media swarms like schools of fish hugging the underbelly of a Great White. Sensing my departure, their questions grow in urgency.

No need to rush...

I slow my pace, a grin forming along my lips. This *is* the greatest achievement of my career, and I've never been one who shies away from the spotlight. In fact, I thrive in it, which is why I almost never advise my clients to settle before going to court. Because I'm *that* good—not only under the eyes of everyone in a courtroom, but under pressure and high stakes.

And there's nothing I love more than watching the opposing side crumble, spiraling fear in the eyes of criminals. It doesn't matter that they're often big names on Silicon Avenue—belonging to wealthy families much like my own— and possess more money than they know what to do with. They all shrink like petty thieves and murderers when the law finally catches up with them. I recognized the same look on my uncle when I made a mockery of him and his slimy company in front of the whole nation.

It doesn't matter that we're related...

"Do you think Bass Mobile will recover from this?"

Evidence doesn't lie.

"No." My tone is matter-of-fact, as I open the driver's side door of my McLaren, which swivels vertically before pointing directly toward the bright sky. Taking my seat low to the ground, I'm careful not to scrape my heels against the car's fiery-red paint job. "Their reach goes beyond New York. There's no doubt other states will follow suit."

And chip away until not even a dollar remains of Silicon Avenue's largest mobile manufacturer.

"Miss Astor! One more que—"

On the smooth seal of my door, their voices turn to quiet

muffles. But even the car's heavily tinted windows don't minimize the flashes ringing along the beige interior. With my auburn bangs framing my face, I flash a smug grin that will surely be the front of every prominent newspaper tomorrow morning.

Flipping down the sun visor, I re-line my lips with deathly precision, a familiar haughtiness I've grown to accept coursing comfortably through my bones. From the corners of my vision, NYPD officers shoo the crowd away, granting me a clear exit.

My departure is swift, leaving the courthouse—and more than a few disappointed faces—in my dust. Not even a minute goes by, when my phone lights up through the opening of my purse.

Mom: *Are we still on for tonight?*

～

DOWN GOES *the Giant*

I stifle a laugh, reading the headline on my smartphone by ByteBuzz, Silicon Avenue's most popular blog, managed by an anonymous pseudonym who writes scathing tech gossip. In only a few short hours, whoever-they-are has already posted about today.

A white-gloved hand slips a martini on the side table next to me. "Thank you, Eustace." I smile at my parents' butler— who happens to be an exceptional bartender—before he zips away.

Taking a sip, I observe the vacant room. My eyes roam over the checkered grooves of the chocolate Chesterfield sofas, then flick to the deep draperies encasing the night sky around large windowpanes. The area's lighting is dim, like always, giving the quaint lounge an almost speakeasy vibe.

While this room's a fairly unused section of my parents' estate, I often found it the best place to study growing up, appreciating the green bankers lamps which allowed me to pretend I was in some pretentious law school before that became a reality.

Grabbing my glass by the stem, I return to the article.

And, no, I don't mean giant, as in Goliath. Rather, down goes Bass Mobile, one of Silicon Avenue's longest-standing tech giants. And by the hands of who, you might ask? Well, the recipient of that award is none other than Lauren Astor, who is no dwarfish David. But a calculated, merciless, data privacy lawyer, whose blood runs so icy, her litigation spares no soul.

Not even her own uncle's, Oscar Bass.

I roll my eyes. *Talk about hyping up the drama. I'm not that ruthless.*

Retrieving the toothpick skewering a pair of olives from my clear beverage, I sink both between my lips.

The world must think that I backstabbed my entire family, my parents are ashamed of me, and I'm the soon-to-be black sheep of upper society. But that couldn't be further from the truth. Both my parents and older brother supported my decision, and it was my mother who pushed the hardest that I accept the case.

Before responding to the state's prosecution inquiry, I spoke with her first, since Oscar *is* her brother, after all. She confided in me that she'd suspected ill-intent from him for years but, giving him the benefit of the doubt, she ignored the hunch. But when my cousin's fiancé, Hannah, exposed unequivocal evidence that Bass Mobile was mishandling data and spying on their customers *and his own family* through their smartphone cameras, there was no denying what a truly evil man he is.

The taste of gin on my tongue is strong as I continue down the article.

Lauren was spotted leaving the courthouse, media personnel trailing her like a swarm of drones, capturing her every move and answer. Departing in her signature red McLaren 600LT, she left behind a hefty *fine for her uncle.*

One-point-two billion dollars, to be exact.

And in case you were wondering, the hotshot lawyer didn't acknowledge a single question about the surmised secret society.

Suspicious? I'd say so...

Yet another ridiculous rumor.

This one started around two years ago, when the evidence against Oscar Bass surfaced. Honestly, I shouldn't be as shocked as I am by the outrageous theories. People are desperate to make things out to be bigger than they actually are. They're so quick to equate shady CEOs—*who have been around since the dawn of capitalism*—to *The Illuminati.*

Nothing like plastering *"secret society"* on blog headlines to reel in the clicks and get people in a craze. As much as the media and raging conspiracy theorists *want* to believe there are mysterious, cloak-wearing masterminds puppeteering the general population like little green army men, there was not a single drop of evidence in our entire case to suggest such a thing.

My uncle was simply spying on prominent figures for his own twisted gain, using tactics like blackmail against his competitors. And in terms of the company as a whole mishandling user data, evidence proved they were only doing so to maximize profits by *grossly* overstepping privacy laws. All to better match customers with targeted advertisements. And, take it from a data privacy lawyer, that's not unheard of around here.

So, no. For the hundredth time. There is, in fact, *not* a secret society on Silicon Avenue.

"Sorry I'm late, dear." My mom's soft voice lulls me from my train of thought. Rounding my chair, her modest teal dress comes into view before taking a seat on the opposing couch. "The time slipped away from me. You know how tumultuous planning our charity auction always is. Hiring the speakers, handling publicity, the press, the list goes on. You'd think after ten years it'd get easier."

Eustace appears in a matter of seconds before I can reply, his dark suit faring well in the dim lighting. Clasping two hands behind his back, he addresses her. "Shall I uncork a bottle of Merlot, Madame Diana? Or bring you some hot tea?"

Crossing heel-clad ankles, her bright green eyes are like looking in a mirror when her gaze slides from him to me. "No wine for tonight. Bring the champagne, a fine bottle—the *Roederer Rose* will do. We have means for celebration!"

"Right away." He nods, disappearing to the full bar across the room.

Pride swells in my chest, but I can't dampen the subtle churn of guilt. "Oh, Mom... We don't have to celebrate."

"Nonsense." Her face doesn't fall an inch. "I'm sure you must think today was terribly hard for me. It was difficult, sure. I must admit, I still have compassion for my brother, but it's a compassion reserved for the man he used to be and a hope that someday he'll return to his old self. But I've come to terms with who he's become—blackmailing politicians, abusing his own son... It's for the greater good he's behind bars and that his company goes down with him. So, yes. It *is* time to celebrate."

With each of her words, the aching feeling lifts, and I mimic her smile. "Thank you, Mom. I couldn't have done it without your encouragement."

"Having you on that trial was crucial in putting us on the right side of the public eye. We couldn't allow ourselves to be a part of such a scandal, family or not. But always remember the most important reason. You accomplished what all of us in high positions can only hope to do—you helped society. Don't allow the media to twist your heart any other way."

I mull over her remarks as Eustace returns with our bubbly flutes.

Although she's a former psychology professor turned philanthropist, meaning uplifting speeches are literally her job, her words are genuine. They take me back to a time when I was only in middle school, yearning to be like my late grandfather—her father—who practiced law. Never once did her support waver when I studied to take the LSATs, when I attended law school, or when I came on as a junior associate at Astor Associates, the firm her father founded.

Yet sometimes it's hard swallowing such praise from her. If only she knew the vanity and egotism ever-flowing through my veins. I won't entertain the notion that the case didn't pique my interest because of its high-profile nature and the way it would glisten in my portfolio. Oftentimes, I catch my drive to excel, to win, being more for the sake of *winning,* instead of my client's or society's sake.

But victory and ambition go hand-in-hand with being a shark.

"To Lauren, my only daughter." She raises a glass, her slender arm splitting between strands of her copper locks. "May today's verdict serve as a cornerstone to look back on for confidence. Cheers to a long line of career successes."

TWO

LAUREN

AFTER A FEW MORE GLASSES OF champagne, I have a slight buzz. Now sitting atop stools, we sip on cups of green tea. Eustace remains behind the bar, cleaning our glasses as jazz music emits from distant speakers.

All is well until I catch my mom gazing ahead of her, blatant worry shining in her irises.

"Is something wrong?" I graze her arm.

She flicks her attention back to me, quickly covering the expression with pleasantry. "Of course not."

"Don't do that—I saw that look."

"Oh... I'd hoped to wait for another time, dear. Tonight's special."

Her tone... My shackles rise at her obvious distress. *She rarely sounds like that.*

"Mom, what's going on?"

She pauses for a moment.

"Forget tonight. We can celebrate again some other time. *Tell me,*" I urge.

Her shoulders droop, turning from me. "Eustace, could you give us some privacy?"

"Yes, Madame," he says, disappearing to another room.

For a moment, save for the music, it's painfully silent between us. *Then more than a moment,* leading my brain to make up the worst possible scenarios, ones I don't have the courage to voice.

"Your father's gone away again."

"Jeez, Mom." Air gusts from my lungs. "Why didn't you just say so?"

I pick my tea back up, a puzzling feeling overtaking me when I notice she still looks concerned. "Come on, don't look so down. What's new? He probably needed a breather." The explanation comes easily, as it's the one I always use when explaining my father's reoccurring disappearances.

But it's true, I remind myself. *He runs the largest cyber security company on the planet.* The man needs time to himself, and if that means he wants to jet off to the Bahamas or some relaxing port town from time to time, then so be it. He's never been gone for longer than a week.

But why is she so quiet?

"Really, it'll be fine. You know he'll be back in no—"

"It's been a month."

My back straightens, disbelief rippling down my spine in jagged waves. "No... No, that can't be right."

"He can't handle the stress, Lauren." Glossiness shines in her eyes, refusing to look my way.

"Did you call the authorities? Did something happen?"

"No, what use would that be? He responds to every one of my texts, says he's in Switzerland—and his phone location records attest to that. This is the same old him, dear, just... I think maybe the stress has finally gotten to him."

Guilt nips at me all over again. Ever since I took on the trial nearly two years ago, the media coverage of our two families has been nonstop. Smear campaign after smear campaign, and more gossip headlines than I can count, they never fail to paint us as either the aggressors or even accomplices of what happened—*and still don't.*

Even before the trial, running Astor Security has never been easy on him, but he's always pulled through. "Why now? Why—"

"There's been talk of an investigation." Her face hardens, accentuating the subtle wrinkles across her aged yet striking features. Then laughter that doesn't reach her eyes rings hollow across the lounge. "The state will use you to win their case, but they'll still turn around and put us under scrutiny. And they don't need evidence to do so. Our familial ties with Bass Mobile alone warrant an audit, probably more."

She's right. Search warrants, subpoenas, sifting through years of data... It could last months, if not longer.

"But he has nothing to be worried about," I state with confidence. "His company has never veered from the law."

"Doesn't matter. You know how these things work. Even if they don't find any criminal evidence—*and they won't*—to suggest otherwise, they'll point their attention on him. All it takes is one small slipup or a poor explanation."

"Couldn't he hire more lawyers and advisors? Or..."

But if they made him testify in court, it wouldn't matter how many lawyers he had on his defense. He'd have to do the talking... I bite my lip, finding myself agreeing with her. *He can't handle that.*

I can't see a proper solution, only to sell off shares before things get out of hand. And he would never do that. The company is our family's greatest asset, a true beacon on Silicon Avenue, raking in twenty times the annual revenue of Astor Associates.

Appraising her, I wonder if she's contemplating the same solution. But I quickly conclude she can't be, not with her looking so torn... Then it hits me—

While he's the largest shareholder by far, he doesn't own over fifty percent. She could sway the board to de-seat him as CEO.

"You're not thinking..."

She places her cup on the bar top, hands revealing a slight tremor. "It's what's best for the family. The board would go through with it on goodwill alone."

Suddenly, my dress's fabric seems too tight at the neck, my toes too cramped in my pumps. There's something uncomfortable and horrid about picturing my father stripped of his dignity. But deep down, I admit it's for the best. Because *he* hasn't been at his best, not for years, with his mind elsewhere—on what, though, is anyone's best guess. But it surely hasn't been on the company, at least since the beginning of the trial.

"And who would take his place?" I dare ask. *We would want the board to pick someone from our family.* "Felix?" I name off the obvious choice by age birthright—my older brother and only sibling.

Her lips thin, annoyed by my suggestion. "He's more absent than your father is."

Like the strike of a match, rage simmers beneath my skin. *"And why's that, huh?* He wouldn't be so *absent* if you and Dad only cared to—"

"Enough." She flicks her vicious gaze at me, sending my heart racing, revealing a rare side of her that only comes out when she feels backed into a corner. "Don't bring that into this. That has nothing to do with the decision, and you know

it. We need someone who can answer the questions, someone who can handle the lawyers... You know what it is I'm asking, Lauren."

As I release a calming breath, the tight cord of tension wound tightly in my shoulders loosens, and I force myself to face the facts. She *is* stuck in a corner, and she wouldn't ask this of me if she knew there was another way.

But there's one flaw in her grand plan.

"I don't know the first thing about computers. I may be a data privacy lawyer, but that doesn't mean I can make the right business decisions for a cyber security company, let alone write code or decipher algorithms."

In light of my protests, her strong presence holds firm, keeping her gaze locked onto mine. Which could only mean one thing. *She already thought of that.*

And then I'm nothing but a sailboat out of wind, navigating treacherously foreign waters, faced with two options. On the one hand, I could continue straight in my deafened ways, abandoning all else for my own personal gain. In essence, do what I do best. Or I could acknowledge the call from the shore, put my ambitions on hold, and help my family.

"This type of life comes with sacrifices," she'd always said growing up. But I'd never felt the weight of the warning, not once, until I hear her next words, practically sentencing me with the swing of a judge's gavel.

The only plausible solution.

"Which is exactly why I've taken the initiative and arranged you a marriage with someone who does."

THREE

TRISTAN

I'M a man of many names.

The first I was born with.

The second I am proud of.

And the third I am not.

"Apex, Apex, Apex!" The crowd chants the third, their words ringing in my blooded ear. Dodging my opponent's wicked left hook—which would surely lay me flat on my ass, given the man's mammoth-like size—I go on the offensive, jabbing right for his jugular.

Choking, he reaches for his throat, stumbling backwards until he makes cold hard contact with the chain-link surrounding the ring. In an instant, spectators press against the other side of the barrier, screaming in both his ears, their eyes glazed with exhilarating hunger.

They're nothing but animals.

And severe gambling addicts, who crunch cash between their fingers, having waged their bets on the winner of tonight's main event. While I'm normally heavily favored, tonight's odds were nearly even, meaning the underground arena's even more packed than usual. And if the word around here is true, some kingpin, who thought he could make a quick buck betting for my loss, flew in my opponent—a Russian UFC fighter.

As sweat mixes with the blood trickling down his pecs, his head droops downwards. *Guess he's never been to a place like the Down Under.*

Deciding that it's time to end things, I glance one last time at the repulsive tattoo marking his entire bald scalp, then deliver a swift kick to the side of his temple, before he slumps to the ground.

The room explodes, with those in the crowd having one of two reactions. Losers snarl in disgust, slapping their money to the ground and stomping on the green. But the winners are the most rambunctious, either jumping in a frenzy or literally *climbing* the cage's fence, meaning to storm the ring.

Knowing it's best to leave before that happens, I exit through the single door attached to the ring. I'm met with a bare white hallway and the familiar face of my best—and only—friend. Squinting, my eyes adjust to the powerful over-hanging fluorescents.

"I'd say that was one hell of a fight, but..." Bryson smirks, tossing me a towel.

"But it wasn't." I finish his sentence.

"*Nope.* You really made a show of toying with him. Seems you may have potential for professional MMA." Pushing up the sleeves of his hoodie, revealing toned forearms, he turns from me, his long strides aiming for the door at the end of the corridor. "Not that you need the money."

Trailing his lead, I snort, running the towel down the length of my bare torso. With only a few drops of my own blood on me, sweat slicks off my skin, leaving behind stone-hard muscles inked with intricate tattoos. After discarding the towel to the ground and shrugging into a black hoodie, we break through the exit door.

My eyes sigh in relief, returning to the dim darkness coating the heart of the Down Under. If it weren't for the tents and stalls lining the perimeter of the underground area, then the smell of tobacco and a very distinct set of foods would inform us we're entering the marketplace.

Staying close behind Bryson, I flick my hood over my head as we weave between bodies of shady marketgoers.

The Down Under brings in a wide variety of people who all share the commonality of meddling in illegal activity. One trip down here, and some alleged nobody passing you by may just be a gun for hire, pickpocket, run-of-the-mill thief, or New York City's most successful crime lord.

Anything goes, really, as long as you don't snitch to the wrong people—though that probably wouldn't do any real harm. Even the NYPD turns a blind eye to this place, never having attempted a single raid. Presumably because they know the absolute shitstorm they'd get themselves into with any number of mobs or gangs, who quite like having a neutral zone away from the police.

I have a hunch about where he's headed as we near the perimeter. And when we break from the crowd, leaving a purple stand with an aged woman I haven't seen in years, my suspicion proves correct.

"Oh, no, Bryson—"

"Cool your jets. It's not what it looks like, man." Whipping his head towards me, he shoves both hands into his pockets, flattening his dark curls beneath the weight of his hood.

"What is it, then?"

"It's only a hobby now." With eyes wandering to the booth as if caught in a trance, his legs follow suit.

Letting out a huff, I follow, until the booth displays what I already knew would be there. *Lockpicks.* Picks of all different sizes and lengths scatter across the table, some with angled tips or winding grooves like a snake.

"*A hobby?* Come on, be real."

"I am," he says defensively.

Usually, I can instantly tell when someone is lying. But never with Bryson. Maybe it's because he's cut from the same cloth, having had a childhood comprising disappointment, struggle, being passed to and from orphanages, and living on the streets. If it wasn't for Bryson's crafty lock-picking skills granting us entrance into grocery stores, we both would've starved more than a few times.

The moment his hand grips around a handle, I clutch his arm, tugging him aside. "I thought you left this behind."

"Get off me, man!" He shakes from my grasp, lowering his tone. "Do you really think I'm breaking into places? Stealing? What are we, fifteen again? Be serious, Tristan. I work on Wall Street wearing five-thousand-dollar suits. If I *wanted* to steal people's hard-earned money, I already got the best job for that."

My shoulders droop as an involuntary chuckle seeps through my lips at his crude joke. "Sorry, I should've believed you. It's just... why here?"

"This place has the best stuff, better than anything online." Returning his attention to the table, he grabs a pick, running a finger through the grooves. "And it's alright. Thanks for looking after me—it's really only a hobby."

I listen to him undergo an intense haggle with the lady

over a few bucks—which is ridiculous, given he's a multi-millionaire. Turning my back, I appraise the market.

We first came to the Down Under at the ages of thirteen and fourteen. *That* I know. But what I'm not too sure of is at what age I decided it was a good idea to enter the cage. I remember it vividly, though, seeing as I got my ass kicked. But some internal fire kept leading me back, until the only hits I received were the ones I would allow.

Sometimes, I feel I deserve them—*the hits.* But I can't quite pinpoint the reason. My five-hundred-dollar-an-hour shrink says I'm unable to move past the guilt surrounding my childhood, which leads to my, and I quote, *"self-sabotaging and compulsive behavior."*

If only she knew I'm Silicon Avenue's most wanted hacker on top of it, then she'd *really* give me an earful. With my own set of ethics, of course. As unbelievable as it may sound, my goal is to always leave a positive impact on society. My methods of doing so? Well, that's where many would bat an eye.

After successfully haggling the price of a kit down to three-fifty from three-seventy-five, Bryson offers the woman cash. Although she wears a flustered appearance, when her palm fills with green, all that fluster turns to contentment—that is, until she looks over our shoulders. I cock my head, watching her smile morph into fear, before she quickly disappears through the curtain behind her.

An icy alertness slithers up my back. Somehow knowing who I'd see, I twist on my heel.

Jace.

I recognize the scrawny man with jet-black hair standing before us instantly. Presumably in his early twenties, Jace wears a plain white-T, ripped jeans, and a wicked grin.

Judging by his outward appearance, he's far from the threatening type around here.

Except for one thing.

The owl tattoo peeking out of his collar.

"Hello, Tristan," he says.

Bryson tenses beside me, and from my peripherals, I catch him reaching behind his back.

"Don't," I hiss.

His weary gaze flicks to mine. "But he's—"

"I know what he is." I swallow. "We've... met before."

His lips fall, a look edging on the side of betrayal shining in his features. But I don't have time for explanations. I don't have time to explain how Silicon Avenue's theorized secret society—whom we've both known exists for quite some time —has had me under their thumb for almost two years. Because all I have time for right now is getting Bryson the hell away from their *all-seeing eyes.*

That *is* what they say.

"The Oculi see all."

Jace seems to read my mind, repeating the society's coined phrase with a monotone that has me questioning if it's really a human living inside his skin. Quirking an eyebrow at me, he takes another step forward, donning a mocking expression. "Did you think that excluded your friend, *Bryson Reed?"*

Fuck.

My teeth grind together, threatening to saw off my enamel. "Bryson, *leave.* I'll be fine."

But his stubbornness prevails as he sizes up the man who's half a head shorter than both of us. And he's not wrong in doing so—we could both take him by the time we'd hear him squeal. But there would be unforeseen consequences.

When Bryson's eyes reach mine, I nod curtly. And to my

surprise, pressing his lips into a thin line, he leaves the booth, disappearing into the darkness.

"Such a shame. The society could find a great use for his skills, if only he wished to serve a greater purpose. You two share that in common."

"What do you want?" I clip out.

"Quite the attitude, aimed towards someone who's only a —oh, how did you so poetically phrase it last time?" He rubs his chin, putting on a show. *"A bitch lackey under the thumbs of those who really matter."*

I cross my arms. "Case in point: here you are again."

"And you're any better? What is it, hacker by day, cage-fighting animal by night? I'd wager you can only count on one hand the number of people who know all your names." He circles me, agitation boiling in my core when he continues. "In truth, I pity you. I can't imagine how fucked up you are in the head. Probably because of what happened to your parents—"

In a blink, I thread the collar of his shirt between my fists, and take another good look at the owl tattoo crawling up his right pectoral. Curving with complicated geometric shapes, a crescent moon wraps around the bird's head, and thick ink accentuates its eyes.

Eyes that appear in my dreams.

Maybe they really can *see me. I hope so —*

I slam him down on the table, his yelp pouring cool satisfaction over my veins. He stares at me for a moment, genuine fear shining in his pupils, before doing what no other man in his position would. *He laughs.* Acting like a complete hysteric, he shakes beneath me, cackles ringing out across our small enclosure.

Loosening my hold, our first encounter nearly two years

ago flashes before my mind. When my whole life turned to shit, and I learned what this mysterious pawn does best—*pushes my buttons.*

"Get lost, buddy," I tell the scrawny man behind me, who follows my footsteps. Shoving between spectators, I slick the sweat off my chest with a towel, as some pat me on my back or roar in my ears. *"I saw that tattoo of yours. Trust me, you won't be the one who finally converts me to their* cause."

I bank a left, freeing myself from the crowd, right in front of the water fountain station near the bathrooms. A random from the crowd approaches us, smiling, but when he catches the tattoo poking out of my new stalker's shirt, his face falls before he gets lost.

"My name's Jace. Nice to meet you, too. And this isn't about conversion, Tristan," I barely hear him say.

For years now, The Oculi and I have had a so-called mutual understanding:

I don't reveal them to the public.

They don't expose my hacker name.

And we don't meddle in each other's affairs.

Simple as that.

While I appear to the society as any other hacker—who steals and gives no thought of the general public—that's simply untrue. But they can never know that. Because if they did, they'd realize it's my sole intention to expose them and, even worse, that I haven't yet. Which could only mean one thing.

I can't.

Admittedly, I do *possess backdoor access to a public channel that would quite literally make them the face of New York City. I have the* power play, *so to speak. The shock-and-awe script waiting for execution. Meaning, even with their vast reach and extensive efforts, there'd be no chance of a cover-up, as the damage to them would be irreversible.*

But that's just the problem...

Who is "them?"

In theory, I could expose a few of their members, the ones I'm aware of, several of whom have flashy names and deep pockets on Silicon Avenue. They'd be thrown behind bars and plastered all over the news. But that wouldn't be enough. That wouldn't dispose of them all, and evidence suggests there are quite a lot of members, with whoever reigns on top being unknown.

"Of course, it's about conversion," I say between gulps, splashing ice-cold water on my face. "What else would it be about?"

"The society has had a change of heart."

"Right, sure they have. What're they going to bribe me with this time? A yacht? New equipment? Maybe some shiny real estate properties?"

He holds out a manila folder. "We have two requests of you."

Christ...

When will they get it through their thick skulls that I'm never joining their ranks? Rolling my eyes, I snatch the folder, letting intrigue get the best of me. They've never requested anything from me...

Turning to the first page, I instantly know what this is about—the Bass Mobile trial, which is no secret to me, including the fact that the society had involvement in spying on their customers. Flipping through, I'm met with a slew of technical jargon, all of which is plain English to me.

Backdoor scripts, database scrapers, encrypted communications and channels linking to offshore accounts... Clearly, all of this was managed from the inside by someone who's technically savvy, no doubt. But now that there's so much attention on Bass Mobile, they need someone on the company's outside: a hacker. And, given the timeframe, they need the best, otherwise they wouldn't come to me.

They want me to erase the society's involvement before the trial starts.

Offering back the folder, I shake my head. "Oscar Bass is none of my concern."

"And he shouldn't be. We have no more use for him. He's going down no matter the outcome, but The Oculi will remain. Meaning, all traces of our involvement must be gone before the trial's investigations."

When he doesn't take it back, irritation pricks at my temple. "What of our understanding, our agreement? What makes your bosses think they can make such a request? This is grossly overstepping the line."

"My apologies, I must've misspoken. This isn't a request. Flip to the last page."

My heart thumps at the ire in his tone, at his new surge of confidence. When I comply, a vile wave of nausea climbs up my throat, studying the picture taped to the final page.

In the darkness of nighttime, through the window of her dorm room, my younger sister—the only family I have left on this earth—lies on her bed, face buried between the pages of a fine arts textbook. Blonde hair tied messily atop her head, she sports a sweatshirt inked with Columbia University's signature-blue lion mascot.

And she couldn't look more peaceful.

To her, I'm nothing but a rich techie who made smart investments, not the damaged mess who frequents the Down Under and encrypted chat rooms. And that's how I've designed our relationship to be, so she never dips a single toe in the life I live.

But, even with all my efforts, all I do is cause her trouble.

Jace's cackle rings in my ears, snapping me back into focus, finding his posture straight and imposing. "Did you really think removing her from the university's public records would prevent us from finding her? Sneaky, sneaky." He wags his pointer finger at me, lips curling so viscously, I only see red. "But not sneaky enough. Just because you two don't share a last name doesn't mean she's invisible to us."

Running my hands through the tendrils of my silky hair, I'm utterly speechless, which allows him to taunt further.

"Oh, how I'd love to meet the young lady. Columbia University? Wow, that's impressive. What a pleasure it was seeping through her records. Did you know she's been top of her class for four straight years? There's talk of naming her valedictorian. Seems she's got the smarts—must run in the family. But also, the talent, with such a bright future ahead of her... Gosh, what a pretty name, too. Aurora Stevens—"

"FINE," I snap, anything to remove her name from his slithering tongue. "You know you have me. It's as good as done. No one on that trial will get a whiff of the society's involvement. Now, goodbye."

"Not so fast." He blocks my way past him.

God, his face is punchable. So much so that I'd love to find out how hard I'd have to squeeze until his head pops right off his neck. With a sharp exhale, through my blinding rage, I recall his words earlier. "What's the second request?"

"Oh, this is where it gets really fun. We need you to enter into an arranged marriage—"

I almost topple backwards. What did he—

"Yep, you heard me right. And here's the kicker. With Lauren Astor."

What the fuck???

Everyone on Silicon Avenue has heard that name. And while I may live only five minutes down the road from her family's rolling estates, nobody socializes with me. And I do mean nobody, seeing as I'm the biggest recluse on Wisteria Drive. Members of high

society may know of me, but no one's knocking on my door and
inviting me to fancy brunches or anything.

I'd chuckle if it wasn't for my dreadful predicament. That's *how*
ludicrous that statement sounds. "Never in a million years would
they agree to that."

"We're thinking they will once the trial's over. Astor Security—
which, might I remind you, is the company your own code kick-
started all those years ago—will need a new CEO."

This is getting out of hand.

"Do you not realize how crazy you sound? Astor Security is the
largest security company in America, probably in the world.
Nicholas Astor would never relieve himself of his position. And, for
that matter, arranging his daughter to marry—essentially, handing
over half their family's shares to a complete outsider? No... There's
nothing you could bribe that man with."

This is no longer plain, life-threatening blackmail. This is abso-
lute nonsense. I pass him by, his weak arm proving an unsuccessful
deterrent. But what does stop me in my tracks, though, are his next
words hitting me square in the back.

"Which is why we won't bribe him. No, when the time is right,
Nicholas Astor will disappear."

I snap from my haze, returning to reality, watching the
man I'm so sick of rise to his feet and dust himself off.

"You'll do what we say, when we say. And you'd best
remember what's at stake for you, Tristan Walker. Your
aliases, your sister, your friend, and anyone else you may get
attached to in this lifetime will be as good as dead if you fuck
this up."

Fear churns within my bones as Jace crosses the space
between us, plunging his hand deep into his pockets. "Full
compliance is our request now. From here on, you're not only

a complacent hacker under the helm of Astor Security, but a loving husband."

He reveals a small black box, an enormous engagement ring and a gold wedding band flashing from inside.

The moment the pair comes into view, a complex mixture of emotions replaces my fear. First, there's a twinge of guilt, having broken my resilient ethical code when I hacked and watched her most private moments. But, recalling the needy temptress she truly is, lust overshadows my shame.

It's true. I should've never crossed that first line.

But I have to know her.

"The arrangement has been made. Your bride awaits. We'll be in touch."

FOUR

LAUREN

"RELAX... *RELAX*, LAUREN, HE'LL SHOW," my friend, Hannah, says, with as about as much conviction as telling someone the Earth is as flat as a frying pan.

Her feigned confidence only makes me pace harder, my heels threatening to plunge through the church's wooden floorboards. My wedding dress—that was fitted *two days ago* —trails in my wake, toppling over boxes of shoes and makeup and ribbon.

"Who shows up late *to their own wedding?*"

My chest heaves, heightening my blistering annoyance. I breeze past Hannah—dear, sweet, sweet Hannah—who, in hopes of calming my mania, holds out a flute of sparkling wine.

Like that'll help.

"Who does he think he is? *Tristan Walker.*" I spit out his name.

The whole cherry on top of being forced into an arranged marriage by my mother to save our family's company is that my husband-to-be is a complete *nobody*. One quick search online spills next to nothing about the supposed crypto-billionaire who lives several miles from my parents' estate—if that's even true, seeing as I couldn't find a single photo of him online.

No one can be that *invisible, can they?*

"Maybe there was traffic..." Hannah's voice wobbles, but not even that dampens my rage.

"Ohhh, sure."

With sunny rays casting against me from a nearby window, I stare at my reflection in the full-length mirror, wearing a frown.

The white dress fits me like a glove, accentuates my curves, and hikes my breasts up with a hidden corset. Professionals have poked and prodded me since five a.m., sparing no details. Eyelash extensions. Hair extensions. Makeup. Nails. A spray tan. The whole nine yards. Meaning, I look fucking hot—*I'm a hot bride.* On top of that, by the end of today, this man's getting half our family's shares of Astor Security.

And he *still* can't give me the time of day.

The heavy diamond looping around my finger feels so foreign, it might as well be a Ring Pop. No, wait, a Ring Pop would be better, actually. Would carry more substance. At least it would've come from some boy who had a crush on me during recess, not from a no-faced ghost.

"What a joke," I scoff, resuming my pacing that's now more like stomping.

Given normal circumstances, this is around the time I'd be celebrating the big moment to come, taking pictures with my bridesmaids and family. But these aren't traditional circumstances. I'll never experience that. I'm lucky I even got to pick my bridesmaids, and that they were in town on such short notice. No, this is nothing but a sham, a downright—

"You're sure abusing that exquisite dress of yours."

I stop dead in my tracks, recognizing the voice immediately. Whipping around, I find my older brother leaning against the doorframe, dressed in an all-cream suit, with his fiery hair perfectly tousled like always.

"Felix!" I run to him. On our embrace, my anger pools around my ankles, relief taking its place. "Thank goodness. I wasn't sure if you'd make it."

Over his shoulder, Hannah whisks by towards the door, offering me a sympathetic smile. I wave her off, pulling away from my brother.

"You never have enough faith in me. I wouldn't miss walking my only sister down the aisle for anything."

The air in my lungs whooshes from me. Never in my life would I have predicted my father missing my own wedding. Even if the ceremony is all a fraud, I'd still prefer him to be the one to hand me off. Maybe that would give me more confidence in this decision.

But it wasn't a decision, I remind myself. *What choice did I have? Let everything my father's worked so hard for crumble to the ground?*

"Plus, Hannah called me in as backup," he adds, pulling me from my thoughts. When I look back at him, he winks, prying a snort from me.

"I'm sure she did. The poor girl had to stomach my hellish mood for over an hour."

His eyes twinkle with amusement before an abrupt silence grows between us. Then his smirk vanishes, a somber guilt clouding his stare.

"Don't," I blurt out before he says anything. "Mom's right.

This is the best option for the family, and none of that's your fault."

"Yes, it kind of is, Lauren... You're the one who's always been so focused. That's supposed to be my job, as the oldest. Yet, I'm the one who never pursued the internships Dad offered me over the years. This sort of pressure shouldn't be on you." He adjusts his cufflinks, avoiding my gaze with an unmistakable waver to his tone. "I've been away too long—"

"No." Tears prick my eyes.

I haven't seen my brother in over a year. He's been abroad in Greece and Italy and Spain and who knows where else, *"living the high life"* in the words of our parents. As if they truly know him. Like they weren't the ones who pushed him away for being gay.

There was never an explosive fight—at least, not coming from their end—and maybe that was the problem. No counseling, no adult-like talks, *no emotions.* Instead, our parents resorted to belittling silence, their rationalizations ranging from him simply being in a *"traveling phase"* to *"he's distracting himself from his future."*

I've never once blamed Felix for being unable to withstand them anymore. Because we've always been so close, I completely understood when he first extended his European trips to two weeks, then two months, until he flat-out moved away. He's created a whole new, happy life for himself, one where he's not treated like some disregarded shadow that our parents can mold into whatever they want.

"No," I repeat. "You know how I feel about that. So, don't get me started." Batting the tears away, I curb my emotions, lest I smudge my makeup and make this whole day even worse than it already is. "I'm going to be fine. Who knows? Maybe I'll get some hot sidepiece to fool around with."

Rolling his eyes, I earn a smile from him, which lifts the heavy feeling in my chest. "Whatever you say."

"And, plus, *you're* the one who's newly engaged." I nudge his shoulder before bringing up his hand, inspecting his gold ring. "Dimitri is one lucky guy."

"Jeeeez." Eyebrows shooting to his fiery-red hairline, he homes in on the diamond looping around my own finger. "I know we're assuming this Tristan guy sucks, and he's a billionaire and all, but that's a *shiner...*" Awestruck, he angles my finger left and right, eliciting thousands of sparkles against the sunlight. "Absolutely stunning."

"You know he sent it to my apartment through the mail?"

"What? No..." His shoulders slouch as disgust lines his features.

"Yep. My doorman delivered the box to my doorstep."

"Yikes." He drops my hand quickly, as if he might catch some bad juju. "Talk about zero class... Hey, maybe it's not too late to lawyer yourself up an ironclad prenup before you two officially sign the papers. Whether he's loaded or not, the real money's in those company shares."

A sad chuckle escapes me. "Unfortunately, I think we're well past that stage."

The shares are the whole reason he's marrying me. Sure, the recluse will have to take the reins on the company, assuming a smooth transition of leadership, but my father's already built the business up to what it is now. And if he's truly the genius computer whiz my mother and half the internet says he is, he'll have no problem calling the technical shots. As for the investigation, he'll have me by his side, answering all the legal questions—which can't be too difficult. My family has nothing to hide.

I can't help but think he got the better side of things.

Music trickles in through the doorway, signaling the sure entrance of the groomsmen and bachelorettes—a whopping *two* on each side.

The ceremony has begun.

My throat bobbles, and unexpected nerves take hold of me. Although hordes of people looking my way never make me the slightest bit nervous, there won't be much of a crowd. My mother planned it that way. *"Less questions the better,"* she had explained. But questions and eyes aren't what have me sweating bullets.

Walking down the aisle towards a man I've never met? That's pushing me to the edge of my limits.

Feeling vexed, and in need of a distraction, I force a laugh. "He's probably ugly." Smugness settles comfortably in my core at the thought of him being on the losing side of *some part* of this arrangement.

"You're right." Felix offers me his steady arm, lips curling upwards. "I'm sure he's positively miserable. Ghostly pale, flabby, acne and all. No wonder he never leaves his house."

UPON OUR ENTRANCE, a reverent silence blankets the room. I clutch onto my brother's arm, the big moment passing at an agonizing yet lightning speed.

"Oh, shit..." I overhear Felix's quiet mumble.

"It's worse than we thought?" I hiss under my breath, lips twitching.

With the thickly embroidered veil covering my head, I'm unable to get a good look at Tristan. Only a vague outline of his suit-clad body standing at the altar, along with a kaleidoscope of colors radiating through the stained-glass windows behind him.

I puff out a breath against the fabric, frustration nipping at me when the film doesn't move the way I want.

Damn this thing.

Kicking out my toes so I don't trip over the dress's front lip, our footfalls glide across the velvety carpet. But with each step, my brother feels less like a comforting chaperone and more like a stiff board.

"Is it?" I pry him again, deathly quiet.

Judging by my impaired vision, we're nearly there, and he still hasn't loosened up.

"H-he's..." His voice dies out.

Wow. He can't even finish his sentence. Satisfaction burns down my core. *He must be downright hideous.*

Felix stops us, and the music fades to a hush. Although we didn't rehearse, I know what comes next. My brother takes my hand, his clammy with jitters, as heavy steps approach.

When Tristan halts before us, my heart thunders. Even without seeing him, there's an unmistakable *presence*, as if we're minor constellations moving to his gravitational pull. Through an opening in the embroidery, I catch deep brown eyes staring back down at me, confident flames eddying beneath them.

"I, Felix Astor," his voice booms across the space without waver, ushering my hand to an unfamiliar one, "in place of my father, Nicholas Astor, hand over my beloved sister in your hand in marriage."

My breath hitches, a wave of intrigue hitting me on the contact. Rough and calloused, his skin is nothing like I would've guessed, and when Tristan's deep tenor thanks my brother, a simmering heat peruses down my spine. His warm thumb caresses along the top of my hand, as if he's branding me, invading my space, crawling underneath my skin and leaving it brightly burning.

Snap out of it, I scold myself. You can't get all hot and bothered before you've even seen the man. Plus, you heard Felix's reaction. He's uglier than dirt. He's—

The veil lifts over my head, dangerously slow, only to reveal something so contrary, my mind can't quite comprehend, leaving my knees weak.

He's... *devastating.*

Lifting my gaze to his impressive height, I'm met with tan skin, a square jaw, and a cocky smirk. His brazen stare roams down the length of my dress before flickering back to my face. And when his eyes drop to my lips, a familiar thrumming between my legs beats to its own accord. Fighting the unwelcome desire, I avoid his haughty gaze, instead appraising his suit.

But that proves even more distracting.

He could've been born in the white tuxedo he wears, because not an inch of fabric hangs loose along his broad shoulders. And it's not until I catch the tattoos peeking out his collar, that I *really* study him.

Before I know it, I'm tracing the black ink with an unashamed precision, up half the length of his muscled neck, then down past his cufflinks on the backs of his hands. My eyes seem to *move* towards them, a blurriness roaming across my vision, before I sway backwards, then I'm—

Falling?

Gasps ring out from the pews, as weightlessness claims me, and I'm helpless but to stare up at the church's breathtaking ceiling. Beige stone gracefully arches through ribbed vaults, converging into a single domed peak, and stained-glass windows depict ethereal scenes with robed saints.

Blackness creeps across my vision, pulling my consciousness from the present, until a pair of strong hands scoop beneath the arch of my back. Held in a dance-like dip, I suspend in the air, curved with my hair cascading down to the floor as the light returns to me.

My heart pounds in my chest when Tristan's striking features come into view. Not a nervous line marks his features, only a cool, collected calm. I furrow my brow. He can't be more than a few years my senior, but there's no mistaking the mature aura he radiates.

Anxiously waiting to be pulled up from possibly the most embarrassing moment of my life, I'm struck with shock when he instead *leans in,* until his minty breath is merely inches from my nose. His dark chuckle sends goosebumps soaring across my arms, flashing me a row of porcelain teeth.

"Look at you, all dolled up and weak at the knees before I've even consummated the marriage."

FIVE

TRISTAN

GOD, *she is beautiful in person.*

Even when she stands at the altar, shooting me a look that could skin me alive.

Easing her back onto the balls of her feet, she scowls, then quickly plasters on a fake smile for the audience. But a seething death wish remains lined behind her pretty eyes, something that could only be caught up close and is enough to make my pants feel too tight below the waist.

"Are you alright, Miss Astor?" the officiant asks, his frail palms grazing Lauren's arm with concern.

Adjusting the veil atop her head, she bats down her frazzled hair, offering him a forced smile. "Yes, I'm fine. Thank you." Her jaw ticks in annoyance. As she meets my gaze, a rosy blush stains her cheeks. "These silly shoes. I knew I shouldn't have worn them."

I collect her hands in mine, putting on the most tender face I can muster. "No need to explain, honey. I was well aware of your clumsiness before I asked you to marry me."

Chuckles purr over our shoulders from the crowd, even

earning a snicker from the officiant. Cocking her head, Lauren glares at me with promises of murder, all while wearing a cordial grin.

Someone didn't take that too well. Bet this hotshot lawyer aficionado has never been called a klutz in her life.

"Ohh, Tristan," she teases sweetly, but with a subtle bite to her tone. Soft digits brush the backs of my hands, catching them in a grip that surely appears affectionate but is much too tight. "You always have a talent for stating the obvious."

A thrill sparks low in my gut at her retort, intense and alluring, and it takes everything in me to remain silent, letting our battle of wits die out on a whisper. A few heartbeats later, she breaks our connection, sweeping her gaze across the church pews.

The wedding is quite small, with only fifty attendees. Thankfully, guests freely picked their sides upon arrival, otherwise mine would be as vacant as a ghost town. My only groomsman is Bryson, aside from Lauren's brother—who looks madly uncomfortable, presumably because he knows the marriage is arranged.

I side-eye my friend, stifling a grin. While there's nothing abnormal about his sharp, faded haircut, with buzzed sides and coarse curls up top, I can't help but raise my eyebrows at his well-fitted suit, loafers, and tie.

Although my Best Man *does* work on Wall Street as a powerhouse stockbroker, strictly rocking Armani suits and fifty-thousand-dollar Rolexes, I hardly see him in a professional setting. But it's obvious he wears the part like a second skin. Chin high, shoulders back, he looks as though he's ready to bust out a heartfelt speech about our amazing friendship and how *it was about time we two lovebirds sealed the deal.*

Bryson is well aware of The Oculi's involvement in today's

affairs, but that doesn't make me any less appreciative that he came. And that also goes for my only other invitee. Flicking my head, I catch my younger sister sitting in the front row next to the aisle, legs crossed neatly, wearing a bright floral dress and an even brighter smile.

My throat bobbles.

I use everything in my power to keep her away from this life, yet there she is, no doubt sitting amongst some of Silicon Avenue's two-headed snakes. But I couldn't tell her the truth of today, or risk damaging our relationship by not inviting her. Because when your family is so limited...

You keep them close.

A trickle of sadness sinks down my middle.

That's where our mother would sit if she were still alive, and next to her, our father. Even though this is all a ruse and against my will, I like to think their souls are in attendance, if that's possible. I've never given religion much thought, but we *are* standing in a church—the most glamorous and expensive venue in probably all of New York City. So, who knows? Maybe they're invisible to human eyes, craning their everlasting gaze from the tops of the church spire or the empty pews.

Either way, the thought is touching.

When the officiant clears his throat, I banish the sorrow, taking Lauren's hands in mine, instead refocusing my attention on her mischievous, emerald eyes. She must hate me. To her, I'm an opportunist thief, acting under my own volition, collecting half of what her father worked for.

If only she knew it's so much worse than that.

"WE MET WHILE STUDYING AT HARVARD," I recite for what has to be the twentieth time tonight, feeling as if I'm an actor in some misfortunate sitcom.

Our reception is in full swing, underneath a ginormous pop-up tent on the outskirts of the church grounds, housing a dance floor and a bar. On the edge of the dance floor, with my new wife, we converse with a finely dressed couple.

I think Lauren said they're distant relatives? I can't keep track.

Lauren backs me up, slinking her arm around my bicep. "We kept it a secret, even from close friends, given the high-profile nature of my recent trials. You wouldn't believe the lengths defense attorneys will go to win their cases, even using the media to slander the opposition."

Their jaws drop in unison. "That's *awful,*" the woman says after they exchange surprised looks, raising her hand to her chest. "We completely understand. People have such loose lips around here."

Lauren nods. "Oh, I'm well aware they do."

After a few more minutes of agonizing small talk, the couple expresses their congratulations and departs for another drink, the woman with a twinkle in her eye like she scored on some juicy secret meant only for the *in-crowd.*

Little does she know, it's the same bullshit story we've been spinning the entire reception, thanks to Lauren's mother. Immediately after the ceremony ended, Diana Astor pulled us into a side room and quickly gave us the rundown of our supposed relationship.

We've been together for about a year.

We initially met at Harvard years prior, while Lauren was attending law school and I was studying to get my Master's in Computer Science.

We were friends throughout that time, but never made it official.

That's why it didn't take long once we started dating to get engaged.

And we can fill in the rest of the details as we like, so long as our stories are cohesive.

What Diana didn't say—but is quite obvious—is she's assuming people won't be nosy enough to look me up on the university's records, or that she'll simply pay the school a lofty sum of money to make it so. The irony is she doesn't realize how easily I could make that happen, to the extent that even those working *at* Harvard would believe it's true. By the end of one night, I could hack my way into having officially attended Harvard University and maybe throw myself two Computer Science degrees, that I don't need, while I'm at it.

Like there isn't anything you can't learn online these days.

I smirk to myself, allowing Lauren to lead us towards the next—and, thankfully, last—table, mentally preparing myself for the next round of lies and *sincere* gratitude for their attendance on such short notice.

Weaving through chairs and tables, we enter back onto the dance floor, crossing to the other side. Lauren's magnificent dress flows behind her, trailing on the ground with a white train that's several feet long. Even in her heels, the top of her auburn-kissed head barely reaches my nose.

Having Lauren Astor on my arm as my wife is like showing off a prestigious award that I didn't earn. One that sparkles, smells divine, eats up the limelight, and every man can't keep their eyes off of. *Even though I wish they would.*

"You could at least smile," she says through clenched teeth.

"And you could smile a little less." I peek down at her,

loving how she bristles against me. "Don't want to crack those pretty teeth of yours."

"*I mean it,*" she snaps. "Might I remind you, there's a lot riding on us working together and appearing legit, including a state investigation. And, not to mention, the board has yet to name you as the new CEO, and they won't do that if they sense something is up."

"Is that so?" I stop abruptly, forcing her to do the same. We're in the center of the dance floor, with more than a few pairs of eyes stealing glances our way. "I'll appear however you wish me to, only because you *are* my wife."

Slowly, I sweep my fingers down the length of her slender arms. "You want me madly in love? Done." Leaning in, I invade her space, and when my lips brush against the hollow of her ear, she shivers beneath me. "Obsessive, so the only name I can withstand hearing from your mouth is mine? Done."

Retreating, her exhales come out in choppy waves, until I'm a hair's breadth from her inviting lips. I loop my arm around the small of her back, giving her a sharp tug towards me, and revel when a sound so close to a moan escapes her.

"Territorial, to the point of ruining another man's life if he so much as touches you?" I crash my lips to hers, finding her body tense like a taut rope. But after a few prods of my tongue, she eases up with a soft whimper, sending a ripple of satisfaction down to my bones. On my withdrawal, our lips resound softly. "Done."

Her eyes flutter open, meeting mine, only for her eyebrows to scrunch the moment I whisper, "But let's get one thing straight. Your precious board *needs me.* If there was someone better for the job, they would've named them by now."

As if she's slipping from a seductive haze, her eyes wander and chest rises, then falls rapidly. And for a moment, I think I've rendered her speechless, until the gears in her brain practically churn in front of me, unwilling to wave a white flag. She nibbles on her lower lip, stealing my attention back to her red-stained mouth.

"You're rather cocky for a man who seems to have zero business experience. How are you so different from any of my father's engineers or technical advisors?"

Fixing her smudged lipstick, I brush my thumb along the corner of her parted mouth. "Because, dear wife, it's my code that runs Astor Security."

SIX

LAUREN

NEVER WOULD I have guessed that my wedding would be so secretive, as if we're criminals on the run from the authorities.

At the end of the reception, Tristan and I drove off in a cute retro car, streamers dangling beneath a *Just Married* sign. Guests lined up on both sides of the church's driveway, all with smiles and pictures and cheers until we were far from sight.

But unbeknownst to them, their newlyweds drove several miles down the road, entered the heart of the city, only to pull into a parking garage and get picked up by a discrete limo. I don't have a clue what my mother paid for our driver's silence, but he didn't say a single word when we arrived, and he still hasn't on our drive to Tristan's estate.

Thankfully, the driver has also kept his privacy wall up the entire ride, or he'd subject himself to our own deafening silence. Not at all the norm of two newlyweds who should be madly in love.

Tristan sits beside me, ankle resting atop his knee, looking out the window as trees fly by. I'd call our scene painfully awkward, but I don't sense a sliver of tension radiating from him, and my mind's too preoccupied to care.

He kissed me...

He kissed me, *and I liked it.*

If I think hard enough, I can still *feel* his tongue dancing around mine, invading my mouth like it's his to claim. In that moment, pressed so close to his chest, I discovered the chiseled body he must have beneath that suit. I shuffle in my seat, my dress suddenly suffocating, rubbing between my thighs in all the wrong ways. And his *hands*, so massive and calloused. I wonder how they'd feel—

No.

I banish the thoughts before they run wild. He's just a pretty face, that's all. Seeing as we don't know the first thing about one another, his smooth talking was overstepping the line and definitely didn't win me over.

I mean, look at him...

Peeking to my right, I study his tattoos, particularly the lines crawling up the side of his neck, almost touching his earlobe.

He's far from my normal type. No prestige. No flashy family last name. And he's got a sort of bad-boy aura about him...

But he does *wear that suit well,* another side of me argues.

My gaze inches up the fabric of his tuxedo, counting each black button until I find the top one unbuttoned, bowtie hanging loosely around his neck. Rising still, I trace his strong jaw and chin, up his straight nose and—

I catch his eyes in the window's reflection, staring right back at me.

Shit.

Noticing I've fully turned my gaze in his direction, I snap

it straight ahead. Although it's nighttime and the limo's interior is dark, I wonder if he can spot my cheeks burning just from the lights glowing off the LED strips lining the floor.

"I'm your husband, Lauren. All you have to do is ask, and I'll give you plenty more to gawk at."

"Stop that." I cross my arms tightly, embarrassment burning along my skin. "Just stop. You don't know me, and I don't care what the law says we are. I'm not your wife."

"Interesting." His eyebrows tick skyward. "I happen to recall you taking my last name today, Mrs. Walker."

"Yes, but—"

"And those rings? Are they not from me?"

I huff an annoyed breath at having to explain myself. *"Yes, but one of them was delivered to me from my doorman."*

"That was your mother's idea, actually." He frowns.

My shoulders fall, a feeling eerily close to betrayal blindsiding me. I know my mom did everything to keep the wedding as close-lipped as possible, but couldn't she have at least let me meet Tristan before forcing me at the altar with him?

I didn't even know what the man looked like.

I don't regret my decision—if I can even call it that— marrying Tristan Walker. Saving my family's legacy. But the real weight of what I've given up is only hitting me now. What I'll miss out on...

The privilege of finding true love. Knowing with certainty he's the one. Shedding joyous tears over steak and wine and the moonlight and an unexpected proposal. Celebrating with close friends, who soon become my bachelorettes, and then partying until the sun goes down in Sin City, all in the name of monogamy. Planning and experiencing a true wedding, with a guest list so full, the venue can hardly compensate.

Arriving in the Caribbean or the Amalfi Coast or Maui or who-knows-where, because neither of us planned our own honeymoon...

All of it.

Gone.

Struck permanently from my life, in the span of two weeks.

My throat tightens, and an unbearable sorrow stings my eyes—

"I'm sorry." Tristan places his hand on my knee, seeping warmth through the thick fabric of my wedding dress. His tone is nearly as serious as the gleam in his eyes.

I chuckle sadly, swiping the wetness from my ducts before tears fall. "You didn't force me into anything."

"No. But I could've made today easier. And, for that, I'm sorry."

I'm taken aback by his remarks, realizing this is the first time I've opened up and heard an actual apology from anyone, aside from my brother. But with him, I *had* to be strong. The guilt was already tearing him apart, which was evident in his gaze before the ceremony, and I couldn't allow his life to crumble. Not when it's going so well, and I haven't seen him so content in years.

As for my parents...

I sympathize with my mother's harsh position, needing to take the family's reins in my father's absence. But, truthfully, I expected her to be more compassionate or acknowledge the monumental sacrifice I'm making for the sake of the family. Marry a total stranger, pass him off as the new CEO, and single-handedly represent the company against a state investigation? And what do I get?

Not even a thank you.

Whether my father even knows of the arranged marriage or not, I *still* haven't heard from him in over a month—not even to check in.

"Thank you," I whisper.

Tristan stares at me for what feels like a lifetime, before his shadowy gaze flickers to his hand still atop my knee. Through the dimness, I spot his throat bobble.

"I admit, I'm often not a good man, and you definitely deserve better. Maybe I'm the greedy, selfish one on our end of the deal. But you...? You were only acting in the best interest of your family. And, above all my many faults, I can understand that." His eyes return to mine. "Doing *anything* for family."

My heart quakes at the sentiment, and I wonder if he can sense the intrigue blooming inside of me through the line of our stare. Doubting our newfound connection, I anticipate an eye roll or a snicker, something that screams *gotcha*. But it never comes. Nothing taints his gaze, which remains unwavering, until I snap my head back to the window, finding the night sky easier to traverse than his mysterious depths.

We remain silent for the rest of the trip through Wisteria Drive, zooming by familiar luxurious estates, their long driveways lit by floodlights in the darkness, most owned by recognizable tech royalty like the Basses and the Vuittons. Once my family's estate is far from view, we enter through a gate, and the private driveway progresses further than I've ever been.

Climbing up a windy, steep hill, I question whether we're really still on Wisteria Drive. With each passing pocket of dense trees, the city lights trickle in through the foliage, and the greenery below seems more and more sparse. While the estates below have pristine hedges and artificial gardens, up here is like stumbling upon a natural oasis, hidden amongst the outskirts of the city.

Once the limo levels out, I'm nearly smooshing my cheeks against the glass, anticipation buzzing around me. When the tree line breaks free, my breath hitches and heart nearly stops.

Wow... is the only thought I can muster, staring in wonder at undoubtedly the most beautiful view of New York City I've seen in the night. From our tall vantage point, the skyscrapers stand proud in the night, glowing magnificent hues of white and crystal-blue, like cloudless stars reflecting off a calm lake.

Sloping down the unobscured bluff, we travel atop a cobblestone driveway that runs through yet *another* gate, this one imposing while gliding open on a muted hum.

"We've arrived," our driver announces over the intercom, before an architectural masterpiece comes into view as we round a central fountain.

Don't get me wrong, my life is not a tale of rags to riches, having been born in one of the most prominent families in the country, meaning I've walked through my fair share of mansions. Contemporary, Victorian, Tudor-style, you name it, and I've experienced it. And, at this point, there are very few that catch my eye. But there's something about Tristan's modern estate that just screams luxury with dark hints of secrecy.

Slabs of black concrete pivot at sharp points, framing the floor-to-ceiling glass panels dominating the exterior. Steel slopes along the near-flat roofs, and polished marble leads to a mahogany front door and a three-car garage. Warm light gleams along the path, giving—

A tuxedo blocks my view from the opposite side of the window, before I spot Tristan's inked hand reaching for the door handle. And it's now that I realize my chin rests on my palm, elbow propped on the side of the door, staring out like I'm Cinderella arriving at the ball at midnight in her pumpkin coach.

How embarrassing. His ego doesn't need further nurturing. Get a grip.

As Tristan props open the door for me, I snap that awestruck, doe-eyed look off my face, and instead opt for an unimpressed, composed demeanor. Jumbling my dress's long hemline above my ankles, I take his outstretched hand, my stiletto making firm contact with the cobblestone. And in what seems like a flash, our driver zips away, as his taillight's red glow disappears through the trees.

It's so calm.

I breathe deep, focusing on the sounds of trickling water emanating from the impressive fountain, which proves quite tranquil in the night's hush.

"So, it's to your liking, then?"

"Hmm?" I'm pulled from my serenity.

"My house. You *are* technically moved in already. You seemed impressed."

"Oh, ya..." I shrug, facing the mansion, whose walls are even taller now that we stand in the driveway. "It's nice."

"Just nice?" His smirk is daring, calling my bluff.

But I double down and fold my arms around my middle. "Look, I'm not some sorority girl who's going to fawn all over your riches. Sorry to burst your bubble, but I've seen real estate that would make your home look like a cookie-cutter duplex. Now, can we go inside?" I make for the front door. "It's getting kind of co—"

"No, wait." Catching my arm, he tugs me back into the crook of his warm body. "A cookie-cutter duplex, huh? Ouch." His deep timbre rumbles against my skin. "Since my new wife has such a sharp tongue and is so hard to please, I have one more surprise for you."

Nobody should be allowed to sound that good.

Gritting through his velvet undertones, I ask, "What, do the porch lights twinkle or something?"

"No, no. It's *much* better than that. See, I knew taking in an Astor, I'd really have to up my game."

"Fine." I audibly sigh. "I'm ready."

Sinking a hand in his pants pocket, a hidden *click* resounds, and the leftmost garage door rises.

Oh, here we go.

I hold in my protest, mentally preparing myself for his rows of sports cars, which he's sure will impress me. But it only takes the door opening just enough to reveal the car's metallic hood for my interest to pique, because—that can't be...

No...

That's impossible...

When the door reveals its prize, I'm left dumbfounded. *Stupefied.* My mind unwinds like a wine cork, primed to pop, before imploding into tiny splinters across the driveway.

"WHAT?!" I shriek.

SEVEN

TRISTAN

"OH MY GOD—OH my God—*oh my fucking God.*"

Lauren's heels clack along the garage floor in rapid percussions as she circles the McLaren Sabre like a hungry tiger. Her long white train trails behind her, brushing along the supercar's steel-gray exterior that's a mere six inches off the ground.

"H-how...? How did you—Nobody could—"

"Words, Mrs. Walker." I call her by her new last name, satisfaction burning through my veins when she doesn't throw me a damning look. "Use your words."

She stops by the driver's side door, her hair matching the car's fiery orange accents. "How did you get this? Only ten exist in the world."

I step towards her. "Nine, actually."

"Nine..." Biting her lip, her gaze sweeps across the vehicle, absorbing every detail, almost as if she's afraid to touch it. She whirls on her heels, facing me. "I know the list of owners, and have made offers to all of them—egregious offers."

"Have you now?" I ask, taking another step, not the least bit shocked.

"None were willing to sell," she says, confirming what I already know. "How did you change one of their minds? It couldn't have been with an offer."

"Clever girl. No, it wasn't. But I'll leave how as my little secret." My next footfall lands inches from her, pressing her backside against the car door. Craning my head down, my eyes flicker to her mouth, still tasting her sweetness on my tongue from the ceremony. "You'll quickly learn that I'm a very convincing man, Lauren, who gets exactly what he wants, with or without money."

Her pupils visibly dilate, and it's enough to stiffen me below the belt.

But the answer to her question...

Blackmail.

After hacking Lauren's search engine histories, I quickly discovered her fascination with the McLaren Sabre, only to further unbury emails she's sent to every one of their owners. Since the car's launch in 2020, she's offered upwards of five to ten million dollars to each of them—nearly triple the car's initial value—with no success.

Once I realized bribery wasn't an option, I was keenly aware I'd cross whatever line necessary to get her what she wanted. I began looking into the owners, most billionaires with recognizable last names. And, turns out, a particular CEO on Wall Street's books are *cooked.* Cooked, as in crooked as hell. Crooked, as in inflating his company's profits via fraudulent accounting to entice investors, creating for the world an unstable asset that only exists to enrich *his* pockets.

All it took was a single threatening email containing proof, spelling out exactly what would occur if he unwisely chose the route of incompliance—which treaded along the thin lines of total and complete exposure. He left the car abandoned in the unmarked location of my choosing the following night, keys still in the ignition.

Guess shareholders and the public wouldn't take too kindly to his actions.

I still plan to leak his precious secret—in due time. A year or so, maybe. Long enough that he can't map the coincidence back to America's newest Sabre driver.

For him, I have no mercy or second chances. Because he's had more than one could count. Because he's a burden on society left unchecked, whose greediness trickles down to those he'll never look in the eye. He might as well steal tuition from a single mother's child or a loaf of bread from a hopeless vagabond, then at least his stomach would get a taste of the damages wrought from his own hands. Suit or tie atop an ivory tower wearing a presidential grin or not, it makes no difference to *me*—his judge *and* jury.

He'll reap what he sows.

And, call me a hypocrite, a thief's a thief.

So...

I pull myself from the aggravating scenario, instead refocusing on the delectable wildcat in front of me.

...Point proven—not that she'll ever know. Guess I really don't *need to bring cash to my negotiations.*

"Is that what this is? A bribe to get what you want from me?" she asks in a near whisper, subtle anger weaving through her tone. But not overshadowing the familiar allure I recognize from all the times I've watched her, giving away just how needy she really is.

Propping my hands against the car, on either side of her head, I trap her between my biceps. She gasps, her dress jumbling around my legs at my nearness, and I'm surprised when I feel not an ounce of guilt at having violated her online privacy. Locking my jaw in restraint, I cast out the thought of taking her over the hood of this car, clad in her silky wedding dress, until she's screaming my name loud enough to know who she belongs to, enough to wake the neighbors down the other side of the mountain.

"I don't need to buy you fancy things to get what I want from you. You *do* own half of what's mine. But, if that's how you'd prefer this arrangement to go, you can have just that. Don't believe that I'm above shoving my Black Amex between your lips and telling you the pin, only so I can have you each and every way I desire. Because I'm not." When she wets her lips, I know I could take her right here, right now, if I pushed further. But I let up, allowing her room to breathe. "But no. I can't bribe you with what's already yours, now can I?"

Left in a state of disarray, her chest rises and falls as she propels herself away from the car. "What do you mean?" She eyes me suspiciously.

Retrieved from my pocket, I dangle a key in front of her, a red bow intricately woven between the metallic loop. Her eyes widen like saucers, jaw slackening before clamping it shut. Rolling her lips between her teeth, she peeks at the car, then meets my gaze, unable to stop the toothy grin spreading across her features.

"You can't mean—"

"I do—mean exactly that." I set the keys in her palm, finding acute pleasure when her fingers slink around the grooves. "It's your wedding present."

∾

I SPEND the better half of an hour giving Lauren the grand tour, which conveniently left out my hidden tech room, lest my new bride finds out I'm the world's most wanted hacker. But I'm sure she didn't notice, seeing as the house is nearly fifteen thousand square feet.

I'll admit, the place was pretty barren before she moved in. Once I found out about our arrangement, I hired the most expensive interior designer from the city to decorate and liven up the rooms—and it seems to have paid off.

"Your house is... amazing."

Our house, I restrain from correcting her.

Craning her neck upwards, she admires the living room's central chandelier, unknowingly giving me a glorious view of her backside.

I don't know if she slipped on that sporty black bodysuit because she means to torture me, or because it was the first outfit in one of the unpacked boxes left by the front door from the movers. But, either way, I'm enjoying the view. Her red hair flows behind her shoulders in tight curls, with every one of her mouthwatering curves on full display.

Christ. My eyes peruse down her body. *The things I'm going to do to her...*

Turning, blatant awe marks her beautiful features—and stays there until we stand in front of the final room of the tour.

"I saved the best for last." When I push open the door, her hushed sigh is the only affirmation I need.

My bedroom has the best view in the house, with a single glass panel lining the entire wall facing the city. Forest trees frame the distant skyscrapers like a painting, their distant lights and the infinity pool glowing blue on the deck below as its focal point. Charcoal gray wallpaper with gold accents wraps around the walls, matching the room to the house's dark aesthetic.

When she wanders into the bathroom, I smirk.

"Uh..." Brow furrowing, her gaze darts across the room, from the additional toothbrush next to mine to the massive closet stocked full of her clothes. "All my stuff is in here."

"And?" I lean against the doorframe.

Her fist snaps to her now popped-out hip, a confrontational look I'm growing to love blooming across her face. "Sorry—let me rephrase that for you." Her tone drips with sarcasm. *"Why* is my stuff in your room?"

"Our room," I correct.

Her eyebrows raise, and a silence encroaches between us.

"I had the movers bring all your belongings to *our* room. Is that a problem?"

"Yes, actually." She crosses her arms. "They clearly forgot the most important item—my bed. What room did they stick it in?"

Mimicking her, I fold my arms over my chest, stretching the fabric of my black tee taut. When I catch her gaze flicker to my biceps for a fraction of a second, hunger sparks inside of me. "They threw it out."

As per my request, I don't add.

"What?"

"Why would my wife need a second bed?" I challenge.

Pacing across the room, she hisses under her breath, something along the lines of *"out of his fucking mind."*

"Let's get one thing straight. What happened today at the altar." The fainting, she neglects to say out loud, embarrassment still creeping up her neck. "That was the pressure and stress getting to me. Nothing else. So, don't get it twisted."

"Mmhmm." I nod, even though I don't believe one drop of

her sudden bravado. "I'm sure a lawyer like yourself is quite unprepared for high-stress situations."

"This is different," she hisses, and I bite my lip to keep from smiling. With a powerful strut, she stops in front of me, before laying down the law. "This is only an arrangement, one that will *not* be consummated. You're representing the company, and I'm protecting it legally. That's all. We're a united—*fake*—front. It would be best if the lines weren't blurred. Meaning, I am, under no circumstances, sharing a *bed* with you. Understand?"

"I didn't ask you to."

Confusion marks her face, so I explain, "I would never let my wife sleep in any other room but the master. If you don't want me in your bed, fine. I'll take the couch or a guest room. You're never to sleep in any room but this one. But let me make *myself* clear." I let my gaze fall down her body, slowly, revealing exactly what I want. "It won't take long before you ask me to join you."

"Arrogant much?" She scoffs, unable to meet my gaze.

Closing the distance between us in one step, I let our bodies graze against each other, so she can feel what she does to me, standing there in that tight outfit. She gasps, her eyes ever-so slowly tracing the long steel subtly outlined by my sweatpants now pressing against her stomach. I watch her intently before cupping her jaw, tilting her head all the way up to look at me, recognizing the palpable lust behind her stare.

"Yes, I am," I say hoarsely, a groan nearly surfacing from the torturous friction. "But that's not why... Something tells me you can't hold out for long."

Her lips part in shock. But before she can speak, I brush my thumb across her soft lips, dragging downwards until the bottom pops back up. "And when that happens—when you ask me to take you in the way you so desire—it'll be too late."

Throat bobbing, her exhales are like struggling mewls. "Y-you don't know me."

"Don't I?" I tighten my grip, the tips of my fingers grooving through her hair. "If I reached between your thighs, would I find your pretty cunt soaked for me?"

A soft whimper passes her lips, the sound in complete contrast to the stubborn expression staring back at me.

"That's what I thought." I chuckle darkly. "So, for now, we'll play this your way. I'll be the CEO you so desperately need and nothing else, only to watch you pay the price to get what you truly want."

By now she's so worked up, she's the one pushing into *me*. "What price?" she asks on a moan.

"That you'll be my good little slut, who won't hesitate to present her needy holes for filling, whenever I want, wher-ever I want."

Her chest rises and falls rapidly, and I sense a war waging inside her brain of whether or not to give in. But I don't let her decide, instead leaning in until my lips brush her ear.

"Now, I'll leave it to you to finish yourself off."

EIGHT

LAUREN

IT'S BEEN a week since our encounter that almost sent me over the edge.

A week of nearly breaking my back against the shower wall, morning and night. A week of suffering Tristan's sidelong glances and knowing smirks before he disappears all day to do who knows what. And, what's worst of all, a week of doing *absolutely nothing*.

As far as the world knows, Mr. and Mrs. Walker are gallivanting their way through a romantic European honeymoon, set to arrive back in New York City on the morrow. Which means we're both strictly house bound. No public outings whatsoever, not even for work.

I don't remember the last time I've sat around and done nothing. Do people really do that—all day? If I watch any more reality TV, my mind might actually deteriorate into something between children's Play Doh and a complacent sloth.

At least I'm getting my tan on.

I roll over with an exasperated sigh, the grooves of the

sunbed kissing my stomach. Pushing my wide-brimmed shades further up my nose, I swipe to the next page of my ByteBuzz article.

I'm usually not much for exaggerated gossip, especially when it's about my family or myself, but I've read their stuff before—only for keeping up on recent tech news. Although, I've never been *this* deep. Over the past week, I've devoured more click-baity blog posts than I can count, even ones of Tristan and me.

Tapping to ByteBuzz's front page, our article plasters along the blog's top banner, no doubt their most clicked news of the week. No reader would ever suspect the supposed paparazzi photos are anything but authentic or that the very man captured in the shots leaked them. But, here I am, lying on a sunbed in the middle of an oasis, never having left New York.

It's quite eerie, really, what artificial intelligence software can do, especially under the mastery of a technological savant. Pursing my lips, I study the photo of us hand in hand, Tristan in board shorts and me in a bikini, walking barefoot along the sandy beaches of Crete, Greece.

The attention to detail is unbelievable.

Zooming in, I even catch the tiny flower tattoo on my ankle I got in Hawaii years ago. And that bikini, it's exactly like something I would wear. Twin triangles accentuate my breasts by a tight knot tied behind my neck. Gold hoops decorate the risqué thong bottoms. And thin ties criss-cross around my tan belly, forming an X pattern.

In fact, it looks oddly familiar...

I cock my head, brow furrowing as I glance towards my cleavage, *discovering the bikini's spitting image already hugging my curves.* Bolting to my knees, icy coldness shoots from my toes up to the hairs on my head.

That fucking asshole.

My gaze whips up high, searching the house's countless windows, trying to spot him lurking in a shadow, or a red dot from a camera, *anything*. But I come up empty.

Relax. Releasing a slow breath, I settle back into my bed, propping myself up on my elbows. *It's probably a coincidence.*

Coincidence, my ass. There's no such thing as coincidences, another, more analytical side of me argues, the side that would usually call the shots if my brain hadn't recently turned to soggy mush. *Way to let a smooth-talking, pretty face get to you. How embarrassing.*

Taking a sip of my 2 o'clock gin mule, I sigh.

Speaking of that...

Peeking around, making sure I'm still alone on the patio, I zoom in on the photo, blowing up Tristan's glorious body. Inked slightly darker than his hair, tattoos crawl across his arms and chest, leaving washboard abs the center of attention. With tan muscles in all the right places, he looks like he walked straight off the cover of *Sports Illustrated*.

It's a fake photograph, I remind myself, but the idea does little for my gawking. Creeping my nose an inch from the screen, I bend my legs at the knees, pointing my toes in the air lazily, as I zoom closer—

"Quite an interesting read, you got there," says a voice like sin from behind me.

I gasp, slamming my phone face-down on the sunbed.

"I know what you're thinking." Amusement coats his words. "That there's no way any of that is real."

Angling my head towards the ground, I freeze like a

statue, lest he discovers my face the same color as a ripe tomato. "It's not, being as it's a *fake* photograph."

"Artificial intelligence *learns,* baby. It can't create what doesn't already exist. Meaning, I had to feed it actual photos of myself. I could send you a few, if you'd like."

My cheeks blaze even hotter, signaling it's time to leave.

"No thanks," I bite out, scrabbling to my feet, avoiding his direction, but he steps from the corner of my eye and—

"Oof." A breath knocks from my lungs, and I struggle for balance.

"Easy there." His chuckle sounds directly above my head, sending a shiver down my neck.

Emerging from my disorienting state, I first notice where my hands are. Or, more like, *what's underneath them.* My eyes move of their own accord, and strong pectorals flex in response, as they slowly trail downwards, confirming every bit of the photograph circling across the web—and now through the most remote corners of my consciousness, igniting a fire that may just consume me whole.

There's no unseeing that.

"Wh-what are you doing?" I manage to ask, staring at his bare skin.

It's been a week since he touched me in the bathroom and made promises that, ever since, have left me like a neglected oven, turned to broiling temperatures. And now he's here, all *in-control and delicious,* with his hands cupping around the small of my back, right above my G-string.

And it's way more than I can bear.

My mind screams at me to move, to flee back into the house where it's safe, but it's as if I'm stuck ankle-deep in hypnotizing cement.

"I thought I'd join my wife in the sun. It *is* our honeymoon, after all. And you really are so tempting in that bikini of yours. Do you always wear swimwear that's so—"

"I'm done, actually." I look elsewhere, over his arm, resisting the subtle scents of cedarwood and spice wafting through my nostrils.

Fuck, he smells divine.

"Really? Are you now?"

"Yep!" I say, two octaves above normal. "Just finishing up."

"Good idea. It's probably time for a shower. Are you sure you don't need any help in there?"

A bucket of ice-cold water dumps over my head, and I break free from his grasp, aiming right for the sliding glass door.

Now that's not a coincidence. How does he know? I thought I was being quiet, but maybe not quiet enough. And he's been sleeping in a spare bedroom. There's no way he could hear from out there.

Unless he's been listening—

My pace quickens towards the house, desperate to be free of his tantalizing aura, as if I can escape the all-consuming fire pumping throughout my body. The thought of him eavesdropping by the door, overhearing every bit of my self-pleasure, including the times his own name uncontrollably rolled off my tongue...

It's wrong.

It's violating.

It's... *sexy as hell?*

No, wait. That can't be right.

I should be flat out disturbed or threatening him with legal action. Not running away all hot and bothered from a thirty-second interaction with the man who's not only my husband but my supposed *voyeur*.

Spotting Tristan in the window's reflection, he trails me with a beaming smile. "Well, I *did* find some unmentionable items in your boxes. Such an impressive collection, too. I'll admit, I didn't tag you as the type. But, don't worry, *I'm* the one who put them in your nightstand—not the movers. Best to have easy access whenever a sudden urge comes on. And, gosh, there *has* been some awful ruckus coming from that bathroom of ours. I can't help but wonder..."

Fuckkk.

At the brash confirmation, right before I burst through the door, my nipples pebble beneath my bikini, pushing taut against the thin fabric, and creating for me an entire world of aching need. I'm thankful when the chilly air conditioning strikes my skin, but soon find it's of little use.

My bare feet clammer across the marbled floor as I aim for our—*my*—bedroom. Tristan's chuckle is at my back, taunting and cocky, full of dark promises and delicious endings.

"Don't you want help out of that lovely bikini, Lauren?" he purrs. "Or, better yet, I'd prefer if you kept it on."

God.

My name on his tongue is a sensuous command, one that every ounce of my being screams at me to obey, to whip around and melt into compliant putty beneath his feet.

By the time I reach the bedroom, I'm practically biting my bottom lip half-off and running a temperature close to boiling. His next seductive call is cut short—by me slamming the door in his face.

NINE

TRISTAN

THERE'S nothing like the smell of worn leather and hard-earned sweat.

Light on the balls of his feet, Bryson circles me inside the confines of the ring, his padded focus mitts absorbing my flurry of punches. He catches them with a controlled precision in our dance of coordination that's only made possible by years of practice and connection.

He knows me through and through, like a brother I never had. Which is why, when I feign to the left and swing a vicious uppercut—a move that would no doubt send another man to an unexpected naptime—he catches the blow with ease, as if he's the choreographer behind my strikes.

"So..." He dodges another, sweat shining below his hairline. "What's your plan?"

"What plan?" I huff out, opting for another tactic—bullying him into the corner.

Three rows of jumper cables encase the ring in a perfect square, and elastic rubber provides a soft yet durable floor beneath our feet. We're sparring in my pull-barn-turned-boxing-gym I had built years ago on my property, where Bryson and I practice twice a week.

Before he's two backpedals away from touching the ropes, he senses my strategy, ducking and dashing underneath my next swing. Flustered, I swivel one-eighty, finding him smug.

Too slow, his self-assured grin seems to say.

"Don't play dumb with me, Walker. The one and only plan —*blinding the eyes that see all.*"

The Oculi.

My feet fall flat, every ounce of energy zapped out of me, guilt drying out my throat. "Nothing. There's nothing to do."

Bryson lowers his mitts, shoulders slouching. He knows the pressure and blackmail I'm under, the real reason I'm in my current arrangement. I tell him everything. Always.

Unable to handle the pity in his stare, I duck underneath the rope, bound off the platform, and head for the water station.

"And what is there to do?" I ask, not expecting an answer or reassurance. Not that he could come up with either. It's obvious I'm utterly and completely fucked. "I've spent the better half of three years trying to find a weak spot in their organization. Their top of command. *Something.* You know that. But I can't keep meddling in their affairs, not anymore, not when Aurora's in their sights."

His presence comes up beside me, resting a comforting hand on my shoulder.

"Don't." I shrug him off roughly.

I recall Aurora at our wedding, sitting where our mother would have, looking every bit her carbon copy. Her floral-inspired style, her blonde hair and authentic smile, down to her optimism which defies even the most dire of circum-stances. But I didn't give her the chance to sniff out Lauren and I's false connection. That day, I introduced my new bride to her in under two minutes, before whisking Lauren away on an apology of having little time, needing to thank the rest of our guests, and a promise of catching up soon.

A promise I don't intend on keeping.

Meeting Bryson's stare, I sigh. "Don't," I repeat, lightening my tone. "I know what you're going to say. That I'm not a burden on my sister. But the harsh truth is *that I am*. All I do is cause her trouble, just like when we were kids. Only now, she's making a life for herself in college and is so close to graduating, while unknowingly being used as a hostage to bend my will in a deadly game she doesn't even know exists. So, yes. She *is* better off without me, even now."

Bryson snatches his gallon-sized water bottle, not a sliver of anger lining his next remark. "We're not kids anymore. We can't change the childhoods we were dealt any more than the things we did to survive. You act as if she isn't cut from the same cloth as us."

"Maybe she is. But I'm the older sibling. *I still am.* She can spout about how she wants to make it all on her own, all she wants, but I know why she turns down the money I offer her. And it's no wonder. If I were her, I wouldn't accept *anything* from me. I was supposed to protect her back then, not be a ball and chain wrapped around her ankles, dragging her down each time we—"

My voice strains, as unwelcome memories invade my mind. They're scarred, jagged around the edges, and all too familiar, slicing and replacing any passing neurons with white-washed walls, fluorescent lighting that sucks the life from your blood, and, above all else...

Shattered hope.

Fighting the telltale signs of the coming on of a panic

attack, I breathe slowly, in and out... in and out... then gulp water like I'm a desert castaway, unwilling to be brought to my knees by a numbness I know all too well.

"So," I croak out. "What's my plan? To allow their eyes to see whatever the hell it is they need from this strange arrangement. And if I need to act as some air-headed CEO for the rest of eternity for Aurora to live the peaceful life she deserves, so be it."

Bryson remains quiet for the rest of our sparring, and it isn't until we sit on a bench outside the building, soaking in the day's last sunrays, that I realize I didn't tell him the whole truth. While I've crossed Silicon Avenue's most threatening society off my hacker radar, there *is* another mystery I'm still working on solving...

"There's been more transfers to the offshore accounts."

Bryson perks up. "Did you find something new?"

"Only that now I know they're connected somehow. The transfers are all coming from the same MAC addresses on an unknown VPN server."

"English, hacker-man. Use English." His lips thin. "I work with stocks and hedge funds. Not cryptography."

I bite back a smirk. "Think of a MAC address like a computer's social security number. Meaning, each server has its own unique address. And when you get down to the nitty-gritty, that's all a server really is—a computer. Before, I thought these transactions weren't connected, but after hacking their MAC addresses and discovering them all the same, I know they're coming from the same computer."

"Which means one person, or one computer, is behind every transaction."

"Exactly."

"Okay..." He leans over, resting an elbow on his knee,

appearing in deep thought. "Then what's stopping you from finding their identity? It seems like you have exactly what you'd want."

"MAC addresses don't reveal any personal information. The big one being their location. That's what I'm currently working on and is the big piece of the puzzle. The simple fact I could even intercept their traffic in the first place means they have to be nearby. Nearby, as in probably in New York City."

Bryson snorts. "Yeah, like *that* helps. You've got it narrowed down to just under nine million suspects." He nudges my shoulder. "What's stopping you from your hacker magic, huh? This seems like the thing you could bust out in a night."

The funny thing is, nine million is quite a small number in the world of cryptography. But I keep the snarky remark to myself.

I cross my arms, resting my back against the bench. "Usually, it would be. But their location hides behind an encryption I've never dealt with before. I'd need the decryption key, and so far, that's proven very challenging to figure out."

And brute force is not an option, I remind myself. I don't go into the details, not wishing to bore him...

But for you? *I render no option.*

Buckle up. Class is in session.

To crack the encryption hiding the computer's location, a decryption "key" of 64 random hexadecimal characters is required.

For example, maybe the key is this:

8F7A35A117C9D7880805F0F-
B355A7D8372B62097751A0871399618E072536046

Or this:

A4C01768CEAE460B9E99511BE4BEC52C3490F-
FA4B214F42D67EF403549FD5EE2

Or, *maybe*, this:

E6BA1DBD8F744D6F107823C3861D7-
CAD9B3023AD9570C5FDE5A8E18A231CDABA

Understand?
It's quite the dilemma.
If you do the math—which I would love to whiteboard out for my friend here but lack the precious time and persuasive skills—*that's a lot of possible combinations.* More combinations than the number of *atoms* in the visible universe or neurons in the human brain. So many, that a thousand supercomputers running twenty-four hours a day randomly guessing the decryption key couldn't solve it. *Not even by the end of our lifetime.*

The magical number of possibilities, you ask?
2^{256}

That's $2 \times 2 \times 2 \times 2$ ... 256 times. (Hence, why it's referred to as a *256-bit key* in modern-day cryptography.)

I'll spare you the effort of inputting that equation into your handy-dandy calculator—which wouldn't be able to calculate it, anyway. Because if it could, the result would be a number so unfathomably large, it has seventy-eight digits.

Yes, *digits*.

In short, if I don't find a weakness in the encryption algorithm to better help me solve the key, there is absolutely *no way in hell* I'm figuring out who's behind these mysterious transactions.

Class is adjourned.

"Well, hey," Bryson says, patting me on the back. "Not everything's turned to shit. At least your arrangement came with *that.*"

He flicks his chin across the yard to the beautiful woman on my front porch. From our vantage point, Lauren is unlikely to spot us, but her fiery red hair stands out through the forest's dense foliage. Pressing a phone against her ear, she paces across the mahogany, hips swaying in a hypnotizing rhythm.

I'm taken aback when annoyance plummets into my stomach, splashing down into a pit full of territorial jealousy. Bryson's eyes track her every movement, and it's enough to swim murder through my thoughts.

Not catching a hint from my impending silence, with a playboy smirk, he continues, "What a smokeshow. And sleeping under the same roof as you? I'm sure you two have been busy. If that was my wife—real or fake or arranged, I don't care—I'd be tappin' that every—"

"Bryson," I growl, shooting him a scathing look, one that surprises me more than him.

Eyebrows scrunching, skepticism lines his features. "Oh, no. Don't tell me—"

"I'm not." Folding strong arms around my chest, my blood pressure pounds between my ears. "There aren't any feelings and won't be. She's a spoiled piece of work with a smart mouth."

That I've spied on and hacked daily for nearly a year now, I don't add. Not that Bryson would scold me for the invasion of privacy, but the confession is just too big. Especially after what I saw following our confrontation at the pool earlier today.

Such a greedy girl....

She was quite pent up after our encounter, seeing as she rode her dildo with extra tenacity. Even if she *did* know I've been spying on her through her phone, it's not like she's trying to hide it. I could've easily listened in on those desperate moans and cries of ecstasy by simply standing by the bedroom door... And catching her ogling my photo in that delicious bikini of hers was more than enough confirmation that she'll be mine for my liking sooner rather than later.

"Right, right. Well, I'm sure you know just what to do with that smart mouth of—" He stops himself short, a dubious grin spreading across his features when he catches my jaw grinding like a millstone. "Quite the touchy subject for you, man. Are you sure you're not—"

"Yes. I'm sure."

"Alrighty, then. Whatever you say."

Relief pours over me when she goes back inside, away from Bryson's prying gaze, leaving me asking similar questions, even after he's long gone and I'm back playing house with my arranged wife.

If sex is all I want from her, then why does one glance from my friend get me so riled up?

TEN

LAUREN

FOR A RECLUSIVE BILLIONAIRE who is rarely seen in public, let alone in his own kitchen, Tristan's pantry is *loaded.*

Snacks and cereals, tortillas, oils, flour, spices, and vegetables—you name it, it's in here—all stacked on high shelves, meticulously placed by whom I'd guess is a professional organizer. And the same goes with his gigantic freezers and fridges.

I raise an eyebrow at the bags upon bags of beans, lentils, and rice. Oversized and sealed in see-through containers, they stack in the corner, nearly touching the ceiling.

What is he, some doomsday prepper?

Nearing the backside of the pantry, which has enough space to fit a nice-sized bedroom and then some, I open a cupboard labeled *pastas.* Heels clacking against the marble with a box of linguine noodles in hand, I round back to the kitchen, only to discover something down-right mouthwatering.

With perfectly dampened locks draping down his forehead, Tristan stands beside the stovetop, eyelids closed, smelling the meal I'm cooking. He sports form-fitting gray sweatpants and a white tee shirt, but he may as well be naked. Stirring the red saucepan, his biceps bulge, veins straining along his tattoos.

"I didn't know you cooked," he muses, his deep voice causing my eyes to drag down to his sweatpants, which are of a tight fit and have the most delicious outline around his—

Shit. Quit staring.

I snap my eyes back up the moment his catch mine. When his gaze dances with mischief, I know I'm caught.

"I do, from time to time." I shrug, battling the heat forming in my cheeks. "I'm quite a good one, actually. This is nothing special."

Lies, a voice chimes in my ears. Since when is a three-course meal starring steamed oyster linguini, scallops, and ribeye steak not a big deal? Not to mention, kicking out all the housing staff for the night, including the cooks, ensuring alone time with him.

"Nothing special, huh?" He smirks. "I got your text. You're making a meal just for me?"

I come up right next to him, grabbing one of the many brass pots hanging above the stovetop. "We're set to meet with the board in two days. We need to practice appearing married."

"Practice?" He chuckles, too close to my ear, seeming almost offended by the word. "We *are* married, might I remind you. There's no need to practice anything." The backs of his fingers trail down my arm. "Unless you mean—"

"That's not what I mean." I bat him away before his touch lulls me into an inescapable trance. Instead, I focus on letting water into the pot through the stove's attached faucet, paying

him no attention. "Enough games. We need to be taken seriously."

From the corner of my vision, he folds his arms. "So, I take it you thought *those* were necessary for *practice?*"

I shoot him a puzzled glance, following his languid eyes wandering down my short dress that's covered by an apron, past my bare legs, and stopping at my feet.

"What—these?" I quizzically stare at my pink manicured toes peeking through my matching pumps, the stilettos so sharp they might pierce clean through the mahogany.

"It's not too late to admit you like to look good for me. First the pool, now this?" he asks, face smug enough to punch.

"No need to read into them." I purse my lips, chin lifting. "I'd never be caught dead without heels. Anywhere. The only brands adorning these feet are Jimmy Choo and Prada. And, for the record, these are my *house-appropriate* heels. They're only four inches."

His mouth opens, no doubt for a snarky response—

"And while we're on the topic of clothes..." I cut him short, my tone dripping with spite. "What are you wearing to the board meeting? Because it sure isn't anything you left in my closet."

Jaw clenching, heat simmers behind Tristan's eyes in a way that has my lips rolling at his nearness. But I stand my ground, weathering his intense stare before whipping my head back to the stove, submerging the linguini into the now boiling water.

"Do you have a problem with my clothes?"

More games.

If he's looking for a mental sparring, I'm more than eager

to play. And he picked the wrong opponent. Reality check. That's my job.

And we're not even inside a courtroom.

Wooden spoon in hand, I shake my head and stir, wearing an apathetic expression. "How could I possibly have a problem with them? They're nowhere to be found. You obviously moved them. You know, all your *real* clothes? Suits, ties, blazers—not the excuse for a high school dropout left hanging from my closet rods. Nothing but cheap hoodies, plain T-shirts, and worn-out sweatpants. What an eyesore. And would it kill you to wear something with color? If I have to keep staring across at a solid wall of neutral darks and grays, I might actually go blind."

An aching tension bounces between us, and I mentally prepare myself for his impending retort. But when a torturously long second passes by, and then another, satisfaction burns its way down my middle—

"That's a whole lot of words for asking me back into our bed."

Sucking in a startled breath, my composure completely blown, I whip towards him, a savage response hot on my tongue—

"I don't blame you, baby. You'll find it comes with many benefits, all of which I'll be more than happy to *practice* with you." His smile is brazen and mocking, branding my skin with rage. But before I can deny his claims, he interrupts me *again*. "Although, now that I think of it, those perks don't extend to the clothing department."

"What?" I burst out, my mind splintering in disbelief.

That can't be possible. He must be lying. Because if what this *billionaire*—my arranged husband, who lives atop

Wisteria Drive in a hidden mansion like some modern-day Jay Gatsby—is alluding to is true, that would mean...

He doesn't own any suits.

"You think I need some fancy suit to convince the board to appoint me as CEO?" he asks, confirming my suspicions, his confident step sucking the air from my lungs and eliminating the little space left between us.

Hands sprawling upwards, he rests them high above my head against the metallic range hood attached to the ceiling. My head trapped between his biceps, he pins me like he did on our wedding night. Only this time, I don't know if the fire sparking between my legs is from my ass cheeks pressing into the stove's bar or from the six-foot-five inked god staring down at me like I'm his next conquest.

"N-no one would show up in anything less," I stammer, heart hammering against my ribcage.

"I'm not just anyone." He catches a red curl, twirling it between his fingers. "But for you, wife, I'll play the part. Wear the suits and the ties. Even though every member of that board knows Astor Security is nothing but a long-term investment to me, waiting to be cashed."

A flicker of anger sparks inside me. He speaks as though he has some type of claim to the company's success, as if he was there with my father during his long nights building the company from the ground up.

But his tone...

Why does he sound so sure?

It's my code running Astor Security, he had said during our wedding reception. The words replay in my head like a vinyl record, spinning at a dangerous speed while running over ominous scratches. I lacked the time to pry answers out of him after he had made such a preposterous claim, and I was too skeptical afterwards.

"What?" He cocks his head down at me when I meet his challenging gaze. As if my thoughts are plain and written in a book for him, he says, "You're wondering how one man's code can run the world's largest security company. I'll admit, it doesn't run all of it. But it's the backbone of Astor Security's most sophisticated encryption systems, the ones used by their Fortune 500 clientele since the formation of the company."

"That's not possible." *Or is it?* My father founded the company twelve years ago, and Tristan's twenty-eight, one year my senior. "That would mean you were—"

"Sixteen."

Sixteen... The math adds up.

Denial winds a tight band around me, plunging me into a hushed stillness.

"Much too young to legally form a business in America. Not that I wanted to. Back then, I needed quick cash. But unfortunately for the big names on Silicon Avenue, I was unsusceptible to their many manipulations. Because I knew what I had—and, even worse, knew how to hide my product from theft. So, when I advertised I meant to sell, a bidding war ensued, one your father eventually won. He paid me a lump sum so high that my final demand before signing was to keep the number and my name from the public. That's why no papers reported on the deal. But many long-standing board members know about it."

"How much was the buyout?" I dare ask.

"Three hundred million."

Quietness engulfs us, accompanied only by the bubbles of boiling water behind my back and Tristan's minty exhales tickling against my forehead. In his nearness, I crane my head upwards, studying his features for a fault. But not a single stress mark lines his face. And no uneasiness sways in his dark eyes.

He's telling the truth.

"I don't believe you. You're lying," I accuse against my sound assessment, weathering the manly aromas of after-shave dancing their way into my nostrils when he leans in closer.

From head to toe, I'm enveloped by his body heat. Stifling a moan, I press harder into the stove, blood pumping below my waistline. Suddenly, when the skirt of my short dress crawls up my thighs, I regret picking this outfit. The bottoms of my ass cheeks touch the oven's cold bar, the rough grooves pushing into my skin.

"Sooner or later"—his growl has my toes curling inside my pumps and goosebumps racing along my arms—"you'll accept that Astor Security is mine, just as you belong to me."

My body gravitates into him, an instrument bending to his will, supple and eager for the taking. "I don't belong to anyone," I pant, mustering up a wave of defiance.

"No?" His strong body brushes against mine, sending my dress even higher. "Then I look forward to hearing others call my wife by my last name."

"A-Astor is the name I use at work."

"Not while I'm CEO, it isn't. I'll ensure every man in my company addresses you as Mrs. Walker, acknowledging you're mine, or they'll sign their own resignations within the hour."

My jaw falls the same instant he grinds his hardened length against the apex of my thighs. And even while he wears sweatpants and my apron, harsh friction still scrapes against my clit through my apron—which hopefully conceals my compromising state.

I cry out from the sensation, fumbling for my rising hem, but he snatches my wrists before I touch the fabric, tightly pinning them against the range hood above my head. Heels scraping along the mahogany, my arms writhe in resistance, but I don't budge an inch and only manage to fully expose the skin below my belly button.

"Keep struggling, baby, and maybe this apron will fall off too."

He grinds into me once more before I can reply, earning another moan as his free hand grabs a fistful of my ass cheek. Yanking me towards him, he works my waist along his shaft, until my eyes roll back into my head and wetness spills over the rim of my panties, dribbling down the insides of my thighs.

In minutes, or maybe hours, I'm unsure of who's grinding against who, before he releases his hold on my wrists. Threading his fingers through my hair, he grips possessively, angling my neck to his liking, right before his lips latch onto the column of my throat.

"What are you doing?" I ask breathlessly.

A guttural growl sounds in my ear. "A ring isn't enough to mark you as mine."

He suctions hard, teeth scraping along my delicate skin, before his tongue darts out, lapping up and soothing the burn. I grind against him hard, gasping in a frenzy, way past the point of caring what the fuck we are or aren't or who's giving in to who.

Reduced to a single need, I untie his drawstrings.

His lips plop away from my neck. "Greedy girl, you want my cock?"

"Yes."

"Will you be my good little slut, down on your knees in worship?"

"Yes."

I yank the loops through in a struggle, desperation crawling up my windpipe, until I'm gripping the waistband, tugging down—

"Are you going to invite me back into your bed?

Sucking in a sharp breath, I stop midway, a response lodged down my throat. He pinches my chin and tilts my head up, away from his mouthwatering situation, trailing a long line beneath his pants. Caught off guard, I meet his gaze, finding an authoritative challenge.

"Hmm? Speak up."

"I-I—"

"Then you don't deserve it."

"But I..." Cheeks burning and chest heaving wildly, my tongue twists like a serpent caught in a hunter's trap.

He releases me, but not before his gaze roams down the length of my body, practically marking me on the spot. "There's a point where my restraint ends, Lauren. Don't invite me to dinner while wearing my ring and a tiny dress again, unless you intend to be bent over these countertops screaming my name."

ELEVEN

TRISTAN

IN MY DREAMSCAPE, there exists three themes.

Black nothingness.

Eyes who see all.

And Whispering Pines Home for Children.

... It's the third I dread the most.

One look at my mismatched socks, and I know where I am.

I propel towards the door, adrenaline hot on my neck. But before I can grasp the handle, a familiar voice beckons behind me.

"Tristan, where do you think you're going?" Her tone is sweet but laced with subtle authority. "We're not done with our session yet. Please, return to your seat."

For far too long, I stare ahead at the door's chipped paint, debating whether to listen or dash down the hall and see how long it takes before I'm locked up in my room. Running would be the norm for me, given how it's the only thing left in my life that gives me any sense of control. But, in the light of recent circumstances, I obey.

The couch's faded upholstery swallows me whole, much too large for my frail teenage frame. My sour gaze sweeps across the cracked linoleum floors and white-washed walls depicted with cheerful lions and zebras. Crossing my arms, I lock eyes with our orphanage's counselor, who sits in front of a wall decorated with impressive degrees, ranging from a Bachelor's in Neuroscience to a Ph.D. in child psychology.

Dr. Jennings is surprisingly young and quite pretty, with an inviting smile and silky blonde hair draping behind her dress. But none of that entices me to spend more than five minutes with the woman, who is clearly only trying to help me.

She should know a lost cause when she sees one.

"Thank you. I know this can be a challenging process." She glances at her clipboard, resting an elbow on her chair. "How are you feeling right now, Tristan?"

Shaking my head, I stare at the wall again, unable to hold her gaze. "All those degrees, and all you do is ask me the same fucking questions."

"These questions are designed to help you open up to me," she explains, unscathed by my aggression.

"And why would I want that?"

"We've been over this many times. I can't help if you won't let me in."

And I never have during our mandated thirty minute, bi-weekly sessions. But my outbursts and snide remarks never sway her either, so I pick another from my arsenal of antics.

Nothing.

I say... nothing.

But she rides out our silence. Tapping my shoes on the ground, I listen to the clock ticking and the buzzing from overhead fluorescents, flickering every so often and casting a dull glow. With the ever-present lack of funds, Whispering Pines doesn't have enough money to replace anything, *let alone the life-sucking lighting that only proves to agitate and isolate.*

"Your sister has found these sessions helpful."

I snap my head to her, the lid on my composure stripped bare. "Has she now? I should strive to be like her, shouldn't I? Aurora Walker. Such a talented young girl. What a stroke of bad luck she ended up with delinquents and a run-of-the-mill physician who couldn't find a job elsewhere."

My words are vicious, masking my hidden guilt, but they're also filled with lies.

Dr. Jennings, having graduated from Stanford and several other prestigious universities, could work anywhere. Which only highlights her taking an almost charitable position, helping distressed adolescents whose families faced tragedy. Like what happened to our parents years ago—that I never talk about.

But my sister sure does, leading her to overcome mental boundaries I've yet to even approach. And I'm nearly double her senior. Despite my words, I'd never envy my sister. I can't imagine going through what we did at such a young age. Even though she doesn't have frequent bouts of rage, she's not without her own personal brand of coping.

Upon our first night in the orphanage, she didn't speak a single word. And not again the next day. And the next day. For an entire year. *Until she finally spoke to Dr. Jennings.*

And talked, she sure has.

Improved in many facets, my sister is the model child. The foster kid parents dream of adopting. Well mannered. Cute. Easily sociable. Impeccable grades. The whole shebang. And it's true. She deserves all the growth she's worked so hard for, including a loving home and a future away from here. She could have it all, if it wasn't for the anchor strapped to her ankle.

Her brother who ruins everything.

To my dismay, Dr. Jennings sees right through me.

"Can you tell me what led to the incident at school earlier this week?"

She means when I beat Ainsley Callahan to a pulp during lunch, until his blood coated my knuckles, shining brighter than his ginger hair. Two security guards eventually pulled me—a malnourished freshman—off him, or else I would've never stopped. Even though he's recovering in an ICU somewhere, I still hear his taunts, like he's right beside me on this couch, wearing the same mocking grin.

Did your new mommy and daddy buy you that coat? What a shame. You won't get to keep it after they trade you back in like all the rest.

And he was right.

This time, we only lasted a week with our new adopted parents. Being well-off, they splurged and bought us whole new wardrobes, among other welcome-home gifts. They were especially smitten with Aurora—rightfully so—until they learned her package-deal brother came with special challenges, including authoritative issues, a hair-trigger temper, and an affinity to talk back.

My outburst at school proved too much for them, and they swiftly shipped us back the same day.

"Did the boy provoke you?"

I shrug.

"Do you feel remorse?"

Yes. But only for my sister.

I can't unsee how she deflated upon hearing the news, or the looks of contempt and anger she threw at me on the silent drive all the way back to the orphanage. It was her chance at restarting the life that was stolen from us. A wealthy one at that.

After ten more ticks of the clock, Dr. Jennings pushes her glasses higher up the bridge of her nose, aiming with a different approach. "Could you talk to me about why you're skipping classes again?"

"Because everything they teach is a waste of time."

Rummaging through my hefty file on the coffee table, she retrieves and flips through a packet of papers. *"Having studied your records before, I must admit, they're awfully unique. Your teachers complain of attendance and missing homework, yet you receive excellent marks on tests. Aside from your math instructor, I must note, who has many wonderful things to say."*

"And? What does it matter if I'm passing all my classes?"

"Do you feel unchallenged at school?"

Right again.

Not that I'm going to let her in on my little secret—on where I choose to go over attending class. She doesn't get the chance to twist the only positive thing I have going for me.

Programming.

If it's not my math class or the occasional science lecture, I'd rather spend my time in the computer lab, submerging myself into coding projects and studying cryptography, among other computer science subfields. My personal textbooks, however, may not be of a positive nature. Many are solely obtainable through obscure channels in the internet's underbelly and contain guides on illicit activities.

All done under the anonymity of the school's internet—using a VPN and an Onion browser, of course.

But I'm not a full-blown criminal. I don't steal or harm anyone, only chat on anonymous channels and look where I shouldn't. Albeit my detached ego, I carry a moral compass in my back pocket. Hacking for me is simply a challenge, to find out if I can do something—or get into somewhere I shouldn't.

Harmless, really.

Call it morbid curiosity.

So, yes, to answer my prying, over-educated counselor's question, I feel unchallenged, which causes me to skip classes. Only *because an endless pool of information doesn't reside in their boring lectures. But online, awaiting my fingertips.*

My gaze drifts off, showing my lack of interest. She tempts me with a few more prompts, all of which I ignore. And right as the clock strikes four, indicating our end of session, I'm out the door without so much as a wave goodbye.

Later that night, my sister and I engaged in a routine, entirely warranted argument. Subjects and accusations ranged from hopelessness and contempt to conspired sabotage. Although in the realms of familiar territory for the two of us, this time was particularly scathing. Because something she said finally struck a chord with me.

Mom and Dad didn't give up their lives so you could throw away ours.

The sentiment burns my throat raw, especially having come from my eight-year-old sister, a girl who sees too much at her age. Because she's right. One of us can control their anger, has the courage to work on their trauma. But the other doesn't, and in their compulsiveness, spoils any and all opportunities for the both of them.

When I assaulted Ainsley, no matter how good it felt in that moment, I may as well have dumped my sister in a volatile puddle of quicksand—at least then she'd have her own chance at escape.

"Tristan?" a concerned voice prods...

So, I'm giving her a break, one she won't talk me out of. I won't give her that option. Because it's better for the two of us. No matter her cruel words, Aurora loves me. We're the only family we have left. And I'm the eldest, meant to look after her in our twisted misfortunes, even if that means making the hard choices, by doing what I should've after the first time a parent sent us back to Whispering Pines, and every other time thereafter when I refused Dr. Jenning's questions:

Freeing her from her burden.

"Tristan!" Urgency overwhelms her tone now. My mind tells me it's my sister, crying for me to come back to bed, but my heart knows it's another...

After leaving a note, I pack light, stuffing a backpack with the few possessions to my name. My plan is simple: never step foot in another foster care or Aurora's life, no matter the pain. Not until she wears another last name, gifted to her by a family who will undoubtedly adore her and allow her the life she couldn't afford beside me.

Shimmying down the fire escape, the night is my sole companion in a new life—

"TRISTAN!"

Air knocks into my lungs, and I jolt awake. Sitting up in a flash, confusion swirling in my brain, I squint in the darkness. Lauren stands near the edge of the guest room bed, wearing a silky robe and a horrified expression.

"Jesus, are you okay?" Her hand trails down my bare shoulder, comforting and warm.

I cock my head, noting my chest heaving up and down, and the sweat slicking across my pecs and hairline. Swallowing, my throat is raw, and I instantly know why she's upset.

"Was I loud?" I ask on a whisper.

She sits on the edge of the bed, pretty locks rolling off her shoulders, unkempt and full. "You were screaming."

Dammit.

Shying away, I focus on the nightstand, feeling as if I'm back in my dreamland. I've succumbed to therapy for years now, but the nightmares still come and go, although less frequently.

"Hey." Lauren brushes my chin, tilting until I look down

into her soft eyes. "It's not a big deal. You can always talk to me about it."

Pieces of the dream come to me in fragments, all unwelcome shards of my past I'd like to keep from the present. An ache weighs down my chest, yearning to open up to her, someone other than a therapist or a pill-pushing shrink or even my dearest friend who faced the same life as me.

"I—"

A chime interrupts me, and my phone lights up from the nightstand. Flicking my gaze, I catch the sender of the text.

That's Jace's number.

Anguish and guilt gnaw at me.

Here's my wife—despite being an arranged one from only a week ago—with compassion and kindness in her eyes, something precious and rare for a woman of her fiery caliber. I know that because I'm well-versed in *her*, having invaded her most private moments for my own pleasure and curiosity.

But that doesn't even scrape the top of my worst offenses, as she's left in the dark about *everything*.

My hacker identity.

The Oculi.

The truth of where her father resides.

Not that I could solve that mystery for her entirely, as I don't have the keenest idea of where he is or *what* the society did to him. "*When the time is right, Nicholas Astor will disappear,*" Jace had said, all the time ago, before making true on his dire threat. And if I don't want my sister to suffer the same fate, then I cannot allow Lauren to evolve past a mere distraction, to plunk her fingers along my heartstrings, no matter how tempting she is beside me now.

For Aurora's sake, I must remember what Lauren really is to me.

A mission.

Astor Security is a mission.

And I'm a dutiful, obedient foot soldier.

"Are you okay to be alone?"

"Yes," I answer with a convincing smile. "It was only a bad dream."

Once she leaves, I pick up my smartphone with shaky hands.

Jace: *Aurora's friends are such chatterboxes. I can learn of her whereabouts just by listening to them. But I'll keep tracking her phone, though. Did you know sweet Aurora's ballet recital is at the end of the semester? Apparently, tickets are sold out, but I'm sure I'll manage.*

My jaw clenches when I see the new round of photographs. All shot from behind, Aurora sits in an auditorium beside friends, dutifully taking notes during the lecture.

Jace: *Two days. I'm eager to meet Astor Security's new CEO.*

TWELVE

LAUREN

"WHERE ARE YOU?" I tap my heel on the concrete, standing outside Astor Security's shining skyscraper.

"I'm almost there." Tristan's voice mixes with aggressive wind, spewing from the other line into my violated eardrum. "Two minutes, tops."

I mumble curses under my breath—not that the most *unpunctual man alive* could hear me, anyway. "You said that the last ten times. I told you the board meeting was twenty minutes earlier than it actually was. And you're *still* late."

More wind is his only response.

Business personnel usher past on the busy Silicon Avenue streets, offering me not so much as a glance. Which is to their luck because, if they did, they'd find me wearing an annoyingly lethal expression—and a satin, all-white blazer suit I had dropped off at the dry cleaners this morning.

And, why did I do that?

Because today is fucking important.

"Would it kill you to roll up your window?"

Pinching the bridge of my nose, I pace the sidewalk,

searching through the rows of grid locked cars on the street. I presume he's behind the wheel of some glitzy sports car, one of many parked beside my new McLaren in his massive garage.

"No can do, baby."

Jackass.

Pacing harder, steam shoots from my ears. "The board is waiting."

"And they can wait a little longer." I can practically see his cocky grin. "For the record, I wouldn't be late if you hadn't sent me to that fancy designer. Bossing around her assistants all morning, making suits from scratch—what nonsense."

I scoff. "You're *lucky* I'm one of Cyna's high-profile clients, or else you wouldn't have gotten a designer piece made and fitted to your size *in one day.*"

Christ! My blood pressure spikes. *Must I micromanage everything?*

"You know I don't need a suit for today, let alone a designer one."

"You're completely out of your fucking mind. You're only embarking on one of Silicon Avenue's biggest transitions of power *ever.* So, *yes,* you need a suit for that, *genius.* And if you're standing beside me as my husband, it's going to be designer. *And—"* I stop myself short, knowing if I don't, I might blow a mental fuse.

This is not the time.

I exhale slowly, my fingers pulling the skin along my brow taut on a slow sweep.

Breathe, Lauren. Breathe.

In. And out. In. And out.

Everything's fine.

"Better now?" His deep chuckle rumbles through my phone. "Listen to us bickering. It's no wonder we're married."

"Where are you?" I ask quickly, ignoring him.

"Five blocks away."

Five? In this traffic?

I walk between two cars parallel parked in front of the building, lifting my chin down the line of motionless vehicles. "Just park and get out and walk. You won't make it far, if you—"

"Three blocks."

Huh?

I search again, feeling dumb when I find zero movement.

"Ha. Ha. Very funny. Now—"

"One. Better move out of the way, baby."

With confusion floating about me, my head zips back and forth. *Does he have the wrong address?*

And it isn't until aggressive revving roars from the distance that I notice a motorcycle soaring between cars. The bike zips across the nearest lane at high speeds, heading straight for me.

Shit—

I dart back to safety between the cars, heels grazing the lip of the sidewalk, before two wheels screech to a halt in front of me. And what I see cracks my mind in half, leaves my smart mouth for tarnished rubble upon the pavement, and betrays every single preconceived notion about what type of man I *think* I'm attracted to.

Reflecting the sun's rays, onyx steel coats the entire bike's frame, almost as dark as the leather jacket worn by the rider. With gloved fingertips gripping the handlebars and a backpack strapped around his large frame, his body cranes over the machine.

In a rebellious display, he revs the engine once more, the roar bolting across the city streets and clattering through my bones. Sitting up, he plants his boots on the ground, swinging his head my way. Clad in an obscure helmet, he makes a show of swooping his neck downward, then back up, tracing the length of my body.

I meet Tristan's eyes through the tinted glass, my heart somersaulting as I notice the attention he's drawn. Curious eyes peek through car windows, and onlookers pull out their phones behind me.

Silicon Avenue's newest power couple has returned from their honeymoon, I remind myself, anticipating tomorrow's headlines as I slap the thunderstruck look off my face.

Removing his helmet, revealing devastating features, Tristan's mid-length hair tumbles in a relaxed yet elegant fashion.

God, help me. What've I signed up for?

"Mrs. Walker," he purrs, sauntering towards me with a cocky grin. He wraps his arms around my frame, the smell of leather foreign and enchanting. "I'm sorry to have kept you waiting."

Before I can conjure up a response, he bends down and kisses me, uncaring of the heads turned towards us. His bottom lip delves low, deepening our connection, until he freezes, holding himself back. When he pulls away, loosening his grip on me, I'm overcome by a fleeting wave of disappointment.

"Where's your suit?" I manage to ask.

"In here." He shrugs off his backpack, yanking the zippers apart, revealing fabric covered in protective plastic and a pair of Santoni Oxfords. "Do you approve?"

"If Cyna had anything to do with it, I do. Now it's just up to you to pull it off."

Zipping the seal shut, he lugs the bag across his shoulders like a sling.

"Well, don't *you* look the part?" Eyebrows lifting, his lips form a proud smirk. As I weather his assessment, he practically drinks in my appearance, fingers brushing against my blazer's lapel, then noting tall heels peeking beneath my long dress pants. "If it was up to me, no matter the men sitting around the table as competitors, I'd elect you CEO."

I flinch ever-so slightly, a hitch in my breath betraying my surprise. No man's ever said something like that to me, especially not one I'm romantically involved with.

He could be lying. Putting on a show for the cameras.

Subtly, I sweep my gaze over his shoulders, finding the cars' curious peepers having passed on. Then, using my peripherals, I note only foot traffic. *But no one's looking anymore.* Much like the typical crowd of New Yorkers, we're old news in less than a minute. The city dwellers must have dispersed after our kiss, and moved on with their day.

I study his stare with the intensity of a detective, feeling much like a mousy schoolgirl pining for praise from her new boyfriend.

"Do you mean that?"

"Of course, I do." His chuckle warms my insides. "Your teeth may be pretty, baby, but they're also savage. I'd relish watching you chew and spit out that board before their lesser minds could even comprehend your power."

THIRTEEN

LAUREN

EVEN BIRTHED WITH THE SURNAME, Astor Security is intimidating. The sheer scale of my father's company is mind-boggling every time I step foot in this building. White marble with gold accents dominates the space, and tall spires shoot upwards of five stories inside the modern lobby.

Too impatient to wait for Tristan, who's changing into his new clothes in the men's room, I make for the rows of elevators. The board has already waited thirty minutes for him. With our luck, they've elected someone present or have left entirely.

Which would mean I entered an arranged marriage for nothing.

If it was up to me, I'd elect you as CEO.

Tristan's words swim in my mind, occupying too much space and contradicting everything I'm familiar with. Even though I questioned him further and found him truthful, the idea is hard to fathom. Because if there's anything I've learned from years of practicing law and co-existing with New York's upper society, it's that powerful men never share the spotlight, let alone shine it on someone else.

Even in marriage, where the two are equals.

With a jittery exhale, I punch the up arrow, retrieving my phone from my Birkin. Dialing my father's number, I don't press the phone to my ear, knowing he won't pick up. He's been gone for nearly two months, and this has to be the twentieth attempt at calling. It's not the first time he's ignored them during his frequent disappearances, so I'm not concerned for his well-being, but I am blindsided and angry that he didn't even bother to shoot me a message.

Sadness weighs heavily in my middle at the sound of his voicemail. Today was his last chance. I thought maybe—*just maybe*—if he picked up this time, I'd forgive him for inadvertently putting me in this position. He could keep his job, hire more advisers, delegate his stress away, and everything could go back to normal.

But it really does *seem like he's given up.*

I read my missed text messages through blurry vision, blinking the waterworks away with haste, glad for a distraction.

Hannah: *Just heard you have to give up your apartment keys today. That's awful, Lauren.*

Sofia: *We'll be there for support!*

I walk forward once the elevator doors slide open, with my head buried in my phone. Reading our girls' group chat, littered with frowny emojis, I find little comfort, only reminders of yet another step back in my life.

It's true. My apartment keys are due by the end of the day. I would've given them up sooner—only to rip the band aid clean off the same night I moved into a mysterious man's mansion—but today is the first day back from our alleged European honeymoon, having romanced our hearts away in Greece and Spain and—

Expecting an empty elevator, I raise my head and lock eyes with possibly the last human being I want to see on this planet.

Oh. Hell. No.

My sadness morphs into blistering annoyance. Swiveling a one-eighty, I rush for the doors, which close before I can escape. For a split moment, I stare ahead, frozen, chanting a silent prayer that the man hazily reflected in the metal leaning against the back wall would disappear out of thin air.

"What a lovely surprise," my ex-boyfriend purrs. A sound that once made me melt like compliant butter is now more akin to nails on a chalkboard or a symphony of disappointment, effectively shriveling up my ovaries.

Seriously, World? Today of all days?

As I meet his eyes through the reflection, adrenaline spiking, I repeatedly jab the open button to no avail.

"Come on, enough theatrics."

Lifting off the wall, his suit-clad body blocks off the rows of buttons. And to my annoyance, before we ascend, he presses the emergency stop button. A subtle redness glows in the surrounding air, and the perpetual hum of the elevator vanishes, trapping us together.

I look elsewhere, crossing my arms.

What a child. Always needing to get his way.

Blistering anger pumps through my veins, but I manage my composure, weighing my options:

I could ride out in silence, hoping he eventually gives up —which is unlikely—and lets me out...

I could scream...

I could kick him in the nut sack and free myself...

Or maybe I could—

"Silent treatment, huh? That's fine. I can do all the talking—"

"And what would there be to say, *Adrien?*" I snap my head towards him, his name on my tongue a vile hiss.

Dammit. I regret the decision instantly. *This would be a lot easier if he didn't look like* that.

Adrien's ebony suit molds to his body like a glove, leaving no mystery as to what lies underneath. Gel slicks his hair straight back, not a dark hair out of place, and a flashy Rolex gleams beneath his cufflinks, impossible to ignore.

When he catches my appraisal, his bright teeth shine in a smooth smile. "I prefer you feisty."

I roll my eyes, his cockiness rubbing me in all the wrong ways.

More than five years my senior, Adrien Vuitton and I are long since history, having broken up with him less than a year ago. Unlike Tristan and I's fake meet-cute, Adrien and I *actually* met at Harvard while I was studying in law school and he was a postgraduate teacher's assistant for my corporate law class.

Ashamedly, attending his office hours led to me asking for tutoring I didn't need, which led to hooking up and little studying, which *then* led to a real relationship that lasted past my graduation and even into my early professional career. Straight out of graduation, Astor Associates accepted me as a junior associate, where Adrien was already well into his career, practicing as a corporate fraud attorney.

Often as the sole associate working under him in cases, my feelings were nothing short of infatuation. He was—*is? Question mark*—my stereotypical type of man. Popular. Intelligent. Impeccably dressed. Takes charge of a room. And has an impressive last name—*Vuitton.* Not a soul in New York's upper society hasn't heard of that name, especially in the tech industry, much like my family's.

So, on paper, the relationship was exactly what I wanted, and everything was great. For a time.

Until I started moving up the ladder.

After several years of busting ass, taking on more cases than any sane lawyer would deem manageable, and deducing myself to a borderline insomniac, the firm promoted me to a senior associate, then to a junior partner, younger than anyone before in the company. The only problem? Adrien previously held that title—that *"bragging right,"* as he used to call it—and he was still a junior partner. Meaning, in veiled resentment, his girlfriend was his equal. Possibly even his match.

And his little ego couldn't handle that.

When people began directing their questions at *me* instead of him at parties and professional events, and it was *my* name plastered on the media and staking claim on all the high-profile cases, his resentment turned into unmistakable envy. His criticisms increased tenfold, my accomplishments undermined and chalked up to my family name, albeit my near-perfect track record, impressive portfolio, and the sheer fact my grandfather died long since I started working at the firm.

His words blaze in the back of my mind, the ones that so easily manipulated me and stole too much of my precious youth, before breaking things off and never speaking to him again...

Always trying to be a mini-me, aren't you?

Come on, doll. You know I assign you the easy cases.

You got a lucky break. Don't let it go to your head.

Must be nice having everything handed to you.

Most of us didn't have a mentor to fuck.

"You're an asshole who couldn't handle a woman over-shadowing you," I spit out. "Not interested. End of discussion. So, you might as well let me out of here. I have important matters that need my attention."

Amusement twinkles in his cobalt eyes, a look that tells me I took a bite on his hook. He sinks his hand into his pocket, leaning against the wall—the spitting image of a type of arrogance only obtainable through extreme privilege.

"Don't act as if you didn't prefer being my subordinate, having an older mentor who favored you." His words form a sick taste in my mouth, but I hold my tongue. "Besides, things can go back to the way they were, now. I *was* promoted to senior partner recently."

Ridiculous. He's just rubbing my nose in his accomplishments.

Seeing as I work at the same company as him, he surely knows I'm aware of that fact. All senior partners have their names engraved on the front door—bold and unmissable, an annoying reminder of his new accomplishment. And fuel for my lethal drive to add my name, younger than any lawyers before me.

You're also years older than me, I don't say, knowing he'd love for me to further feed the fire of our argument, so he can twist my words and rewrite them into me being jealous of him.

He doesn't deserve my congratulations.

Instead, I scoff an unimpressed breath. "I've moved on."

"I heard, I heard. You're recently married. To a... Oh, what's his name...?" He refrains from laughing, making a show out of brushing his chin, lost in thought. *"Tristan Walker,* is it?"

Eyebrows ticking, I rest a hand on my hip, putting my

impressive engagement ring on display. "What, did that take a hit to your precious ego?"

After stealing a rapid glance at the diamond, a shadowy darkness emerges from behind his eyes. "From who? A reclusive nobody I've never heard of? As far as I'm concerned, he doesn't exist. Not in our world. *Not beside you.* And I must say, gossip spreads quick, doll, and the story of how you two met...? Doesn't quite add up."

My stomach drops. He's one of the few people who could piece the puzzle together. *He knows too much.*

"You met and were close friends while at Harvard? Not possible, not with me by your side. You forget, I worked at that school for the entirety of your attendance."

I hold his gaze, not giving up my position.

"Come on, Lauren, we're in the same field. We see the same things. When holding positions of power, nothing is out of the picture or too extreme." He lifts off the wall, stalking towards me. "Even if you won't confess, I know an *arranged marriage* when I see one, especially one whose alleged relationship started *before we broke up.*"

Shit.

I break his stare, an uncomfortable iciness crawling up my back, reducing me to some kid caught red-handed with my fingers buried in the cookie jar. But I fight through the jarring feeling, whipping my head back, finding him a hair's breadth from me.

"Enough with the charades, Adrien. I've changed and want nothing to do with you."

Exuding a condescending expression, his familiar cologne is a nostalgic wave into my nostrils, now violating and repulsive. But I don't back down, don't move an inch from his show of superiority.

"Whenever your little arrangement finishes, I'll be right here, ready with open arms to take you back."

Deceptive asshole. Take me back, like I'm not the one who ended things.

"Disgusting. I'd rather date my mailman."

"What does he have that I don't?"

I ignore him.

"It can't be looks."

Debatable.

"And he doesn't have more money."

Definitely.

I don't hide my smirk, reveling when I catch his jaw tick.

"Well, I won't ask if he satisfies you more in bed, because I know that can't be true."

"I—" Stopping myself short, I pray the embarrassing blush doesn't shine through my foundation.

"Ohhh," he drawls in delight like he struck gold, an irrepressible grin spreading wide across his features. "I see. You two haven't...?" His snicker bounces off the walls of our tight enclosure when I don't respond, igniting fire atop my skin.

I hate that he knows me so well. He probably even knows that after our breakup, I was such a complete mess that I called off men entirely. No romantic relationships. No dates. No hookups. For nearly a year, I ensured a sound mind and a clean slate, one without a man who can't accept an ambitious woman.

"Gosh, you must be real pent up, then. But, I'm feeling generous and can't bear watching you downgrade yourself next to such a loner. I'll cut you a deal. How does that sound? I'll overlook your *fake* marriage and the little thing I have going on with my new secretary, and every Friday night or so you can swing by my place and I'll help you get off—"

"No."

I jerk from his vicinity, but he eats up the distance in one step, trapping me in a corner. Heart palpitating, claustrophobia claws its way up my throat, and the metal bar lining the elevator spears into my backside as I shy away.

"Come on, dollface. There's no need to play hard to get." His eyes flash with a repressed anger, not a care for the clear boundaries set between us. "Nobody's here to judge you. Nobody's listening."

His hand moves to my throat, and I freeze in fear. Gently, he caresses my skin with the backs of his fingers, pupils dilating with lust. Sending chills down my body, his voice is a near whisper.

"Don't worry, Lauren, I'd never force myself on you. But why wait? I know how you *really* like it, what it takes for you to come undone. More than any other man, especially your husband. And we have all the privacy we'd need, right here and now. I just want to hear you say the words. Ask me to take you—"

The elevator's hum returns, and the lights brighten to their normal intensity. Over Adrien's shoulder, the doors swing open, unveiling a large man.

In what feels like slow motion, I appraise him from bottom to top. Polished Oxfords peek out from below his pressed slacks, catching my eye, only to be stolen from a charcoal suit clearly crafted by an expert tailor. And it's not until my gaze reaches his chin, strong and freshly shaven, that I know it's Tristan.

Who wears a face like murder.

FOURTEEN

TRISTAN

BLINDED BY RAGE.

Such a misleading phrase. On the contrary, I see quite well.

Maybe a little too well.

Albeit under a hazy concoction of adrenaline and compulsiveness—the back of my mind a volatile maelstrom—some of what my eyes perceive is reality. Like Lauren pushed up to a corner, her features dripping with fear. And the suited backside of a man who's invading her space and putting his hands where they don't belong.

And others are only enticing illusions—like how his tongue might look pierced into a shish kabob or how easily it would be to blot out all recollections of his name from this earth, then find out who actually cared about his lack of existence. A low existence, really, that came to an overdue end after one minor mistake.

Touching. My. Wife.

Before I can comprehend my actions, I'm inches from the two of them, yanking the man from the back of his collar. A choked breath shoots from his lips, his feet slipping on the floor as I drag him across the space, then heave his body against the opposing wall. He cries out, the metal bar digging into his skin, as I shove his cheek into the wall. Catching my gaze, his single eye quakes with terror.

Noting the crowd of spectators who watch through the door, I use all my effort to control my volume. "You want to know what I have that you don't?"

Lauren's gasp is hardly audible over the blood pounding in my ears. "How did you know—"

But she's drowned out by the clash from me slamming *pretty boy's* back against the wall again, preferring to look at him dead-on. My fingers clutch onto the front of his suit, lifting him until he's at eye distance, feet dangling beneath him.

"Less value on your life and a Glock 19. Touch my wife again, and you'll stare down the barrel."

Silence spreads around us, accompanied by the distant footsteps outside the elevator—and his pathetic attempt at a response. His lips sputter, throat bobbling.

Coming out of the bathroom, I expected to find Lauren waiting with the same fire she had outside, toes tapping impatiently. But when I didn't, and she further ignored my texts, I tapped into her phone's audio, hearing her speaking with a man whose name was familiar.

Adrien Vuitton.

See, even though we've never personally met, I'm well acquainted with him, like many others who are—or *were*—a part of Lauren's life. Charming and good-looking with an imposing surname, Adrien is the epitome of societal elite. From the outside, he appears courteous, likable, and probably donates to charitable foundations, all with a gallant smile. But pluck twenty seconds from their conversation and Mr. Perfect is now a sleazy fuck, whose jaw—I'd wager—has never met the backside of a clenched fist.

Luckily for him, I'm well practiced.

Today's his day.

Releasing him back to the ground, I deliver a blow to his face, swift and brutal, narrowly missing that proud nose of his. He grunts before dropping to the floor, his suit jacket sprawled about his figure. I loom over him, each of his wounded groans only a raindrop doused on my internal fire. When I pick him back up, he holds out his palms, attempting to surrender, unable to speak.

"What? Cat got your tongue?" I taunt, jostling him, earning myself more stutters. "How about I cut *you* a deal? Either I'll *cut off* your tongue and teach it how to speak to a lady. Or, I'll let you keep it, if I hear an apology."

"I-I-I'm sorry."

I laugh. "Not to me. Apologize to *my wife.*"

"Tristan…" Lauren's voice seems distant.

Adrien cocks his head, cheek now shining an angry red. "I-I'm sorry, Lauren."

Liar is my first instinct. *It's not enough.*

Touching what's mine has dire consequences, enough to ricochet throughout his entire life. A bruised face and ego won't suffice. He's due for a blow where it'll really hurt—to his sparkling reputation. One click, after hacking into this building's security cameras, and his predatory elevator scene would soar across the cyber sphere, personally landing on the inboxes of every New York Times editor.

Hell, I could make him world news.

I raise my fist again, savoring another blow—

"Tristan." Lauren's soft digits graze my shoulder like a

calming wave, extinguishing my fire in an instant. "That's enough," she says under her breath. "People are watching."

As I peer over my shoulder, I find dozens of phones aimed our way and more than a few heads poking through the elevator doors. I release my grip on him.

Regaining his footing, a few moments pass before he wipes that horrified expression off his face, replacing it with an unphased aura, as if he wasn't moments away from being beaten to a pulp. He dusts off his slacks and arm sleeves, meeting my glare, a wary caution still shining there.

"I'm pressing charges."

What a daddy's-money response. How boring.

I grin. "I'm looking forward to it."

"You got a lot of nerve handling me the way you just did." His gaze flickers towards the doors.

"You think their cameras scare me? I'd do it all over again, without thinking twice—right here in the lobby, out on the street, in a courtroom, *anywhere*. Name a time and place."

"How civilized," he sneers, dragging his eyes from me. "Next time, Lauren, put a leash on your dog before you bring him to work."

"At least my dog's loyal." Birkin hanging off her crossed arms, Lauren's chin tilts upwards, an assertive confidence seeping back into her tone in just the way I like. "Have fun with your assistant. Such a *lucky* gal."

I thread my fingers through hers, tugging her close, a chuckle breezing past my lips.

Adrien bristles, then leans in, his voice low and menacing. "Don't forget, I know this is all an act. You'll never be what I was to her. You won't satisfy her needs the way only I can."

Electricity sparks hot along my skin, a growl forming deep in my throat.

"And I *do* mean in bed." Then he has the nerve—*the gall*—to pat his hand on my shoulder, as if we're long-lost pals and he's not about to say something that'll book his teeth a one-way ticket to the floor. "From time to time, I still hear her sweet cries screaming my name. Something you'll never experience. After me, she's as good as ruined."

I spring forward, aiming for him again—

"Enough." Lauren steps between us, hands pushing against my chest. "Leave, Adrien. Our attendance is wanted elsewhere."

He smirks, as if he won some battle of wits and proved a point, before turning on his heels.

Good fucking riddance.

I fold my arms along my chest, never wishing to be in the same room as the man again.

"Oh, Lauren? One last thing." Suit swinging in the doorframe, he faces us one last time, smug and content. "I forgot to mention—I'm heading the investigation team against Astor Security. You're their representation, I take it? I *so* look forward to spending more time together."

His words hit me like a two-by-four, straight to the jaw, freezing me in place as my fingernails dig their way through my palm.

Then he *winks* at me. "Goodbye, for now."

"WHAT A *FUCKING* LOSER. Why did you date that guy?"

We stride down the hallway, my head swimming with numerous insults, all scheduled to fling Adrien's way.

And he's heading the investigation? I don't ask, unable to voice the truth. How fucking typical.

There goes my grand plan of ruining his sparkling reputation by making him a national headline. There's no exposing that man's true colors with evidence that just so happens to make Lauren—who's now his opposition—look like some victim. That couldn't look more fabricated. In fact, even if I dug up past dirt on him that didn't involve Lauren, it would likely be spun by the media as conveniently timed, dismissed as a smear campaign, and probably shift the narrative in his favor.

I huff an irritated breath, nostrils flaring.

"Will you calm down?" Lauren pats down her hair, plastering on a composed, no-bullshit expression that doesn't quite reach her emerald eyes.

"No, really." My volume is utterly unchecked, steps furious and loaded like a hair-pin trigger. She quickens her pace, heels clacking against the laminate, sticking by my side. "He wouldn't last one day the way I grew up, and I'm sure he's had it coming for a long time. What a slimy fucker. How could you put up with him? What was going on in your head—"

"I don't know!"

She combusts, eyes flashing with untamed frustration, as we pass by a ridiculously large secretary's desk. Constructed with a single slab of white quartz and beneath moody lighting, three similarly dressed women peek their quizzical eyebrows over their monitors, soaking in every bit of Lauren's sudden outburst.

"I was young and in law school, and I lied that I needed a tutor. He was so attractive to me and charming at the time, I'd never thought he'd..."

My jaw ticks, but I keep a lid on my composure.

"And I worked under him on so many cases later in my career, like I had some forbidden romance with my boss..."

Christ. I shouldn't have asked.

"And he was so much older than me..."

Okay, that's all I can take.

"And—" She stops herself before I do, heels screeching against the floor, anxious worry returning to her eyes. "There's no time for drama! So forget about what happened."

"Sure, like that's possible."

"I'm serious," she hisses under her breath. "We're forty-five minutes late. For all I know, given the importance of the people on this board, they've already left."

"Oh, they haven't left, I assure you that. You and I could go enjoy a cup of coffee, maybe even catch a movie, and we'd still come back to a full room. The offer is on the table, by the way. I'll take you anywhere you like. I *do* own a plane."

Eyebrows raising, she points a finger at my chest. "You see? It's that kind of arrogant attitude that'll screw up this entire plan."

"Will it now?" I stare down at her manicured nail and the diamond glistening on another finger, absentmindedly puffing out my pecs. "You only said I needed to wear a suit— which is entirely unnecessary, but I digress. I didn't know this arrangement came with a personality change on top of it—"

"Tristan." She growls my name, a sound that has my chest lifting in anticipation. "We are *not* doing this right now. Seeing as you're a grown adult, you can behave and act cordial, I take it? Good. Let's go."

I bite my lip when she whips around, strutting further down the hall, leaving me in the dust. Hypnotized, I watch her hips sway, tight curls bounce, and ass cheeks imprint against the fabric of her pantsuit. Catching up to her, I match her powerful steps, noting the hallway narrowing. I sweep my gaze across the new scenery and my brow furrows in confusion.

With dozens of single-door private meeting rooms on either side, the corridor twists and turns, but what's most peculiar are the impossibly high walls. Vertical slices of laminate protrude from them with geometrical shapes cut into their sides, opaque and white. In fact, the entire space is starch white. The floors, the intricate sidings, even the ceiling, projecting subtle lighting, making me question whether we slipped into the pages of a science fiction novel.

"Are we heading to the helm of a spaceship?" I ask, banking another turn, finding more of the same shapes.

Lauren's gaze stays pointed straight ahead, focused and serious. "Only you couldn't recognize the fine artistic works of Étienne Leclair when they're right here in front of you. My father commissioned him for over *two months*. These walls are his originals—do you know how much that cost?"

"Antoine La-what-now?"

She shakes her head, the corners of her tight lips pulling. "Unbelievable..."

Rounding what seems to be our twentieth corner, this time, imposing gold double-doors face us from the hall's dead end.

Lauren exhales sharply, and gives herself one more pass over, speaking in a confident yet hushed tone. "The board is aware of the seriousness of the investigation—and that it's starting any day now—so they'll most certainly make their decision today, relinquishing my father as CEO and hopefully passing the company into your hands. So, it's important we cater to their requests and act professional. First, I'll introduce you to each of the board members, who you'll *profusely apolo-*

gize to for being so late—make up some excuse, if you have to. Then we'll enter negotiations—which will be nil on our side —then move onto the other itinerary until the board votes. Can you handle all that?"

Coming near, I face her, loving how her neck cranes upwards at me.

Fuck.

She's so jaw-droppingly beautiful. And the best part is, she knows it. But doesn't she understand she can get whatever she wants without playing games? No matter who sits in the powerful chairs around a table behind these doors, they'd eat out of the palms of her hands, if only she'd outstretch them, staking her birthright as CEO.

But that's not part of the deal. Not the role I'm unwillingly playing. And definitely not the type of profession Lauren has worked so hard for. So, I'll be what is asked of me. *Be the* real *leadership a thriving Astor Security needs.*

"Yes, I understand. There's no need for my pretty wife to worry. I'll take it from here, with only one revision..." I stare into her wanting eyes, starkly aware of the desire towards me that she might never admit and I'd never pry from her. Not until she's ready.

"I never apologize—*and neither does my wife.*"

FIFTEEN

LAUREN

TRISTAN WALKER IS A SILICON HEIR.

Or, that's what I would conclude if I didn't know any better, given what I've witnessed in the past twenty minutes.

Keeping true to his startling promise upon his entrance, Tristan didn't utter a single apology. In fact, aside from a blunt *good evening,* he didn't try to win over the board members at all, his worst offense being that he sat at the head of the table... in the chair purposely left empty... The CEO chair—*before he's even CEO.* He then wheeled another chair next to him, stating that his wife only sits by his side.

Gone is the reclusive nerd who only wears hoodies and T-shirts, exchanged with an unashamed intellectual yet evenly tempered businessman who accepts nothing less than his demands. And, I must admit, I'm having a hard time deciphering which version of my arranged husband I prefer.

The compulsive motorcycle-riding bad boy?

Or the sophisticated and authoritative executive?

Pick a side, Lauren. Leather jacket or suit, leather jacket or suit, leather jacket or suit...

Oh, screw it.

There's no reason a girl can't appreciate both.

"Mr. Walker, I'm well aware you're exceptionally versed in our cryptographic systems and can handle the pressures of investigative questioning," says Mr. Henshaw, who sits several seats down from us and is Astor Security's third highest shareholder—behind my family and now Tristan, who owns half our shares. "But what of your business credentials? Might I remind you, many of us have been on this board since the company's infancy, meaning we know of your *real* background."

I straighten in my chair. *He's calling Tristan out for not having attended Harvard?*

Although it comes as no shock the board is aware of our arrangement—given the information Tristan shared with me about his code founding the company—I still didn't expect them to be so upfront.

"I don't need an MBA from some prestigious school to identify this company's weak points."

"It's that easy then, huh? You're the sudden financial expert, are you now? Just waltz on in here like you own the place and solve all of a Fortune 10 company's problems. As if we don't have advisers." Mr. Henshaw scoffs, folding his arms across his navy suit, while other board members wear similar, skeptical expressions.

He does *own the place,* I nearly correct but keep my mouth shut. At least ten percent of it, which is astronomical for a top ten Fortune 500 company. More than anyone else here at the table besides me.

"Then your advisers are ill-informed and need replacement. The root causes of your financial problems *are* errors in computer science."

"Sure, sure. And how's that?"

Tristan turns to me, our chairs so close I can smell the mintiness on his breath. "Mrs. Walker, can you please reiterate to the board what you explained to me earlier—what are the two types of information the investigation team will require access to?"

The weight of ten pairs of eyes locks in on me, igniting a familiar thrill I rarely feel outside of a courtroom. Before me, anticipation crackles down the table's long line of elite group business executives and industry investors, all awaiting my expertise.

To my left is an impressive, straight-shot view of Silicon Avenue's busy streets. Astor Associates, our immediate neighbor, peeks through the corners of the window, the skyrise a solid sheet of cerulean glass gleaming in the afternoon sun. I can list off each one of the towering buildings and the tech mega-corporations they house, as well as their founders and CEOs by name, having worked on trials either for or against all of them.

As a data privacy lawyer, my late grandfather's firm will always be my second home, where my future lies. But I've put aside my cases until my family's security company gets back on track and out of the public eye, meaning the investigation has captured a highly sought-after commodity. My full focus.

I bask under their gazes as my attention slides from one board member to the next.

"It will be the investigation team's main goal to find substantial evidence to start a trial, and they will most definitely have preconceived notions, given the recent imprisonment of my uncle, Oscar Bass. Their agenda will be as follows. First, they will gain access to company logs. Which includes records of network activities. User data. User access. Data transfers. System changes..." My words are like the strikes of a hammer, plunging the board members deep into worry.

Personally, I have no doubts about the company's ethics, but handing over free-rein access to company logs is like opening Pandora's box. There's no telling what information, in the right hands, could be misconstrued, especially given the sheer bulk of clientele and data the company protects.

With thousands of companies as clients worldwide, Astor Security supplies cyber security software, including firewalls, antivirus protection and intrusion detection systems. From the beginning, our crown jewel has always been our cutting-edge encryption solutions. Companies hire us to store their users' sensitive data—their passwords, addresses, names, social security numbers, et cetera—in our server warehouses, all located a short plane ride out of New York City.

Such data is a colossal liability and certainly the investigative team's best angle.

"And the second?" Tristan asks beside me, his self-assured eyes roaming over their faces. A hungry predator awaiting his final blow.

"Incident reports." His hum of approval skates across my skin before I continue. "This would include general security incidents and breaches in our systems or our server databases."

On my closing words, Mr. Henshaw returns to the offensive. "And how does this pertain to our apparent *financial problems?* Might I add, our stocks are at an all-time high."

Tristan stands, all eyes looking up to his impressive height. "They are now. But what about last quarter?"

"They took a short dip in February, yes. But errors in security were hardly the culprit."

"Weren't they?" Tristan rounds my chair and paces down the line of others. "What about the server breach in January? Do you think that had no effect?"

"The breach was minor and resolved within twenty-four hours. Besides, occasional breaches among all companies—even security companies—are common."

Unable to avert my gaze, I watch Tristan with a pounding heart, wetting my lips as he rounds the next corner, the front side of his powerful torso swinging into view.

"Common but unacceptable. And avoidable. You want to know why you should vote for me as your CEO? *Because you need me.* You're right, Mr. Henshaw. I *haven't* been here long, yet I've already identified the reasoning behind January's incident. And, contrary to your company's publicized findings, it wasn't someone acting on the inside."

"You're suggesting a hacker? That can't be possible," a sharply dressed woman in red speaks up. "Our team found no evidence of outside tampering. Our encryption secures all sensitive data, even as it's being delivered to our databases. Even if a hacker *were* to intercept a transmission midway, they wouldn't obtain any revealing data."

"No, you're right. They wouldn't. But hacking is about being creative and finding another angle, not tackling encryption head on. For example, what if instead of intercepting, a hacker acted as a *user*, sending their own data to the server?"

A hush descends upon the room, one he lets draw out.

"What if this user's password being sent to our servers for protection is actually a line of code? From there, if they have equal knowledge as a database administrator, they'd merely write up a SQL one-liner, querying for a thousand other passwords or home addresses or social security numbers. What-ever they feel like, really, is at their disposal. All without ever leaving a trace of outside tampering."

The jaws of more than a few members aim for the table, and Mr. Henshaw's shoulders deflate along with his ego.

"H-how are you so sure?" he asks.

"Because, Mr. Henshaw"—Tristan takes his seat beside me once more, this time closer, his body warmth invading my skin—"I'm not a businessman."

More silence.

Wow. We pulled this off. We actually pulled this off—

"Before calling a voting intermission, my wife and I have one final condition," Tristan booms beside me, his hand resting on my knee beneath the table. At first, I think he's acting, feigning our connection, but then his palm runs up my thigh with an unmistakable possessiveness. "For my new leadership and Mrs. Walker's representation during the trial, we demand a transfer of one percent of company shares from each of you."

WHAT?!

My mind roars, and by some miracle, I manage a straight face, stifling the explosion from bursting through my lips.

What the hell is he doing?! This wasn't part of the plan! One percent from each of them? Is he insane? That's ten percent, half of what's shared between us in marriage. That's unheard-of. Outlandish. Absolutely—

He grips me hard, his calluses notable through my thin pants fabric.

He's trying to throw this all away...

His hand delves down the inside of my thigh.

No one's going to agree to...

Sweeping ever-so close to my sex.

I-I need to speak up, s-say this is all a mistake...
Then he *stops*. An inch from my clit.
Is he...
And rubs tight circles.
Oh...
Ohhh, fuckkk...

My brain clatters and clashes under deep fog, overshadowing the enormous bomb he just dropped on everyone in the room. Their gasps ring out around the table, their raised voices talking over one another, but I hardly hear their remarks, can only focus on the infinitesimal amount of friction working against my clit, caused by the tugging of my pants.

I've never fooled around in public—*especially* in such an important business setting—but the risk of being caught, against all odds, only heightens my arousal. I'm used to being the center of attention, the one calling the shots, but here's Tristan, commandeering the board members' assets as if they're simply his for the taking, while putting me under the same pressure.

Light like the brush of a feather, he grazes across my clit as he switches over to the opposite thigh. I bite down on my lip, stifling a moan, a small puddle forming in my panties when he starts up the same slow rhythm. From the corner of my eye, I steal a glance his way, finding him staring straight ahead, eating up the chaos of the room.

I'm aware I could leave at any moment, but lust overruns my every thought, desire flowing through my veins, begging for more. Resisting my urges, my blazer is suddenly suffocating, my breathing erratic, as his digits swirl with masterful precision. They're *right there*, right where I want them, yet a million miles away. A veiled yet tantalizing offering.

And one I take against my better judgment.

I scoot my waist forward, sucking in a sharp breath on contact. Tristan's low growl sounds beneath the commotion, sending my toes curling in my pumps and my arm hair standing on end. Rolling my lips together, suppressing the need to cry out, I plaster on a calm expression as pleasure soars across my body, winding me up so tight I might burst.

Feeling my tension, Tristan eases up some pressure and switches to vertical sweeps, the pads of his fingers exploring down my middle, further and further, forcing my legs wider. Meant to tease, his speed is agonizingly slow. I stifle another moan, as haughty need consumes me like wildfire. But when his digits come back up, his touch is rough, scraping against my apex hard enough that I jolt backwards.

Gripping my thigh, pinning me to the chair, he leans in, whispering against my ear with a low chuckle, "Relax, baby. You can take it."

And I do.

For another minute or five or twenty or maybe an hour—not that I can decipher time anymore—I'm reduced to a single desire. Where my limited set of skills consists of maintaining neutral emotions, disregarding crucial conversations, and snapping back to reality when the entire board rises.

"We'll return in fifteen to inform you of our decision."

SIXTEEN
LAUREN

THE DOUBLE DOORS CLICK SHUT.

"So..." I avoid Tristan's intense gaze, blood raging between my legs. His motions have stopped, but his hand still grips a fistful of my thigh. "Did you make all that up...? About the hacking, I mean."

"No." His deep tenor only worsens my situation.

I push through the mental fog, thinking of *anything* other than the specimen seated beside me, who's staring down like he can see through my clothes and knows I'm seconds from bursting—which I am. The wise side of me is aware the only way I won't is by physically leaving. And while Tristan isn't holding me hostage, the door is ten steps away, and the intermission is technically for everyone, including us, I find myself glued to my chair, teetering around a question stuck in my throat.

If circumstances were different, I'd recognize the suspiciousness of his hacker knowledge and grill him endlessly until he offered an acceptable explanation. Except, in this moment, that kind of cognitive clarity is miles over my head.

"H-how did you know, then?" I ask instead, hoping his reasoning takes the heat down several notches.

"The technique is called an SQL injection," he explains, completely dodging the *how* part of my question. "This company certainly has talented programmers and data scientists who could sniff out the vulnerability in the database structure—*and probably already have.* But they obviously haven't implemented the changes into the code base yet, probably because management downplayed the incident as an overreaction. From my research, Astor Security's upper management is much too business focused. Bosses and team managers should have science backgrounds. Not business. Preferably both."

I blink when he stops talking, staring deep into his dark eyes.

Oh, God. I didn't hear half of that.

He smirks, reading my expression. "But was that really the question you had in mind, Lauren?"

Not exactly...

Swallowing, I squirm in my chair, finding my throat void of saliva, my true desire trapped deep down.

"Ask me," he commands, the setting sun shining through the windows, basking his features and sharp suit in a tan orange.

"What if we hooked up, and it meant nothing?"

His grip tightens around my thigh, rekindling the pulsations between my legs, a reminder of just how wet I am beneath my pantsuit.

Eyes flashing with lust, a devious grin marks his lips. "Friends-with-benefits—with your husband?"

An awkward knot twists in my stomach, a blush creeping

through my cheeks. It *does* sound ridiculous, having now breathed life into the offer.

"Yes." I hold my ground. "You obviously want it, too."

"No, baby, that won't work for me."

"Why not?"

He swivels my chair, facing me towards him. Prodding between my closed legs, I note the tattoos emerging through his suit sleeves on the backs of his hand—and the satisfied look he wears when I open my thighs for him. My heart palpitates as he pulls my chair closer to his, until mine hits his parted knees, forcing my legs to spread even further.

"Because there's a price for getting what you want."

Puzzled, my brow furrows, until I recall his words last week, the ones engraved in the back of my mind every time I finish myself off in the shower:

You'll be my good little slut, who won't hesitate to present her needy holes for filling, whenever I want, wherever I want.

"You remember, don't you?"

"Yes," I say breathlessly.

He leans forward, his nose grazing the tip of mine, staring deeply into my eyes. "Then ask the right question."

"What if..." His alluring cologne invades my senses, leaving me dazed as I wet my lips. "What if I was your whore?"

"If?" He chuckles deeply. "Oh, baby. You already are. Look at you, spread so wide for me. You couldn't beg any harder unless you dropped to your knees."

My lips part right as he palms my pussy again over the fabric of my pants. A moan breezes past my lips, and I'm so caught up in my need that I instantly grind against his hand. Pleasure explodes from my sex, trailing all the way down to my toes.

"So greedy, aren't you?"

A struggled cry is my only response.

Removing his hand, leaving me aching and bare, he yanks my waist further down the chair, until my neck rests atop the chair's low headrest and my tailbone sits at the very edge. My heels dangle off the ground, the backs of my knees propped over his thighs.

"Undo your zipper."

Done.

"Good girl."

The praise solidifies into my bones, warm and zealous. When he catches the top of my red lace panties peeking through the opening, his gaze darkens before he rests his hands below my belly button.

I squirm with struggle, waiting in anticipation.

"Now invite your husband into your bed."

We lock eyes, his with assured confidence that I'll cave this time. He sweeps his digits over the lace, a teasing touch that has my teeth sinking into my lip. Then he grabs the panties by the band, triggering a wave of confusion, which quickly morphs into panic.

"Wait—"

He yanks them upwards, the fabric plunging then scraping straight through my slick folds, as pain mixed with ecstasy expels the air from my lungs.

"My bed is yours!" I cry out on a labored breath.

"A good slut wouldn't hesitate," he growls in my ear, shifting the angle, and tugs once more.

"I'm sorry!" I writhe in my chair but find no relief. "Please, Tristan, come into my bed, please, I need—"

"Don't worry, wife, I'll be beside you every night." The band snaps against my skin on release, right before he plunges his hand deep into my pants. "Fucking you senseless until you've learned who you belong to, until you freely give yourself over without question at any time of my choosing."

I buckle forward, my palms shooting to his suit-clad chest, the sensation too much.

"Hands on the armrests," he scolds, and I settle back down. "Yes, just like that. Now quit grinding your waist... Such a perfect slut, aren't you? Giving me easy access."

Holding still, my nails dig into the leather, every muscle wrung taut while he works all the way down my pussy, then comes back through the center to my clit, the slickness audible between us. Panting in a wild craze, I expect him to latch his tongue onto my throat, but he only watches me with hungry eyes, pleased as I combust into a million pieces beneath him.

"*So. Fucking. Wet,*" he grinds out, clenching his teeth.

Up. Down.

Up. Down.

Up. Down...

Whimpering, I can't hold out much longer, my legs quivering, spasming in mid-air. But that only satisfies him further. A growl rumbles in his throat, and his touch grows more purposeful, more possessive.

"*You're mine and no one else's.* This pussy is mine. Your perfect ass and perky tits, even your smart little mouth. Every part of you is *mine.* Do you understand?"

I nod vigorously, words beyond me.

"To the public, you're my wife. But to me, you're my obedient slut." Retreating his hand, he flicks his chin towards the conference table. "Now bend over and show me what's mine."

Madly driven by lust, I all but dash from my chair, leaning

over the mahogany, ass pointed upwards and pants pooling around my heel-clad ankles.

Sunlight trickles across the table in gold streaks. I trace them until my gaze lands on the double doors, anxiety flickering in my chest. Because it's only now that I've even thought about our time restraint—and the floor-to-ceiling windows, for that matter, putting us on full display for anyone with a handy set of binoculars. But, somehow, that only raises my backside higher and spreads my legs further, wetness dribbling down the insides of my thighs.

Lazily, he sweeps my panties aside, exposing my flesh. A deep groan follows suit. "Are you always this wet for me, Lauren?"

Yes.

"We don't have much time," I whine, waiting for his cock, anticipation churning inside me. "They'll be back any minute."

"A minute is all I need."

Grabbing two fistfuls of my ass cheeks, he spreads them before thrusting home. The impact is aggressive, sending me lurching against the table with a moan on my lips, but what surprises me is the sensation. It's not the fullness I expected—but slurps and groans and a suction so divine, my eyes roll to the back of my head.

Ohhhhh....

My mind turns up blank, entering a place that's entirely foreign. My ex ate me out a few times, sure. But that was all, and it never felt like *this*.

Tristan wraps his muscled arms around my hips, pinning me to his mouth and lapping up my juices like a starved man. And if it weren't for the moans rumbling against my clit, I'd think he was suffocating himself. I match his volume, biting down on my lip, reveling in the way he swirls in clockwise motions before rubbing vertically with the flatness of his tongue.

"Mmmm." His breath tickles my skin. "You taste even sweeter than I imagined."

Squirming, the inside of my sex clenches around nothing, as need crawls up and out of my throat. I grind back onto his face, propping myself up on my elbows, only to be pushed down flat by his heavy arms. Then he *sinks* his tongue into my pussy and brutally pumps. Losing control of my volume, my cries bounce off the walls, the sensation too great.

Fingers plunge between my lips, silencing me, as his pace turns punishing, more desperate, my breasts slipping across the wood. Although concealed by my blouse, the subtle friction against my peaked nipples has me sucking against his fingers, taking them all the way to the knuckles. His digits explore my mouth, purposely sweeping and invoking my gag-reflex as an intense wave builds inside of me.

Feeling me tense up, Tristan's free hand darts for my clit, flicking roughly until the wave triples in size and topples headfirst off the ledge. His groan vibrates against my flesh as my inner walls pulsate hard along his tongue, my intense reaction stifled against his fingers.

When my climax subsides and he releases his weight off me, I whip around with haste, grappling for his belt buckle. Dropping to my knees, I stare straight ahead, salivating as I trace the impressive erection outlined through his pants.

Rough calluses snatch my wrists, tugging me back onto my feet. "There's no time for that, baby."

My stubborn nature yearns for an argument until I catch distant chatter seeping through the conference doors. Alarm bells rattle inside my head before Tristan and I both pull up my pants, a triumphant smirk gleaming across his lips.

Returning to my chair, I cross my arms, as if we've been anxiously waiting for the past fifteen minutes, and not throwing our bodies at each other in front of a gigantic window and agreeing to *ownership* over said body.

"Don't pout those lips before they name me CEO, or I'll gladly take you to another room and use them."

TRISTAN and I return to our chairs after shaking the hands of every board member. Not only did they vote him as CEO, but they actually handed over the requested one percent shares from each of them, without negotiation.

Not that Tristan gave them any room not to.

Beneath the table, he threads his fingers through mine, and a surprising warmth blooms across my skin. Then he leans into my ear, and whispers something that has my jaw dropping, even in light of the attention on us.

"Marriage or not, the extra ten percent goes to you and you only. Share with your family, if you like, seeing as they're the reason I'm in this position."

I meet his gaze, utterly stunned. Isn't greediness the whole reason he agreed to an arranged marriage? Sure, he got his cut of our original shares. But there's ten extra percent of a Fortune 10 company he just threw my way.

When his head returns down the table, his thumb rubs the backside of my hand with gentle strokes, nearly bringing tears to my eyes.

Mr. Henshaw clears his throat. "Mr. Walker, before the board adjourns, there's one more announcement."

Tristan simply nods.

"As of today, there's a new board member whom the rest of us met earlier today."

As if on cue, one door opens, revealing a surprisingly young man who can't be older than twenty-five. Beneath a striking black blazer, a burgundy turtleneck presses against his small frame, and spectacles rest on the bridge of his nose, affording him an intelligent appearance, despite his youth.

Stiff like a board, Tristan freezes beside me, staring straight ahead at the man. As I study him more closely, he relaxes, but not enough to stop his Adam's apple from bobbling halfway down his throat.

"Mr. Walker, I'd like you to meet Jace Cavendish."

SEVENTEEN
TRISTAN

GUILT SURPASSES the intensity of fear.

At its root, fear is an obstacle. A mere hurdle for the jumper. A train that should be met head-on and refused to run off course. But guilt is that which you cannot undo. The decisions you can't take back. The words you can't unspeak.

Guilt is shaking Jace's hand, congratulating him on his new board seat, then watching his eyes trail down to my wife. A wife I should only think of as an asset, or a means to an end. *An arranged wife.* But, in that moment, I couldn't get that through my head, could only taste the fear any husband would when a poisonous widowmaker gazes upon its next target.

Except...

Her most dire threat isn't Jace, whom she just met and knows as the charming young businessman who recently came into newfound wealth. Not the psychotic puppet master, who pulls strings attached to misfortunate heads, and the chameleon who roams the slums of New York City and the Down Under and now Silicon Avenue tech dynasties.

No.

She should be wary of the person seated right beside her. Who adorns her with a lavish ring he didn't buy, invades her digital privacy every night, keeps secrets regarding her own father's well-being, and is a ruthless knight upon the chess-board of higher players—who most certainly seek power over her family's company. All the while staking claim and devouring every inch of her body.

So, yes.

Guilt is a merciless bitch.

My opponent's fist hits me square in the jaw, the roaring of the crowd blasting through my brain as I stumble. The cold chain-link digs into my back, and I prepare for another blow —or rather, *don't prepare.* This time, the contact hits the corner of my chin, but it's still not enough to douse the sickness simmering inside my gut.

I don't know how many years it's been since I've thrown a match, probably sometime before my sister and I regained our connection, and I audibly heard her forgiveness for my abandonment as children. After that, I've only come to the ring for ninety percent pure sport and ten percent self-loathing. Following our recent betrothal, I hadn't stepped foot in the ring, even though I could've covertly broken our one week in-house honeymoon with ease.

Only if the truth were an option for Lauren, without the expense of my sibling. If she knew any better, she'd run far, far away from me, leaving her ring on her nightstand and her family's company for the wind. And if I had the gall, I'd add Lauren to my ever-growing list of women whose lives would be better off without me. Instead, I can't help but grow attached to her—giving her reasons to do the same with me—

when the only sensible outcome for us is pure and utter destruction.

After another flurry of unsatisfying punches to the face, I sway, my body yearning for the ground, until a fist catches me by the hair, the fingers pulling taut against my scalp. My cheek slams into the chain-link, meeting the countless hungry eyes of spectators, so close their screams spew saliva across my face.

"What gives?!" My opponent rages into my eardrums, barely audible over the ringing inside my brain and the hollers of those who placed their bets on this match. *"The infamous Apex doesn't land a scratch on me!"*

Then I meet his fist one last time before the ground.

"YOU WANT TO TALK ABOUT IT?" Bryson asks over the loud music.

In hindsight, maybe it would've been better to nurse my post-knockout shiners with a glass of single malt scotch at home, where I can play anything *but* heavy metal and grant my ears some much-needed peace. But, out of habit, after my spectacular loss, Bryson and I rode on over to the Blacktop Tavern, our favorite biker bar.

"No."

I take another sip, the whiskey stones clinking against my glass. The spice burns down my throat, a stark contrast from the ice pack pressing against my temple.

Bryson eyes me above his beer bottle, caution swirling behind them. "I'm not stupid, you know."

"I didn't say you were." I avoid his stare, roaming my gaze across the bar.

Riding from the Down Under to the Blacktop Tavern is quite the shell shock. While the crowd here is undoubtedly tough, it's a different *type* of toughness. Although they're rough around the edges, sporting tattoo sleeves, muscles, and leather jackets, I'd trust these people any day over the crime lords and thieves found below ground.

But that's going off pure instinct, which I've always relied heavily on, seeing as Bryson and I are typical loners here. Sitting in the back corner in a booth, my stare peruses across the bar, noting the Harley Davidson posters and the *road and route* signs littering the walls so heavily there's not an inch of visible paint beneath them.

"Really? So, you're just assuming I don't think you threw the match, then?"

I return to his gaze, finding him leaned back and annoyed. A complex mixture of colors glows atop our table and his skin, shining through the Tiffany lamp suspended above us. Discarding my ice pack, I fold my arms across my chest, matching his demeanor.

"Everyone has off days."

"No. Not you."

"Yes, even me. Maybe you'd understand that fact if you ever stepped foot in the ring."

Earning a scathing look, the words sting on the way out of my mouth. I know I'm being a dick, but Bryson can handle the heat. And I obviously don't want to talk about it right now.

Although, in his defense, when do I ever?

Standing firm, Bryson leans forward, defiance emerging from behind his eyes. "And why would I do that? So lowlife goblins can wage their bets on me? So I can relive the beatings we received living on the streets? To feel alive? News flash, I have other ways of coping, and none of them involve self-infliction."

A dull throb aches between my ears, empowering his words. Returning the ice pack to my skull, I look anywhere but at him.

"Fine. If you won't open up with me, then at least do so with your therapist."

A laugh bubbles out of my mouth, cold and full of ire.

"And say what? Hey, Mr. Shrink, *who could legally break our doctor-patient confidentiality if I so much as blabbed a single piece of the wrong information*, things have been rough lately. A secret society you're not supposed to know about—and wouldn't believe, even if I told you so—is threatening my sister's life for the exchange of my services. And, by services, I mean hacking skills. Yep, I'm a criminal. Got a pill for that, Doc? Didn't think so. That's alright. Even if you did, it wouldn't change the fact that my *arranged wife* is in their sights, and I can't save her or tell her the truth without jeopardizing my sister. And it's all my fault because I bought some stupid textbooks I shouldn't have in high school."

"...Wow." Bryson releases a heavy breath, eyes widening slightly. "So you *do* have feelings for Lauren."

He manages to pull a laugh from me, dulling my sour mood. "Is *that* what you got from that whole thing?"

"I don't hear you denying it."

I'm surprised when my lips snap shut, confirming his suspicions. I *can't* deny there's nothing between us, but I also can't admit if there *is* something. Not when I'm only a liar and bad news for her.

"It's... complicated."

"Isn't everything with you?" Bryson grins, before his lips soon lose their curve, morphing into a sympathetic expression that I find unbearable. "Now I see why tonight happened..."

A heavy knot constricts my gut, leaving me speechless. Faced with the truth, a gnawing silence grows between us, one we let drag out for a few minutes, instead nursing our drinks.

"So..." I count the whiskey stones inside my near-empty glass, stooping low to my tried-and-true tactic for lightening the mood. "I'll conveniently segue into an opportunity for you to finally admit to your no-good Wall Street habits."

"Not this again." A smile tugs at his lips, one he conceals by sipping his beer, before providing me with a familiar *answer yet non-answer.* "We're really not all bad."

"Sure, sure. Ever the stand-up stockbroker, aren't you? Be straight with me. You never slipped a little extra in your pockets?" He shakes his head. "No Jordan Belfort, *Wolf of Wall Street* action?" Eye roll. "No hard-selling penny stocks?"

My teeth sink into my bruised lip as he exhales sharply, irritation pricking at his temple as I stifle a laugh. *"No, man. For the hundredth time, no. There's zero trickery involved. I play the game by the books, fair and square. I make my clients' money by advising them on smart long-term invest-ments and, I, in return, make a percentage over time."*

"Bummer."

Contrary to my prodding, I've always known Bryson made his millions legally. We wouldn't be such close friends if he crossed outside the line of the law, and he only tolerates my illicit hacking activities because I'm out for the greater good.

But the accusation is just as funny every time.

"Then what *is* your way of coping, *oh wise one?"* The ques-tion comes out innocent and light. But, at my core, I hope he has unforeseen knowledge, some magical remedy for my guilt.

Eyes flicking across the room, he lowers his voice. "You really wanna know?"

I nod.

Tugging his black backpack off the floor, he sets it on the booth beside him. The zipper eases open at a slow pace, fueling the mounting sense of anticipation echoing through my chest.

Why's he being so secretive? Is it drugs? Weapons? Wads of cash?

When he reaches in, a jingling sound soon follows, making my brows furrow in confusion. With a laugh, he slings a pile of miscellaneous gold and silver metal across our table, uncaring of who might see. And it's not until he retrieves and unwinds a roll of felt fabric that the familiar tools unveil.

Oh, you've got to be kidding me...

Lock picking? *That's* his secret to coping?

"Come on, man." His snicker bounces between us. "What'd you expect?"

Now *my* eyes roll, catching a pair of bikers sitting at the end of the bar, their disapproving gazes pointed our way. I ignore them, studying the ten or so brass cylinders locked to a metal safety clip. "Don't you tire of picking the same locks over and over?"

"I would, if that were the case."

Choosing one from the loop, he stands it on its side, facing the opening towards him. Like a skilled surgeon, he picks a tool with an L-shaped tip from the pile without so much as looking, shoving the end into the lock. He holds steady as he guides another tool into the opening beneath the first.

"I always choose the lock at random, and I never pick the same lock twice in a row. That way, I'm essentially learning a new lock each time I pick, instead of memorizing."

"There are only ten locks, Bryson."

"Ten *on me.*" Angling his ear to the device, wearing a concentrated expression, he wiggles the second tool vertically, until there's a subtle *click.* Inching outwards a hair, he repeats the motion, and so on. "I guess you could call me a bit of a junkie or a hoarder. Everywhere I go—shops, used market-places, online retailers—I buy or trade for another and add it to my collection. Because every lock differs from the next, even ones from the same manufacturers. Meaning, they're all another opportunity to learn and improve my craft."

Craft.

While, I admit, he *does* take the hobby seriously, I'm having a hard time grasping the point. It's not like we're still hungry kids living on the streets, breaking into supermarkets and gas stations for food. *There can't be* that *many doors he's locking himself out of.*

"But why keep up the skill?"

"The same reason you still hack," he answers quickly, confusion floating about my brain. "And don't say it's because you're helping people. It's a respectable byproduct, sure, and I'm glad you have a moral compass, but that's not the real reason."

"And how do you figure that?" I cross my arms. "I've donated hundreds of millions to charities—upwards of billions, if we're counting the anonymous wire transfers made by all the corrupt billionaires I've blackmailed throughout my career."

Career. Eerily, I note as the word leaves my lips...

We really are *cast from the same mold.*

"If that's not my driving force, then what is?" I ask.

Another *click* resonates across the table, this one louder than the rest, before he rotates the first tool and tugs the metallic top loop free, unhooking the lock from the safety clip. Balancing the loop atop his forefinger, he meets my stare, his pooling with satisfaction.

"To go where you're not allowed."

A shocking wave rattles through me as I hold my friend's stare, and I chew his remark between my teeth. That look... that gleam in his eye is no different from the one I wore following my first successful hack.

At age twelve, my very first culprit was none other than my principal's printer, located in his office. I saw the machine quite often, being the unruly child that I was. But my next disciplinary meeting with him was much more tolerable when his printer began printing out pictures of dicks. *Lots and lots of dicks.* So many, in fact, that I programmed a web crawler with the sole purpose of finding even more. And it did. *For days.* No matter his efforts of unplugging the machine —which proved fruitless, given the handy wireless backup power I also tapped into—the prank carried on, until he literally smashed the printer to pieces on the pavement the following week.

In the courtyard.

During lunchtime.

In front of dozens of students.

Pressing my lips firmly, I contain a laugh, banishing his angered red face and the epic rumors that spread like wildfire after the incident from my mind. Instead, I focus on the beginning, sitting alone in the computer laboratory when I should've been at English class.

My sole motivation truly *was* curiosity. Choosing the principal's printer was only a last-minute decision, as the lab's printer would've been substantial motivation. Because I wanted to know if it could be done, if I could do what I set out to.

In essence, *to go where I wasn't allowed.*

I nibble on my bottom lip. "It's more complicated than that."

"Is it, though?" Bryson sets his instruments down. "What I'm getting at, Tristan, is something your therapist never could. That hacking *is* your coping mechanism, the extension of yourself that overcame and still tethers to our childhood. Regardless of what occurred today, you're not some brainless meathead pining for a beatdown in front of drug addicts, criminals, and gamblers. No. Deep down, you and me? We're still rebellious teenagers who talk back and defy authority. Even as an adult, you *challenge* authority—the CEOs and politicians who make pretty speeches and play respectable roles no one would question, unveiling them for what they really are."

My heart lifts to his confidence, chipping away at the mountain of darkness clouding my insides, until reality sinks back in.

"Ya. Right." A bitter laugh seeps through my lips. "Even if your teenage assessment is right, it does nothing for my predicament."

Nothing for the guilt, I don't add.

"Wrong again." His tone shifts, definitive and knowledge-able, like I'm opposite of him in the sparring ring, learning an MMA move from his seemingly endless repertoire. "As children, it was Ainsley Callahan on the playground. Now it's The Oculi on Silicon Avenue."

My lips part. *He's calling The Oculi my bully?*

"Bryson, this is getting out of hand..."

"Then I'll ask you one question—what do bullies do?"

And it's as if he sucker-punched me straight in the ribcage, whooshing the air from my lungs. Ainsley tormented me for months. He'd never miss an opportunity to remind me of my place, to call me society's leftovers, a waste of space, a no-good foster kid, who'll never find parents who would love me. And that notion extended to my younger sister.

Until I fought back.

Then he never spoke another word to me.

"They never stop."

Sickness rises up my throat at the realization. Because if that's true, then Aurora will never be safe. *Lauren* will never be safe, no matter my compliance with their demands. They'll use me until there's nothing left, and like the tongues of liars in the wake of a nullified contract, they'll do away with those who are disposable.

Bryson must read my face, because he clutches my wrist, staring straight through my eye-sockets, his intelligence felt in the remote corners of my soul. "Then stop playing dead. Stop acting as someone I know you're not. You're treating their society like you initially handled your bully. Doing as they say, letting them throw the punches, hoping they'll grow bored and forget about you and your family."

"It's not as simple as it was back then. I don't even know *who* makes up The Oculi—at least, not all their members. There's no way of knowing if I'd successfully expose them all, and I'd risk putting Aurora in harm's way."

"Then comply with their demands," he says calmly, choosing his next lock at random. Confused, I protest, but he cuts me short. "For now. Gather evidence, investigate, lie low, and revel in the opportunity provided by *their mistake* of getting too close to you. Until the time is right."

"For what?"

He shoves his instruments into the lock, rougher this time, peeking at me through his lashes.

"Your one and only strike—*a knockout.*"

EIGHTEEN
TRISTAN

AFTER PAYING our tab and waiting until the booze wore off, Bryson and I exit the bar, meeting the New York City nightlife. Small crowds of men and women lean against the bar's brick-walled exterior, smoking cigarettes and swigging beer glasses pressed to their lips. Rows of bikes line the streets facing outwards, their metal frames illuminated a deep red shade by the neon sign above the door.

Helmets in hand, we saunter past the bikes. Some are low riders with handlebars higher than necessary, others cruisers or choppers, unlike our sports bikes near the back. Sleek, aerodynamic and both Dacatis, Bryson's is a flashy red while mine is jet black, with an aggressive design, sharp lines, carbon fiber and—

Someone sitting on top?

We stop in our tracks, noting the figure, who's turned away from us and wears a leather jacket much like ours. Not wanting any trouble, I give him the benefit of the doubt. He looks quite young. Maybe he's drunk or is just curious.

"Hey, buddy, I think you've got the wrong bike."

He doesn't move. "No, I've got the right one."

My jaw clenches at the sound of his voice, but Bryson backs me up, stepping right behind him. "You don't want any trouble with us," he warns.

But when the man turns around, flashing the owl tattoo crawling up his neck, nearly as dark as his slicked back hair, Bryson shies away.

"Oh, but it just so happens that I do."

Jace smiles, resting his elbow on a handlebar and propping an ankle across his knee. Leather jacket falling open, his white tank and rusted dark jeans come into view. I even spot a dog tag dangling off his neck and ink across the backs of his hands that couldn't have been there this afternoon.

I fold my arms over my chest. "It seems you have more identities than me, Jace."

"But only one name. That's the key." He wags his index finger at me, as if what he said proves anything at all. "Though, you might have lost one tonight. Apex implies you're on top, right...?" He sucks in a sharp breath, tapping his cheekbone. *"Ouch.* Quite a shiner you got there."

Rolling up my sleeves, my tone is friendly. "You want one to match?"

"How'd you come up with that name, anyway?" he asks, ignoring my threat. Retrieving a cigarette from his pocket, he lights the end, before bracing the orange filter between two fingers. *"Apex..."* The tip glows a subtle red on his inhale, smoke billowing out of his nostrils and between his lips. "So edgy. Although, I'd wager you came up with the name when you first entered the cage. Thirteen, fourteen, or so? But, still. Almost as edgy as your hacker name, Gh—"

"Is there something you want? Or are you just here to taunt me? Is that the reason you joined the board, too?

Because you can't stand being apart? *Mr. Jace Cavendish.*" I sneer out his fake executive name. "You say you only have one name, but that can't be it."

"Maybe it is, maybe it's not." He shrugs, taking another drag.

"Well, you look like a nobody to me," Bryson chimes beside me. "No friends, I take it?"

"There's power in being no one."

His pupils dilate for a fraction of a second, as if he said too much, before a slick calm washes over him. Eyes narrowing, I mean to pose more incisive questions, but he beats me to the mark.

"It seems you're holding up your end of the deal," Jace says, a content smirk stretching his lips wide. "Little Red doesn't suspect a thing about her father, does she? Otherwise, you two wouldn't have looked so chummy sitting next to each other today."

A fire blooms across my skin, red-hot and volatile, at the mention of Lauren on his tongue. It's enough having him on the board, in the same room as her, breathing her same air, but it's crossing a whole other set of lines calling her by a nickname I've yet to claim.

"You act as if I'm getting something out of this." I steer the conversation away from her.

"Don't you? As far as I'm aware—which is quite literally her every whereabouts these days—your younger sister is still safe and sound at Columbia."

More bait. All he wants is for me to lose my temper like always, but this time, I won't give him the satisfaction. "What do you want, Jace?"

Disappointed, his lips thin. "Well, I'm here to give you your assignment, now that you're CEO." Yanking his jacket sleeve back, he exhales sharply, eyeing an expensive-looking watch wrapped around his wrist. "But it seems to be running late."

Late?

I pinch the bridge of my nose.

"Move aside, twig." Bryson jerks his thumb in a pointed direction. "You're wasting our time."

"Any minute now, any minute now..." Jace ignores him, mumbling to himself under his breath, heel tapping against the pavement impatiently. Not a minute goes by before he shoots to his feet and paces on the sidewalk, his head whipping back and forth like some aimless pendulum. "People just can't follow simple orders and be where they're supposed to be, can they?!" His arms flail outwards, gravity pulling them back to his sides with a flustered *smack.*

I catch Bryson's gaze for a split second. He only shrugs.

"Uh..." I inch myself towards my bike. "Is this not something you could shoot over email?"

"You're the hacker here," Jace hisses. "I'm sure you can figure out why we leave as little digital footprints as possible."

"Okay..." I take another step. "Maybe we could meet up at work? As much as I hate the idea, it's better than—"

"Finally!" he practically shouts.

Eyebrows scrunching, I look around, finding the road silent and completely void of cars. Until I follow the line of his gaze and land on a bike in the distance. Not a motorcycle. But a *bicycle.* With a black hoodie atop his head, the rider pedals hard, emerging through a haze of thick fog. And the closer he gets, the sicker I feel.

Because he's quite... *small.*

I cock my head, studying his scrawny frame, until the bike

squeaks to a halt right in the middle of us, off the edge of the sidewalk. My mouth goes dry when I appraise his youthful, chubby cheeks, and my heart goes utterly still at the owl tattoo inked up his neck, in the exact spot as Jace's.

He can't be older than eleven...

In a rush, he shrugs off his backpack, fumbling for the zipper with shaky hands. "I-I'm sorry—"

"Don't say anything," Jace reprimands harshly. "Remember your place. You haven't earned your speaking privileges yet."

Speaking privileges...?

The kid nods and lowers his gaze, offering Jace a manila folder. Shaking his head, Jace snatches the folder. "Your superior will hear of this."

My gut sloshes with vile at the revolting scene, threatening me with sickness that will, more likely than not, end up all over the pavement.

Chin trembling, the kid rides off back the way he came, away from Blacktop Tavern.

"Why the sour face?" Jace asks me.

"He's just a kid."

"And?"

My anger bubbles to the surface.

If he wants a reaction out of me, fine.

"Is that another one of your roles? Dressing up as a kid, luring them into your games? You're sick. A fucking predator." The Glock concealed at my lower back stings against my skin, begging to put a bullet between his eyes.

"Don't be so dramatic." He unwinds the string on the folder's latch, avoiding my murderous gaze. "Kids like Tony are eager to join our cause. They need strict rules. We give their troubled lives direction, a higher purpose. He had no one who cared for him before us. He had nothing."

"Is that what they've taught you to say? What're you, some fucking trained monkey? You're *stealing* his future, not giving him one." My hand shoots to my chest. "I know what it's like to have nothing."

"Yet here you are. Frequenting the Down Under, the cage, letting strangers bash your face in from a little guilty conscience. From my perspective, your life could do with a little order and discipline. And your skills could *actually* serve society."

My vision blurs with red, fingernails dig into my palms, and heavy feet move of their own volition, towards the man who would most certainly serve society better *dead* —

A hand clutches my shoulder, jerking me in the opposite direction. Bryson's stern face comes into view, the only solace able to bring me back to sanity. When my heart rate returns to a manageable rhythm, I release a heavy breath through my nostrils, turning towards Jace. Lips sealed airtight, I outstretch my hand, ready for my assignment.

More like my sentencing.

Jace only grins, as he—*yet again*, with a flawless record— wins our battle of wits.

"The society thanks you for your efforts," he says before handing over the manila folder. Swiveling on his heel, he strides two bikes down, takes his seat, straps on the helmet hanging off a handlebar, and rides off through the haze.

Blinking, I assess the hefty packet—and the two words etched across the front in red ink...

Project Dupe

NINETEEN

LAUREN

"HOW ARE YOU FEELING? EMOTIONAL?" Sofia asks me, an unmistakable tease to her tone. "We can step out if you need to—"

"Cry? Oh, no. I don't cry."

Hannah and Sofia chuckle in unison, their laughter bouncing off the walls, echoing in the empty space.

While it's odd seeing my apartment this way, barren and sparsely staged for interested renters, I admit keeping it is not in the best interest of my current arrangement. In the words of my mother, *"A married woman has no need for an apartment in the city, when she has a husband waiting for her back home."*

My two friends, who I met several years ago on the night Hannah just happened to enter into a *fake* engagement, have been in this apartment on numerous occasions. It's been our go-to party spot, with so many memories I could barely count.

"It's alright. There, there." Hannah rubs my shoulder as the three of us look out at the city skyline through the floor-to-ceiling windows, a rawness prickling at my throat.

"I'm fine." With a sharp sigh, I refuse the tears that want to form. "But... it *is* sad, though." My gaze sweeps across the space, from the oak floors to the impressive kitchen, across the perimeter dominated by glass, then arriving on the wrought-iron spiraling staircase leading to the second story.

I love that staircase, I think somberly. *We've taken so many pictures on it. Christmas, New Year's parties, potlucks, and spur-of-the-moment get-togethers...*

Christ, who knew I was this *attached?*

I don't even own the place outright, having only rented the apartment for the past few years. Initially, I thought it was too small, but settled due to its convenient location near Astor Associates. If I had known I'd get so sappy over moving, I would've put the money down without hesitation. But it's much too late now to put in an offer, given my arrangement.

And, so, the keys of the girls' notorious, drunken head-quarters are being handed over to another lucky renter.

As if she can read my sad expression, Sofia joins me in my mourning, asking, "Remember that time when Sterling shoved Damien's face into his birthday cake, right after he blew out the candles?"

I snicker, recalling my two cousins smearing each other with icing like a couple of kids and all the polaroid pictures of their heinous aftermath.

Hannah chimes in, "What about when we built a two-story beer bong out of PVC pipe for Halloween? What a mess."

I roll my eyes, a grin spreading along my lips.

"No, no." Sofia shakes her head, dark hair tousled around her shoulders. "The *real* mess was when Jenna brought over that new guy she was dating during our New Year's Eve party, who drew whipped cream dicks all over the windows."

We all bust up laughing, tears lining our eyes. And, before long, I'm practically gasping for air between choppy breaths, heaving my next words out. "It was so bad, people in the apartment over called and complained to our property manager."

"Ah!" Hannah barrels forward, her hand pressed against the glass for support. "You can't... be... serious?!"

"No, really." My face stretches taut with a wide smile, enough to crack into pieces. "It took weeks to get off. I hired professional cleaners and everything. They were *not* happy with me."

Our laughter echoes across the empty kitchen and through the main hallway, until it simmers down and a sad aura surrounds us.

"We're all just a bunch of frat lords, aren't we?" I ask, trying to lighten the mood.

Sofia's smile is solemn. "'Fraid so."

When a hush descends upon us again, I sigh, retrieving my main and spare keys from my pocket. Heading to the kitchen, I set the pair on the counter.

"So, do you know who will take over the lease?" Hannah asks me.

"Nope. But someone already did. The property manager obviously can't tell me their name. Whoever they are, they're one lucky son of a bitch, who will never know how good they got it."

Hannah shrugs. "Who knows? Maybe they will."

"Doubtful."

"Mmm..." She avoids my gaze, the slightest smirk lifting her lips. "No, I'd say likely, even."

Confusion wraps around me, but then when a chuckle seeps out of her, my eyes narrow into slits. "Hannah..."

She doubles over as her palm smacks against the marble, body shaking with laughter.

"Hannah. You did not —"

"I got you!"

Sofia's jaw drops to the floor at the same time mine does.

"What?" My hand flies to my hip. "You're the new renter? You could've just told us that from the start!"

"And where's the fun in that?" Hannah pulls out her own set of keys from her purse, swinging them around her forefinger with a dubious grin. "Come on, I was only testing you, seeing if lawyers really *do* have a funny bone."

"I can't believe you got so lucky. There were dozens of applications."

"I wouldn't call it luck, per se. Damien said he was looking for another investment property, so..."

"Oh my God." I roll my eyes in disbelief. "Tell your fiancé to leave some real estate for the rest of us. What is he trying to do, buy up every high-rise in New York City?"

"It's his new hobby, allegedly, since taking some time off work. Anyway, no matter that I'm the new owner, the place is always yours." Her gaze ping-pongs between me and Sofia, who appears perfectly content. *"It's all of ours,"* she corrects herself.

Aside from the ruthless bait-and-switch, relief washes over me. "Thank you."

"No need." She hugs me, her hair smelling of fresh lavender and a hint of lilac. "You *are* my future cousin-in-law."

I smile at that, mentally equating her to the sister I never had.

Hannah heads over to the fridge and tugs back the handle,

revealing a champagne glass positioned on the inside of the door. And in less than a minute tops, the three of us clink glasses bubbling to the brim and toast to the many more memories to come.

TWENTY
LAUREN

MY ARRANGED HUSBAND suffers from chronic lateness.

Even when joining his wife between the sheets.

Lying atop the California king, I appraise my body, annoyance pricking at my temples. Adorned in my most revealing nightgown, breasts kept at bay by a flimsy tie, my freshly shaven legs slide against the black silky sheets. Without needing a mirror for confirmation, I know my hair falls perfectly at my shoulders, somewhere between the realms of *just-heading-to-bed* effortless and *I-want-you-to-fuck-me* glamorous.

What have I become?

After today's events, there's no denying my intentions for tonight. In my head, the scene went something like...

Tristan walks through the bedroom door.

Finds me twelve notches past hot.

And then fucks me.

A simple, three-step process. We wouldn't even need to speak to one another, only give in to our carnal urges and finish where we left off. He couldn't mess that up, right? No man in his sound mind would miss a date with his horny wife who—apparently—wears *lip gloss and perfume* to bed.

But no. He's late.

And I hate waiting.

Whipping the covers back over my body, I return to my phone. For the past several hours, I've reduced myself to a mere gossip addict *again,* reading click-baity and over-exaggerated articles. Several were about me and Tristan—mostly rumors of our love life tagged with photos taken in the street outside Astor Security. I wouldn't have read them if it weren't for the mouthwatering view of Tristan in those riding pants...

I huff a breath, scrolling through articles at random.

Innovex Microchips' Stocks at an All-Time High

Swipe.

Silicon Avenue's Most Eligible CEOs

Swipe.

New Shocking Evidence Supports Silicon Avenue Secret Society Conspiracy Theory

I roll my eyes.

Swipe.

Swipe.

Swi—

Unmasking Gh0st: Silicon Avenue's Most Feared Hacker

Intrigued, I shrug my shoulders, clicking on the article.

In the shadowy depths of Silicon Avenue, where lines of code weave the fabric of secrecy, emerges a mysterious phantom who strikes fear into the hearts of tech moguls and cybersecurity experts alike.

His name? Gh0st.

Whispered in hushed tones across the digital realm and left encoded in the aftermath of cyber exploits, his hacker name is synonymous with elusive brilliance and unparalleled hacking prow-

ess. Unseen, unheard, and virtually unstoppable, Gh0st's trail is that of encrypted chaos, sending shock waves through tech elite. Whether infiltrating corporate databases, exposing covert dealings, or disrupting the digital status quo, Gh0st operates in a realm where anonymity is his greatest ally.

But who is Gh0st, and what motivates this feared hacker?

Some speculate he's a disgruntled tech insider seeking revenge, while others believe he's a rogue genius fighting a covert war against the overreaching, upper tech society. But the answer remains elusive, with the public's sole lead stemming from an incident last October.

For those unaware or in need of a memory refresher, after the CEO of CodeCraft labeled the hacker a "coward who hides behind pixels" in a social media post, the hacker responded with his notorious, cryptic humor—by sending a picture of himself directly to the man's inbox.

Feast your eyes, ladies.

My eyebrow quirks. *Feast my eyes...?*

Scrolling down, I'm met with an intense image. With black-and-gold wallpaper as a backdrop, secrecy cloaks the man in the photo, who adorns a face mask beneath a black hoodie. LED strips glow vibrant red along the facial covering, crossing X's over the eyes, swooping out one nostril and into the other, and diverging into a wicked smile.

A twinge of fear rises inside of me as I stare into his veiled eyes—a fear that proves short-lived. Curiosity takes over, trailing my gaze to the parts he *does* reveal. The zipper of his hoodie hangs considerably, exposing the inner sides of defined pecs and a strong throat.

Biting my lip, I study his skin further, the rough ridges forming taut muscles. The image takes me back in front of Astor Security on the busy street, staring wide-eyed at the man atop a stealth motorcycle, feeling the weight of his blacked-out helmet perusing up and down my body.

Not that I believe Tristan's some masked cybercriminal, but I must admit, from the parts I *can* see, the two share an eerie resemblance. And the way the man in the photo tilts his head in a cocky manner—like he *knows* he could watch me at any moment, if he so pleased—has the bottom of my nightgown jumbling between my thighs as they rub together.

Quit it, I scold myself. *What are you doing, Lauren, unlocking some new fetish? No. You've only worked yourself up for the past three hours. That's all.*

Shaking the image from my mind, I continue on with the article.

CodeCraft's CEO shared the headshot on his social media. The post quickly gained traction, spreading like wildfire across the internet, which only pried even more scrutinous comments from the business executive.

Guess he doesn't share an affinity for masked men.

I digress.

One fact remains undeniable: Gh0st is not a faceless entity confined to the digital ether. He could be your colleague, your neighbor, or even the person you unknowingly brush shoulders with at a local coffee shop. Anyone's fair game.

So, dear reader, stay vigilant.

Signing off for now. But don't worry, your next dose of tech drama is only one byte away.

- ByteBuzz

I gnaw on my lower lip, creeping back up the article until I'm face-to-face with Gh0st once more.

Stay vigilant...

Eyes crawling across his skin, my heart flutters in my

chest, then returns to a steady rhythm when I come up empty.

See? Just paranoia.

I'm about to swipe out of the article, until I spot something I hadn't in the photograph. Black and tiny, it's no wonder I missed the tip-of-a-sewing-needle-sized tattoo peeking out of the zipper's metallic teeth. With my heart rate picked back up and my throat suddenly dry like sandpaper, I zoom in. Pixel by pixel, the area enlarges, revealing a slight upward bend in the ink, pointing towards the man's mask.

It's just a coincidence, I tell myself. *Millions and millions of men have tattoos.*

But do those men mention hacking techniques at board meetings? the opposition challenges inside my head, dripping with mental clarity. *Do they live in remote mansions? Disappear all day long, doing God-knows-what? Know parts of conversations in an elevator with your ex that they shouldn't? And allude to your private shower habits?*

"Something tells me you can't hold out for long," Tristan had said, taunting me with his knowledge.

He was so confident... *How?*

Stop it, stop it.

I toss my phone halfway across the bed, knees snapping to my chest in comfort. These are all assumptions. Mere speculation. I don't have Tristan's tattoos memorized, so I'm only painting some unfair narrative on him. There's no way of knowing or comparing the two photos. I shouldn't assume—

Except there is, the thought beams in my headspace.

I *can* compare them...

Grappling for my phone, body shimmying across the silk sheets, I scour for a particular ByteBuzz article, which proves easy enough, seeing as it's still plastered across the top of the blog's main page. Zooming down the blog post, text flying across my screen, I stop on the picture of Tristan and me hand-in-hand on the beach during our supposed honeymoon.

Instead of gawking like the first time I saw his mouthwatering, tatted body in this picture, I zoom in, with one target in mind, uncaring that artificial intelligence fabricated every pixel. The waves of the ocean, my red bikini and glorious tan all dart from the screen, replaced by chiseled pecs. And, to my horror, not only is the center completely vacant of tattoos, but ink decorates the outer side of his right pec in beautiful, unexplainable patterns, one particular strand stretching further than the others, *in the same exact spot as the hacker's photo.*

I hurl my phone yet again, fortunate when the device doesn't plummet to the hardwood, teetering on the edge of the bed.

It's fake, it's fake, it's fake...

Artificial intelligence learns, baby. It can't create what doesn't already exist. Tristan's words form a feedback loop in my brain, leaving me frazzled and anxious as I spring out of bed, heading for the kitchen on brisk, bare feet.

I just need a snack. I'm cooped up, is all. Waiting and waiting and waiting and waiting—I mean, that'd drive anyone crazy!

As I pass through the living room, a slight chill brushes against my skin, a reminder of my scandalous nightgown. Looping my arms around my middle, annoyance simmers deep inside me.

What is it, nearly midnight, and he's still a no-show? What's he doing all night, huh? Got somewhere better to be? Got someone else to—

Ugh! Jealousy flares my nostrils wide. Rounding the

corner to the kitchen, my soles eating up the marbled floor, I—

Stop in my tracks.

Sporting his leather jacket, looking the complete opposite of crawling out of the spare bedroom—*more like crawling out of some bar*—Tristan props the fridge door open, back facing me. With not a single light turned on in the space, the fridge illuminates against his unkempt hair, which he drags a smooth hand through, before grabbing a leftover container.

"And where have *you* been?" I ask, just as sharp as I intend, my voice ping-ponging in the large area. I don't care if I sound like a jealous wife, because... *well, because I am.* One who yearns for a groveling session once he turns around and sees what he's been missing.

His back straightens. "Oh, uh..." He shuts the fridge. "Out."

Out? What is he, some teenager?

He shuffles leftward without turning my way, grabbing a plate out of a tall cupboard. I narrow my gaze, as I note the weird hobble in his movements.

"Out where?"

"I... got caught up."

My jaw tightens at his vagueness, and irritated heat scatters down my arms. I bound across the space, fury pumping through my veins when he *still* doesn't turn around, even when I'm two steps from him.

"Oh ya? Is that what happens all day, too? You know, when you're never around the house?"

"Lauren..." His voice carries a menacing warning I couldn't care less about.

"Just spit it out, *Tristan.* What is it? Got a girlfriend?"

"No."

"You sure?" I ask his backside—*who's really the one I'm conversing with*—drenched in spite. "Well, contrary to your big promises, seems you didn't intend to take me up on my offer earlier. And you sure as hell don't intend to right now. Looks like you're all talk."

"That's not true." His deep growl nearly has my toes curling, but I hold my ground.

"Then why aren't you looking at me?"

His shoulders tense, and silence encroaches the space between us.

"Turn around."

"Lauren—"

"Turn around."

On reluctant feet, Tristan twists at an achingly slow pace, revealing himself in a gut-wrenching state. Our eyes connect for a fleeting moment before we both take in each other's appearances. Bruises shine along his handsome features, and medical gauze covers what I presume to be a split lip. My breath hitches in his wake, and anger oozes straight out of my pores as thick worry seeps back in.

If it weren't for his unabashed, darkening gaze scanning down the length of my body, I would forget how on-display my body is. With a ticking jawline, I catch his knuckles whitening against the ledge of the countertops. Weathering the thrill sparked by the much-needed attention, my concern comes out ahead.

"What happened?"

"I crashed my bike." His voice comes out thick and distracted, which would usually serve as an effective deterrent for me sniffing out his lie. If it weren't for one thing...

"Your clothes look fine."

Closing the space between us, he says nothing, eyes

drinking me in. His nearness sends shivers bolting down my arms, devising tempting scenarios where I'm bent over these countertops or down on my knees batting my eyelashes up at him. When he grips my spaghetti strap between two fingers, noting the flimsy tie concealing my breasts, I nearly tug it for him, until an unfamiliar aroma of tobacco, sweat, and rubber floats into my nostrils.

"Tell me where you were," I demand.

"We can always talk later, baby." He rolls the strap between his thumb and index.

"No..." I resist the heat pooling between my thighs. "I want to talk about it now. *Where were you?*"

Dropping the fabric, he shrugs, avoiding my gaze. "It's not a big deal, okay? Bryson and I went out to a bar, and I crashed on the way back, taking a corner too fast."

He's still lying.

"Look at me."

His eyes flicker before locking onto mine. Craning my head back, I search them, tapping into my near endless supply of discernment, earned from years and years of working beside clients with deceptive tongues. And what I find shocks me, sends hard-earned compassion, and floats countless questions about my consciousness. Contradicting his nonchalant yet arrogant façade, hurt swims through his eyes like a lost soul in a fishbowl, as guilt bobs up to the surface before diving back down to a shadowy refuge.

"Please, talk to me."

"I..." He looks away, his aching tone weighing down on the marrow of my chest. "I can't."

Cupping his jaw gently, I turn him back towards me. I brush my thumb along his skin, wary of his injuries. "You can tell me anything."

Wetting his lips, anticipation wrapping around us like a constricting coil, he seizes my wrist softly, his gaze nothing short of penetrating.

"Lauren, stop," he whispers. "Don't care for me or look after me. Don't get close. If you want more, only let it be physical. If you know what's good for you, *you'll stop asking questions.*"

He retreats from my grasp, leaving me empty and stunned. Because for the first time tonight, absolute truth passed through his lips. Dazed with confusion as words fail me, he saunters and disappears from the kitchen. Snapping from my haze, I dart forward, tracking his footsteps, swinging around the corner, only to discover him doing the same around another.

"Tristan?"

My steps quicken, banking left at another turn, but *again* finding him just out of sight.

"Tristan!"

I dash down the hallway, narrowly catching him passing through the library doorway. Huffing between breaths, prepared to find him trapped and skulking atop one of the lounge chairs with no escape, I break through the open door frame. But upon my entrance, I'm engulfed by an over-whelming fog of confusion, and I question whether the past twenty minutes were a part of a dream. Because if my twenty-twenty vision doesn't deceive me...

The room's empty.

I PACE IN THE KITCHEN.

People don't just vanish out of thin air. He must've gone

through a different doorway, and I narrowly missed him. Then my brain filled in the blanks.

Yes, yes.

It's one a.m. on the dot. Hours past my usual bedtime. Sleep deprivation can lead *anyone* to unexplainable situations and play tricks on *anyone's* mind. I'm nothing special. Fatigue is the culprit, no doubt, and contorted my reality.

Except...

I'm not tired.

...fuck...

In thirty seconds flat, I'm in the library, pulling books off the shelves like a woman possessed. What a horrific sight for any self-acclaimed bookworm, their pages and leather-bound spines clattering against the ground, forming heaps of unsung knowledge. Moving to the next in line, I tear at the shelf with veracity, the paperbacks soft butter and my hands sharpened blades, ripping them from their cozy nooks with no resistance.

The Art of War?

Gone.

The Odyssey?

Gone.

Pride and Prejudice?

Goodbye, Mr. Darcy.

1984?

G—

Fingers slipping along the cover, air whooshes from my lungs before I crash backwards on a self-made pile of novels. "Uuugghhhh," I groan out in pain, rolling off the mound.

What a stupid idea. Have I gone mad?

As I brace against the floor, my guilty gaze scans across the mess. The first shelf lies barren, the next nearly as sparse, and the third looks ravaged, with books trampled over another and teetering off ledges and—

Defying gravity?

Jaw dropping in disbelief, I arch my head backwards, meeting *1984's* captivating eye, uneasiness building in my chest beneath the scrutinous blue iris. Tilted ajar, a curved metal rod pokes beneath the novel's pages and into the wooden shelf. Prying myself from the oddity, I look past the eye, to the fourth bookshelf now swung open on its hinges, unveiling a dimly lit corridor.

And a single elevator door.

TWENTY-ONE
LAUREN

I'M a curious cat who may just get herself killed.

But without the nine lives.

My inner rationale screams at me to turn around, clean up the mess I made of the library, go back to bed, and forever wipe this little secret from my brain. But to its dismay, when the elevator's smooth doors glide open, I enter with no hesitation.

Clean with sterile air and a slight chill, I fold my arms along my middle, thankful for the oversized cardigan and fuzzy slippers I threw on after encountering Tristan while wearing next to nothing. My gaze sweeps across the space, at first noting the sheer size of the lift.

You could fit a car in here...

Then my eyes land on the second peculiarity, where the collection of buttons should be on the wall. Except, there aren't. No up arrows. No downs. Only one—with no floor number. I quirk my eyebrow as the doors seal shut, wondering if the machine will move on its own, and wait in silence... until I finally cave and hit the round knob, which lights up like normal.

Casually leaning against the wall, I prepare for ascension, despite my heart pitter-pattering like hail thundering atop concrete. But when the elevator hums and my stomach flutters, I realize I'm heading *down*, not up.

But the library is on the main floor...

Tristan *did* mention having a basement full of cars. Maybe this whole time he's what every typical billionaire in his late twenties with too much money and time on his hands is—*a car junkie*. Not a... I can't even form the thought in my brain, seeing as it makes this all too surreal, too haunting, that I willingly set foot through doors that might actually open to a fearfully renowned cybercriminal. And how such an alleged individual would react when caught in the act?

It's anyone's best guess...

Always hating the sensation, I weather the feeling of weightlessness, anticipating the pushback against my feet on the deceleration. But when the machine surely surpasses the vertical threshold of a basement, the slow doesn't come. Claustrophobia seeps into my bones, sudden and confining, like the slithering of dirty fingers up my windpipe, gripping me tighter with every second passing into the abyss.

Down...

And down...

And down...

Until—to my immense relief—the steel plate flooring pushes against the soles of my slippers. Mumbling prayers and running clammy palms against my cardigan, I stare a hole straight through the double doors as time slows to an aching crawl.

"Please be cars, please be cars, please be—"

Ding.

My heart plummets, and what I see might as well weave tripwire between my ankles or smack my face with a sledge-hammer. Instead of the rows of McLarens, Lamborghinis, and Ferraris I had hoped for, are actually rows of *server racks*.

Paling, I exit the doors, stepping into an entirely different realm. Made up of tall racks, I walk down the main path, with floors so clean there must not be a speck of dust on them. Numerous red and green dots of light flicker through the racks' cages, just as neat as the floor, with not a cable or loose end in sight.

My pace is languid through the deep azure glow coating the surrounding air, emanating from the ceiling of endless white panels and reflecting off the identical floor below. With an ethereal vibe, the space can only be best described as wandering through hazy blue clouds or some meticulously arranged world where stillness and the soft murmurs of tech live between sheets of ice.

Halfway down the line of racks, I hit an intersection. Head on a swivel, one path leads to several more rows of the same, and the opposite leads to yet another door, which I pass through and find a myriad of *even more doors.*

Upon their inspection, most reveal utilitarian rooms like a modest kitchen, a full bathroom, and even a workout area. But each swing of a door feels like another trigger pulled in a deadly game of Russian Roulette, counting down the seconds I have left before coming face-to-face with the *real* Tristan Walker.

My wedding band weighs heavily around my finger as I grip another knob, this one at a dead end of a corridor and notably warmer than the rest.

An unexpected wave of emotions knocks against my

temples. Feelings not of fear, but of *sadness*. Because what's even scarier than unveiling a ghost, who I now share a last name with and is surely sitting somewhere beyond this doorway, is coping with the aftermath and the shock waves that will ripple through us.

Whatever *us* really is.

And it's in this moment that I realize Tristan *has* pried feelings from me, whether they're small or substantial, and has either mutually latched them onto himself or discarded them completely. In just two short weeks, Tristan—who is quite literally my opposite "type" in every way—has become a comfortable presence beside me, by ways of his self-assurance and assertiveness.

But is anything real?

The possessiveness. The jealousy. The lost guilt and simmering heat behind his eyes. Is the Tristan I'm getting to know a complete lie? An illusion masking motives I can't stomach to fathom? Accepting the sorrow and uncertainty, I take deep breaths, in and out, until the shakiness vanishes along with the fruitless questions in my mind that may forever remain unanswered...

Until I twist the knob.

AND THERE HE IS.

Gh0st.

Silicon Avenue's most wanted hacker. No doubt the object of ire for dozens of CEOs. Right here, beneath the mansion I moved into mere weeks ago, hidden in a bunker far underground. Behind five monitors littered with code and graphs and even a digitized world map with red heat signals, his back faces me through an ergonomic office chair, headphones cuffed over his ears.

Maybe movies gave me the wrong impression, but this isn't quite the hacker lair I expected. No dingy walls. No ominous green glow. No suspicious odors or a gazillion wires running across the floor and dangling from the ceiling. Only a tidy workstation surrounded by whiteboards occupying half of the wall space, adorned with mathematical equations, diagrams, and nearly illegible handwriting. And while the endless hacking textbooks and loose papers sprawled across the floor may *look* haphazard, with a second glance, there's actually an organized chaos to them.

Not having moved an inch from the doorway, words caught in my throat, my gaze crawls past the papers, drawing a zig-zagged line my way, hitting the nearest wall—

Wrapped in wallpaper.

The exact same wallpaper in the ByteBuzz article. I freeze, staring at the black shapes with gold specs in them, a final confirmation for what I already knew. Like an electric shock to my system, the mask-wearing man flashes through my thoughts, a deadly reminder of who it is I'm really dealing with.

Who sits ten paces from me...

Heart pounding and toes recoiling in my slippers, my eyes flicker to Tristan, who's dressed in a fresh white tee and sweatpants. His arm tattoos are on full display, running down his skin in intricate patterns. Like a sixth sense, his back straightens ever-so slightly, and I know he's aware of my presence. Closing the manila folder laid before his keyboard in a definitive swoop, he rests his headset across the back of his neck, swiveling in his chair.

And meets my gaze.

A shiver courses down my spine, unlike any I've ever felt before, somehow calm and controlled in this moment.

He speaks first. "Do you know who I am?"

A nod is my only answer, and I catch his throat visibly bobble, an anguished expression morphing across his face. One that must be well-practiced.

"Lauren—"

I whip up my hand, silencing him. *Enough lies.*

"Now, are you going to answer my questions?"

There's a pause.

"Yes." His voice comes out thick.

"What do you want with Astor Security?"

"Nothing..." He runs an anxious hand through his dark hair. "Nothing, Lauren, please. There are no bad intentions. I'll admit, I took the agreement for the shares out of greed, craving a portion of the success I laid the groundwork for. But that doesn't mean I don't recognize your father's hard work. I want the company to keep thriving—and for your family to remain in it, for that matter."

I recall his negotiations earlier, and the shares he willingly handed over to me, essentially paying my family the exact amount of shares they lost from the marriage.

That could've been an attempt at winning me over, I caution. *To cover his ass if this exact scenario ever played out.*

"What're the server racks for?"

"Mining cryptocurrency. Bitcoin and Ethereum, mostly."

It's public knowledge that Tristan is a crypto billionaire. However, a trace of doubt still lingers within me. "Is that all?"

He averts his gaze, crossing his arms. "Some store sensitive data. This bunker is low enough to protect the data center from natural disasters, if anything was to ever happen."

Sensitive data. I frown, thinking of the worst.

Building an iron-clad wall around my heart, I move on to the prosecution's pivotal moment. "Do you hack me?"

Jaw unclasping, he makes to his feet. "Lauren—"

"Don't move." He freezes midway before sitting back down, hands gripping tightly on the armrests. "Stay in that chair. Now answer."

"It's not—"

"It's a yes or no question."

"...Yes."

I knew the truth when I walked in here, but his affirmation still swings a blow. "What do you know about me?"

"Everything."

A thrill that I loathe sings in my gut at his possessive tone, at the thought of someone on this earth possibly knowing more about me than *myself.* Unable to resist, I imagine him breaking into every one of my social media accounts, my work and school records, tapping my phone calls, reading my emails and text messages, even setting his gaze upon my bank accounts and numerous investments.

Everything... He truly knows *everything.*

I recall Tristan at our wedding. *Territorial, to the point of ruining another man's life if he so much as touches you?*

I appraise the man across the room, who seems compliant with my interrogation and yet somehow still in control, with a smoldering fire blazing behind his gaze, practically marking me on the spot as his.

He's untouchable. *And I'm his obsession.*

I let that sink in, gaining some sense. "Do you hack me while I'm in the shower?"

"Yes."

Another blow, one I don't let twist into an intriguing scenario that could disrupt the balance of power that I'm struggling to hold between us. *He invaded my privacy,* I force down my brain. *In the worst way possible.* That's disgusting, and anyone else in my position would run straight for a police station without looking back.

Except...

I *can't* turn him in, even if I convinced myself to. What would become of my father's company? Disrupting the investigation now would most certainly land us a court case, where the prosecution would be heavily favored against us from the get-go. And, investigation or not, threatening his exposure might earn retaliation.

Baring my teeth, my final question bubbles an inch from the surface. *Do you hurt people?* I don't ask, fearing an answer I'm perfectly capable of conjuring up myself.

He's a hacker, Lauren. What do you think?

Reading the fault in my expression, Tristan perks up, desperation dripping from his lips. "Lauren, I don't—"

But he's cut short on my slamming of the door, his protests muffling through the wood. When several seconds go by and he doesn't bust through, I know he's keeping his promise by remaining in his chair. So, I depart the hacker's den alone, passing through the humming crypto towers, taking the lift back to normality, and slipping into bed, all with a quiet, numb conscience.

One that can't comprehend the past two hours of my life.

TWENTY-TWO

TRISTAN

ADRIEN VUITTON IS a dead man walking.

Well, any man who flirts with my wife is, especially when he's her *ex-boyfriend.*

"You're thoroughly missed back at the firm," Adrien says with a sly grin, leaning back in his chair, propping an ankle up on his knee.

Seated across from him in the conference room, Lauren remains silent. But, after a moment's thought, she feeds into his bait. "Really?" she asks, all too enthusiastically.

Annoyance simmers down my middle as I watch her placate him.

A week ago, she'd be rolling her eyes at his advances and giving *me* all her attention. But that was before she confronted me in my hacker's den—which I like to call my Bunker. Seeing her down there, witnessing who I really am, was a sucker-punch straight to the gut, even though I technically allowed her entrance.

The Bunker keeps my identity safe as well as millions of dollars' worth of mining servers—which are all legal, overlooking the times I occasionally use them for brute force attacks, and are how I make the bulk of my money. I'd be quite the fraud if a not-so-randomly-picked yet randomly-placed book on a shelf was my only safety precaution—an example of what we as hackers refer to as *"security by obscurity."* To set the record straight, no, I don't, in fact, leave the haven of all my deepest, darkest secrets in the hands of chance.

But I did that night.

Maybe the guilt finally got the best of me, or it was the anguished look in her eyes when she discerned my inner turmoil. I don't know. But after I broke away from the kitchen, a part of me ran a little *too* slow, got a little *too* careless. Like when I disappeared through the secret entrance and intentionally left the elevator's security system unarmed, a slim corner of my being hoped Lauren would figure me out and track my footsteps. And, in my head, when she'd hypothetically find such a passage, she wouldn't need to bypass a triple-locked system by offering her eyes, fingerprint, *and* face to a scanner.

She'd just walk straight through.

While our encounter plunged shards of ice right through my heart and most definitely broke a new connection between us, there was something *freeing* about it. She saw me raw, as my truest self, my bones stripped down in a neat pile before her feet. Something few people on this earth can attest to.

Not that I earned any solace.

Since our encounter, she hasn't spoken more than two words to me, let alone looked my way. Day after day, I initiate a conversation, one I'm not even sure I'd know how to navigate should she not quickly disappear after my attempt. And the only times she *is* near me for longer than two seconds is when she applies makeup to my bruises in the mornings before work, all the while wearing a detestable expression and paying no heed to my futile efforts.

I wish she would chew me out, slew hatred my way, demean my skill by labeling me a lowly script-kiddie, or call me a fucking creep or criminal or both. *Anything.* Anything but silence. If she would just talk with me, I'd at least explain that I don't hurt innocent people—quite the opposite, actually. Then maybe she'd warm back up to me, or at least look me in the eye right now.

"Oh, yes." Adrien's gaze meets mine for a fraction of a second before sweeping back to Lauren, whose chin is now resting in her palm. "Chester is handling your cases until you return. Poor guy, he volunteered for the role and can hardly keep up with your workload. I heard he's already requested an extra junior associate for help."

Lauren's snicker ignites jealousy deep within me, and it takes all my strength to stay in this chair, my piqued gaze flicking back and forth between the two of them. I hate that they have history, and I especially hate that Adrien is the head of the investigation team. I'd say it's too improbable to be a coincidence, but he likely assumed the position with the sole intention of having another opportunity at Lauren.

I recall his words in the elevator last week. *From time to time, I still hear her sweet cries, screaming my name. Something you'll never experience. After me, she's as good as ruined.*

My jaw locks, the springs holding me back, my composure tense and wild.

"How many junior associates does he have under him now?"

"Three."

"You're kidding." She laughs again. "Maybe he should've asked for your help instead."

She's brushing his ego now? *This guy.* Who I know to be an arrogant man-child who couldn't handle watching Lauren surpass him professionally?

Wow. I bite back a smirk, noting the hint of disgust lining her stare as she holds his eye contact. *She must really want my attention... or she really fucking despises me.*

I'll gladly take either over silence.

"You think so?" Adrien purrs across the table. "I would if it weren't for my other cases, many of which are nearing trial, and I've yet to find a co-prosecutor. The two of us litigating like old times? We'd be unstoppable—"

That's enough.

"Don't you have questions for us?" I interrupt, folding my arms across my suit-clad chest. "You *are* the one who called for this meeting."

Taking longer than necessary, drinking in Lauren's appearance for a few more seconds, he slides his smug gaze to me. "Oh, right. So quiet over there, Tristan." He chuckles like we're best friends. "I nearly forgot you were here."

For a split moment, I catch Lauren's stare, clearly expecting my reaction, before she snaps it back on Adrien. Even though my fists clench under the table, yearning for pretty boy's face, satisfaction burns through my veins.

That's right, baby. This is all about me, isn't it?

When he doesn't earn an outburst, Adrien interlocks his fingers atop the table and clears his throat, addressing me. "My team needs access to your database servers."

"They already do."

"Full access." His eyebrows tick upwards. "Some segments are still restricted to them."

I clench my jaw. Although I'm complying with their investigation, the idea of disclosing total privacy goes against my very nature as a hacker, something akin to a king digging a moat around his castle, only to lower the drawbridge for his enemies.

"We'd need to take a trip down to the data centers, then."

Adrien's lips thin, not believing a word. "This isn't my first rodeo."

"Do you think I'm being untruthful?"

"Yes." His tone is honest. "Or, if you're not, bring up an engineer who'll have a better idea of working the permission settings remotely." A smile tugs at the corners of his lips. "It *is* your second week as CEO. There's no shame in letting them fill your gaps in knowledge."

Ohhhh, what a great challenge it is, keeping my poker face tightly fastened around my head. Because unfortunately for Lord Narcissist here...

I have no gaps.

Ignoring the fact that I was already well versed in the layout and security measures of Astor Security's databases—and the databases of every company on Silicon Avenue, for that matter—*before* assuming this role, I still studied. For my first week as CEO, I called upon every advisor in the whole security company, paraded them around the office, and questioned them endlessly on the ins and outs of security protocols, technological infrastructure, employee training, the corporate hierarchy, research and development, partnerships and clientele... *The list goes on.* Then I made like a thirsty sponge and soaked up their insights with zest.

I adjust my cufflink, unphased by his pathetic jab, relishing when his eyes catch sight of my wedding band. "And why would I allow high-level permissions to be changed remotely? So any overeager intern in the software engineering department can grant themselves admin access with one line of SQL?"

His face falls.

Uh, oh. Seems you've entered my domain.

"Fine. The data center is two hours south, yes? We'll take the company's helicopter, and you can hand over admin today." He turns back to Lauren, dismissing me.

"Today won't do," I say.

Head snapping back, his eyes flash with annoyance. *"And why not?"*

"The data center is undergoing maintenance for a few more days, which means privilege powers are immutable."

"Cut the bullshit. *Maintenance?* How convenient."

I lace my fingers together atop the table, my tone calm and placating, which only riles him further. "Mr. Vuitton, I'd only ever be transparent with you and want nothing more than seeing your investigation run smoothly. If you'd like, I could call up a database dev and have them explain the necessities of index and data integrity maintenance, which are thoroughly recorded and scheduled for the first week of every other month."

His lips part, a snarky response obviously stuck in his throat. Regaining composure, he asks, "And what's stopping the state from assuming that you're stalling the investigation?"

"Maybe becau—"

"Don't answer that." Lauren's hand juts out, interjecting me, yet she *still* doesn't look my way.

Silence fills up the room, and Adrien's eyes flicker between the two of us, noticing her avoidance of me. His smug aura returning, he appraises my wife. "I should've known I couldn't slide that one past you. I taught you well, Lauren. Maybe even a little too well."

His words are like a match striking over a pool of gasoline, igniting a fire in my veins while I simultaneously catch Lauren's green eyes widening.

"Umm..." She fumbles for her purse as an uncomfortable expression peeks through her façade, somewhere between embarrassment and disgust. She walks a tight line to the door, her heels clacking against the ground. "Let's take an intermission." Her voice is small and unfamiliar as she struts out of the room before the door swings shut and leaves me alone with Adrien.

Great.

I rise to my feet, buttoning my suit jacket, intending to follow her tracks. But as I round the table, Adrien's snicker rings across our space. My soles scrape against the carpet, and I'm stuck between chasing after Lauren—and most likely getting ignored—or staying with this piece of shit and possibly getting into a physical altercation that'll land me in police custody. Against my better judgment, I choose option two.

"Something funny?" I ask, meeting his stare. He's resumed his cocky persona, ankle propped atop his knee while leaning backwards, wearing an oh-so punchable grin.

"I guess I couldn't help but notice... It didn't take you long at all to piss her off, did it?"

On second thought...

I'm not staying for this shit.

Without a word, I aim for the exit again, my fingertips grazing the brass knob—

"Even if your marriage wasn't arranged, I could still win her over."

My grip tightens around the metal. "She doesn't want a single thing from you."

"Is that so? She sure wanted my attention ten minutes ago."

"That wasn't about you," I growl into the door.

"Come on. With her, it's *always* about me."

Like the last tug on an overstretched rubber band, his taunt snaps my patience in half. I whirl on my feet. *"She's the one who ended things with *you*. Not the other way around. She had a year to take you back, and she didn't. Why do you think that is?"*

He shrugs. "Maybe because she saw me with other women. She's such a stubborn thing, who tried her best to replace me and is now realizing that's not possible. *Especially after ending up with the likes of you.*"

Her look of betrayal in the Bunker flashes before my eyes, and an inkling of doubt creeps its way into my heart before being overshadowed by anger. Taking another step, both his feet plant back on the ground, caution swirling in his gaze, most definitely recalling the shiner he received from my fist the last time we met in the elevator.

"Do you need another reminder of what happens to men who touch my wife?"

Adrien sits up straight, and although he doubles down on his arrogant exterior, I catch his Adam's apple bobble. "Go right ahead. Let the security camera on that wall over there catch the whole thing."

I nearly laugh. *How amusing.*

I could have the logs wiped before he stepped foot in the lobby, and I wouldn't even have to be CEO. Fists clenching, I want nothing more than to wipe that smug look off his face and ensure that he'll never speak to my wife again, but

Lauren can't afford to have the man leading the investigation against her family's company be purple and bruised, only so the media could fabricate a firestorm of accusations.

"Just like the security camera in the elevator?" I don't hide my smirk. "I'm still waiting on those charges you threatened to press me with."

With his confidence resurfacing, he stands to his feet, chest puffing outwards as he grabs his leather briefcase from the adjacent seat. "I don't need to take your money in a court-room or damage a reputation you don't possess to get what I want from you."

Lies. You're just too proud to press them, I don't say, knowing exactly what—or who—it is that he desires.

"You're never going to have her, Tristan. Not like I did. And the quicker you come to terms with that fact, the better. So, I'll cut you a deal, and we can stop this little game. Sound good?"

"Whatever it is, I don't want it."

"Yes, you do." His eyes dance with mischief. "During the investigation, if I find anything malicious, I'll shove it back under the rug. And afterwards, you'll file for divorce and send Lauren back to who she really belongs to."

My teeth grind like sandpaper.

"Lauren's hand may have been arranged for me, but she's still *mine*. And whether or not she accepts that truth, doesn't concern you, because when she finally *does* give herself over to me, she'll hardly remember your name. And as for your offer? I'd rather light the match myself and watch this company burn to ashes than divorce my wife."

His lips quiver, pressed firmly together, before he combusts in a fit of laughter. Tears line his eyes, and he practi-cally slams his briefcase onto the table. "Wow." He flips open the dual latches. "I guess I'd be delusional too if I married someone so far from my equal."

Shuffling through papers, he pulls out a business card, his fake smile visible from here, plastered across the laminate. Closing the clasps, he returns to me. "When you change your mind, and finally realize you're not her type and I'm her equal in every way, give me a call. Then we can follow through with our deal."

He slips the card into my breast pocket, then saunters his way to the door, briefcase in hand, apparently calling off the rest of the meeting. Pausing in the doorway, he pivots on his heel for one final gibe...

"You'll never fuck her like I did."

TWENTY-THREE

LAUREN

WHAT THE HELL *is wrong with me?*

I run the faucet as cold as possible, tracing the icy spout up my bare arms. One by one, I rip five paper towels from the dispenser in a manic state, then scrape my skin until it's beet red, trying to pry off the thousands of bugs crawling all over my limbs. Their tiny feet puncture clean through like a thousand needles, sharp and torturous, while simultaneously calling me a complete *idiot*. Or... that's how my body feels after flirting with my narcissist of an ex-boyfriend. As if I'm nothing but some harbinger of dirty, unwelcome infestations.

After practically slam-dunking the towels into the wastebasket, I huff an aggressive breath, staring at myself in the mirror. Looking every bit how I feel, loose strands of auburn hair poke out of my low bun in tendrils, and my lipstick—that's usually lined so sharply it could kill a man—smudges at the corners, accompanied by the erratic rise and fall of my chest.

Get it together. You're lucky no one walked in during your little temper tantrum.

Fine. Maybe I overstepped a boundary I'd *never* cross in a million years by inflating Adrien's overzealous ego, but Tristan deserved it. In fact, he's had it coming and so much more. I can't fathom how many lives he's destroyed, how many companies and innocents have fallen victim to his treacherous skills.

Including myself.

I don't know who I'm angrier at. Tristan, for hacking and watching me when he shouldn't. Or myself, for gaining an affinity for the idea.

For the past week, alone in my bed at night, instead of banishing the thoughts of the hacker sleeping in the other room, I *fantasize* about his dark prowess, of how his eyes have watched me through a camera lens in the worst possible moments. And since that fateful night in his lair, the dangerous thoughts rush through my brain every time he's near, making me afraid of what might come pouring out my mouth if I *do* decide to talk with him. Which is why I'm distancing myself from him at all costs.

But, forbidden voyeurism kink aside...

He still hurts people, I reiterate to myself. *And that's something I could never accept.*

Once I finish touching up and curb my emotions, I slide my blazer across my shoulders, then my Birkin down my forearm, and exit the bathroom. But on the door's swivel, I come face-to-face with Tristan—all six-foot-five of him, hotter than sin in an Armani suit.

Alarm bells ring between my ears as I avoid his intense gaze, aiming straight for the meeting room.

"Where are you going?" he asks, catching up beside me.

I don't answer.

"The meeting's over."

I stop. *Over?*

Dozens of questions bubble into my head, and I nearly voice one, until I realize that would involve actually speaking with him. Instead, I accept the fact that Adrien must've gotten all the answers he needed and the two of them must've gone ahead with scheduling the data center visit. On a swivel, I head for the elevators, my strides long and powerful. I have my temporary office in mind, where I can draw the blinds, lock the door, and bury my head into a pile of investigation paperwork or a law textbook or maybe a pot of sand—if anyone's got one of those handy.

Glued to my side in silence, Tristan rides the elevator, annoyance nicking at my temple when he doesn't press another button and also gets off on the tenth floor.

"You'll have to talk to me, eventually."

Like a brooding storm, I march through a row of desks littered with computers and techie types. Employees poke their heads above monitors or side glance our way, aware that Astor Security's new CEO is in their midst, and who's currently hot on my trail. Offices wrapped in glass line the back wall, with mine nestled in the corner, seeming miles away.

"You can't ignore me forever."

You'd be surprised, I don't voice, rummaging through my purse.

"Lauren, *I'm sorry.*"

I shoot him a look that screams *a thousand apologies wouldn't be enough.* His eyes flash with hurt, and when compassion bubbles inside of me, I quickly glance away. Fingertips grazing cold metal, I retrieve my office key from my purse.

Almost there...

My legs pump harder.

"If you'd just give me a chance to explain—"

My office door—that's supposed to be locked—swings open from the inside, and out comes Jace, Astor Security's newest and youngest board member, trailed by—

Mom?

Diana Astor, looking as regal as ever in a silver business dress, strides from my office, copper locks flowing off her shoulders in glossy waves. The pair laughs at something unheard, before my mom turns her attention our way. Eyes flickering between myself and Tristan, her smile falters momentarily before it quickly lifts back up.

"Sweetheart." Her tone is warm, a dose of comfort I didn't know I needed until this moment.

"Mom." I return her grin as I look past her shoulders into my office, appearing exactly how I left it.

"Oh..." She reads my gaze. "I hope you don't mind. I was showing Jace your office. He's thinking of taking it over after the investigation."

Jace pauses, swallowing against his burgundy turtleneck. The fabric peeks between his opened blazer and tucks neatly into his checkered slacks, giving him a sophisticated chic rarely seen inside a tech company, which I can appreciate. Meeting my stare, his irises overfill with hesitation, as if he's questioning whether I might brawl over some office.

"It has such a wonderful view." He pales.

Fighting back the lawyer in me, who yearns for anything and everything prestigious, including highly coveted corner spots, I shrug. "I don't mind. It's only a temp and would better serve as a full-time office, anyway."

"Thank you, I really appreciate it." Relief pours over him, a nervous chuckle seeping past his lips when he peers past my right. "If that's alright with you, of course."

Turning, I discover Tristan staring down Jace, like he may just strip his coat off and tackle him to the ground.

For Heaven's sake, what is with him? Now's not the time to get territorial. It's just an office. Is he really so pent up over my silent treatment that he can't fake it for two whole minutes? While my mother and several older board members may know of our arrangement, Jace surely doesn't.

After several painful seconds pass with no response, I brush my palm down his suit jacket. "Honey?" I ask through beaming, clenched teeth, the term of endearment like acid on my tongue.

"Hm..." He pulls out of his angered trance, his eyes veering off from Jace. "Yeah, it's no problem."

"Second week, am I right?" I force a laugh, earning rushed smiles from both of them. "They have him working like a dog."

"I have no doubts about that." My mother clasps her hands, ensuring a seamless flow in the conversation. "I'm sorry I couldn't make the board meeting, sweetie. I had Charlie put in my vote, which was perfectly fine by me, as attending wouldn't have swindled my decision." She winks before slowly drifting from us. "Well, I'm nearly finished giving Jace the grand tour, then I'll have to get back to more planning. The date's almost here, and things are getting hectic as usual—our caterers called and canceled on us last minute. Figures."

I almost forgot. Our family's charity event is in two weeks. And speaking of family...

"Oh, Mom?" My call twists her on her heels. "Can I speak with you for a moment?" *Alone,* the flicker of my head says.

"Of course."

She files into my office behind me, shutting the door. As a precaution, in case things get emotional, I draw the blinds, and the last thing I see is Jace smirking at Tristan, who wears an uncomfortable expression.

"Is everything okay?" she asks.

Is everything okay...

I nearly laugh, but stop myself, knowing the sound would come out sour.

Oh, nothing. I hold my tongue. Did you know my husband was a hacker before you arranged my hand in marriage? No? Didn't think so. Well, seems now I'm forced to cope with him for the sake of the family business. No pressure. Thanks, Mom. Maybe vet your eligible bachelors under a stronger microscope next time.

Instead, I pose a different question, one that's closer to my heart and wields a scalpel, ready to slice it in two:

"Have you heard from Dad?"

Her sigh sends me crumbling into my chair, my Birkin dropping to the ground beside me. It's been over two months now and weeks and weeks of my calls, only to hear the same voicemail answer. He's never been gone so long, and to say that I'm worried, is the understatement of the century.

"Yes."

What???

I perk up, the ache in my chest vanishing. "When? What did he say? Is he okay? I mean, where is he? Did he say when he's coming back home and why—"

"He's not ready for all that." Face falling, she takes a seat on the lounge chair in front of my desk.

"Then what *did* he say?" I ask again.

"That he's okay, and that we shouldn't worry."

Betrayal hits me hard.

I'm relieved to hear of his safety, but why hasn't he picked up *my* calls? What about *my* reassurance? My mind wanders into territory that'll only bring more hurt, like the thought of him calling my older brother or his colleagues, leaving me solely on read. But I quickly banish the notion. He'd never do that. Although we sometimes didn't see eye-to-eye growing up, we've always bounced back and maintained a strong relationship.

Like the mind reader she often is, my mother says, "He's embarrassed, sweetie. That's why he hasn't picked up."

My heart skips a beat. *So he* did *mention me...*

"He's not a man who admits to failure, especially not to his only daughter."

But he didn't fail, I want to argue, but my emotions get the better of me, tightening my throat. *Why can't he see that?*

Just because the pressure mounted too high, doesn't diminish all his achievements and hard work he's put into this company over the years. And even if all our material belongings and good fortune were to be stripped from our hands tomorrow, no powers in this universe could touch the lasting effects of a loving father. Which is why I yearn for his call, for his voice, so I can share what might lead him back home...

Everyone has good and bad seasons in their lives; it's only a matter of weathering out the storm for dawn's coming light.

"Tell him I love him," is all I say when she opens the door.

On its swivel, Jace appears in the doorway, so close he was probably about to knock. Yet... he doesn't react, doesn't turn his head towards my mom, who's standing inches from him. He only stares straight ahead into nothingness, like he's in some far-gone dimension, seeing something invisible in this reality.

An uncomfortable sensation blooms inside me, as if shadowy fingers trace icy patterns down my spine or a ghostly figure whispers eerie messages into my ear.

When a few moments pass with no acknowledgment, my mom speaks up. "Jace?"

Nothing.

"Jace, come on," she says, this time calm. Almost... *too calm*, with an undertone I've frankly never heard from her. "You have work to do."

His head snaps to her. "Of course. My apologies, Mrs. Astor." Then his eyes lock onto mine, content and with his usual alertness. "Thank you again, Lauren."

I simply nod before they see themselves out, leaving me alone.

Finally.

Looking for a distraction from the oddities of the past five minutes, I fetch my laptop from my purse, meaning to—

My door creaks open, and in walks Tristan, donning hunched shoulders, harrowed eyes, and a defeated expression. His tone is soft, stripped of its usual fire, and I sense he's gearing up for possibly the last shot at my forgiveness.

"I know I overstepped unthinkable boundaries and that I'm not worthy of your trust or forgiveness... But if you'd just take one last chance on me, you'd find that I actually help people."

Then he walks out the door.

YOU'D FIND *that I actually help people...*

Lying atop my silky sheets, with a conflicted conscience yet again, Tristan's words gnaw their way into my heart.

How could I take a chance on him? What would that even mean? I may be a lawyer—a data privacy lawyer, at that—but I can't scoop into his brain and dissect indisputable evidence of his innocence. And how could he explain otherwise? What could he say that wouldn't be nothing but hearsay to me? I'd be acting on pure faith, and that's not something I do often. If ever. I prefer cold, hard facts, which, in this case, only prove his *lack* of morals.

As I chew on my bottom lip, pondering the conundrum, an idea hits me square in the face, one so obvious I should've had thought of it sooner. Whipping out my phone, I pull up ByteBuzz and type a single keyword into the search bar.

Gh0st

Staring at the spinning loading circle, anticipation courses through me. *It's going to be more of the same. Don't get your hopes up*, I think, right before the queried articles send my heart plummeting to my feet. Because the titles don't enforce Tristan's cunning and heartless narrative at all...

They turn it upside down.

Could this CEO's charitable donation be the workings of Gh0st?

Gh0st Strikes Again

Gh0st: A Modern-Day Robin Hood or Cyber Menace?

Hacktivism: Gh0st's Legacy

Gh0st's Code of Justice: Hacking for a Cause

Hacking for a Better Tomorrow: Gh0st's Benevolent Exploits

...

Down and down and *down*, the articles go, with publications dating back years. But I don't read them. In fact, I don't click into a single one, because their titles alone are a welcomed downpour of relief over my head.

I'm not married to a monster.

Guilt nips at me, for having treated him so poorly this past week, when all he was trying to do was reach out and explain himself.

I should apologize. I hop off the bed, aiming for the door, but then stop abruptly, a dubious smirk spreading across my lips. Or maybe... actions speak louder than words.

I pivot, heading for the bathroom.

Specifically, the shower.

With my phone in hand.

TWENTY-FOUR
TRISTAN

HOLLYWOOD GOT HACKING ALL WRONG.

My hands don't skate across a keyboard in a flurry, and they definitely don't finish an exploit in two minutes flat, moving like some crazed machine on Adderall going ham on *hackertyper.com*. No, really, go to hackertyper.com right now and let your fingers run rampant, let them produce a myriad of vague code in matters of seconds, only so you can bask in the effortless glory that real hackers positively *do not*.

On the contrary, what I said to the board members is true. Hacking *is* creativity. It's thinking outside the box. It's wafting through prohibited textbooks and staring at a whiteboard for hours on end, dissecting an asymmetric algorithm into minuscule, malleable parts until a vulnerability emerges. It's outsmarting your enemies, catching them in their slip ups and laziness, then exploiting them through a backdoor, before leaving without a trace.

Unless you want to leave one.

I'll be the first to admit that I love the attention, and intentionally leave a digital footprint somewhere in their code base. Call it egotism. Or mocking. But gaining a reputation lands impressive titles and whispers among the cyber sphere, all of which bring fear into the hearts of malicious CEOs and politicians who have overstepped their jurisdiction for far too long.

They quake with fear when their admins discover my footprint, no doubt anticipating my demands. For days, I leave them wondering, sometimes leading them to skip work or flee the country entirely. But it's no matter. Wherever they go, I'm there with them. And with me, are my demands. When I reach out, I send an anonymous, encrypted email or, if I'm feeling particularly jaded, I call them directly, using a voice modifier that makes me sound like some dark overlord.

Their defenses are always the same. They'll wire transfer me a lump sum of money, if I turn a blind eye to their criminal activities and their burden on society. The numbers range to astronomical heights, with low ends starting at seven digits. But I couldn't care less if they had eight, nine, ten, or twenty. Because I don't want their money, never have, even when I was dirt poor. Blood money is just that, and it doesn't belong in my hands, but *elsewhere.* Where it can do good.

Charitable organizations.

Underfunded schools.

Community programs.

Public libraries.

Medical research foundations.

Educational scholarships.

Anywhere. Literally anywhere but between their greedy, slimy, unlawful fingers.

So, my demands are usually simple, with the intention of counteracting their wrongs. Instead of forking me the cash, they'll anonymously wire transfer the money they stole from society to one of the above of my choosing. Or else face total exposure. The choice is theirs. And over the years, they have met my ultimatums with less and less backlash, probably due to recognizing more than a few public scandals being orchestrated under the helm of my fingertips. Because if there's one thing hardened in the minds of every Silicon Avenue tech tycoon and others across the globe...

It's that I never bluff.

Project Dupe glares at me from my table like a menacing predator catching a whiff of its prey. Somehow, a plain manila folder is the most dangerous commodity in the entirety of my Bunker. I've already read all the files, and unlike all the other papers scattered across the floor or shoved inside textbooks or taped on my walls, I concealed every document of *Project Dupe* right back where they came from.

As if that'll make my troubles go away...

The Oculi's assignment for me is simple, really, as I've already got an undiscovered backdoor into Astor Security's databases, one I've had years prior to becoming CEO. And that's just it. They *need* my invisible skills, someone on the outside, to erase away a particular type of data manipulation that was done by someone on the inside. While they were clever with hiding their manipulations, it won't hold up once the investigation team gets admin access and digs deep. *And,* apparently, whoever-they-are's randomized database username ended in...

I check my notes one more time, then quickly close the file...

9F2M.

Should be easy enough.

I write up some code, querying the user's activity. A twinge of *wrongness* eddies inside me, until photographs of my sister flash behind my eyes, then memories of Jace walking out of Lauren's office follow suit, forcing me to hit enter.

Jaw clenching, I anticipate the return.

They're probably stealing rich people's credit card information, I theorize. *What better way to fund a secret society?*

But when the batch of transactions display on the screen, I lean in with a furrowed brow. *Wow... That's a lot of users. There have to be thousands.*

I scroll through the transactions, which contain more than just credit card information. Phone records, passwords, social security numbers, addresses, photographs, even public traffic camera information. Anything and everything that Astor Security may keep protected for outside companies—all being sent to randomly encrypted locations.

Another batch of transactions generates, bigger than the last.

My jaw drops.

Again, the size is exponentially larger.

Then another.

Oh, fuck...

I stare in disbelief, heart pounding as evidence of millions of users' information being siphoned pours in, dates ranging backwards over the span of years. And again, all with random encrypted destination addresses. I chew on my bottom lip. Even though my intentions are to comply, I thought I'd be able to gain some ground, learn something new about The Oculi I could potentially expose later. But even if I could decrypt just one address, they all appear different.

These will take days to erase.

I force my mind into a mode which holds no emotions,

where I don't think of the catastrophic consequences of letting something so terrible continue to slide by undetected, instead focusing on the people who matter most to me. It's the selfish choice, maybe, that allows for collateral, but it's the only one I can live with.

Writing up some code, I tap into the Bunker's supercomputers, which mesh in between the server racks, hoping to speed up the process. When I launch the program, the oldest entry from user 9F2M ticks away, then the second oldest, then the third, forever erasing the trace of those peoples' stolen information and decimating my chances at defying the society.

I lean back in my chair, feeling as if I'm nothing but what Lauren must chalk me up to be. Needing to rectify *some* of my currently huge faults, I focus on another monitor, which displays my current personal hacking project—the one I info-dumped onto Bryson outside my sparring outbuilding.

The offshore accounts.

They're of a similar predicament. Large sums of cash funneling into offshores—which usually always rings *illegal* alarm bells in my head—all from one encrypted start location. A location I so desperately want, as I've yet to come across such loaded offshores. The encryption algorithm has been hard to crack, but over the weeks, I found a vulnerability that may just cut enough probability off to allow for brute forcing to find the start location. Writing up yet another script attached to the supercomputers, I let this one run, with not a clue when it'll stop with the answer, if ever.

With a sigh, I watch the two programs run side-by-side.

One for the innocent.

And the other for eyes who see all.

Both set to text me upon completion.

Bile rises past the lump forming in my throat, saliva thoroughly coating my tongue. Breathing through my nose and out of my mouth in powerful huffs, I combat the nausea, until I'm able to look at the screen without feeling weak at the knees, and instead stoop to dark humor.

It's fine. I was already going to Hell anyway.

Switching to a free monitor, I—

Ding.

Lauren: *Which hole do you prefer, Robin Hood?*

My mouth falls open at the message.

She can't mean...

Opening the text, I scroll down and find an image that slices my mind in half, right down the middle, and has blood surging to my cock.

Oh, fuck...

The shot is a closeup of Lauren's shaved pussy, with her manicured nails parting her flesh ever-so slightly. The camera angles upwards, providing the best view of her perfect lips dangling past her entrance. Water drips off her sex and dribbles down her inner thighs in long streaks, telling me exactly where she is.

Like a man hypnotized, it's short of a miracle that I notice the top of another photo peeking below this one. With my cock now raging against my sweatpants, I scroll to the next photograph and nearly fall off my chair.

FUCK. ME.

My mind turns up utterly blank as I stare into the palpable lust shining in Lauren's bright green eyes. Dampened hair sticks to her skin and frames her face like some mermaid goddess, whose only life goal is to torture me and currently has her *tongue stuck straight out.* The picture cuts off just above her nipples, and her upper teeth gleam beneath her lip line, taunting me, begging for her pretty face to be fucked. My length throbs beneath my pants, leaving me frozen in my chair.

Ding.

Lauren: *One or two? I'm waiting...*

My immediate instinct is to inform her about how I don't have to choose. That her body is mine at any moment of my choosing, and whether I'd prefer to fill her mouth or pussy or stretch her tight ass or fuck her perky tits, is left entirely to my discretion. But I'll play her game. For now.

Except, there's one little problem.

I can't choose, I can't choose, I can't choose...

I flip between the two photos at rapid speeds, as if I'm undergoing a life-or-death decision. Uncertainty clouds my judgment, rendering me useless, until I picture my cum dribbling off the corners of her tongue, tears shining in her eyes after taking me like a good slut would—at full force.

Me: *Two.*

Lauren: *Watch me, then.*

Watch her...

Heart shooting to my throat, I clear my central monitor with haste, moving the now thoroughly forgotten programs out of sight. In less than a minute, I hack her phone camera, using the same backdoor I always have, and put her on full screen. At the mere glimpse of her, my veins flare along my forearms, and I grip my mouse with brutal strength, left surprised when the device doesn't crumble like an empty soda can between my fingers.

Because Lauren—*my wife...*

I'd worship at her fucking feet.

With fingers wrapped around the base of the pink dildo I've watched her use countless times, she sinks the tip past her lips, looking straight into the camera. I presume her phone's standing inside one of the shelves cut into the marble of the massive shower, seeing as the angle is flawless and swiveled downward just enough to see her hair drawing wet locks around her peaked nipples. Withdrawing, the grooves of the tip *pop* out from her lips, a line of saliva following in its wake.

Now throbbing to the point of pain, I pull out my cock, unable to withstand the tease. Caressing a hand down my shaft, I watch in awe as she bobs once more, faster this time, then twirls her tongue around the tip. Blinking into the camera, water trickling down her devastating features, she repeats the motions, pumping what feels like straight serotonin mixed with red-hot testosterone straight to my groin.

Fuck...

If she were a camgirl, she'd swindle me for every penny. Hell, I'd write her into my will, if she weren't already my wife.

Mind swimming with lust, I pry my fingers off myself and onto my keyboard, hacking into her microphone and speaker before dragging my free-standing mic to my lips. "You can take more than that, baby. I want to see those pretty eyes water."

Shock flashes in her pupils at the sound of my voice, soon followed by a glaze of desire. Gripping the base with two hands, she pushes *into* the dildo, further now than ever. My hips buckle at the sight, straight through my clenched fist, and I imagine it's my cock burying down her throat instead.

"Such a good slut for me, aren't you? Deeper... Yes, just like that. Now hold."

With the base nearly touching her lips, her eyes line with moisture as she stares back at me. But I make her wait as I thrust my cock into my hand again... and again... and again... until I'm satisfied when I hear her soft whimpers plea for mercy.

"Out," I command.

She whips the silicone from her lips on a struggled gasp, coating thick saliva down her chin. Her breaths come out choppy, and her chest rises and falls, conveying just how needy she is. Every fiber of my being screams for me to rush upstairs and fuck her senseless.

But I wait...

"Who owns your body, Lauren?"

"You do," she pants.

"Then show me where I want it, and I might come up there."

Without protest, she unclasps her lips again, tongue shooting out all the way. When I remain silent, her brow furrows tightly as a whine seeps from her chest.

"On your knees," I growl.

In a flash, she drops to her knees, head craning upwards at the camera while she wears the same expression. Water rains down from the showerhead attached to the ceiling, clattering against the marble, then landing on her skin.

Christ, she's fucking perfection. No painter or master sculptor could ever do her justice. And I have her all to myself.

Desperate for her mouth, my fingers clutch around the armrests before I make one final demand.

"Now touch yourself."

TWENTY-FIVE
LAUREN

MY KNEES WOULD STING RESTING atop hard marble...

If it wasn't for the fiery lust raging through my veins.

I hold back a moan as I swirl two digits over my clit, sucking my lower lip between my teeth. I'm not sure how long I've been staring into the camera lens or since Tristan last spoke, but each agonizing second only fuels my desire.

Eyes flickering through the glass, I catch Tristan leaning against the doorframe, dressed in sweatpants and a black tee. In a flash, he peels the shirt from off his back, leaving behind defined, tatted muscles, then saunters to me with slow and controlled steps.

I bite my lip, stifling a mewl as I work my clit, before he props open the massive glass door, his dark eyes staring down at me.

"Did I say you could close your mouth?"

Excitement soars through me, propelling my tongue straight back out. My gaze wanders to his impressive length, outlined through his sweatpants and inches from my lips. He pinches my chin between his thumb and forefinger, forcing my head skyward, until I meet his captivating stare.

"Look at you, touching yourself, on your knees for my cock like a good little whore. You want to be filled, baby?"

Caught in his grasp, I nod as well as I'm able.

"Of course you do." He grips my jaw tighter. "That's why you sent those pictures, isn't it?" When he sinks a thumb into my mouth, my lips instinctually wrap around. "Why you set up your camera and teased me with that tight body?"

"Mmhmm," I moan against his skin. Mimicking what I did for the camera, I bat my lashes up at him, swirling my tongue around his thumb.

His dark chuckle rumbles across my skin. "You're just begging to be taken rough."

Answering, I swirl my tongue again, this time with an open mouth.

"Fuck," he groans, jaw clenching when he withdraws his thumb. My eyes trail down to his length, to his gray sweatpants now littered with dark dots of water. "See what you do to me?" he asks, while I practically salivate at the black boxers peeking above his drawstrings.

A thrill rushes through me, similar to what I felt after coming while in the meeting room—when I hurried to my knees to make us even. Just like that day, my fingertips creep to his drawstrings, slipping across them with my own juices. Peeking up and finding no protest, I'm overcome with hunger, undoing the strings in one tug before I jerk his sweatpants to the floor.

My heart pounds in my chest as I make for his boxers, ever-so slowly peeling them down until he springs free and causes my lips to part. While I knew he was hung, judging by the outlines, it's a whole other thing seeing his cock up close, with no fabric acting as a barrier.

Jaw hanging low, I watch in awe as he discards his pants, tossing them across the bathroom tile. And when he finally steps in and joins me, my mouth waters before I lurch my head forward, my lips touching his tip—

Fingers thread through my wet hair, yanking me away. Annoyance surges through me, and my mouth opens on a whine, but a pink dildo shoves my protest back down my throat. I nearly choke, the sensation sudden and invasive. Eyes stinging, I clutch his thick wrist with both hands, abandoning my clit.

"Relax, baby. You can take it." He retreats, then slowly pushes the silicone back in. "I want to see those pretty lips kiss the base." His voice coaxes me into submission, and I widen my throat for compensation, hands loosening around his forearm.

"Good girl." At the sound of his addictive praise, my pussy clenches around empty air, as he pushes back in, further this time. "Finger yourself," he commands. "I want you wet and open."

Eagerly, my fingers dart for my sex, a moan rumbling around the toy upon their entrance. Tristan's face shines with hunger as he watches my every move, possession flaring in his eyes as he tightens his grip on my hair, working the dildo faster.

Pumping into myself, my inner walls grip my fingers and coat them with a wetness that's been steadily increasing since I flicked on my camera. Stretching my mouth taut, I take the silicone all the way, earning a low groan from him, one felt throughout my whole body when my lips touch the base.

"Fuckkk, yes."

His words burn satisfaction inside me as he smacks the base against my lips, in and out, savage and relentless, prying sloshing and gurgling noises deep from my throat, louder than the water thrashing against the marble. With watery eyes and an unwillingness to yield, I add another finger, thrusting hard, right to the knuckles.

He rips the dildo from my mouth, just in time to hear my cry ricochet throughout our enclosed space, bouncing to and from the glass and marbled walls. Shameless, I pound into myself, slapping my palm against my clit, knees scraping against the floor, until my legs quiver and eyelids flutter while seeing stars.

"Not yet," Tristan growls. He stands me up by my bicep, causing my fingers to slip out of me, my pleasure dying out with them.

"Why not?" I whine into his chest, then tilt back to meet his stare, studying his features.

He really *is* devastating, the stereotypical bane of most straight women, and the very definition of jaw-dropping hotness. Water slithers down his cheekbones and straight nose, falling off his strong jaw, only to peruse down pecs and abs so intricately inked and defined they should be illegal.

"Because I want both your holes filled to the brim."

"Both?" I choke out.

His chuckle races shivers up my spine, right before he suctions the dildo onto the glass in the exact positioning I always do, reminding me just who it is I'm dealing with. Curious, I watch him stride through the waterfall of steam, taking a seat on the protruding, cube-shaped slab of marble in the corner, merely two feet from the suspended toy. Arousal flares inside me when he leans back, cuffing a hand around his length, then flicks his chin towards the dildo.

He wants to watch while I...

Teeth sinking into my lower lip, I line myself up to the toy, head pointing in Tristan's direction. Like normal, I ease onto it, letting the silicone stretch the front of my opening with short back-and-forth motions. Eyes locked onto Tristan, whose hand runs across his enormous shaft in languid strokes, I push past the tip, my mouth forming an *O* on the intrusion.

"Mmmm... *Fuck*," I curse under my breath as my inner walls grip around the toy, its girth significantly larger than my two fingers, stretching me wide.

Tristan's gaze is molten fire, consuming me whole. Giving him more to appreciate, I stand taller, brushing my hair off my breasts, content when his eyes trail down my body. Reveling in the feeling of control, I twist both of my peaked nipples, letting a cry slip free, taking more of the dildo. Tristan's free hand grips the marble's lip, knuckles bleaching starch white, as he rolls his lips between his teeth in restraint.

A restraint I want reduced to splinters.

Twisting rougher, I tilt my face high, throwing myself backwards, hard enough now that my ass cheeks smack clean against the glass. Again, and again, they rattle the wall at a brutal pace, until my moans become desperate cries and the whites around Tristan's eyes widen like saucers.

Bursting to his feet, he bounds across the shower and threads his fingers through my wet hair. Tugging taut, he brings my face an inch from his, so close I can smell the mint on his breath. His gaze drags down my body slowly, dark and possessive, eliciting goosebumps along my arms, despite the steam cloud surrounding us.

"Are you going to be my good slut and take me rough?"

Yesss. I nod vigorously, unable to form a single word.

I gasp before he plunges my head down, his cock prying past my lips. Unlike the dildo, this time I'm prepared, and I instantly relax my throat, taking him deep. Pleasure bursts through me when he growls, his grip tightening on my scalp as I throw myself back against the dildo, then lurch forward and take him far down my throat.

"You like having both your needy holes filled?" he asks, earning an eager moan that vibrates around his length. "Ooh, yes you do. You take me so well, baby." Feeling him lurch over, a sharp *smack* whips across my ass cheek, followed by the other.

A surprising thrill passes over me, having never been filled in multiple holes at once and treated so roughly.

"Fuck, Lauren, your ass is so perfect pounding against the glass."

At the sound of his praise, I swing harder, surprised when the glass doesn't shatter as it rattles on its hinges. A growl rumbles above me, raising another round of tingles along my arms and all the way to my toes. He grips the underside of my neck and squeezes—gentle enough to not cause pain, but hard enough that it may just leave a mark.

"Look up at me... yes..." He bucks forward, right as I'm on a forward sway, plunging his cock deeper than before, smacking his skin against my lips. Squinting, I hold his gaze through the sting. "Such a good girl. I love seeing my wife's pretty eyes water. Now hold still for me."

Wife.

The word rattles inside my brain in his same deep tenor, making me realize I want nothing more than to hear him say it again.

I slow my movements until we're both utterly still. Then his hands grip my hair on either side of my head, locking me in place, before he drives in slowly. His hard length sweeps down my tongue in a tantalizing way, grazing the back of my throat, then searches further when I relax. Withdrawing, I wrap my mouth tightly, sucking hard.

"Your mouth... is so... *tight.*" His fingers tug hard against my scalp before he pumps, bottoming out once more. "Hollow those cheeks, baby. Do it again, do it again," he practically begs, earning an immediate response from me, this time sucking harder and lapping my tongue against his underside on his retreat.

"Fuckkk," he growls, driving home, then again, faster than before, until he's face fucking me at full force, and I'm thoroughly coating him with saliva that trails out my mouth and down his shaft, reaching his balls. Eyes flashing to his, I cup them with one hand, satisfied when I find them smooth and shaved.

His mouth parts in surprise. "Lau—"

I scrape them with my nails, lighter than the tickle of a feather, and it's his undoing. He topples over, pounding so hard that if it weren't for his stifling size, my screams would surely reach the other side of the house. Smacking my ass, he grabs a fistful and jerks me back, commanding me to continue fucking my dildo. In a flash, I'm swaying with full force, eyes squeezing tight, taking his cock and my toy to the max, reveling in the sight of an orgasm bright on the horizon.

"Eyes on me," he growls, bucking on my upswing.

With a choke, my eyes pry back open.

"That's right. Look at me while I fuck those beautiful lips. You're my needy little wife, aren't you?"

There it is again. My moan vibrates against his skin, as the pressure builds and builds, discarding any sense of sanity I have left.

"Come for your husband."

When my legs instantly quiver at his command, Tristan's mad and victorious laugh barks over me, before his hand ducks low, wraps around my middle, and goes straight for my clit. On his masterful touch, my vision blurs and crosses in two as he flicks roughly, tearing a euphoric release right through my body. As if he can read the future, Tristan supports my hips a second before my legs shake profusely as I come. With ragged breath, my inner walls pulsate around the silicone, grinding out every last sensation.

Lessening the pressure, Tristan sets me fully back on my feet. Heaving between exhales, he withdraws his still raging cock, and asks, "Are you oka—"

Energy courses through me, and I plunge him back down my throat, every ounce of my being yearning for his release, craving his saltiness on my tongue. Not waiting for him to adjust, I bob my head back and forth in brutal swipes, staring up at him with an unblinking, confident gaze before I sweep my nails across his balls, rougher this time.

"FUCK!" Tristan roars, and I know he's there.

He grips my scalp hard, his body going rigid while I work him, until he's whimpering a desperate sound I know is my new addiction. On a deep groan, slapping a hand on the glass for support, he spills warmth into my mouth. Quickly, I drop to my knees and loop my arms around his strong waist, lapping up and swallowing his seed like sweet nectar, moaning in the process as I watch him come undone.

When he subsides and I'm sure I've tasted every drop, I grab him by the base, then lick the backside of his tip. Gritting his teeth, he shivers before I lap once more, this time with my lips sheathing his tip.

"Lauren," he warns, and I plop him back out with an innocent chuckle.

"Wow..." I dismount, standing tall, his hand still threaded through my hair. Heart racing from my own release, I look up at him with a giggle, a dubious grin spreading across my lips. "I guess I don't need to ask if that was good for you, too."

But instead of his normal fire, I find his pupils blown wide and serious, his gaze flickering between my eyes and lips at rapid speeds, a response caught in his throat. Breathless, my middle swarms with butterflies, all taking flight when he crashes his lips to mine. Then my eyelids grow heavy, falling closed of their own accord, and my body lifts to his when a strong arm loops around the small of my back. A moan breezes past my mouth and into his, high-pitched and minty and full of untold passion, as I dart my tongue past his lips at the same time his does mine.

Then my fingers are in his hair, nails tracing lines through his every lock, down his neck and across his jawline, silently marking him. He groans at that, a pleased rumble vibrating my insides while our tongues dance to a swift beat of intimacy. An unexpected warmth blooms in my middle, more comforting than the water sweeping down my back or the haze building in the air around us. And it's in this moment I realize I've never felt lips so attuned to mine, ones that make seconds seem like minutes, and minutes seem like hours, all the while we forget to question if time has ceased completely.

Until we make our withdrawal.

Slowly...

And I stare into his eyes of wonder.

Not an inch separates us. With my head craned back, our noses graze, and my palms rest against his pecs while heavy arms wrap around my waist, shielding me in a pool of calmness and protection. A stillness grows between us, one not of awkwardness or regret, but of mutual fascination, as if we had a conversation without speaking and whispered secrets into the ether that only time might unveil.

Mouth parting, I think he's braving the first word. Instead, he cups the back of my neck, bringing me closer until my forehead meets his warm lips. Sucking in a quiet breath, sudden emotions tug on my heartstrings, forming a lump in my throat.

I don't care what we are or we aren't. Whether he's my arranged husband or real, or if he's Robin Hood or the next goddamn Destroyer of Worlds... None of my exes kissed me so tenderly. Or held me with such care. As if their life might sever in two if I were to vanish.

Blinking, a tear falls from my eye, mixing with the moisture already present on my cheek, before his lips retreat on a mumble.

"I must've done something extraordinary in my past life to deserve you, because I sure as hell don't in this one."

TWENTY-SIX
TRISTAN

"GOOD MORNING, SLEEPYHEAD."

My eyes flutter open, taking in the master bedroom I haven't slept in for weeks. Squinting, I study the blurry yet familiar space.

Something's off...

I sweep my gaze across the room.

It's more than just the now feminine touch mixed in with the area's dark color palette—like the sheepskin rug peeking out from the foot of the bed and the sweet smell of lavender in the air. And it's not even the goddess to my left, dressed in a silky nightgown, who snuggles in the covers with her knees propped up, holding a cup of coffee in one hand and a book in the other.

No, it's something else...

My lips part. *I didn't have a nightmare.*

"Not a morning riser, I take it?" Eyeing me with curiosity, she takes a sip, leaving a rosy lip mark behind on the mug. "I guess it *does* go hand-in-hand with your night job. Must be hard to balance, now with your day job."

Blinking in disbelief, I'm at a loss for words, staring up at her perfectly curled hair, when mine must be more akin to a blown-over mop.

I *always* have nightmares. Sure, not every night is a struggle over life or death, reliving my years on the streets or in and out of foster care, before awakening to the sound of my own blood-curdling screams. But... there's always *something* unpleasant about them, something I can't control. A harrowing memory. A deal gone wrong. The gnawing feeling of starvation inside my gut, trickling its way through my dreamscape, reminding me I'm still a teenager, scavenging for food.

But not last night.

Last night was... a blank. Yet, a blissful one. Like I truly, *truly* slept, maybe for the first time in years. Although I frequent counseling and have—in my mind—conquered many of my past traumas, there's always a very subtle hint of fog in my brain, a tiredness I can't seem to shake.

Until now...?

Sitting up, the plush comforter slides down my bare torso. I'm amused when Lauren sneaks a look at my chest, then her gaze flickers to my hair as I trail my fingers through the silky strands. A blush creeps across her cheeks, which she fights, swinging her head back between the pages of her book.

"You're lucky it's a Saturday, or you would've slept through your third week as CEO." She nibbles her bottom lip, not daring another peek when I scoot closer. "I mean, it's twelve. Is this what you do every weekend—sleep? How boring."

No, I don't say, refraining from informing her that most weekends I'm either hunting down an online trail of my next target, exploring encrypted chat rooms and criminal hangouts like the Down Under, or sparring and shooting the shit with Bryson.

My chuckle comes out low and groggy, which only deepens her blush. "And what shall I do instead, dear wife? Follow in your footsteps and read"—I sway forward, raising an eyebrow when I catch the title of her admittedly beefy book—"*Advanced Approaches to Jurisdictional Intrastate Law?* Now *that* sounds boring."

I pause, letting the accusation sink in.

Despite my mocking tone, I couldn't devise a more intriguing woman, tailored just to my liking, even if I possessed the power of shaping life. While I may not be her typical type, Lauren sure is mine. Preppy. Confident. Brains equal to that of her beauty. All wrapped up in a sophisticated, sharp tongue.

Unimpressed, she purses her lips, not meeting my eye. So, I push further. "That's gotta be the driest title I've ever read. I mean, *look* at the size of that book—or, should I say, *tome*. And here you are, treating the beast like some romance novel on a Saturday morning."

"*Afternoon.* Saturday afternoon," she corrects, sparking a playful fire in my gut. Setting her coffee on the nightstand, she flips to the next page. "This is my light reading, I'll have you know, which touches on *many* interesting subjects."

"Does it now?" I have to bite back a grin as I snatch the book from her grasp.

"*Hey!*" She swipes her hand out, missing mine by a hair.

Keeping to the page she's flipped to, I read aloud the first words my eyes come across, sounding as dull and tedious as humanly possible.

"*In the examination of intrastate jurisdiction*"—I dodge her next attempt—"*we methodically scrutinize the unremarkable terrain*"—Fumbling over the sheets, she practically barrels into me, only to meet my stiff-arm—"*where state boundaries seamlessly transition into mundane legal domains*"—Mouth wide in shock, she struggles some more, gaining zero ground —"*while simultaneously acknowledging the intricacies of this...*" Squinting, I bring the text near. "*...milieu...?*"

"Meelyee...?" I sound out the word, weathering a beating against my forearm, kind of how I'd picture a chihuahua chomping at a pitbull's ankles. "Milyaw...?" I try again.

"It's pronounced *meelyoo*, dimwit!" Lauren shouts on a raggedy breath, working herself into a fit. With a final, exacerbated huff, she topples back onto her butt.

"*Dimwit? Ouch.*" I feign offense, pressing my free hand to my chest. "For the sake of your glamorous social life, I hope you don't know what that means."

She rolls her eyes. "Of course, I know. It quite literally means someone's social environment—the setting, the atmosphere, like a social backdrop. And, wow, would you look at that? How convenient, in aiding when describing *your* social life," she taunts with a sassy head bobble, a smile on the tip of her lips. "Let me use it in a sentence for you. How's that sound?" she asks rhetorically.

Tapping her chin, her gaze points to the ceiling with an exaggerated *hmmm*, before shooting back to me with a triumphant gleam. "My husband is a solitary hacker who confines himself in a digital *milieu*, utterly detached from conventional social environments."

My lip plops open. Not from her crass example, but because she said...

My husband.

Shock courses through me, sweet and inviting, as the word

swims through my mind, taking up an abundant amount of space, effectively kicking out any chance of a retort. It's the first time she'd referred to me as such in private, and it takes me back to last night, when we shared a kiss unlike any I've had before. No matter our situation, in that shower—if our tongues could speak—they confessed their love.

Whether she realizes the weight of what she said, she doesn't show it. Instead, she uses my dazed state against me, and makes to snatch the book from my hand yet again. But this time, my reactions are slow, and she grazes the spine, before her hand slips and she topples over...

"*Oof,*" she gasps.

...*Right on top of me.*

With my back sinking into the mattress, Lauren's body cranes over me, her long locks and limbs entangling with mine. "O-oh my God," she fumbles against my skin, pressing her palms to my pecs. Nudging herself up, her eyes widen when she finds her mouth an inch from mine, which curves into a wicked grin.

Soaking in her frantic state, I study her gaze ping-ponging between my pecs, eyes, and lips, all the while her chest rises and falls to an erratic rhythm. When she settles on meeting my stare through wild bangs, I reach a hand to her gorgeous face, causing her to freeze like a stone as I pluck a strand of hair off her glossy lips.

She shakes her head in a quick burst, clearly fighting off a wave of mental fog, and pushes her palms against my pecs, nudging herself up. Instinctually, I wrap my arms around her back, trapping her in my embrace. Breathing deep, I savor this moment together, basking in her light touch and lavender perfume.

Catching her blush, I wink. "If you want round two, baby, all you have to do is ask."

"Quit it." She squirms, cheeks flaring deeper. "Your leg is digging into me."

"Oh ya? You poor thing." I lock around her tighter, bucking my hips upward, loving when a sound so close to a moan escapes her. "You think that's my leg? I'm taking that as a compliment."

Jaw dropping, she realizes her mistake.

"I'd blame morning wood if it weren't for your skimpy outfit." I trail my gaze down low, catching a pair of peaked nipples through her nightgown's now drooping neckline. "Fuck, Lauren." She shivers at the sound of her name. "You really love tempting me, don't you? Is that why you kept this lacy thing on until I woke up?"

"N-no," she stammers. "I just haven't taken my morning shower yet."

"And why's that? Were you hoping I'd join you?"

Biting her lip, she looks elsewhere.

Ohh, yes, she was.

Creeping my hand down the small of her back, grazing along the smooth silk, I grab a fistful of fabric until the smallest hint of her ass peeks through. With the other, I pinch her chin, bringing her back to me.

"If I flipped you over and tore off this little dress, would I find your panties soaked for me?" When she hesitates, I press my thumb into her bottom lip. "Huh?"

On a sweet whimper, she whispers, "If I were wearing any."

Fuckkk.

My cock hardens to the point of pain. Gathering more fabric in my fist, her bare ass cheeks fully expose, confirming her confession. Jaw locking on its hinges, hunger pumps through my veins, fueling the need to relive last night and mark her as mine.

"Such a naughty girl, always begging for my cock, even when you're acting innocent. But you're not, are you?" She shakes her head and squirms in my grasp. "That's right, you're nothing but a tease, a greedy slut who needs to be filled with her husband's cock every morning to start her days. Does that sound about right?"

Panting, her eyes fill to the brim with lust, a response trapped in her throat.

"That's what I thought." I grab a fistful of her ass, pushing down until her wetness touches my shaft. Moaning on contact, she clutches my traps, straddling me as she rocks her hips, coating my length. Gritting my teeth, I fight the urge to thrust into her. "I'm not going to ask you again. Yes or no, Lauren? Do you want me to join you?"

Then come the questions I don't ask...

Do you want me to fuck that tight mouth again? Watch you ride your heart out, trapped between your toy and my cock? Combust into a million pieces until you see stars only I can shape? Then intertwine our bodies, letting our lips make love in a way we can't admit to?

No... I don't speak such candor.

Because it's obvious.

"Yes."

TWENTY-SEVEN
TRISTAN

I'M the epitome of a satisfied man.

One who really *shouldn't* allow his wife to cook, not after the unholy events that transpired in my shower only thirty minutes ago. No, she shouldn't set foot in a kitchen. Maybe not even *use* her feet, at least for the rest of the day. The only words in her vocabulary should be *yes* and *no,* directed at servants who will attend to her every need, *including me.* But, alas, here I am—*at Lauren's request*—sitting on a barstool, watching her sauté chopped bell peppers, mushrooms, and onions.

"You really didn't need to make me breakfast. I could've called in the chef."

After a masterful flick, the colorful blend soars high into the air, then rains back down into the pan. I raise an eyebrow, second guessing my suggestion.

"I don't need a fancy chef's help to make an omelet." She cracks an egg on the counter, before breaking the shell in half with one hand, dropping the gooey inside over the vegetables. "Who do you think I am, my cousin?"

I cock my head. *That's an oddly specific comparison*, I think, but don't implore further.

Instead, I drag my gaze over her new outfit. Tight jeans, a cropped white tee, and a scrunchie cinching her hair into a high pony. Strands of auburn locks flow downward, kissing her shoulders, and gold hoops dangle off her earlobes, glinting in the sunny rays beaming through the giant windows. It's hands-down the most casual thing I've seen Lauren wear, yet I'm even more appreciative, starkly aware I'm getting a glimpse into a rare side of her.

"No, I misspoke." With my chin propped on a fist, I sigh when she cracks another egg with one hand while simultaneously working a spatula with the other. "You clearly don't need help."

God, she's just divine.

Swooping the spatula around the edges, she lowers the heat, then disappears around the corner, mumbling something about basil. When she returns to the stovetop with a jar in hand, a light air floats about her, bringing energy to her steps, almost like a giddy kid who scored big in the candy aisle.

"Your pantry is magnificent. Honestly, the best I've seen."

Sudden pride swells in my chest, the compliment having come from the best person possible. "It's no thanks to me. I hired a professional organizer."

"Well, they had their work cut out for them, then." She laughs, a tease to her tone. My heart drops, knowing where she's headed. "Why do you have so much food, anyway? The gigantic bags upon bags of beans and rice? There's no way you'd go through all that, even in five years. I mean, are you preparing for the apocalypse or something?"

Amused, she slides the perfect omelet onto a plate, swiveling on her heel to—

Stop in her tracks.

"...Tristan?" Her voice is achingly soft. "Are you okay?"

Dammit, couldn't I have kept a straight face?

"Oh, of course. I'm fine." I feign a smile, masking my uncomfortable state, but the words come out twenty shades of *wrong*. "Thanks for breakfast. It looks delicious."

Lips pursed, her eyebrows shoot to her hairline. "And I'm supposed to believe that?"

My heart thumps as I yearn to open up to her. But I bat the urge back down, realizing I'd only be trauma dumping on someone who couldn't fathom my childhood.

I shrug, holding her skeptical stare. "It's nothing, really."

Expecting a lashing, I harden my emotions. But then she does the exact opposite. A sliver of hurt sparks in her eyes, shoulders slackening, as if she's accepting that we're not at the level. That *I* don't see her as someone I can share sensitive topics with.

"Okay." Setting my plate in front of me, her smile is so forced it might crack her front teeth. And in the first ten seconds of her gathering up dishes in silence, I cave.

"We had different childhoods, that's all," I explain, hoping she'll leave it at that.

She gives me an incredulous look, tilting on the line of offense. "That's what you were so anxious about telling me? I know I may come off prestigious, but I wouldn't think of you any differently if you didn't grow up wealthy or didn't go to some fancy boarding school."

Oh, she really doesn't get it...

Cutting a wedge off the omelet, I avoid her heavy gaze, swallowing hard. "I guess I mean they were *polar* opposite."

Weariness glosses over her eyes, and before she can prod, I rip the bandage clean off. "I was a foster kid."

Her lips part.

"Then lived on the streets," I add.

It doesn't matter how many counseling sessions I've attended, or how many hours I've talked with Bryson—who always seems to have it all together—nothing stops the bundle of shame twisting down my center. That's all it takes. One confession, and I'm just a kid on the playground, admitting to something I never should have, damaging my chances of fitting in, landing myself in a pit of loneliness.

Clinking the pan into the dishwasher, she stays quiet for a moment, and I don't blame her. What does someone say to that? *They're sorry?* Sorry for what? For not donating large sums of cash to the misfortunate? I do that myself, more so than quite possibly anyone else in this state—and that doesn't even account for those I *blackmail* into donating. Yet, children still go hungry, live on the streets, lose their parents in broad daylight, and dance to and from foster care with little to no control over their well-being.

No amount of money will fix that.

And those peering in from the other side of the glass must realize it, too. Curating themselves guilt-free explanations, all teetering on the edges of *that's life* or *you're just looking for handouts* or *everyone gets dealt shitty hands at some point.* Whatever needs to be said to provide a buffer. In a way, I don't blame them for their reactions, for steering clear of such touchy subjects. And I won't hold a grudge against Lauren for doing the same. Because what can she do to change the past?

I harden steel around my emotions, preparing for the sympathetic yet loaded response. The judgment. Or, worse, *the pity.*

"Wow..." she says, much like everyone else before her. "I've never known someone so strong."

My head snaps to her, a blankness swimming through my mind as I sputter for a response.

No one's ever said that...

"Do you mean that?"

Slipping from my lips, the question feels silly and unnecessary. Because the moment I search her eyes, I find them without so much as a flicker of fault. Rounding the island, she takes a seat on an adjacent stool, her hand coming to rest on my knee.

"Yes," she answers truthfully. "I remember you saying you sold your code as a teenager because you needed the money. I just assumed you were taking the opportunity that most would, opting for a life of luxury. Not a life where you *just had food to eat*. I can't imagine what it must've taken to survive, to pull ahead and end up where you are now."

I bat down a sour laugh. *If only she knew...*

Not that my life is one of glamorous parties and upper society, given that I hunker myself down in a literal bunker for days on end, but... I'm far from in control of my life, as if I'm back on the streets, unknowing of what tomorrow will bring—*in a bad way*. The Oculi have their talons dug into me, into my sister, so deeply that I don't know if I'll ever pry them out. And that fact scares me, worse than before, because now it's not just my sister I fear for.

It's Lauren.

The society may not be threatening her life, but they've surely been tampering with her family's company. And the way Jace eyed her outside her office had my skin crawling, as if he placed her on his personal, fucked-up chessboard, in a position where he knows every one of her moves. And I can't even warn her without turning his wrath on my sister. Which is why *this*—Lauren and I, having such an intimate conversation—is a bad idea.

But, like a lovesick fool, I carry on anyway...

I pick at my food, fighting the intense instincts that sometimes arise whenever a meal is in front of me, shouting at me to devour the nutrients while I still can. "It took a long time to get where I am now, and I don't mean financially. Even if I hadn't made millions early on, I could've always made money. Eventually, I would've gotten off the streets. But it's the mental scars... No amount of money heals them any quicker."

To my surprise, she doesn't break down, doesn't bathe me with praise and sympathy. Only her simple touch remains and, somehow, it means more than a thousand words ever could.

"Do you feel you still have them?" She sweeps her thumb slowly, back and forth, so tenderly it brings tears to my eyes. "The scars."

Batting away the emotional onslaught, my voice still comes out raw. "Yes."

"Like what?"

The omelet pulls my gaze like a gravitational force, the eggy goodness sparking salivation across my tongue. Jerking my head aside, I swallow hard. "The food... Truthfully, the cravings aren't usually there, but I guess they gain a bit of power when we mention it head on..."

"So, you think you have a hold on the fear, for the most part?"

I snort. "Well, if I did, I wouldn't be such a hoarder, now would I?"

"I guess not." She bites back a grin. "But, to an outsider, you're just *extra* prepared—smart, even."

I roll my eyes, earning chuckles from the both of us. "Okay, sure, sure. Explain away my mild insanity however you like, baby."

When our laughter dies, her seriousness returns. "Then that's it, then?"

My pulse jumps at the subtle innuendo, hinting she already knows the answer.

"Any guilt?" she asks.

A crater the size of the moon splashes down in my gut. Questions race through my mind, all deadlier than the last. Does she know I'm working with The Oculi? Has she snuffed out all my lies this entire time? Maybe she's contacted her father and-and—I can't finish the rest.

I wet my lips. "I-I don't know what you mean..."

"Yes, you do."

Fuck...

I freeze, caught in the trap of her unreadable stare, which loops my heart strings around an electric chair, her next remark primed to finish me off—

"I heard you that night. When you woke up screaming." I loosen a breath, only to be plunged back underwater. "You were... muttering things in your sleep, in between the howls."

Oh, no...

"What did I say?"

"I'm sorry, over and over and over again... Why?"

Embarrassment eats at me. I *really* didn't want to get into this, but I can't ignore the voice from deep in my soul calling for help.

"...Because of my sister."

Then the floodgates throw open, pouring out all of what I

can afford to share with her. Bouncing between foster homes and adoptive parents. My outbursts, and the consequences they had on my sister. And my abandonment of her.

"...We managed to repair our relationship when we got older, but that doesn't mean I'm not still a burden on her now. Because the harsh truth is I *could* do more, *be more* for her. My victories carry such weight now, affecting not just myself or my limited friends and family, and I'm afraid of what might happen if I *do* fail, now with such high stakes."

To my luck, Lauren doesn't pry further, accepting my vagueness regarding stakes, presumably chalking it up to me needing to catch every big, bad, evil CEO. Not what'll happen if a secret society she knows nothing about grows too powerful to stop.

Complex emotions mark her features, bordering on a sense of pride, grateful for my rare vulnerability, before dark shadows take over. "I used to feel the same way with my clients, especially when, regardless of the evidence, I knew in my gut that the opposition was guilty or my client was innocent. But no matter my efforts or track record, sometimes, innocents do time and criminals walk free."

"But that's different. In the courtroom, you're only doing the best you can."

"And you're not?"

A breath breezes past my lips, and my heart beats to the rhythm of her passion.

"How can you so easily pass me grace, yet neglect to offer yourself the same? At the end of the day, I'm only human, doing the best I can do—same as you. And there's always tomorrow, which brings another round of second chances."

Stunned, I soak in her wisdom, a weight lifting from my shoulders. For the first time, I feel myself *relating* to Lauren, who might just carry similar pressure. Except she has the courage to do something about it.

She notes my untouched omelet, offering me a gentle smile. *I'll leave you to it,* she seems to say. She stands to leave, but not before she presses a warm kiss to my forehead, bringing tears to my eyes, and whispers...

"It's not your job to save the world."

FOR THE FOLLOWING TWO DAYS, I breathed an air of strange freedom. Lived life with a guiltless conscience. Until reality caught up.

Ding.

And informed me of my program's success. At forever erasing The Oculi's footprints inside Astor Security.

TWENTY-EIGHT
TRISTAN

I'M the Astor Charity Auction's most generous donator.

Who hides out beside the server's door.

The spice of my single malt Scotch burns down my throat before I place the glass back on the bar top. I'm sitting at the very edge of the bar, doing my absolute best to disappear from thin air.

Despite the general assumptions regarding my loner status and the fact that I spend most of my time below ground like some hermit, I don't have social anxiety. And I'm not crippled with fear in large crowds. On the contrary, I'm quite charismatic—*when I want to be.*

And tonight is *not* such an occasion.

Every year, instead of gallivanting through the hordes of people just here for business, I enter through a back door, then disappear up the stairs to one of the private balcony boxes for bidding. But this year, at Lauren's demand, I walked the red carpet out front, fought off paparazzi, and politely denied the dozens of microphones jutted my way, only then to be flocked by a slew of business personnel upon my entrance.

Their words were charming and appearances perfect— until they asked what they really wanted from me. An investment. A position on their board. Or sparking some new business venture or startup.

But, still, that's not the problem. The problem is that they think they're talking with Tristan Walker, the new CEO of Astor Security, when they're actually speaking to a cyber ghost who knows *everything* about them. Their shady deals. Tax evasions. Unlawful firings. Offshore accounts. Connections with the mob. You name it. If they're a corrupt Silicon tycoon, I know them better than their wives or husbands do —or more than their adulterous lovers, for that matter.

And in the short span of thirty minutes, I was approached by several business moguls and politicians who I'm either actively finding dirt on, have relations with the society, or I've already blackmailed into handing out *actual* charitable donations. All the while, they're assuming I'm just some tech kid in his late twenties with lofty amounts of time for twiddling billions between my thumbs.

So, I've decided the servers' corner is better.

"How'd I know I'd find you here?" a male voice asks.

Swiveling on my stool, I find the king himself.

Damien Bass.

Who's quite possibly the first face I'm not repulsed by, seeing as Lauren's cousin has a flawless reputation—that I can vouch for. We've met a handful of times at tech conferences, but it's been years.

"Lauren put you up to this?" I grumble into my Scotch, resting an elbow atop the bar.

"She did." He smirks as both hands sink into his pants

pockets. Our suits are in brash contrast, his coated in long navy-blue and cream stripes and mine a solid white from head to toe. "Unfortunately for you, my cousin's an over-achiever in all aspects of life, including socially, and excels at these types of things."

More grumbles. "And you do too, I take it?"

"Normally, yes. But I could do with a little less ass-kissing."

I nearly spit out my drink, which erupts a fiery laughter from him. Regaining my composure, I ask, "They swarmed you, too?"

"They always do. But tonight is relentless. Nothing like conversing with CEOs—who I've never seen throw up a single bid here—spout about their charitable deeds before offering me a backhanded deal."

"Exactly!" I combust, my hands jutting out in the air. "Thank you. Finally, somebody gets it."

Although I'm not much of a partygoer, I *do* appreciate tonight's Roaring Twenties theme, which allows for a bold array of colors. Men don loud suits they wouldn't otherwise wear, some even adorning rounded bowlers or top hats on their heads. On their arms, women flaunt short dresses with lace, beads, and matching headbands, mimicking the *flapper* style of the twenties.

The servers' door swings open, kicked by the foot of a woman dressed in all black, carrying two trays full of bite-sized hors d'oeuvres and champagne flutes. She splits us in two without a glance, before two others follow in her shadow, dispersing into the maze of guests.

Damien's gaze tracks their movements. "According to Lauren, I'm supposed to wingman you. I'm assuming to show that Astor Security is still in good standing with the *in-crowd*, even under new leadership."

I snort, taking another sip. "Sounds like my wife."

His head flicks to me, and I instantly know he's aware of our arrangement. I guess that shouldn't surprise me. Lauren *is* best friends with Hannah, Damien's long-term girlfriend, so he must've heard it from her.

Before he can speak to the subject, I jerk my head to the empty seat beside me. "Or you could camp out here with me."

He opens his mouth on a protest, then clamps it shut. Rolling his lips between his teeth, head on a swivel, hesitance swims through his eyes, until he meets mine once more.

"Fuck it."

"COME ON, just try it. One sip." I hold out my drink before Damien, clinking the whiskey stones against the glass.

His nose scrunches. "I'll pass. Single malt Scotch tastes like a campfire. Or the underside of a rubber wheel."

I bite back a laugh, the alcohol in my brain making his comment that much funnier, given I *did* start drinking Scotch after frequenting the Blacktop Tavern. I flick my chin his way. "Those are some fighting words. Unexpected, at that, coming from a fellow whiskey connoisseur."

"No, no." He shakes his head. "I'm a *Bourbon* man."

"Mmhmm, sure. Sounds to me like you can't handle the heat."

His eyes bulge in a way that has me clamping down on my bottom lip. He holds out his hands, palms facing outwards with a gleam to his eyes, as if he's waited a millennium for my exact words, having prepared a lengthy exhortation comparing the two whiskeys.

"Now, wait a minute. Bourbon's got a special sweetness, thanks to the charred oak barrels they use during the aging process. I've tried many Scotches, but it just can't compete, with an earthy profile that's an acquired taste for sure. So, both have heat, but Bourbon is noticeably smoother."

"Wow..." I feign astonishment, rubbing my fingers along my chin. "That's a whole lot of words just to agree with me."

"Hey, that's not—"

I bust up laughing, unable to contain myself any longer. Mouth dropping, he watches in horror, until his lips sputter as well, bellowing deep from his chest and forming tears along his eyes. Admittedly, the joke wasn't that funny. If anyone else was here, they'd probably scoff or fake amusement. Unless, however, they were already *this drunk*.

"Lauren's not gonna be happy when she finds us," I choke out.

"No." He dots a napkin in his tear duct. "She won't be— with either of us."

When we regain our composure, the room's ever-present chatter and soft music resonates over our silence until Damien clears his throat. "You know... I hold nothing against you for taking over the company. Although it doesn't diminish his hard work, my uncle was struggling for years. It was about time someone stepped up, and I'm sure you're more than capable, just going off your reputation."

A knot forms in my stomach at his honesty.

With subtle, threatening undertones, he adds, "If you're treating Lauren right, of course."

...But then it vanishes.

Because despite the horrible predicament I'm in, Lauren and I have... *something*, even if we won't admit to our feelings out loud. Under different circumstances, I would've by now.

The attraction between us is undeniable, and over the past few weeks, it's grown past just physical. Into subtle flirting at home. Longing gazes during investigation and board meetings. And deep conversations that constantly remind me of the dangerous trapeze I'm blindly leading Lauren down.

"I am," I say, focusing on the truthful part of the lie.

"Good." He nods. "For what it's worth, I know what it's like—if Lauren hasn't already told you of how Hannah and I met.

"She's mentioned the fake engagement between you two before, yes."

He smiles. "I forget about it sometimes, because that's far from what we are to each other now. To the media, it seems like we've had a long engagement—almost three years. But to us, we've just been dating that long, even though it really *does* feel like I'm engaged to Hannah, like I've known her my whole life."

An ache weighs down on my chest at the sincerity and passion in his voice when he continues. "I couldn't imagine my life without Hannah, let alone breathe."

"You intend to marry, then?"

Taking a quick peek over his shoulder, he opens his jacket, retrieving a small black box. Although what lies inside is obvious, that doesn't change how shocking it is when he opens the delicate box. What has to have carats in the double digits is a flawless ring sitting comfortably between two black cushions, glistening in a thousand different directions, even under the dim lighting of the bar. Smaller diamonds trail around the loop, giving the ring an inherent uniqueness.

"Wow," is the only thing I manage to say.

"I know... It's a lot." His hand shakes slightly as he closes the box, slipping it back into his coat. "At first, I demanded to buy her another diamond, but she's so in love with this one that we settled on keeping the diamond but having it set in a new band."

"That shows she loved you throughout your fake engagement." I swallow down the rest of my drink, thinking of Lauren, suddenly despising the ring she wears, as the society gave it to me before we married.

"I've been carrying it for weeks, waiting for the right moment. I'm taking her to dinner tonight after the auction, so maybe then... Do you think she'll like it?" he asks, and I'm taken aback by the nervousness dripping off his question.

I offer him a warm smile. "I don't think there's a woman in this room who wouldn't gawk at that ring."

I've never been a sentimental man, but it's undeniable the power love has. Here's Damien Bass, the crowned king of Silicon Avenue, sweating bullets over asking a woman he's been with for three years to marry him—who he's technically already engaged to.

And then there's me...

Trapped between the threats of a deadly society and balancing my sister's future on my fingertips. Yet, I'm *still* unable to stop myself from pursuing Lauren. Staying away should be common sense, should be the easy choice. But she's melted me down, piece by piece, and now I physically don't know if I can resist her advances, or from stopping *myself* from making her mine—body, mind, and soul.

Because I truly... *Truly*...

Might be falling for her.

Might be a fool in lo—

"There you are."

My heart contracts at the sound of Lauren's voice, and

sings a melody I never want to stop hearing, before I swivel in my chair and—

Positively forget how to form syllables.

"We've been looking all over for you two. You were supposed to network with him, *Damien,* not join him in becoming a wallflower." Hannah folds her arms, shooting Damien a look he's bound to hear about later. His laugh fades off into the distance.

Because all I see is Lauren.

Wrapped in intricate stripes of black and gold, Lauren's dress hugs her body like a latex glove. Staying much to the theme, long frills dangle off her skirt and the black gloves running up her arms that stop an inch above her elbows. My eyes trace the flowing waves of her hair, which are styled in a way I've never seen before, framing her face to perfection, all topped off with long rows of pearls drooping off her neck.

"The ceremony starts in five minutes." Hannah's voice breaks me from my trance. "We'll meet you at our table." After shooting me a knowing smirk, Hannah leads Damien in the direction of the stage.

I stand to my feet. "You look..."

Lauren twirls a strand of hair between her fingers, mischief sparking in her gaze. "Beautiful? Divine? Breathtaking?"

"Ooh, you know, don't you?" Running my hands up the length of her velvety gloves, Lauren bites her lower lip, confidence radiating from her in thick waves. "Yeah, you do. And I love it."

"Cyna *did* spend three days handcrafting our dresses. And you know what a perfectionist that woman is."

"I do, unfortunately." I take my time looking her up and

down. "But even with all her expertise, I think she missed something."

"Not possible."

Unbuttoning my suit jacket, Lauren's eyes sparkle when I retrieve a thin blue box. "Yeah, she did." I offer her the gift, which she takes with a hesitant smile.

"You really shouldn't have."

Anticipation dances in my middle, and I hate the way I immediately start comparing all the gifts she's received from previous lovers. Lauren could buy herself almost anything. So... to put it lightly, I may have gone a little overboard.

"Go on. Open it."

Snapping the square box up on its hinges, Lauren gasps, gaping at the necklace inside. Adorned by halos of smaller white diamonds, a string of emerald jewels forms a two-tiered band, glowing a vibrant green shade that nearly matches her eyes. When she sweeps across an emerald that's larger than the tip of her gloved finger, brushing gently, I know she's impressed.

"What do you think?"

"It's the most gorgeous necklace I've seen," Lauren admits breathlessly. "I hope you didn't spend too much."

Four hundred thousand.

"Nah, it wasn't too bad."

Brushing her hair off her shoulders, I unhook the chain, looping it around her neck. With her body grazing against mine, I breathe in her alluring perfume, savoring the subtle hints of citrus and amber dancing through my nostrils. When I retreat, I find a blush staining Lauren's cheeks above the choker, now sitting perfectly at the base of her neck.

Satisfaction burns its way down my center at the sight of her wearing something that brands her as mine. And she knows it, too, evident in her stare, which fills to the brim with desire and a dark wanting. Looping my arms around her waist, I pull her close, and lean in for a—

She jerks away with a playful smile. "Tristan Walker," she scolds, fueling the fire already present in my veins. "You're going to get lipstick all over yourself."

"You think I care? Mark me all you like, baby." I brush a hand down her backside, my touch a coiling hot wire, charged with possessiveness. "I'd love to give the men in the room something else to gawk at besides my wife."

With a smirk, her hands graze my chest, running across the seams of my coat. When her emerald eyes flicker up to my mouth, I do what I only can.

Kiss her.

TWENTY-NINE

LAUREN

YOU KNOW when a man just screams dirty sex?

That's Tristan.

I can confidently say that fact has little to do with our current stature sitting right below the stage, front and center, at the most important bidding table in the auditorium. And it's not because he's wearing a magnificent, all-white suit that most men couldn't dream of pulling off—even if they were half as painstakingly handsome as him. Even so, none of those reasons are why, with one look into Tristan's eyes, I know that's exactly what I'm getting later tonight.

It's because he's untamed and wild, a deadly phantom amongst ignorant elites, who will cross every line in pursuit of what he wants. And, going off his possessive mannerisms over the past several weeks, I'd wager what he wants is *me*. That tension—along with his hand resting on my thigh under the table and the hefty choker weighing along my neck—makes every other prospect in the room seem inferior, possibly even boring.

Warm lips brush against my ear. "The next man I catch

staring at you will wake up tomorrow to their bank accounts drained."

I clutch the stem of my martini glass too tightly, stifling a reaction. "Now that's not very charitable of you, is it? And the bidding hasn't even started yet."

"They should know what happens when their eyes wander where they don't belong."

He grips my thigh, then traces his fingernails down and back up my shin, raising goosebumps in their wake. Through a blurred lens, I watch the flappers on the lit-up stage, who wear sparkling dresses and kick their T-strap heels merrily, performing a twenties-inspired rendition.

Battling through the haze, I gulp ice-cold water, earning a knowing smile from Tristan—even one from Hannah sitting to my right. Beside her, my cousin Damien lounges in his chair, draping an arm over the backside of hers.

"You have any charities in mind?" he asks Tristan.

"Typically, I focus on organizations that support efforts against child hunger and homelessness." His hands come to rest above the table, leaving me bare. "But this year, I think I'll let my wife have free rein on our biddings."

That's news to me.

I raise my eyebrows, almost as high as Damien, who chuckles, resting a hand on Hannah's knee. "Careful. I did that my first year, too, and she sure knew how to hit me where it hurts."

Laughing into her fruity drink, which must be her signature Tequila Sunrise, the straw plops free from Hannah's lips. "*And* last year," she adds. "Don't get your hopes up too high. This year won't be any different."

Damien pales, sparking laughter from the three of us, right

as a dark-haired woman walks in front of our table, craning her head our way. If it weren't for her flowing dark hair and gold hoop earrings, I'd recognize Sofia solely by her violet dress, which might be the flashiest in the whole room, reflecting rays of light in all directions like a twinkling disco ball.

"I thought that was you guys!" She flashes a radiant smile, eyes roaming down our seats, until she reaches Tristan, and her grin falters. Tristan tenses beside me, and they stare at each other for the slightest second before the oddest thing happens.

They both resume to their normal states.

Her smile returning, Sofia's gaze darts to Hannah, and Tristan slackens against me, propping his ankle on his knee. Worry swims through me as I plaster a pleasant look on my face, feigning ignorance of their little moment.

Hannah shoots to her feet, rounding the chairs for a big embrace, patting her on the shoulders. "You should've told us you were coming."

"I know, I'm sorry. Some mutual friends invited me last minute," she says as they break apart, her eyes drifting from our table to the dancers up on the stage, only feet from us. "Seems you all got the best seats in the house."

"You can thank Lauren for that." Hannah winks at me.

Not feeling the humor in my bones, I chuckle, thankful when the act resonates through my voice. "You can join us, of course." I give her the only plausible response, which feels less like speaking with a good friend and more like chewing on battery acid.

"Ooh, you know I'd love to, but I don't want to ditch the group I came with." My shoulders relax, but tense back up again when she rounds the table, wrapping her arms around me from the backside of my chair, giving me a hug. "Love your necklace, by the way," she murmurs in my ear.

Although her tone is genuine, and her normal warmth sinks through my skin, I can't ignore the ache in my chest over what transpired moments ago. And the heaviness sticks with me, even when she says her goodbyes and leaves us. From my peripheral, I catch Hannah turn towards Damien, engaging in a conversation I can't hear.

I take it as my cue, whipping my intense stare at Tristan. "What was that?"

"What was what?" He scrunches his eyebrows.

"Don't play stupid." I cross my arms. "I saw that look. You recognized Sofia."

Explanations dart through my mind, each worse than the next. *Maybe they knew each other as children?* No, that can't be right. They would've greeted one another, not shared a secretive glance, which led to an unspoken agreement of silence. My heart twists like a rope at the thought of them being past lovers. Even though Sofia is now one of my closest friends that I love dearly, the idea still sickens me and churns jealousy around in my core.

My mind drifts into darker waters, solidifying the theory. *They both—relatively—work in the same field...* Sofia is an engineer at Damien's company, Innovex Microchips. Maybe they met at a conference and bonded over their shared love of technology—mutual interests Tristan and I *don't* share. Possibly around the same time we *allegedly* met at Harvard, given that our whole marriage is a sham, and he probably doesn't even—

"Lauren," he whispers, gently grazing my arm. "It's not what you think, I promise."

I jerk away, uncaring if anyone notices our quarrel, far too consumed by my irrational anger. "What is it, then?"

"Now's not the time."

I huff a breath. "Sure."

Hesitance swims through his pupils as he flicks them around the room, which only further fuels my annoyance. And then my impending outburst is like a hairpin trigger, poised for rapid fire, until he leans into my ear, his voice a soft breeze.

"Sofia's a hacker."

Jaw falling, I whip to face him.

"Don't." His eyes bulge. "Tell. Anyone."

I shake my head. "You're lying."

"Am I? Do you remember Priscella Vuitton's little video that got leaked?"

My stomach drops. *No way.*

And then the puzzle pieces lock into place, all at once. I recall my first encounter with Hannah and Sofia two years back, on the night Damien fake proposed to Hannah. They were at the bar, seated by me, cussing up a storm after a heated encounter with Priscella—whom I knew from boarding school and who was my current boyfriend's younger sister. And it just so happened, later that evening, word got around that her sex tape got leaked. After the three of us became closer friends, whenever Priscella's name would be brought up or the mention of her having bullied Hannah, Sofia always put it simply.

She's taken care of.

When I see they're still chatting, I whisper, "Does Hannah know?"

"Probably not. Hackers keep their identities hidden at all costs."

Bile rises up my throat as I seek to protect my friend, picturing Sofia overstepping boundaries, taking advantage of their closeness. "We have to tell—"

"Lauren, baby..." He smirks. "You really think I'd let a malicious hacker anywhere near you? I've known you two were close for nearly a year, and would've dealt with her accordingly, if she meant either of you harm."

Deal with her.

My soul sings to his darkness.

"So, you're saying she's... like you?"

"Yes." His hand returns to my leg, seeping comfort through my bare skin. "We're aware of each other's online presence, but keep a safe distance, on the knowledge that we have similar goals."

Holy fuck. He's telling the truth.

Sofia's a hacker.

Applause thunders through the auditorium, yanking me from my shock. Linking arms, the flappers all curtsy in sync as two massive red curtains draw across the stage, bringing the show—and my worries—to a close.

APPROACHING THE PODIUM, a man taps on the microphone and clears his throat.

"Thank you, everyone, for joining us this evening. We, at Sonata Hall, are sincerely honored to host this exceptional event annually and appreciate the opportunity to contribute to such a noble cause. Before the auction commences, you'll have the pleasure of listening to the woman of the hour, who deserves every ounce of credit for orchestrating New York City's most magnificent philanthropic endeavor. Ladies and gentlemen, please join me in welcoming Dr. Diana Astor."

The room resounds with applause as my mom appears from behind the curtain, and walks across the stage, her champagne dress glittering in the spotlights. On soaring heels, her steps are powerful yet graceful, each movement swaying the fuzzy poms on the ends of her elbow-length gloves. Beaming a pearl-white smile on her way, she waves at the crowd, earning a roar of cheers and whistles.

"Wow, she looks incredible. What does she have her doctorate in, again?" Hannah asks me, admiration emerging from behind her eyes.

"Psychology. She used to be a professor."

"Impressive. Successful women run in the family, it seems." She grins at me, and pride swells in my chest.

Diana Astor is my looking glass. Her power reflects my own, forged through the blood we share. Before a crowd, I'm the ego, turning the heads of spectators and soaking up their gazes like a hungry artist devouring inspiration. But where there's a flashy apprentice, lies the master, for whom applause is a familiar melody—upheld by a stage that has surely housed no equal.

She awaits the falling hush of the room, letting anticipation linger about the air, before her voice stands alone.

"Each year, as we come together for this extraordinary event, we reaffirm our commitment to making a positive impact on the lives of those who need it the most. Philanthropy, at its core, is a celebration of humanity's collective strength and compassion. Tonight, as we embark on this journey of generosity, remember that every bid, every contribution, is a step toward a brighter future."

As she continues, I don't need to turn around to know that

she's earned the unwavering attention of the entire room, including the four of us. With squared shoulders and an elongated back, she exudes flawless posture, enunciating every word with precision. Her manicured nails rest on the corners of the podium in comfort, weaving through the air periodically, giving particular phrases a greater impact. It's a common strategy taught in many speech classes, including the prestigious ones I unwillingly attended as a child—and am now grateful to have taken.

"It is my privilege to stand before you as we unite for a cause bigger than ourselves. Together, we strive for ripples of change that extend far beyond these walls. So, tonight, let us open our hearts—*and wallets*"—she pauses, smiling at the chuckles resounding across the room—"not only for the auctioned items, but for the lives we will transform. On behalf of the Astor Family, whose full attendance we regrettably miss tonight, I extend our deepest gratitude for your continued support. Thank you."

Applause rings out around the room as she exits the stage, but it's nothing but a backdrop for me as I stare at the empty chair across the table.

For the first time since our family started this auction, my father is missing from that chair. Sadness creeps into me, for his mental well-being and also for him still not contacting me. I called again today, knowing my attempts at communication would be the same. I never leave a voicemail, usually because I'm too angered or embarrassed once I hear his same ringtone —the only voice of his I have left to converse with.

Since hearing of my mom's contact with him, I abandoned calling him altogether, accepting with a heavy heart that he'll return or reach out himself when he's done battling whatever mental demons he's dealing with. But, much like the day the board elected their new CEO, I thought today would be different.

He wouldn't miss tonight, right? He never has...

But I was wrong.

A soft touch pulls me from my fixation. I find Tristan's eyes flickering to the empty chair for a brief moment, before they return to me. A heaviness reflecting my own darkens his features, obviously pitying me.

Full of playfulness I rarely hear from him, he says, "Hey," and plants his elbow on the table, then his chin on his fist. "You know, I wasn't kidding about the bidding. It's all you, baby."

His tone chips off a piece of my sorrow. "Are you sure? I have my own money I bid with each year. I don't need to spend yours." I gaze down at our bidding sticks, his with the number four attached on the end, and mine with three.

Appraising my necklace, he holds my stare, creeping warmth up my neck. "My money *is* your money. And I'd be damned before I let you spend a penny of yours."

My heart rate escalates, and I feel a blush coming onto my cheeks.

While I may be the literal definition of a trust-fund baby with every privilege one can get in life, anything outside of long-term investments, I pay for myself. And that includes my living expenses prior to marriage, my clothes, even my car. Being one of New York's top lawyers comes with its perks, most notably status and income. But nothing compares to Tristan's wealth.

He's self-made, and no doubt on a similar economic status as my parents, seeing as I'm now living at the top of Wisteria Drive, *on acreage*. So, no matter my lofty investments gifted to me via my inheritance, that's not expendable cash—something Tristan surely has in abundance.

"What's your ceiling cap for tonight?" I ask.

In layman's terms, how much can I spend?

"You're asking the wrong question."

My brow furrows. "And how's that?"

"If I'm not bidding, you have some rather large shoes to fill." Picking up my bidding stick, he wraps my fingers around the base, forming butterflies in my chest. "You'll never have a limit, baby. Not with me. And especially not tonight. You have a *minimum.*"

TEN MILLION.

That's the *minimum* amount I must spend tonight, according to Tristan. That's double Hannah's—and nearly five times more than my—donations the previous year. And I'm still eight-hundred thousand short.

After my mother's speech, time escalated to top speeds, and everything faded into a blur of wielding my bidding stick like the raised hand of an overeager student. Except, there's one problem...

The teacher's pet on my right.

"Do I hear two hundred thousand?"

Exceeding her reputation, Hannah flings her stick in the air, without a second thought, to the absolute horror of Damien, who buries his face into its newfound home these past few hours—*his palms.* On the call of four hundred, I match her enthusiasm, sparking laughter from Tristan on my left, who's found our relentless battles this evening downright hilarious.

Hannah and I are no doubt tonight's largest bidders, collecting vintage cars, celebrity meet-and-greets, culinary experiences, sports memorabilia, and luxurious vacations as if they're knickknacks to display in our offices. Will we take that trip to Paris or Dubai or Amsterdam? Take pictures of one of the Seven Wonders of the World? Or drive down Silicon Avenue in that shiny 1929 Bentley? Who knows? *But we want it*, and Hannah and I will wage war—especially over the *priceless* piece up on stage now.

This one-of-a-kind item in question?

A painting.

A god-awful painting.

If I had any children, I'd say my fourth grader could do a better job, given the canvas looks like a child bundled up ten random-colored Crayons in between their tiny fingers, proceeded to scribble indiscernible shapes until the tips went dull, and then called it art. But, hey, in the name of a visionist and abstract technique that goes beyond our feeble, closed minds or not... This painting? To her and me?

May as well be life or death.

"Do I hear five hundred thousand?"

Hannah calls.

"Six?"

I raise my stick, the commotion from the spectators behind us—and Damien's painful groans—growing ever louder with each swing, until it's Hannah's turn on a ghastly one million dollars for a hideous, 24-inch painting. The whites of her eyes shine as she looks my way, a hysterical laugh hot on her tongue, as she swings—

And gets the stick snatched right from her grasp.

Gasping, her lips form an *O*-shape as Damien hucks the stick in the air, the roar of the crowd deafening when it clatters to the ground, two feet from the podium. Amidst the commotion, Hannah smacks Damien's arm with a napkin, laughing hysterically, all the while the auctioneer stands there gaping.

"Umm..." His voice comes through the microphone. "Going once...?"

Turning in my chair when the room grows louder, I find what should reside in a madhouse or a rambunctious bar. Patrons stand to their feet, whistling and clapping towards me.

"Going twice."

Tristan smacks the table, doubled over in laughter.

"*Sold!*" The auctioneer points his finger our way. "A grand total of nine hundred thousand to tonight's most generous lady in gold."

From the corner of my vision, Damien dabs a handkerchief on the crown of his shiny forehead. "I think you nearly gave your fiancé a heart attack, Han."

Slurping on her straw, the bottom of her glass gurgles, void of liquid. "Damien? Oh, nooo. He's fine! I think he just got excited, didn't you, babe?" She nudges him with her elbow, earning herself an incredulous look and an earful of unintelligible grumbles.

She gives me a side-wink as she pats him on the shoulder. "I'll admit, you bested me that round, but there are many more to come. Plenty of time to win Damien and I our own *gorgeous* painting for the penthouse. I think such an abstract style would look lovely on our walls, preferably hanging above the mantelpiece in the living room. Don't you think?" More grumbles. "Oh, good, good. Now, if only I can convince the next speaker to fetch me my stick, then I'd be back in business."

I shake my head, eyes rolling on a smirk.

"You're relentless with that thing, aren't you?" Tristan's deep tenor sounds in my ear, racing shivers across my arms.

Twisting in my seat, I twirl a strand of hair between my fingers, his undivided attention boosting my confidence. "I am when you hand me over an unlimited line of credit. What're you trying to do, go bankrupt?"

Full of delight, his chuckle warms my insides as he traces a light finger down the small of my back. My toes squirm in my heels at his touch, and I notice just how close we are to each other, and how natural that feels. He leans into me, his head several inches higher than mine. I study the tattoos peeking out of his white sleeves, scrawling across his veins while he swirls a fingertip around the rim of his whiskey glass, almost as slowly as the ones marking my backside.

"Maybe I wanted to give you a taste of how a life with me would be."

My lips part, and before I can respond, his press into my temple. The sound of him breathing deep thaws my heart to liquid amber, which beats a study, calm rhythm.

On his retreat, I'm left stunned by the realization that he just did that. Not in the shower, in the heat of the moment, where we're slaves to our urges and ruled by passion. *But in public.* Then he smiles down at me—not a cocky smirk, not a lust-driven innuendo—but... *a smile.* Charming and affectionate, like he kissed me goodbye for the thousandth time before leaving for work, knowing when he comes back home, I'll be there.

"Want anything from the bar?" he asks. "I'm fetching Damien and I a round of water."

"No more whiskey for you?" I say the first thing that comes into my mind.

"Someone's gotta drive you two ladies back home."

I blink, wondering if I'm caught up in some dream escape, where I'm with a man who actually cares for my safety more than whether he'll score big later tonight. *Do men like that exist?* Because, for the past year, I've been positive that they don't, that relationships, deep down to their core, are only ever transactional.

But then I hope against the odds.

And return that smile. "I'll have my usual."

THIRTY
TRISTAN

"A VODKA MARTINI, EXTRA DRY."

"Right away, sir." Nodding, the bartender disappears down the wall lined with impressive liquor, her blonde pony swinging with each step.

Twisting around, I rest both elbows behind me on the bar top, studying the enormous auditorium. Craning my head, I spot the sky boxes dotted around the perimeter, high above the room, draped in red curtains and secrecy. Unknown bidders watch the scene below, some holding mini binoculars attached to sticks—

"Extra dry, huh? Sounds familiar." A man chuckles to my right, and in my peripheral, I catch him swirling towards me on a barstool. I scrunch my eyebrows, puzzled, unsure of where I've heard the voice. But I have before, I'm sure, seeing as the sound boils my blood on instinct. With one look, I grit my teeth, finding Adrien sporting a wicked grin. Clad in a flashy suit, he's every bit the spitting image of high-society royalty that he is. "I've ordered that once before. Actually, more than a few times."

From our last meeting, his final words ring in my ears. *You'll never fuck her like I did...*

"But you're not ordering it anymore now, are you?"

He turns from me, leaning back against the bar. I follow the trail of his gaze, and at the end of it, lies Lauren doubled over in laughter, hand pounding on our table over something Hannah said. Possessive anger burns through my middle, and I suddenly want nothing more than to knock his arrogant persona clean off his face.

"Have you thought about my offer?" He sips his cocktail, not veering his gaze.

My fists clench. "Of handing my wife over like some brood mare? No, in fact, I haven't."

"Time's ticking, Mr. Walker."

That almost sounds like a threat.

Feigning boredom, I adjust my cufflinks. "It's been two weeks since you've gained admin access. I think I'd know by now if you discovered any incriminating evidence in our database."

He shakes his head. "Now, why would I give up such confidential information before you've even agreed to our deal?"

He hasn't found anything. I smirk. *He's not the type of man who would resist an opportunity to dangle dirt in front of my face.*

His lips part, forming a crack in his self-assured mask, when he realizes I see right through to his timid core. Swiping a hand through his slicked-back, dark hair, he changes tactics. "I have a feeling we'll both have our eyes set on one of the remaining auctions."

I quirk an eyebrow. "Doubtful."

"I wouldn't be too sure about that." He grins, a glimmer in his stare telling me he knows something I don't.

Not biting the bait, I opt for an easy response. "Well, if it's a bidding war you're insinuating, it'll only be for a good cause."

"Oh, you won't be thinking of charity, especially not after I win."

This is getting ridiculous.

"You mean when your father wins? That *is* who I'll be bidding against, really."

My insult blows a fuse with him, noting the thick vein popping out along his forehead. *"You're not one of us."* His voice laces with venom, skin paling with unkempt anger. "Not part of this world. I mean, who even are you? Before your little arrangement with Lauren—*Lauren fucking Astor*— I'd never heard of you. Tech billionaires don't just go unnoticed on Silicon Avenue, bypassing headlines and upper society."

Wow, he's really working himself up.

Amused, I bite my tongue, which yearns to tell him of all the headlines I *do* make, more so than maybe any billionaire here. But that would involve informing him of my *other* name, which is quite tempting, seeing as, if I spilled my secret, he'd never lose another taunt from his lips again, let alone allow himself to be in the same room as me.

Encroaching his space, I lean in slightly, reveling when he shies away. "So, what's your grand theory, then?"

Gaining a surge of courage, he stands to his feet with hostile eyes, shooting daggers from several inches below mine. Adrien's a tall man, sure, and is undoubtedly a successful womanizer, but I've got the height on him and at least forty pounds of muscle. Meaning, his bravado is just that—and he won't be looking for a physical rematch any time soon.

"That you're a fake."

I smile wide, beaming a sparkling row of teeth down at him. "Am I now?"

"Yes." He doubles down.

Retrieving a wallet from his pants pocket, he pulls out a Black Amex—identical to the one inside my own wallet and earned without my Daddy's help—then places it on the bar, without so much as a glance towards the server. Taking a brave step closer to me, he seethes under his breath.

"While you may have Lauren fooled, I know your type. Your money's all a lie. Makes sense, too, since you haven't thrown up a single bet throughout this entire auction. After tonight, when she sees you're all a front, she'll know who her formidable match truly is. And, *ooh,* how I look forward to reminding her of *everything* she's been missing. Whether or not you accept my deal, I'll have her again—*taste her again*— until she's screaming the only name she ever has. *Mine.*"

My blood rages through my veins, and I lock my jaw hard, resisting the urge to punch his sleazy words back down his throat, or to smash his head against the bar top, for even speaking my wife's name. Instead, I watch him fish out a crisp bill from his wallet. Pinching the two corners, he snaps the paper in front of my face.

I don't bat an eye. *A thousand dollars? Is he serious? I make that in sixty seconds.*

Then he slaps the green on the bar, as if he's proven a point.

"Tell Lauren her drink's on me."

THIRTY-ONE
LAUREN

"SO..." Hannah grins at me, pushing earrings through her lobes. "When were you going to tell me about you and Tristan?"

Puzzled, I say, "You already know about our arrangement, Han."

Dressed in black work clothes, a makeup artist stops in the middle of us, dabbing powder on Hannah's nose, who awaits beside a large curtain backstage for the auctioneer to finish the current item's biddings. Pulling out a lint roller from her belt of miscellaneous tools, the woman sweeps along Hannah's silver gown, collecting dust that's invisible to the naked eye.

"Oh, don't play that card on me," she says when we're alone again. "I'm the one who was in a fake engagement. Sometimes things can evolve past contracts."

Deny, deny, deny, my natural instincts kick in, steering the conversation elsewhere. "I thought you called me back here for a pep talk." But the words taste wrong the instant they leave my lips.

Why would Hannah Lockwood need reassurance? Aside from my mother, of course, Hannah is the best public speaker I've seen. Running an auction must be the least of her concerns, having been first approached with the opportunity after her impressive donations last year. I don't know what she's auctioning off as she's kept the secret locked up tight.

With crossed arms, her eyebrows raise and lips purse, much like a disapproving parent who's about three-point-five seconds shy from delivering a scolding.

"Okay, okay," I admit defeat. "We've been... hooking up. That's all."

"Right. And does hooking up go hand-in-hand with flirtatious touching, smoldering gazes, and new jewelry?"

She notes the necklace weighing heavily around my neck. Unable to contain my giddy smirk, I recall Tristan's lips against my temple, an obvious display of affection, right smack dab in the center of attention before the stage.

"He said the necklace wasn't too expensive."

She huffs a breath. "And you believe that?"

No. "Maybe it was on clearance."

She rolls her eyes. "That man can't keep his eyes off you, Lauren. You really think he doesn't have any feelings for you?"

I shrug, against my better judgment. "He's a billionaire. And I know Damien's the exception, but a lot of them just want everything they can get."

"So you think it's only physical for him?" I nod. "He doesn't get jealous or anything? He'd be fine with you seeing other men?"

Hell no. "Probably."

She shakes her head. "I'd call you crazy if I hadn't been there myself."

I huff a breath. "Sure, let's go with that. Now, what did you want me here for, again?"

Applause fills the auditorium, signaling the item has sold. Hannah watches the auctioneer step off the podium, then swings her head back my way, mischief sparkling in her gaze.

"So you can watch me prove you wrong."

AT THE END of Hannah's beautiful opening statement, the guests clap in unison, their applause echoing backstage, where I still stand with a myriad of questions buzzing around in my brain. When the commotion ceases, she continues.

"As many of you are aware, I have the honor of choosing what I auction off, which has proven a rather tough choice. While there's been many exquisite items sold today and over the past several years since my attendance, I ultimately chose something a bit different."

Cocking my head, my pulse picks up a notch when she throws me an almost triumphant look from the podium.

"Which is why I'm so thrilled to announce that my dearest friend and I came up with a unique solution, something this auction has yet to sell in its history—an all-exclusive dinner with a beautiful young woman of importance."

Oh. Fuck. Me. She BETTER be referring to Sofia.

I twist on my heel, my heart now halfway up my throat. She couldn't possibly mean me. *I'm married.* She may have worded it politely, but she's selling a *date*, probably on some rooftop restaurant beneath moody lights while enjoying an all-expenses paid, five-course meal.

And who'd want that with a married woman?

"Please, welcome to the stage"—nearing an exit door, I

pump my legs harder, fingers gripping around the handle
—"*Miss Lauren Astor.*"

My jaw falls slack. In the midst of shock, I whip a one-
eighty, catching several backstage workers raising their
eyebrows at me, aware of my identity. On unsure legs, I creep
towards the stage.

Astor? She used my maiden name?

Forcing strong steps, I brace the spotlights with confidence, shooting Hannah a look that appears content from an
outsider's perspective, but really says *I'm going to kill you later,
you brilliant, sneaky bitch!* She only beams back a radiant smile,
motioning her hand to the right. Following her guidance, I
round the podium, finding a tall black stool on the other side.

With a sigh, I play her little game and sit, pulling down
the hem of my short dress before crossing my legs. At this
angle, in front of so many people, I'm suddenly thankful for
the compression shorts I sport underneath. Otherwise, those
in the front row could count themselves lucky, having been
unexpectedly granted a peep-show—starring my bedazzled
red thong.

When my eyes adjust to the lighting, they immediately
search for Tristan, who I spot sitting next to Damien, wearing
a similar expression to mine when my name was called. Jaw
ticking, he turns his head down the line of front-row tables.
Tracing the path of his gaze, Adrien sits at the end, two tables
down, flashing the smile of a hungry tiger right back at
Tristan.

"The youngest child and only daughter of the lovely
Diana Astor, Lauren graduated top of her class at Harvard
Law School, frequents the covers of tech news, and..."

Hannah's presumably self-made list of my accolades and
personal interests goes in my left ear and out the right, her

voice fading into the distance, as my gaze flicks between the two men. One would think I'm in a glorious predicament—what woman *wouldn't* want two billionaires fighting over her? Wouldn't hide a laugh of glee as they wage their bets for a single night of your attention?

But it doesn't have quite the same appeal when one of them is your *ex-boyfriend*.

Adrien combs his fingertips through his jet-black hair and runs languid eyes down my dress, a curve tugging on the corners of his lips. But when I appraise him, I don't see the heartbreaking, stereotypical Casanova that he is. I see a major setback—one that'll ruin all the hard-earned progress I've made the past year, building myself into the woman I was before him, piece by piece. A woman who'd never squash or downplay her own intelligence to appease a man who interprets a female's success as casting a shadow upon his. A woman who is at the pinnacle of her career.

And has her sights set on someone else.

"Would anyone like to start the bidding?" Hannah asks sweetly.

Tristan's stare is molten fire, projecting searing heat from below the stage. "Five thousand," a man shouts from across the room, but he stays calm, not averting his possessive gaze. "Ten thousand," another yells, but Tristan props both elbows on the tabletop, resting his chin atop his folded hands.

Whether the bidders in the crowd care or are even aware of my marital status, they don't show it, as their numbers climb higher and higher—alongside my blood pressure.

"One-hundred thousand," Adrien barks.

Hushed whispers sweep across the room, and *still,* Tristan only smirks. *Is he not going to bid?* Anxious, I nibble on the inside of my cheek. And as the auditorium fills with silence,

I'm overcome with dread as I accept my fate. Hannah and I share a glance, hers dripping with worry and regret.

"Going once..." she says, allowing for a lengthy pause.

"Going twice..."

"S—"

"Three hundred thousand."

Gasps ring from the mouths of nearly everyone in the room, their stares snapping onto the devastating man in white. Tristan sweeps his gaze back over to Adrien, this time cocky and brewing with a challenge. Some of my dread breaks off my shoulders, but only a piece. Although Tristan's entered the arena, it may be too big for him, because if there's one thing I know...

A Vuitton's pocket is never-ending.

"Three-hundred and fifty thousand," Adrien counters with an unimpressed yawn.

"Four hundred," Tristan answers.

And up and up they go, raising the hairs on my arms and grabbing the attention of every person in the auditorium, their heads snapping left and then right like turbulent waves, the numbers growing more obscene with each new call. But when Tristan hollers next, skipping several hundred thousand—to a staggering one million dollars—Adrien pauses.

And so does my heart.

One million dollars? Is he out of his mind?

"Going once..."

Tristan stands from his chair and takes taunting steps towards Adrien, who looks up at him with contempt.

"Going twice..."

"One-point two," Adrien calls, his knuckles visibly whitening from here.

Tristan gets closer. "One-point five."

With his new call, Adrien's cheeks darken. And when he's a foot from his chair, Adrien cranes his head up at Tristan, face red enough for his ears to spout steam and pop his head off his neck like a rocket aiming for Mars.

"One-point seven," he grits out.

Hands on his knees, an inch from his nose, Tristan *laughs* at him. "*Three million dollars.*"

Slamming the table, rattling the glasses and silverware, Adrien bursts to his feet, hurling his chair far enough to disturb the guests sitting at the table behind him. Without a word, he darts from Tristan, legs eating up the floor in a fit of rage. Camera flashes ring out on his dramatic exit, following him all the way up the auditorium stairs and out the door.

"*Sold!*" Hannah's voice splits across the hush, erupting cheers and whistles.

Thank God.

Shoulders sagging, I let loose a breath, standing to make my way back to our table. But when I spot Tristan, I stop dead in my tracks. With a fiery gaze locked onto me, he bounds across the space, weaving between tables, until he takes the stairs up to the stage in two. My eyes ping-pong around the room—from Tristan to the shining spotlights and back to Hannah, who wears a dubious smirk—as if nothing can stop whatever my charged-up husband is about to do.

"I didn't—"

He sweeps me off my feet—*literally*—then carries me over his shoulder like I'm a bag of sand. Whistles fly from the audience as I suspend upside down, hair dangling towards the floor. I desperately bat the locks from my face to no use. My peripherals sway with each of his steps, which pass the red curtain, and enter the backstage area.

"*Tristan Walker!*" I hiss.

"You like making me crazy, huh?" he growls, before a *smack* sounds against my ass cheek.

WHAT???

First, my best friend coerced me into being a prized pony, and now *I'm* getting spanked?! Enraged and not caring that from his point of view his reaction is justified, I pound fists against his back, which only earns me another punishing *thwack*. Pain blooms across my skin beneath my dress, before he kicks open an exit door with the butt of his Oxfords, revealing the warm nighttime air.

"You just want to find out what happens to misbehaving brats, don't you?"

A frustrated moan shoots from my lips. "Hannah tricked me into the whole thing!"

"I don't care."

Pavement roams across my vision, and I swear I catch the flashing of cameras off in the distance. *Great,* now I get to look forward to *that* with my morning cup of coffee.

"You're acting ridiculous!" I squirm.

"Am I?" His grip tightens around my legs as we enter a parking garage, glitzy valet cars lining up the incline. "I've had enough men ogling you for one night."

My next response cuts short as he plops me back down onto my heels—right in front of his motorcycle. My jaw hangs on its hinges. Hannah drove me here, and I assumed I'd hitch a ride back with her or that Tristan drove one of his dozens of sports cars.

"This can't be safe."

To answer, he retrieves two helmets from behind the bike —one larger and a matte black matching the intensity of the bike, and the other mauve. An unexpected thrill scatters through me, before he sinks the purple helmet on my head and flicks down the visor, plunging my world two shades darker. Reaching behind once more, he pulls out his signature leather jacket.

"Turn around," he commands, his voice rough.

Sucking my lower lip between my teeth, I obey, anticipating the sleeves before they're sliding up my arms. Twisting on my heels, he tugs me close, and I find him wearing his helmet with the visor up. His eyes bore into mine as he zips up my jacket achingly slow, the act foreign yet intimate, sparking need below my waist.

Flicking down his visor, he reads my thoughts.

"Don't worry, baby, you'll have your fill of me soon enough."

THIRTY-TWO
LAUREN

I BOLT it down the driveway, my laughs echoing in the night sky.

I'm not sure what convinced me it was a good idea to run from Tristan—maybe the adrenaline from my first time on a motorcycle or the anticipation of what he was going to do with me when we got home. I don't know. But the moment he parked us in front of the house, I removed my helmet and jacket, shot him a sultry smile like always, then took off in a dash.

In hindsight, I'm positively *not* dressed for the maneuver, seeing as I'm clad in thin, six-inch heels, while running at impressive speeds over the granite brick. Turning left, hugging the perimeter of the house, every internal sense tells me he's hot on my trail, and maybe even holding himself back to prolong the chase.

"Where do you think you're going, Lauren?" From behind, his laugh is menacing and full of enjoyment, hiking my pulse even higher and prying more giggles from me.

Banking another left, the backside of the house comes into

view, the pool glowing dark blue against the breathtaking backdrop of New York City off the hillside. Taking the stairs up in two, I burst through the gate onto the patio, and spot my escape—the enormous sliding glass door, which would prove oh-so handy for locking Tristan outside.

Almost there, almost there...

Tension grips me like a brewing storm on the horizon, ripping a squeal from my lips when I grace the handle—

"Oh!" I shriek.

Large hands slap the glass on either side of my head before Tristan's body barrels into mine. Adrenaline pumps through my veins, and I squirm to no use, earning myself a thrust against my backside, trapping me against the door. When I'm totally spent, chest heaving up and down, he collects my arms, brings them high above my head, and bundles my wrists in his firm grasp.

"You like running, baby?" he whispers into my ear. Brushing a free hand through my hair, he chuckles darkly. "Go ahead, I'll always catch you."

Fingertips tracing down my back, excitement buzzes along my nerve-endings on a moan when he hikes up my skirt. "Interesting..." He tugs the band of my compression shorts. I suck in a breath as an unexpected wedgie scrapes between my folds, before the fabric snaps back against my skin. "These aren't allowed in my house." He yanks them down in a single jerk, exposing my ass.

"Fuckkk," he growls on discovering my glittery red panties, tightening his grip on my wrists. Pushing my skirt higher, he grants himself a better view. "You're just testing my patience, aren't you, baby? Hmm?"

Whimpers are my only confirmation as need swims through me, blurring the kitchen through the glass. Releasing my wrists, his front presses against my backside, enveloping me, and locks a strong arm around my waist, surrendering me to his control.

"All you've done all night is play games. First, you auctioned yourself off, making me bid against your pathetic ex." Tugging the front of my dress, he frees my breasts. "Then you ran from me." He yanks down my panties, pooling them around my ankles. "And now I find you wearing *these?*" I cry out when his fingers descend upon my clit, rubbing harshly. "And—what a surprise—you're a needy slut like always, dripping wet before I've even touched you."

Overcome with desire, I grind into his hand, coating his skin with my wetness. Adjusting his grip on me, he snatches one of my breasts, pinching the nipple hard. Panting in a wild craze, I brace both hands on the glass, swaying my hips as pleasure erupts through my whole body. With a groan, he pushes back against me, his hard length rubbing between my ass cheeks.

"Finger me."

"What makes you think you're in the position to make demands?"

Past the point of protecting my dignity, I beg, *"Please, Tristan."*

His pleased laugh sounds in my ear. "That's right. You know who owns this pussy, don't you?"

I nod vigorously.

"Tell me who."

"You do," I whine. *"You do."*

"Mmm," he growls in agreement. "You're mine, Lauren. Every inch of you. And I *paid* for your pussy tonight."

Loosening his grasp, he withdraws, leaving my sex bare and throbbing, as he unzips my dress from the back, all the way down, then tosses the fabric on the ground. Threading his fingers through my hair, he pulls taut, angling my head towards the sky, before reaching over my body once more. Collecting my juices at my entrance, he returns to my apex, flicking faster than ever.

"*Fuck!*" My mouth falls open, eyes crossing at the seams.

"Yes, let it out—let it out until you're soaked for me."

He dips again with a satisfied grunt, finding exactly what he wants. Slipping back up my sex, he continues working me, brutal and purposeful, until I'm screaming *yes, yes!* up at the night sky. Legs shaking, I anticipate the denial of my orgasm, bucking into him with desperation, racing towards the finish line, until I'm inches away—

"Come for me like a good little whore."

Biting down on my lip, stifling my reaction, I squeeze my eyes shut as a colossal wave of pleasure topples over my head. Exhaling on struggling puffs, I grind against his hand, riding out the fire coursing through my insides as my pussy clamps around thin air with every pulse.

I sigh with a grin, shoulders slouching as I come down from my high, before he flicks my clit again, forcing a gasp. He wraps his arms back around my middle, holding me captive as he delivers another flick against my overly sensitive clit. I grit my teeth, writhing in his restraints on the next punishing touch.

"*Tristan—*"

Cutting me off short, he delves between my folds, then drags back up to my apex. "I love how wet you get after you come. So perfect."

His praise solidifies into my bones, melting me like malleable clay. My head falls back to rest on his shoulder, giving him easy access. With each stroke, the pain eddies from me, dissipating into the warm night air, stoking another fire of need, until I'm moaning and swaying into his masterful touch once more.

"Your body is so eager to please me, Lauren."

I sink into his skin.

"Open the door," he commands, and I instantly listen, revealing the magnificent kitchen inside. "Go on."

Clad in nothing but soaring heels and a heavy necklace, I strut inside, driven by lust yet laden with power. Hearing the door shut, I turn, blushing when I discover his eyes tracing my movements with hunger. Sweeping my hair over my shoulders, I walk back to him until I'm close enough to smell his intoxicating allure. Wetting my lips, I loosen his tie, dropping it to the floor, and move on and do the same for his dress coat, then unbutton his long-sleeve undershirt—all without a single word. On the final button, he shrugs off the fabric, leisurely unveiling an upper body painted with ink.

His breath hitches when my curious fingertips graze along his core. The intensity of his gaze weighs down upon me as I explore his muscles, brushing across defined pecs and down the hard grooves of his abs, reveling when they flex beneath my touch. Inching towards his belt, he groans a deep tenor dripping with restraint.

"The countertop. On all fours."

My head snaps up. *Did I hear that right?*

"I bid three million dollars for you tonight. Show me what I paid for."

Arousal dumps over me, willing my legs into motion. Bracing the marble, I hoist myself onto the center island and wait for another round of impending demands. Instead, when all I hear are languid steps atop the mahogany behind me, anticipation crawls across my skin, leaving a trail of fire.

He crosses my vision, hands sunk into his pockets, studying me like a fine painting. One that draws dark possession from behind his eyes.

"Fucking hell," he growls, coming to a stop in front of me. "I would've paid triple."

When his thumb presses against my mouth, I bat my lashes at him with a smirk. Dragging down, popping my bottom lip back up, his gaze flickers across my face, surging a sudden confidence in me.

Standing on my knees, I sink low until my wet lips meet the marble. Then I wrap my arms around his shoulders and run nails through his hair, eliciting a groan from him. Slowly, I kiss him, using an ample amount of tongue, sweeping and twisting in his mouth, before I shy away, finding him in awe. Snatching his veiny forearm, I guide his thumb back against my mouth.

And wait...

Spreading my knees wide, giving him the perfect view, I touch myself. His teeth grit, pupils blown wide, hungry and shining with lust, as he watches. Making a show of it, I sway my hips against my fingers and moan through pouty lips, pressing them against the pad of his thumb. On the edge of a growl, his mouth parts, meaning to speak—until I suck in his finger.

And then he's all mine.

What borders on the line of pure devastation marks his features—a man hypnotized, while I work myself and simultaneously jerk my head. Greedily, I take his thumb to the knuckle, brushing my tongue along his skin.

"Mmm," I moan against him, sinking two fingers past my entrance.

His eyes darken at that, fingers gripping the corners of my

jaw, clearly gaining back a sense of control. Ripping his thumb from my mouth, he forces me flat on my back, and I naturally plant the butt of my heels against the edge of the island, pointing my knees high in the air.

Leaning over, his touch follows the curve of my necklace, earning a squirm from me. With a deep chuckle, he tugs lightly, eyes fixated on the emerald choker and pooled with satisfaction. Taking his time, he trails a calloused hand down the center of my body, leaving me flushed when his penetrating gaze settles between my thighs.

"Such a good whore, opening yourself up for me."

I whimper at the attention, then hear the clinking of a belt buckle. Angling my head up, I watch him slide off his pants, leaving behind boxers outlining his glorious cock.

My motions stall.

"Keep fucking yourself," he commands, forcing my knees down, spreading me wide on the countertop. When they contact the cool marble, I resume. "Yes, just like that. I want you ready for my cock."

Propelled by excitement, having yet to take his impressive length, I thrust aggressively, hard enough to sway my breasts back and forth along my chest. Desperation crawls up my throat, needing to be filled to the brim and stretched to my max until I can hardly breathe.

Panting, I add another finger, eyes watering on the intrusion. Fingernails groove into my knees, and I find Tristan grinding his teeth on the last pin of his restraint, as I drive further, far enough my head lightens. Determined, I push again and again, until I'm nearing my knuckles and hurtling high-pitched moans through the air.

"That's enough."

Clutching my ankles, Tristan *slides* me off the marble until

I'm upright. But my feet don't touch the ground for longer than a second, before he whirls me around, cranes my body over the countertop, and crashes his cock into me, bottoming out. Sucking in a startled breath, my reaction stuffs all the way back down my throat—lying somewhere between the planes of pleasure and pain—having never been so full before.

"Shhh." He sweeps my hair to the side, whispering in my ear. "Relax, baby. You can take it."

I bite my lip, stifling a moan, when he retreats to the tip slowly. Then he pumps back in, stretching me further, stealing a breath from my lungs. And, this time, when he pulls back out, my inner walls respond eagerly, gripping around his shaft, blooming heat that I can feel in my toes.

"Fuck," he curses. "So fucking tight."

My hips buckle against the counter on his next swing, harder than the last.

"That's it. Take me all the way."

Freeing a moan, I thrust back against him.

"Such a perfect slut—in nothing but heels for me." He spanks my ass cheek. "You want it rougher?"

"Yes," I pant.

He smacks the other, sharper than before.

"Awe, you poor thing," he taunts. "Are you sure?"

"Yes!—"

He clutches a fistful of my hair and yanks, standing me up with him and colliding my backside into his taut abs. His other hand wraps around the front of my neck, applying noticeable pressure. Barreling into me at full force, he thrusts upwards, hitting a newfound spot, one that has me screaming and bucking and unraveling beneath him with no shame.

And then his name is hot on my lips, clattering against the

walls and rolling my eyes back until my world is a black vortex and, in it, is one audible noise, dominating the rest—*his laughter.* Dark and victorious in my ear, his response only heightens my arousal, only sends my wails rattling further down the empty hallways.

"*YES,*" he growls between thrusts. "Tell me how much you love taking this cock. Louder, baby, louder. Scream my name!"

And I do.

THIRTY-THREE
TRISTAN

I'M a man who'll never see the light of Heaven.

But my name on Lauren's lips is surely my glimpse through the golden gates.

"Fuck!" I holler, powering into her once more. Releasing my hold, she collapses onto the marble. Lying there, she squirms and pants like an animal in heat, begging for me to take her again. Blinded by lust, driven solely by the testosterone raging through my veins, I jumble for my coat and retrieve three things from the breast pocket.

Her red panties.

My phone.

And Adrien Vuitton's business card.

Whining, she props herself up on her elbows—only to receive a mouthful of her damp panties and the abrupt intrusion of my length. Her cry muffles through the fabric, and I shove her back down onto her stomach, granting myself full access to her. Transfixed, I stare down, sweat slicking off my brow, watching her bare cheeks respond to each of my blows.

Her body is fucking perfection, like she's handcrafted

solely for me, her pussy molded just to my liking—so much so, that she could ruin *me*.

Not waiting for her to adjust, I drive into her roughly, wrapping a tight grip over both her shoulders. Reaching across the island, she clutches the opposite lip, holding herself down as I ride her without mercy, until she's screaming my name once again the best she can through the panties.

Satisfied, I retrieve the business card, lying the laminate flat across the marble. At the sight of Adrien's glistening smile, possession swirls through my blood. Collecting all her hair, I twist the silky strands around my hand until they mimic a ponytail, and I can see her four-hundred-thousand-dollar necklace swinging to the beat of my thrusts. When I tug her hair, I earn even more muffled wails.

"Quiet, my little whore." I slow my pace, shoving her panties further in her mouth. "I need to make a phone call."

Dialing her ex, his words sing a vicious melody.

You'll never fuck her like I did...

Ring.

You'll never fuck her like I did...

Ring.

You'll never fuck her like I did...

Ri—

"Why, hello, Tristan. I was wondering when you'd call. Lauren's decided she prefers me, after all, I presume?"

I only laugh, tossing the phone onto the counter, inches from her lips. "I'll let my wife tell you herself."

Now on speaker, he asks smugly, "Are you finally ready to admit that he doesn't satisfy you the way I did, babydoll?"

Yanking the fabric from her mouth, she gasps before I return my brutal pace, prying moans from her lips, until they're just as loud as moments ago. "Tell him who you belong to," I growl, smacking her ass.

"Tristan!"—thrust—*"Oh!"*—thrust—*"Yes!"*—thrust —*"Tristan!"*

The screen goes dark, signaling the call ended.

I laugh again, satisfaction burning through my middle as I force her upright, driving into her still. Reaching over, I rub her clit harshly. She writhes against me, snatching my wrist, but I don't relent, pinning her against my skin, soaking up every one of her struggled cries.

"Give me another, baby."

She clamps down on her lower lip, grinding desperately.

"Come on my cock," I command, rubbing faster, reveling when her legs quiver atop her heels as I climb my own mountain of ecstasy. She lurches over, signaling her release, and I'm right there with her. Molding my body to hers, hands clutching the island over her shoulders for support, I spill into her.

Groaning, my thrusts are slow and purposeful, pulling all the way out, then sheathing back inside her warmth. She rocks her hips beneath me—matching my pace and weakening me at the knees—as she grips along my shaft from her own release, milking every last drop. On my withdrawal, cum and wetness coats my length, dribbling out her opening, rendering me completely and utterly spent.

Until she twists, dropping to her knees.

And her tongue throws open those stubborn golden gates.

~

LAUREN IS GLOWING.

"I can use my legs, you know." She giggles, then asks, "Really, though. What're you doing?"

Hands propped beneath her knees and back, I carry Lauren like a queen, whisking her from the kitchen, through the stately living room, then bank a right, aiming down a long corridor. A cheeky smile marks her lips, clearly enjoying the pamper treatment.

Nearing the open door of the master bedroom, I murmur, "What I should've the first night you were here," and carry her through the threshold.

Understanding the innuendo, her lips part and the blush already marking her cheeks deepens, swelling pride in my chest. Entering the bathroom, I set her on the countertop, then make for the white free-standing tub and swivel the handle, allowing water to clatter against the base. By the time I return with a warm washcloth, steam coats the silent air between us with a thin film. Gently tugging her to the edge, her head cocks in confusion at the cloth.

"Open." I tap her knee. "Good girl."

Her eyes shine at the praise, and she sucks in a breath as I swipe the cloth up her puffy center. I brush a hand down her thigh, my soft touch telling her to relax. When her shoulders droop and that lovely smile returns, I tend to her again. With precious care, I sweep up her center another time, then again on either side of her folds. Tracing upwards, through her mound, I absentmindedly rub tender circles across her thigh. Smirking, arms falling limp, she rests her head on the wall behind her in bliss.

"Tomorrow, I'll call the masseuse."

Her lids flutter open, eyebrows scrunching tight on a protest.

"No buts."

Rolling her lips between her teeth, obviously pining for some snarky retort, she fails to conceal a smile, then lets euphoria claim her once again.

When the water nears halfway, I pick her back up, walk a straight line to the tub, and set her down into the water. Rounding the bath, I step in behind her, the surface rising as I sink in low, before enveloping her in my arms. Lying back on me, she rests her head between my pecs, sighing deeply.

After several minutes of basking in the perfect moment, I whisper into her ear, "You were the most beautiful woman in the room tonight."

And every room, any other day, I don't say.

Twisting her head, our eyes connect, hers filled with genuine passion—but with a flicker of hesitance. "You really mean that?"

"Yes." I cup her jaw.

What're you doing, Tristan? a voice warns, questioning the foolish foot I hover over the line—the line which separates solitary lust from the possibility of something more. *Are you trying to dig yourself into even deeper shit?*

Chest lifting, she turns, until she faces me head on, straddling me. Her hands roam up my arms, over my traps, then delve into my hair, her fingers brushing through my locks like a puppeteer pulling every one of my heartstrings.

Too late, is my answer.

Before my lips find hers.

THIRTY-FOUR

TRISTAN

"CAN I ASK YOU SOMETHING?"

Pulling me from my afternoon slumber, my eyes flutter open at the sound of Lauren's voice.

Today has been my laziest day on record. No hacking. No Down Under. No impending doom. Just... *bliss.* And by bliss, I mean watching Lauren prance around the pool in her skimpy red bikini, sip gin mules, and tan beneath the summer sun all day long—after she had her scheduled at-home massage, of course.

Propping onto my elbows, I find Lauren sitting criss-cross on the daybed we share, her sun-kissed skin shaded beneath the canopy. I remove my shades, discarding them on a nearby table.

"Of course, anything."

"It's kind of serious," she warns, a subtle apology emerging through her tone. "But... I've been wondering for a while now."

Pulse hiking, my chest tightens. *Never mind. Bring on the doom.*

I simply nod.

"What happened to your parents?"

I release a breath.

While my relief may seem odd, I've spent years coming to terms with their deaths. Albeit my anguished time in foster care, unwilling to speak to a single soul about their passing, I did eventually. To Bryson. To my psychiatrist. To my sister, who I co-attended counseling sessions with, at her own request over the years, mending our rocky relationship. And, although time doesn't necessarily heal all wounds—add talking to the mix—it *does* prove to be a rather effective medicine. Which is why her question isn't off-putting, even on a day like this.

Before I can respond, she chuckles nervously, shrinking into an embarrassed state that's unbecoming on her. "Oh—I'm sorry. I-I shouldn't have asked." Shaking her head, avoiding my gaze, she makes to get up. "Stupid, really. What a ridiculous question, when we're having such a lovely day—"

"No, stay." I catch her knee, my touch soft.

Her shoulders droop, and she settles back down, meeting my gaze with hesitance. "You don't have to tell me, if it's too hard..."

"It's okay." Getting up, I sit at the edge of the daybed, letting the sun's powerful rays blind me. "Although it's difficult, I've had to tell their story many times."

"What happened?" She sits by me, her tension easing slightly.

"They were murdered," I say without wavering.

"Oh my God..." She rests a hand on my knee, seeping comforting warmth into my skin, remaining silent.

I pick at the corner of my nail, avoiding her sympathetic gaze. "The story's simple, really. They went out for date night, leaving me in charge of my little sister at home. We were twelve and six at the time. I didn't think much of it when they didn't return before we went to bed. Thought maybe they'd got caught up having fun. Until the knock everyone dreads arrived on our doorstep the following morning."

I side glance, finding her face drained of color. "Did they say who did it?"

"The police never figured that out." I return to my nails. "Said a thief hijacked their car and left them on the side of the road. They never found the car or the driver..."

Anguish laces her tone. "I couldn't imagine dealing with something like that, especially at such a young age."

"You never get over it," I admit. "It only hurts a little less over time. I like to say it's because of therapy, but a part of me wonders if it's because I've slowly lost what it *felt like* to have them there in the room with me. I don't know. But, I never denied their deaths, especially when none of our distant relatives offered to take us in. That gave me an eye-opener of how life truly is."

"No." She shakes her head. "Someone should've been there for you." *Family is family,* she seems to say—words I, myself, take to heart, and would no less fall on a sword for.

"Taking in two kids is a huge responsibility, so I don't hold it against them. Although, then again, I've never reached out to them later in life, either. But... the hardest part was having no one to blame. It would've been easier to cope, I think. Hating someone other than God. Or the universe. It's like fate threw our lives into a spin of roulette, just for the fun of it, and we came out on the losing end. Because, at the end of the day, that's what their deaths were—*unlucky.*"

She nibbles on her bottom lip, defiance flaring in her stare, choosing her next response carefully. But I know what she's thinking—my wife, an Astor Associate, who may as well cuff the criminals herself after solidifying their sentencing in a courtroom. Because it's what I thought during most of my time in foster care: Their deaths weren't a mistake, not when they were at the hands of a human being who possesses free will.

And who deserves to pay.

It wasn't from a lack of trying that I didn't find them. Even with near-limitless power beneath my fingertips and the ability to traverse the outer reaches of the web like a digital wraith with the master key, I can't make evidence appear out of thin air. And when I let that fruitless fight go, I set my mind free for healing. Because the truth is, my parents wouldn't want me chasing after their deaths.

They'd want me to move on.

Sweeping her thumb across my knee, I meet her gaze, before she chooses the safe—yet honest—reply.

"I love that you're so open with me."

And they pierce me right through my spirit.

Because all she's received from me are silent lies.

"WOW, that was seriously amazing. I think you're better than our personal chef."

With a stomach full enough to pop like an over-inflated balloon, I lean back in my chair, sweeping a napkin at the corners of my mouth. Staring from the head of the table, I recount the meal. Roasted duck. Asparagus. Wild mushroom risotto. Mashed sweet potatoes. And a pomegranate glaze that may as well have been honey.

Seated on my right, Lauren chuckles. "Oh, please. You're exaggerating. It was good, but not my best."

"That can't be possible—*look* at my plate." Her eyebrows lift, appraising my empty dish. "Between the two of us, I nearly had the entire bird, and don't even get me started on that risotto."

Pleased, she rolls her lips, concealing a grin. "Okay, but look at *you*. You're double my size," she teases. "And eat enough protein daily to fuel a small army."

"Now you're calling me some *roided-out* junkie?" I narrow my eyes, feigning offense. "Well, I guess I can't blame you, seeing as you'd lick these muscles about as clean as I would this plate."

Jaw unhinging, her cheeks blush a deep scarlet. With a shriek, she throws her napkin at me, scoring a hit against my chest. "No! That's not what I'm saying!"

A hearty laugh pries from my lips, and when she catches my gaze, she can't help but chuckle too, the tops of her teeth beaming against the light of the chandelier. In our silence, I rest a hand on her knee beneath the table. "But, really. It was delicious. I know we had a pampered day, so I hope you didn't feel pressured to go through all this trouble."

She shrugs. "You could say that."

"Oh, ya?" I smirk, squeezing her knee. "Who should I give my thanks to, then? The masseuse or the bartender?"

Her smile fades slightly. "Neither."

My breath stalls at the sudden seriousness of her tone, and a powerful ache weighs down my heart, knowing where she's about to go with this. Before I can interject and sway the conversation, she wets her lips nervously.

"That's not why I did all this, Tristan. Don't you understand?" She lowers her gaze, fixated on the band she twists around her finger.

A diamond I didn't pick out.

A band gifted to her by shadow.

Fused together by *eyes who see all.*

Vulnerability swims through her pupils on their return, shredding my soul in two, as she wears a genuine smile I want so desperately to reciprocate. "I know our marriage is a lie, but that doesn't mean we couldn't be more. *Feel more* for each other, because I do—"

"Lauren, don't..." I caution.

Sadness trickles into her features, like a perfect painting splattered with black ink. "So, you don't feel the same?"

Swallowing down the burn in my throat, I continue. "We agreed it'd only be physical."

Then all that somber turns to sharp ice. "No, you know what? You're full of shit." She laughs a twisted, jagged sound that makes my stomach churn. "Tell me, does an arranged marriage—even one with *friends-with-benefits*—consist of passionate make-outs and cuddles? And aftercare? What about jealousy, huh? Doesn't it seem a little odd to you that you'd rather pay *three million dollars* than see me on a date with my ex?"

She shoots from her chair, her voice raising. "And what about today? I know you wouldn't share what happened to your parents—or anything of your childhood, for that matter—with just anyone. But you are to me, then go around and say *we're just physical?* Bull. Shit. And what about now? Are we just—"

"I'm *not* saying that I don't feel the same."

I bolt from my chair too, combing a shaky hand through

my hair, the lid on my composure—and my common sense—busting through the seams.

"What *are* you saying, then, *Tristan?*"

"That we just *CAN'T!*"

Her pupils blow wide, the gears of her brain practically blowing smoke from her ears. "I don't understand. Why are you so afraid? What's holding you back? I *know* you're a hacker. That you spied on me and invaded every sense of privacy I had."

"You don't know everything. And you shouldn't."

She bounds towards me. "Tell me."

"It's dangerous."

"I don't care," she seethes, taking another step.

"You won't forgive me."

She stops in her tracks, worry slipping through her fiery mask.

And then I'm walking the deadly tightrope once again, with one side presenting the easy option—breaking Lauren's heart and leaving her in the light, where she's safe. Yet, I'm tempted by the other, more so now than ever, of ensnaring her in my grasp and diving headfirst into the darkness, only so I can flirt with tasting her heaven for the rest of our lives at the small price of imminent peril.

Are they truly listening?

If so, then we're both dead.

THIRTY-FIVE
LAUREN

IT ONLY TAKES a single match to ignite a stash of TNT.

And blow up your whole fucking life.

"Lauren... Please, say something."

But how did that stash come into existence, you ask?

Great question.

Well, in my professional experience, these mounds of destruction don't build themselves. No, they're meticulously placed by an outside party, right in plain sight. Someone close. Someone conniving. Even someone who's weaseled their way into your heart and slips a stick of dynamic under your feet, every time they fail to voice a lie. Until those sticks pile so high, the perpetrator switches up tactics, and shoves them between your life's precious nooks and crannies. Anything's game for maximum fallout.

Then they light that bitch up.

"Lauren, please. Let me explain." The male voice drifts out into space, a mere echo in the backdrop of my muted analysis.

Let's go over the facts, shall we?

That silly secret society on Silicon Avenue the conspiracy theorists blow out of proportion and I love to roll my eyes at? Real. I say that with the acute knowledge from my arranged husband—Silicon Avenue's most wanted hacker—who would undoubtedly be well versed in such things. And, I *would* wager he's lying, but that look on his face of pure mortification and dread says he's telling the truth.

Next fact.

Tristan knew they had my father the whole time.

On top of that, the society blackmailed him into our arranged marriage. Yep. Although, that's where things get fuzzy. He *says* he was blackmailed but, for all I know, with a lack of evidence, *he's* the one who voluntarily married me so he can take over Astor Security. Which makes a whole lot of sense, given that he's already admitted to *erasing evidence of their tamperings inside our databases.*

So, after soaking in his twenty-minute-long confession without a word, following our exquisite meal I cooked for us, I'm left with a decision... How do I feel? Do I feel...

Heartbroken?

Betrayed?

Maybe scared?

His hand grazes my knee, his touch soft like a feather—

Nope. I'm fucking pissed.

I burst from his grasp and to my feet, my skin so hot that he might scorch into dust upon touching me a second time. Strutting as fast as I can in heels, I make for my bedroom.

"Lauren!" he shouts from behind, his desperation bouncing off the walls of the hallway. "I was blackmailed—"

"Were you now?!" I don't give him a single glance. "Gosh,

you've really seemed to have taken that well. And I wonder why. Oh, maybe because, for all I know, you're one of them!"

"No, I'd never join—"

"*And my father?!*" My heels pound against the ground in a vicious rhythm, threatening to spike right through the floorboards. "You've seen me call him! For fuck's sake, you're *sitting in his company chair.*" Passing through an archway before the master bedroom, I grip the handle—"Why would I believe a *single word* of your *lies?!*"—and throw the door closed.

"*BECAUSE THEY HAVE MY SISTER!*"

His shoe wedges between the doorframe, anguished features peering through the thin slit in the wood. I study him in disbelief, but all that skepticism turns to sadness when tears stream down his skin, before his face falls into his palms, shoulders quivering, the weight of his sorrow palpable.

Oh, Tristan...

Perhaps against my better judgment—acting solely on instinct—I collect him in my arms, earning another sob from him. Mumbles bubble from his lips, a contorted, wet version of *I'm sorry*, over and over and over again, jumbled in between a harrowing explanation regarding the eerie photographs he's received of Aurora, and the threats against her life.

"Shhh." I press him to my chest, threading fingers through his dark hair. "I believe you."

Erecting to his full height, strong arms loop around my neck, embracing tightly. "You do?"

"Yes," I answer honestly.

"Thank you," he mutters into my hair on a sniffle, still

bordering on the ledge of hysteria, blabbering on with hope. "We just need to lie low for a while." My eyes shoot open. *Lie low?* "Let them get whatever it is they want from this arrangement, so they can move on from us."

I push off from him, meeting his red eyes. "Tristan, while they're threatening your sister, they physically have my dad."

Wary, he cocks his head, the sorrow slipping off him in seconds. "It's the same thing. No one's out of their reach."

"That doesn't matter. I'm going after him."

Twisting on my heel, not waiting for a reply, I make for the bathroom, sensing him close behind. Banking a right, I enter our enormous closet—which mostly fills to the brim with my clothes. Walking up to a wall lined with blazers, I choose the first one my hand lands on, then move on to the skirts.

He blocks my path. "You don't know what you're going up against."

I side-step around him.

"I'm serious." He catches my arm.

I whip my gaze up at him. "I assumed you'd understand. I recall you saying you'd do anything for family," I challenge, watching his shoulders sag. Releasing me, I continue my path.

"But what if it *is* your family who you should be afraid of?" Halting, my head grinds on a swivel. "Your parents," he corrects, leaving my brother out of the question.

"You're suggesting my parents are like Oscar Bass— connected with *The Oculi?*"

The name tastes foreign yet dangerous on my tongue, as I instantly understand the innuendo the moment it leaves my lips. The Oculi. *Eyes* in Latin. Quite fitting, given how they allegedly *see all.*

Tristan locks his jaw, but he might as well scream *yes*.

"And do you have any proof of this?"

"No," he admits.

"Then that's a shot in the dark. I was arranged to marry to save the company. Simple as that. Nothing more, nothing less."

I turn, stopping *again*.

Or could it be more...?

"What is it?" Tristan reads my body language.

Meeting his gaze, I exhale a considerable breath. "My mother says she's spoken with him. That he answers her calls. She told me the day we saw her in my office."

"And what did she say?"

"Same as always. That he's fine and needed time away from work."

His lips part. "How long has he been doing that? Leaving work unintended?"

My heart skips a beat. *No...*

"Several years, at least. He'll leave for a short time, whenever he's stressed and needs a break, then return to business as normal."

His voice drops to a near whisper. "I don't think that's a coincidence."

My throat closes, and I swirl around, aiming back at the wall of skirts. Running my hands through them, I think of my father, and the lovely memories we've shared during my childhood. For years, I've watched him suffer, struggle at the helm of a ship he couldn't steer.

Except... *maybe that was a front. A distraction.*

The thought is sickening and goes against every notion I have of him, theorizing my father might be involved in heinous acts bordering on the corruption of Oscar Bass, who I now realize was most definitely linked to the society. My uncle leveraged his powerful position as the CEO of Bass Mobile to spy on innocents through their smartphones, primarily upper elites. But, with my father, running Astor Security—the largest security company in the world, whose software sits inside the largest companies on the planet...

He'd truly *see all.*

Through blurred vision, I snatch a skirt and a pair of tights.

"Where do you think you're going?" Tristan steps in front of me.

"I may have a lead." I shrug on my blazer.

"A lead? What possibly for?

Plopping onto the center bench, I unlatch my heels and trade them in for a business pair. "We could be wrong. What if he's in trouble?" I ask, denial coursing through my stubborn veins. "Or... if he *is* who we fear he is, then we need to collect evidence."

He smooths his brow with an anxious finger. "You're pining for a shadow, Lauren. I've been after the society for years, and although I may know a few of their members, there's no way of prying information out of them. Not to mention how dangerous that would be."

"Are you so sure?" I strut to the full-length mirror, smoothing out my skirt. Hooking a beige Birkin on my arm, I exhale slowly, banishing the girl who relaxed for hours by the pool, then replacing her with the one who's spent years in the courtroom and double that between the pages of textbooks. "The *active* members won't blab. But I got a feeling one will."

His arms fold across his chest. "And who's that?"

Swiping lipstick across my mouth, lined with precision, I smirk. *"Oscar Bass."*

Catching my gaze, his glint with a sudden thrill, and the corners of his mouth lift like a chess player before moving his queen into checkmate.

"I'm going with you."

And for once, I don't argue.

THIRTY-SIX
TRISTAN

SILICON AVENUE'S former king dons an orange jumpsuit.

And eyes my wife as if she's the one who stitched it tight.

Sitting on the opposite side of the glass, Oscar Bass wears a scowl, flinging his miserable gaze between the two of us. With an irritated sigh, he picks up the phone attached to the privacy divider. Seated in the same cheap metal chairs as him, we grab our own set, holding the phones along our jawlines.

"Come to gloat, Miss Astor?" His voice is haunted and loaded with disdain. With shaggy gray hair, Oscar is far from his normal domain of speaking at tech conferences, commanding board rooms, and frequenting political news events. "Or, should I say, *Mrs. Walker?*"

Frowning, he notes the wedding ring wrapped around her finger, and I stifle the disdain that nearly marks my own lips at the sight of the band. From the beginning of our arrangement, my opinion has remained black and white. I love marking her as mine, but not with a ring that wasn't picked out by me.

I watch her study the band with hesitance, an ache

weighing heavily upon me, as she's surely recalling the moment I came clean to her about it.

When Oscar's lethal stare settles on me, I return an unreadable expression. *"Let me take the lead,"* she had said on the way in.

"Either is fine," she says simply.

"Really?" he presses, holding my gaze. "I'd wager your hacker boyfriend here possesses some choice words on the matter, given that I know him quite a lot better than he thinks I do."

Ignoring his bait, I fold my arms, shooting him a smirk. I'm unsure how long Oscar ran with The Oculi, but it's apparent that he was a man of importance, so he's aware of the mutual agreement the society and I shared for years—of staying out of each other's affairs. Even now, when he's clearly exiled from their ranks, I'd bet he's aware I'm currently under their thumb.

"I thought you'd be happier to see us, Oscar," Lauren's tone is sweet, successfully dragging his cold stare onto her.

"And why the fuck's that?"

"Well, I heard you haven't had a single visitor. We must be better than no one."

Gritting his teeth, redness flares across his cheeks. His fists slam against the glass as he lurches forward, rattling the acrylic on its hinges, and nearly earning a flinch from me. Pupils blown wide, hair in disarray, Oscar looks more like a caged animal than a calculated criminal.

"You're the one who put me here, bitch."

I grind my teeth, biting away the vicious response hot on my tongue.

"No," she states calmly. *"You* put yourself here when you breached the trust of your clients, and your family. I'd say the law finally caught up with you, but you were your own downfall. Your emotions made you sloppy."

Anger flashes behind his eyes. "You'd know all about killing your emotions, wouldn't you? You're an Astor, through and through, just like your late grandfather. A merciless, power-hungry lawyer." His gaze fixates on her hand resting atop the table, focusing on the ring sparkling around her finger. "You two are perfect for each other, aren't you?"

He's calling me merciless?

Well, he isn't wrong.

I *have* blackmailed more than a few of the shady CEOs he likes to call friends—if insider trading, threatening competitors, and bribing politicians is really something you do with *friends*. And I would've gladly aimed my unyielding tactics on him over the years, but running with the society made him untouchable. That doesn't mean he isn't aware of my reputation on Silicon Avenue, though. And while I agree with Lauren regarding his emotions, I'd say it was his unchecked power that truly made him sloppy.

Disregarding his outburst, Lauren takes on a tone more suitable for a misbehaving child throwing a tantrum—dismissive and matter-of-fact. "Although you're such a wonderful conversationalist, Oscar, we didn't come all this way to trade insults."

He settles back into his seat, lips thinning. "Oh, you're here with an ulterior motive?" he deadpans. "You don't say. And what might you want from a locked-up billionaire, stripped of all his titles and earthly possessions?"

"Information..."

His eyes narrow into slits.

"...on The Oculi."

Sitting up straight, he hisses, *"Don't speak that name here."*

Genuine fear shines in his eyes. Fear that Lauren taps into. "So, it's true... You're no longer one of them?"

"You might as well leave. I'm not answering any of your questions."

In a voice as still as death, she asks, "You really want to find out what'll happen if you don't?"

Eyebrows springing to his hairline, he laughs—*actually laughs*—in her face. *"Stupid brat,* thanks to you, I'm in prison for life. And, if I speak a word, and they hear, I may as well sign my worthless life over. I'm lucky they didn't off me the second my compromised position weakened their anonymity. In fact, I'm counting down the days, wondering when the order *will* be carried out, and I'll awaken in my cell to a knife kissing my throat. So, let *me* ask a question. What more could you possibly threaten me with?"

Stirring with anticipation, my eyes land on her. As she leans into the glass, that familiar calm she's been wearing like a second skin slides off her shoulders in a flash, and a ruthless demeanor takes its place. "If you don't comply, *I'm going to kill you myself."*

Silence oozes from both ends of the telephones...

Followed up with hysteric laughter.

Oscar combusts in a fit of mania as he smacks the table, tears lining the whites of his eyes. Swiping the wetness with a finger, he tries to speak, only to succumb to another round.

"Wow!" Exhaling deeply through his nose, a few chuckles seep through. "Didn't expect that one. What's your master plan, huh?" He knocks against the glass. "Bust through and bludgeon me with the sharp end of your heel? Maybe claw my eyes out with your pink nails? Right. Okay. Knock yourself out. I'm *quaking* with fear."

Lauren meets his taunts with her own. "I put you behind

these bars. Don't think for a second I can't sit you on the chair."

The electric chair. My stomach drops at the calmness with which she delivered the warning.

For a fleeting moment, terror clouds his features, before he leans back, seemingly unphased. "The trial's over."

"And who's to say new evidence won't appear, regarding your involvement with The O-cu-li?" She makes a point of enunciating the syllables, daring to speak their name. "I wonder how the Court of Appeals might feel about such a discovery."

"Don't threaten me with something that's not possible, *girl.* Ask your new boyfriend here, and he'll confirm. Didn't he tell you how he erased every trace of my involvement prior to your precious trial against my company?"

I *did* tell her—on the way here.

Smirking, I ask, "You think I can't make all that return?"

His head snaps to me, his panic palpable. "You're lying."

"Want to find out?"

Dread shines in his gaze, and I can practically see the gears churning inside his brain. A man on the cusp of a monumental decision.

Discerning he's about to crack, Lauren prods, "We only want answers."

Swallowing, he leans in, his voice lowering. "Fine."

My heart skips a beat. *We got him... We actually got him.*

Lauren wastes no time. "Who runs the society?"

Oscar's face falls. "I don't know."

"You expect me to believe that?"

He scowls. "Let me rephrase that. *No one* knows. Even high-ranking members such as I was don't ask such questions, unless you're looking for trouble. You simply receive your orders and do as you're told."

I take the next, a complete shot in the dark. "And what of their affiliation with Astor Security?" When his lips part, showing he's aware of their database tamperings, I press further. "What are they doing with the stolen data?"

Sighing, he meets my eyes. "I'm not completely sure. Although that wasn't my assigned project, it was clearly one of importance and highly top secret. Mostly everything I know of it is based on a pure hunch."

A hunch?

"Tell us anyway," Lauren demands.

His voice drops to a near whisper. "For years, they've been doing something in the Down Under."

"The *down-what-now?*" she asks, at the same time my hand grabs her knee beneath the table, as if that's going to keep her from the clutches of the thieves and criminals and killers who roam such a place. Eyes narrowing, her head rotates on a swivel, flicking back and forth between the two of us.

"Ooh," Oscar drawls, lips tilting. "She doesn't know?"

That I'm a cage-fighting madman? I think. *No. Only that I'm a hacker. One step at a time.*

I bypass his taunt, ignoring Lauren's piercing gaze. "How can you be so sure?"

"Well... Either Miss Palm Reader is running a booming business, deciphering dozens of hands per hour, or she's harboring a secret."

Oscar continues, unveiling the intricacies of his hunch, which only further intrigues and stokes Lauren's passionate fire. A fire that could strike the ends of our feet and set us— and all those we love—ablaze. But, despite the dreadful consequences of snooping our noses where they don't belong, if there's one thing I know...

It's that I'm not letting her go alone.

Before we depart, Oscar leaves us with a final—curious—instruction.

"Bring lab coats."

THIRTY-SEVEN
LAUREN

"SO... You thought you'd grab a snack before delving into the trenches of New York City's underbelly?"

Shoving my hands deep into my hoodie packets, I follow his lead down the aisle. My combat boots—yes, that's right, *my combat boots*—smack against the red-and-white, checkered flooring, as we cruise by shelves loaded with miscellaneous, unorganized items. Canned goods. Odon noodles. Hefty bags of rice. Tea. Spices and herbs. Any produce one might need in Brooklyn's Chinatown is right here, in this surprisingly busy —and somewhat sketchy—supermarket.

Tristan weaves between shoppers. "Not exactly."

I huff a breath. *Again with the non-answers.*

He's given them all day, providing me with slim-to-none information regarding the mysterious *Down Under*. After prodding him relentlessly for an explanation, all I've scored is a vague "*bad people go there.*"

Maybe Oscar was lying, I think. *I mean, what kind of name is that? The Down Under. How bland. Absolutely zero fear-factor.* What, do *bad people* let uncreative artificial intelligence come up with the names of their secret hangouts now, or something?

"Look"—I catch up to his brisk pace—"I didn't dress up like a high school dropout, tear holes through a perfectly good pair of Balmain jeans, and rat-up my hair into a horrible low-bun, just to take a tour of Chinatown." He banks a left. *Is he even listening to me?* "I know you said you didn't want to take me, but if you could just point me in the right direction, I'd apprec—"

He grips the handle of a door labeled *Employees Only.*

"Hey, I don't think we're allowed to go in—"

When he tugs back, my heart shoots to my throat, revealing... a completely normal grocery backroom, lined with shelves of overstock.

Exhaling, I roll my eyes.

What was I expecting?

Hitting the back wall, he roams down a long row of freezers, each so cold, their fogged glass hides what lies inside. Nearing the edge of my patience, I ask, "Would you quit throwing me for a loop?"

He twists on his heel, donning a serious expression. "Rule one. You will not, for any reason, leave my side for the rest of the night."

I scrunch my eyebrows. *Don't leave his side? We're in a frickin' grocery store.* "That's a little over-drama—"

"Rule two." Shrugging off his backpack, he pulls a handgun from an inside pocket. My blood freezes, hiking my adrenaline to overdrive. "Ignore anyone trying to sell you anything."

Cocking the barrel, he sinks the weapon between the tight band of his boxers, concealed by the backside of his sweatshirt. "And rule three." Taking a step, closing the distance between us, he flips on his hoodie before tugging mine over my head. "Never pull this down."

I blink. "Okay..."

"Are you ready?" His eyes harden, flickering with subtle regret as he searches mine.

With pursed lips, I observe the frozen glass. "Ready to pick out a salmon filet, you mean?"

He only smirks, eyeing the freezer third from the right, then tugs back the handle. And this time, reveals something far from ordinary. No cold seeps from the freezer. No food sits atop shelves. In fact, *there aren't any shelves,* only a gaping hole off the backside of the artificial freezer, leading to a set of stairs.

Wordlessly, I follow Tristan down the steps, squinting at the poor lighting, until we meet flat ground. After walking completely straight for what must be a quarter of a mile, a dead-end appears up ahead. Except... there's a sound emanating in the direction.

Like laughter.

The hair on the back of my neck stands on end, and nearly springs off my skin when an indiscernible person walks *across* the far wall. Nearing closer, I realize the dead-end isn't a dead-end at all, but an intersection of tunnels.

"Holy shit..."

I peer down the new pathway, this one wider, encased in concrete walls, lit with dark red LED strips lining the ceiling, *and busy with foot traffic.* Another group passes the intersection once more, before we follow in their steps. Stealing a glance back my way, Tristan shines a toothy smile, obviously finding the scenery much more agreeable than I do.

"You haven't seen anything yet, baby. Although, I remember when Bryson first brought me here. I didn't quite believe him when he said there's some labyrinth of tunnels below the city, and dozens of entrances in the most random of places. Nope. I was a total skeptic—until he showed me."

"How old were you?"

"Thirteen."

My stomach drops. *By the looks of the others, this is certainly not a place for teenagers.*

I remain silent for another five minutes, trudging down a tunnel that might very well have no destination, until we reach the first sign of modern civilization. *An elevator.* One fitted right into the cement with an iron cage for a door, as if plucked from the walls of an old-timey hotel.

Filing in behind the others, we find the space packed to the brim with what I'd wager are *regulars.* Adhering to Tristan's side like feathers stuck on glue, we squish between the crowd of leather jackets, hoodies, bandanas, tattoos and smoke, sandwiching ourselves into the far-left corner. When the tight area couldn't possibly accommodate another soul, a man at the front swings the iron gate shut on a *clang,* and with it, rockets my heart into my windpipe.

Sensing my paranoia, Tristan's calloused hands intertwine with mine, basking calmness through my skin.

On our descent, rough chatter weaves between the dense smoke curling in the glowing red air, pluming out the mouths of presumed criminals, gang members, and petty thieves—or maybe eccentric, punk-rocker types looking for a good time. Like this woman to my right, sporting spiky neon hair and a pierced septum, whose languid gaze peruses up the length of my body. Meeting my eyes, she smirks, as if she sees right through my front, to my timid core, and deems me a preppy, rich kid who's hopped over the wrong set of tracks.

Until she looks over my head.

Spotting Tristan, she quickly glances elsewhere, smacking on gum and inspecting her black-tipped nails, suddenly sporting a bored expression.

Ding.

The floor pushes against the soles of my feet before the caged door rattles open, pouring in what sounds like a roaring crowd. Anticipation knots inside me as I crane on my tippy toes, trying but failing to see above the heads of those in front of us. Shuffling our way forward, I theorize an illegal gambling room—like a speakeasy for underground criminals looking to socialize and try their luck at a game of craps or poker.

But, there's a minor flaw in my hypothesis...

Why would a bar—even a casino—be this *loud?*

The pair ahead of us disperses, leaving my answer in plain sight. An answer which has me questioning my reality. Wondering if my name's not really Lauren but Alice, who's tumbled down the rabbit hole into a place of wonder. Except... in this Wonderland, nowhere stands the grinning Cheshire Cat or the Queen of Hearts or red-painted roses.

Only Mad Hatters.

Hundreds—maybe thousands—sit on bleachers, watching two fighters brawl inside a metal cage at the bottom of the arena. Some spectators encircle the enclosure, pounding their fists against the chain-link, tossing coins and green dollars in the air. After a stern tugging on the sleeve of my hoodie, I find Tristan giving me a stern look.

I got the gambling part right, I don't tell him.

Stuck to his side, I descend the concrete steps.

"Didn't peg Oscar for the cage fighter type," I say.

"There are plenty more reasons to be here. But you could call this the main event." Tristan waves off a cheery man, who wears a red-and-white striped vest, standing on the edge of the sidewalk, beside an unmarked cooler.

Passing him by, I recall rule two—*ignore anyone trying to sell you anything*—then say, "He didn't seem too bad. Like a hotdog seller at an MLB game."

Tristan's dark eyes catch mine. "Except instead of hotdogs or popcorn, he's selling unmarked drugs. Drugs that turn you into these freaks."

"Oh..."

Reaching the bottom, we round the outskirts of the hungry spectators. Just being in the vicinity, their sweat and crazed energy seeps through my pores, heightening my awareness and—

"Apex!" a deranged man screeches, his bloodshot eyes fixating on Tristan. Stripping himself from the crowd, he grips Tristan's shoulder, who merely shrugs him off and continues on our way. But the man doesn't quit and sticks to his tail.

What the hell?

"I-I never t-thought I'd g-get the *pleasure,*" he blabbers, practically foaming at the mouth. "The reigning champion. The *apex* of all who've graced the pit."

Eyebrows cinched, confusion warps about my brain.

"Get lost, buddy," is Tristan's only response.

The man's high-pitched cackle rakes up my back. "Ooh, you're just as threatening outside of the cage. Tell me, when will you enter again? It's been quite some time—since your last match, I'd say. Don't let the loss keep you away. I've bet on you every week now for years. Better not be too long! You've made me plenty of cash—"

Tristan whirls around, stopping the man in his tracks. "I'm not who you think I am." Towering over him, he looks him dead in the eye. *"Now I said get lost."*

"Come on, I know you're—"

Tristan reaches behind himself, hinting at the cool metal concealed at his lower back. Noting the threat, the man holds his hands out in the air and shies away, then disappears into the crowd without another word.

Meeting my gaze, hesitation flashes in Tristan's eyes. Playing back the crazy man's words, my head snaps to the cage, soaking in the brutal fistfight occurring inside. I imagine Tristan in the place of the brutes, dodging and ducking in the way I've seen him once before, upon walking in on one of his and Bryson's sparring sessions.

"He had the wrong guy."

Taking him back in—all six-foot-five, inked tattoos and raging testosterone of him—the puzzle pieces form, trying their hardest to click together.

"He seemed pretty confident."

"He had the wrong guy," he repeats. "I mean, look at these people. They don't know left from right."

The truth doesn't quite reach his eyes, but something unexpected does—embarrassment. And then all I see is him, that night in the kitchen, with bruises marking his face.

When I fold my arms, he deflates, sinking both hands into his pockets. Beneath his hood, an uncomfortable expression marks his handsome features. Drawing closer, he lowers his voice, seemingly more concerned with hearing himself speak his next words than one of the maniacs surrounding us.

"What do you want me to say, Lauren? That I'm some cage-fighting freak?"

Even though I knew it deep in my gut, it drops all the same. My eyebrows tick upwards, craving the truth—the whole truth. "But why? Why enter the ring at all?"

"Because..." Shame forms shadows along his face. "It helps."

Could he be any more cryptic?

"Helps with what? Making money? Closing shady deals? Getting your teeth knocked out?"

"No." He avoids my stare. "With the guilt."

My heart stings with sorrow, and I realize he can't be referring to the secrets he kept from me, but a regret that's long-standing. His relationship with his sister.

Oh, Tristan...

I grab his arm, hoping the soft touch seeps comfort through the fabric. "I'd never want my brother doing that to himself over me."

His head snaps back to look at me, surprise lacing through his eyes. "She doesn't—" He stops himself, the defensiveness waning off his shoulders in waves. "I don't enter the cage anymore. Not since marrying you."

Warmth envelops me at the sentiment, that he's essentially admitting to helping himself because of me, but then confusion quickly takes over. I catch another swing from one of the fighters, and I swear I spot a golden tooth dart out of the other's mouth. Shaking my head, I endure the following roar from the crowd and the bizarre idea of seeing Tristan up there in the spotlight.

"Then what of that night in the kitchen? I saw your face. You're telling me you really got that from crashing your bike that had no damage?" I give him a pointed look, and he pushes out a breath.

"Okay, okay. I've had one slip-up since meeting you. But that's all, I swear."

Even though I believe him, I press harder. "But what brought on the relapse?"

"Not what." His lips purse. "But who."

"IS THAT... *JACE?*" I pale.

Seated at a table in the Down Under's marketplace, Tristan and I share—more like pick at—a sandwich. Because what we've really been doing is scoping out one of the many tents lining the perimeter.

Mrs. Peggy's Palm Readings.

Given the innocent name and questionable location, from the outside, I'd think the palm reader was nothing but genuine, if it weren't for Oscar's words ringing true. For the past hour, we've peeked our curious gazes at the tent's dangling red curtains, specifically at the dozens of men and women who pass through them—an unfathomable number of hands to read, given the timeframe.

Some appear to be the average lurker types down here, sporting draped hoods, leather jackets and cigarettes between their lips. Confirming Oscar's advice, others wear white lab coats and the signature owl tattoo I'm now familiar with—like the man standing in front of the tent, pressing a smart-phone to his ear, looking an awful lot like Astor Security's newest, and youngest, board member.

"Yes." Tristan ducks his head down. "That's him. He's down here so often, I thought there was a good chance we'd run into him."

That's why Jace always wore turtlenecks.

No wonder Tristan never liked him...

A shiver scatters across my body, leaving me weightless and consumed by shock. Exhaling a slow breath, I banish the sickness writhing in my stomach at the very first, undeniable proof of The Oculi's encroachment in my family's company.

Pulling my hood lower, I mutter, "We don't have the owl tattoos."

How're we supposed to blend in?

"Not all of the scientists we've seen have the tattoo."

"Does that mean Jace is high up in the society?"

"I don't know..." Caution marks his features. "I don't know what he is. He's like a chameleon, always acting with a different personality, taking on different names. Jace is the one who took the photos of Aurora at college, as if he was some other student in her class."

Another wave of panic hits me, but I bat it back down, reminding myself why we're here, and of the stakes and unknowns which surround my family.

I need answers.

Hanging up the phone, Jace scowls and stalks off in the opposite direction. We both exhale in the same breath, as possibly the only man who could identify us struts down the line of stalls and disappears into the crowd of marketgoers.

Tristan shoots to his feet, throwing off his hood, exposing his strong features. "Let's go."

His urgent tone propels me to mine, and in a matter of seconds, we're sauntering through those same red curtains, beads jangling off the silk on our entrance. Beyond lies a tent clashing with spiritual decorations. Dream catchers and astrological tapestries hang on the walls and ceiling, while incense burns in the corners, fogging the air with whiffs of lavender and myrrh.

"Hello," a young woman's monotone greets us from behind the front desk. "Unfortunately, our reading rooms are full at the moment. Would you mind coming back later?"

On our approach, sweat pricks along my hairline, recalling Oscar's instruction—the line he said he'd heard from a member of the society, which supposedly grants access. Doubts creep into my mind. Maybe he fed us lies, essentially setting us up for a trap.

But it's too late now.

Tristan props an elbow on the table, his voice unwavering. "Not a problem. If you could, tell Mrs. Peggy that I drew the High Priestess today."

"Of course. Such a lovely tarot." Reciting the words like an overused record player, the woman smiles, and the light doesn't quite reach her eyes. "Follow me, and we'll inform her now."

My heart clenches, and I weather the nausea churning in my stomach. *That actually worked.* When she swivels, Tristan and I share a glance, and I find his eyes full of hidden surprise. On his nod, we follow her down a hallway with more beads and silk for doorways. Reaching the end, she draws back a curtain. "Right this way."

Once Tristan and I file in, we turn to—

She's gone.

We exchange uneasy glances.

"This isn't really what I expected..." I appraise the space, which appears to be a normal reading room. More tapestries decorate the walls. More incense burns. And candlesticks stand atop a small table, surrounded by three chairs with faux fur and silk draping off their backsides.

Tristan threads fingers through his hair. "There has to be something."

As we search about the room, my hands grow sweaty, anxiety practically dripping from my teeth.

Oscar set us up...

How could I be so stupid...?

I brought this on the both of us...

We're so de—

"Bingo."

Tristan pulls a large tapestry aside, revealing yet *another* hallway. One definitely detached from the rest, with starch white walls and modern, fluorescent lighting. And at the end, we discover a single door.

A locked door.

THIRTY-EIGHT
TRISTAN

"CAN YOU DO IT?"

Bryson hums, crouched low to the ground, inspecting the door's lock.

By some miracle, Bryson not only was in the Down Under when I called, but he was in the marketplace. Whether he was buying another set of tools, I don't know, but he *always* has them on hand. The real miracle, though—given the foot traffic we witnessed during our stakeout—is that no one's walked in on us yet.

"Yep."

I release a breath at the same time as Lauren. Our hoodies discarded, we each wear a lab coat I brought in my backpack —which now hides inside a chest in the corner.

From the corner of my eye, Bryson takes out his kit, unraveling the fabric until dozens of metallic tools shine against the flickering candlelight. His hands move like a well-oiled machine, jamming one tool into the lower section, without a second thought, then meticulously wiggling the other in, just as he did at the bar.

Lauren catches my eye through a pair of false glasses, and my heart thumps in response. Approaching, I cusp her face with both hands, angling until she looks up at me.

"It's not too late to turn back," I murmur what feels like the very last opportunity to persuade her to go back home, where I'll know she's safe. She could send me inside, and allow me to take the fall, if necessary, as I'm the one who deserves such a fate—*not her.*

But her eyes glint with determination. "Whatever lies behind this door, we'll face it together."

Swallowing down another protest, I nod, sweeping a thumb across her jaw. Planting a kiss onto her forehead, I say a silent prayer to a god I don't believe in, swearing my devoted allegiance, if only some divine source protects Lauren at all costs.

On my withdrawal, she catches my wrist. "It's going to be fine."

"You're right." The words burn on the way up my throat. "We'll get the evidence we need and then get out."

Click.

"Got it." Bryson stands, leaving the door closed. Shadows form along his features, taking us in, a somberness clouding his gaze. "Are you sure you don't want me to come? I could watch your backs."

"No." Lauren beats me to it. "We're the ones caught up in this mess. Not you."

Arms folded over his chest, his defiant gaze flicks back and forth between us, then settles on Lauren. "If Tristan's involved, it's my mess too."

A lump forms in my throat. *Oh, Bryson. What would I have done without you all these years?*

"You've already helped more than enough." Sincerity drips

from her tone. "And besides..." She forces a chuckle, unveiling the nerves she's guarded until now. "We only have two lab coats."

His shoulders sink. "Yeah, I guess you're right. Well... don't let Tristan sacrifice himself for the greater good or some shit, okay?"

Her lips curve into a genuine smile. "I won't."

Swallowing hard, I pat his shoulder, appreciation thick on my tongue. "We got it from here."

His eyes turn glossy.

"Don't you get emotional on me."

"Shut up, man." He laughs on a sniffle. After a bittersweet goodbye, he disappears through the beads.

Candles *pop* in the silent air between us, as pressure mounts from the waning of time and space, floating about the iron door handle like the ominous clicks of a grandfather clock.

"Are you ready?" I ask, fingers grazing the knob.

Her nod is the strike at midnight.

LAUREN GASPS. "OH..."

"...*fuck,*" I finish her thought.

Wires.

Server racks.

Lab coats whisking down the maze.

The door seals shut behind us, as we gape up in wonder at what is most definitely the world's largest underground data center.

Dials flicker between neatly packed rows, with distances so vast, my sight can't reach the end. A deep azure glow blankets the facility, just like in mine, except ten—no, *a hundred*—times the size, making my hacker Bunker look like some doll playhouse.

We walk down an aisle, keeping straight faces. Head tilting, I catch boots strutting across a metallic grid above our heads, running parallel to our path. *This place is as tall as it is long,* I realize, noting the servers lining the grid, a level above us.

"How is this possible?" Lauren asks, breathless beside me. "What is this place?"

Fighting the fog of amazement clouding my brain, I swallow the bile in my throat, on the cusp of a monumental discovery.

"Project Dupe incarnate."

Her head snaps to me, aware of the sheer weight of such a discovery, because she knows of the project, having told her during my myriad of confessions the other night. Knows I hid The Oculi's tamperings inside Astor Security, forever erasing whatever they were doing with all the company's data.

And here lies the answer to that burning question. *They found a better way to "see all."*

Astor Security has data on *everyone*. Phone records. Addresses. Names. Device authentications. Social security numbers. Credit card information... Why use Oscar Bass's authority to see through smartphone cameras, when they could have that and *much more?*

Guilt gnaws at me. *How didn't I foresee this?*

I couldn't have, the sensible side of me argues. All I saw was a vast amount of data duplicating over to *random destinations*. Not one. And I didn't have the time to study them, to realize those destinations were truly all the same, hidden in an ever-changing encryption, obviously designed to throw off detection if anyone were to find the evidence.

"So, you're saying..." Her eyes crawl around us, blown wide, as if she's staring in horror at a newly cracked egg sac, now spewing out a million tiny spiders all around us. "All the data housed here is from my father's company?"

"Yes."

Her face plummets into darkness, no doubt drawing conclusions. Then her expression lifts, eyes pointing ahead of us. A woman cloaked in a lab coat walks our way, staring down at a tablet in her hand. Plastering on a casual look—one that screams *we're supposed to be here*—we make our way down the row, in her direction. Her gaze lifts, noting us, and my heart skips a beat, only to resume its rhythm when she returns to her screen, passing us by as if we're just another pair of scientists.

Alone once more, Lauren's shoulders sag. "Let's get to it," she says, discreetly pulling out her phone. Switching to video mode, she motions a panoramic view of our surroundings.

And that's what we do.

Act our parts. Blend in. Gather evidence.

Repeat.

For hours.

∿

"WE SHOULD LEAVE," I warn. "We have more than enough evidence."

"Just a little longer." Lauren pivots, craning her gaze down an all-white, long, empty hallway, void of technology—or *anything* except for doors. "This looks different."

Banishing the danger slithering up my back, I follow her

across the bleach laminate flooring. Fluorescents beam from the ceiling, depleting any and all of the blue light emanating from the data center. With each step, I feel less like we're inside an underground lab and more as though we've entered a psychiatric facility.

"Lauren, it's time to go..."

She keeps walking, passing by the first door. A single, square window sits beside the entrance, granting visual access to quite an odd room. Dominated by white like the hallway, the empty room stores only three things.

A door on the opposing wall.

A metal chair.

And a ridiculously large, curved television.

Before I can protest, Lauren tries the handle, discovering it unlocked. Gnawing on my lower lip, I stay in the hallway, in case anyone takes notice. Immediately, she goes for the other door, this time finding the knob unmovable. Arms crossed, clad in her lab coat, Lauren's eyes sweep about the room, until they hit the window.

And don't meet mine.

With scrunched eyebrows, she approaches—her footsteps surprisingly audible from the hallway—stopping an inch from the glass, her gaze looking anywhere but at me. Exiting, her report is short. "It's a one-way mirror. You can only see through from the outside."

But I can't make any sense of it.

Continuing further, we don't encounter a single soul, yet my steps are like trudging through thick cement, positive a disaster looms over our shoulders. Occasionally, we pull out our phones and snap pictures, even though they're only of the same type of rooms. Empty. One chair facing a dark television. A locked door. And a one-way window.

Capturing another photo, I—

Ding.

As the sound bounces between the walls, Lauren freezes, swinging her head. "You don't have your phone silenced?" she hisses through clenched teeth.

"I do," I counter in a low tone. "...Or I thought I did."

Glimpsing at the banner at the top, intrigue gets the best of me, and I click it. But the information stops me in my tracks, sending my heart plummeting to the ground.

"What is it?" Lauren reads my reaction.

I fumble for my words, my exhales shooting out in choppy waves. "I-It's the... It's the off-shore accounts I told you about. The ones transferring large sums of money from a single, encrypted start point. The decryption is done."

Which is why my phone went off, bypassing the ringer settings, given the high importance I allocated to such a discovery. I didn't know when the decryption would finish— *or if it even would.*

Pursing her lips, she continues on our route. "Don't you think your little side projects can wait?"

Like a magnet, I stick by her side, the shock coursing through my veins so palpable, I forget my legs are even in motion. "That's the thing..." I swallow, finding my saliva as thick as honey. "The origin address is 492 Aria Sonata Street."

"Sonata...?" Her forehead furrows in confusion. "Isn't that Sonata Hall?"

"Yes," I whisper.

"But that's where the Astor charity auction is held."

My silence drags her features down further, riddled with pain and denial. "No... That can't be right. Your program made a mistake—a false positive. Those happen, right? Because..." She shakes her head with fervor, stubbornly increasing her pace, approaching the next door like normal, as if she can walk away from the terrible realization. "Because that would mean—"

I snatch her in my clutches, wrapping a hand around her mouth, stifling her loud gasp just in time. Shaking against me, Lauren stares wide-eyed through the glass, finding this room like the others—*but occupied.*

With two familiar figures.

Nicholas and Diana Astor.

THIRTY-NINE
LAUREN

"WHO ARE YOU?"

Carrying a black baton, my mother slowly encircles my father, who's strapped to the chair by leather restraints. With pupils dilated like black voids, he stares straight ahead at the television displaying hundreds of tiny screens, each of which plays a different scenario, altogether forming a picture that's indiscernible at our distance.

"No one," he answers in a monotone.

My exhales power through Tristan's hand, his grasp still taut around me, probably—correctly—assuming I'd sway and topple onto the ground. Because what I'm witnessing can't be happening. Can't be real. *But it is,* I force myself to accept, while my brain interprets yet rejects nearly everything in the room before us.

The room displaying my mother, who... *doesn't look like my mother.* Who wears a bland, gray dress and an authoritative expression I've never seen, eyes icy and controlled as she appraises my father below her.

My mother...

Who funds The Oculi with the charitable donations of others.

My mother...

Who is The Oculi.

A kaleidoscope of colors projects from the indiscernible screens, drowning the room with an intensity that could only match being hurtled through starry space at light speed. Encircling the opposite direction, she holds the baton tight at her back, as my father gapes an unyielding gaze at the screen, jaw drooping low.

Tristan records with his free hand, right before she speaks.

"State your baseline."

"The Eye covets shelter for the mice."

A chill quakes through my entire body. The words are nonsensical, but his monotone forces a tear from my duct, the warm wetness zipping down my cheek.

"How does one walk amongst their dreams?" she asks.

His response is imminent. *"The Eye covets shelter for the mice."*

"Does the wife pull the strings of her husband?"

"The Eye covets shelter for the mice."

"What's an owl without mice to hunt?"

"The Eye covets shelter for the mice."

"How does it feel to lose your life's work?"

"The Eye covets shelter for the mice."

"Who are you?"

"No one."

"Does the population need an iron grip?"

"The Eye covets shelter for the mice."

"Do you loathe our time together?"

"The Eye covets shelter for the mice."

"Does your daughter call you, to no avail?"

Blinking, he pauses...

SMACK!

Fighting his grasp, my cry muffles into Tristan's fingers. Tears stream down my face and collect into his palm, watching in horror as my father writhes against his leather restraints. Head lurched backward, teeth snarling on a silent scream, agony twists his features, and his hands flex in pain at the bulbous redness spreading across his forearm.

She whips the baton behind her back, smooth and efficient, then continues pacing. "Does your daughter call you, to no avail?" she repeats.

"The Eye covets shelter for the mice!" he chokes out.

Louder, she asks again, *"Does your daughter call you to no avail?"*

"T-the Eye c-covets shelter for the mice."

"Does your daughter call you, to no avail?"

Once again transfixed by the light show, his dreadful monotone returns. *"The Eye covets shelter for the mice."*

"What's it like being a loyal footsoldier?"

"The Eye covets shelter for the mice."

"Do you dream of our sessions?"

"The Eye covets shelter for the mice."

"Who are you?"

"No one."

"Do nocturnal wings glide over Silicon Avenue?"

"The Eye covets shelter for the mice."

"Do you wish to kill your wife?"

"The Eye covets shelter for the mice."

"What's society without the usurper?"

"The Eye covets shelter for the mice."

"Has your pride been stripped from you?"

"The Eye covets shelter for the mice."

"Who are you?"

"No one."

"Say I am no one."

"I am no one."

"Say I am no one."

"I am no one."

"Say I am no one."

"I am no one, I am no one, I am no one, I am no—"

"Silence."

His lips snap shut.

Rounding the chair to the front, heels clacking in her wake, my mother stares down at him, void of any and all emotions—the farthest cry from the woman who raised me, who calls herself a philanthropist and recites pretty speeches in front of generous crowds.

"Sleep."

And he does so, his head falling forward instantly, dangling off his shoulders. Then my mother twists on her heel, opens the door on the opposing wall, and exits.

On its *click* shut, Tristan releases me, before I spill all of my stomach's contents onto the floor. Groaning, I wobble, slapping my hand against the glass for support. Through the mental haze, the only thing I see is Jace's blank stare, that day in my office, and the only thing I hear are my mother's words to him, before he snaps out of his random daze.

"You have work to do," she had said...

How could the woman I've known my whole life—who raised me—be a lie, a fabrication in every sense of the word? A manipulative abuser. And I'd never spotted the signs? We never spotted them, as a family? The worst part is, I truly don't think there were any, aside from the way she handled

Jace. Growing up, she always supported me. Challenged me. Loved me. Or so it seemed.

But in there—that woman.

She's incapable of love.

Another wave of nausea hits me, saliva coating my tongue, but I swallow harshly, banishing the temptation to hurl. Lightheaded, my knees wobble, before strong hands keep me upright by the pit of my arms.

"Easy there," Tristan soothes, eyes filled with pity. "Can you stand?"

I nod, stabilizing myself. When he releases me, I brave another look into the room. Reading my gaze, Tristan's tone heads with warning. "We need to go, Lauren."

"No."

Not waiting for his protest, I rip back the door and rush to the chair. Squinting at the flurry of lights, I shake my father's shoulder. "Dad?" His neck wobbles in response. *"Dad."* I shake harder, desperation clawing up my back. Lids fluttering, his head props up on a groan. Fumbling for his restraints, Tristan appears across the chair, determination darkening his gaze as he works on his other bound wrist.

"Dad? Can you hear me?"

His glossy eyes meet mine. "Lauren?"

Thank God—he knows my name.

"I'm right here, Dad." I offer a pitiful smile.

"What're you doing?" His normal tone returns, pumping blood back into my veins.

"We're gonna get you out of here, okay?"

A tight line forms between his eyebrows. "Lauren, why aren't you at school?" *I. Stop. Breathing.* "Did Loretta forget to drive you again? Damn that woman, what am I paying her for? Well, that's alright. Go get dressed, and I'll take you to work with me. How's that sound? I'll even sit you in on my meetings today, like last time. And I'll show you..."

I catch Tristan's eyes, his mouth ajar, searching for a response he clearly can't form words for.

Abandoning the restraint, I thread my fingers through my hair, pressing hard against my scalp. Nearing hyperventilation, I stumble away, looking anywhere but at my father's delusional state. Focusing on my exhales, I breathe in through my nose and out my mouth.

Blinking, I take notice of the television and the clattering visuals protruding from the pixels. More than double my height, the screen is gobsmackingly massive, taking up the entire wall, rivaling the sizes one would find at a local theater. Transfixed, I'm unable to look away.

Cocking my head, I inch closer, doubting what it is I truly see. Inside the screen, lies hundreds of others. Rectangular and void of a single sound, *people* and their random surroundings make up the space. Each screen entirely different from the next, I'm suddenly a fly on their wall, or on the street corner, or on the ceiling of a supermarket.

My gaze flickers down a particular row, a revulsive sickness standing my every hair on end, as I take in the scenes, and those unknowingly inside.

They're eating at restaurants. They're driving in their car. They're taking the subway, staring straight down into the lens. They're taking a shower. Or attending a lecture. Or sitting in a cubicle. Or cooking dinner. Or having sex with their girlfriend or boyfriend or husband or wife or some random they met up at a club with—I don't know with who, but if I took it upon my liberty, at the hands of this horrifying, god-like machine, *I would*.

My now-dry eyes crawl to the next, finding—

"Magnificent, isn't it?"

Every drop of blood drains from my veins at the sound of her lifeless voice. Whipping my head, I catch my mother standing by the door she exited through. Hands clasped at her middle, she's so still, it's like I'm staring at a fucking Sim. Eyes flickering, I meet Tristan's alert gaze, who now stands beside my father, abandoning the final restraint looping his ankle to a chair leg.

Facing her, I infuse courage into my bones, hoping it'll resonate in my tone. "Who are you?"

"Your mother."

"No, you're not. Did someone do this to you?"

"No, sweetheart. I am who I've always been."

She smiles brightly, the seemingly real joy reaching her eyes, at last revealing a sign of the woman I've grown up with. A woman who's apparently an exceptional actress. To the point where she fooled her own family, including her brother, Oscar Bass, who admitted he didn't know who reigned at the top.

Emotions caught in my throat, I change the subject, flicking my head towards the screen. "What is this?"

"Oh, Lauren." She laughs a fractured sound. "You already know the answer to that question." Angling her head, she allows the kinetic colors to paint her skin a million different shades. On a whispered sigh, she gazes up in wonder, as one might revere their god or deity or life hero in the flesh.

"This is The Oculi. The one eye."

Who sees all...

Tristan barks from across the room, "No man or woman should ever possess this type of power."

A wicked smile curves on her lips. "How rich, coming from you, who, each day, breaches the privacy of others."

"This is on a different level." From his powerful voice, I summon strength in my core, building a defiance I yearn to unleash. "I aim to better innocent lives."

She struts towards him, each step slow and deliberate, like the falling of a hammer. "And what difference is that to us? If you'd obliged to one of our *many* recruitment attempts and opened an ear to our cause, you'd know we strive for the same thing."

He folds his arms, irritation pricking across his temple. And then it's as if Diana Astor is on stage, reciting a well-rehearsed speech, filled with confident words.

"Innocents can only be helped from positions of power. That is known throughout history. Even today. People without government are like children without parents. Humans need guidance. *They need order.* But what if we could take it to the next level and reap the benefits of such leadership? That possibility isn't out of reach. Not anymore. In this modern century, we possess technology that wields opportunities our forefathers could only dream of."

Still bordering on the edge of denial, I try but fail to block out her words, which scrape their way down my brain and are too foreign on her lips. Lips that normally advocate for hope and a brighter future for the misfortunate by ways of charitable acts. Not by robbing them of control over their lives.

"Enough," Tristan hisses. "There's no benefit to such a world. Your society would only breed power-hungry dictators—*like yourself*—who prey on those citizens, leaving them with no rights. No protection."

"No protection?" She hums curiously, encircling him and my still zoned-out father. "I'll name you one of our key motivations."

Shaking his head, he says, "Go ahead. Spout your nonsense."

She smirks, mischief glimmering behind her eyes. "Imagine a world where no crime goes unseen..."

His lips part.

"...Where no criminals run rampant. Where victims always receive justice..."

They lock eyes.

"...And children don't wind up in foster care without answers, after Mommy and Daddy get left for the birds off the side of a country road."

Growling, Tristan's cheeks bubble with red-hot rage—

She twists, completely ignoring his impending outburst, instead working her way back to me. "Sweetheart," she muses, again in a fake tone. "I'm so sorry. I admit, I used him to protect the company during the investigation, but along the way, I thought I found you the perfect match. Paired you with a man who'd eventually understand our cause."

"Our cause?" I nearly laugh. "Are you out of your mind?" *Yes,* I answer that question, first and foremost. *Most definitely, yes.* "How could you possibly think I'd see as you do?"

"Because you *are* me. You're my blood, my only daughter, sharing a similar power and likeness. Everyone says so. Believe me, if not now, in due time, you'll share my perspective, too, and seek to take action."

I hate the sprinkle of truth in her words. Everyone always *has* compared me to my mother. Even I, myself, have, watching her on stage, commanding the room, soaking in their gazes like a flower does the energy of the sun. And her *eyes.* They've always been mirrors. Except, now, when I gaze upon their depths, for once in my life, I don't see myself in their reflection.

I see lies.

"You're sick," I seethe.

She only smirks. "Lauren, don't resist your birthright."

My birthright?

"Ahh, yes. Did you think the society was born yesterday? Or last year? No, you have your grandfather to thank for that."

My gut drops.

"He knew your potential, even at a young age, when you followed in his footsteps and attended law school. All but naturally, you put yourself in a position to aid our cause, at the very firm he founded, around the same time he also founded The Oculi, and let affiliated court cases and their evidence slide under the radar."

Yet another person I looked up to.

Their image—*shattered.*

"That's your future, Lauren. Helping society."

"Just like you're helping Dad?" I counter.

Her eyebrows tick upwards, donning an air of righteous innocence. "I'm helping expand that man's mind. Allowing him the opportunity to see the *correct* way."

That man.

On the cusp of a realization, sadness reduces my throat into sandpaper. "...He never went on trips, did he?"

He was never stressed.

Her smug silence says all I need to know.

"Go to hell."

She sighs. "What a shame."

"I don't see it that way."

"Not you, sweetheart. What a shame for Aurora Walker." Tristan's gasp rings across the room. "Didn't you know she has a recital tonight? Too bad she won't grace that stage, poor girl. I set my dog loose, and *my goodness*, is he hungry, having waited for so long to tear into that—"

Cutting her taunt short, my mother stares down the black barrel of a Glock, sporting a feline grin. On the other end, Tristan huffs and puffs like a madman, fingers wobbling along the trigger.

"WE'RE LEAVING. RIGHT NOW."

She only laughs, spiraling the guilt already growing in my conscience, as I'm the one who kept us here longer than necessary. And now that greed, that foolish determination, might actually land someone dead. Someone who has absolutely nothing to do with any of this.

A true innocent.

Tristan's sister.

"I wasn't planning on keeping you two here. Oh, but you'll have to leave your father, dear. Don't worry, I'll take great care of him. But... yes. What a splendid idea. Go right ahead. *I wouldn't want you to miss the show.*"

FORTY

TRISTAN

REMEMBER when I said guilt was worse than fear?

I was dead wrong.

I barrel down a backstage hallway, running solely on instinct. An instinct that's pumped lethal amounts of adrenaline through my veins the moment Aurora's name slithered past that snake's tongue. And it's only risen on our way here, boiling my skin hotter and hotter with each passing second.

Because we ran and ran and ran...

Out of that treacherous hypnotism hall, out of the Dupe data center and the Down Under, leaving with phones loaded with priceless evidence. Then I rode full throttle with Lauren strapped on me like a backpack, skipping red lights and pushing wild speeds while on the phone with Bryson, until we arrived at Columbia University's Miller Theatre. We split into three—Bryson, Lauren, and I—each with the same goal.

Finding Aurora before Jace. And getting her the hell out of here.

Dread pushes my legs harder, rendering me blind, contorting my visuals into streaky blurs. Turning a corner, I race down another hallway, zooming past startled looking girls wearing matching tutus, leaving their murmured gossip in my wake.

Dressing room, dressing room, dressing room...

Gotta find the—

THERE!

As I burst through the half-open door, gasps erupt from inside, before I meet five pairs of widened eyes and more tutus. The girls whip their heads, stopping midway through blotting powder on their cheeks or snapping strands of hair between iron clamps. Mouths ajar, their conversations die out on whispers, all taking in the wheezing man clad in a black zip-up and worn-out sneakers filling up their doorway.

My gaze scans frantically.

A mature woman carrying a clipboard folds her arms. "Sir, I'm going to have to ask you to lea—"

She's not here.

I dash off the frame, sprinting down the rest of the corridor, emotions burning my throat raw, then turn a corner into an empty hallway, and—

Ding.

Heels screeching on the floorboard, I whip out my phone.

Bryson: *Found her.*

My heart nearly escapes my ribcage, and a mountain of pressure slinks off my back like rushing water. I type up a response, hitting each letter with shaky thumbs.

Me: *W-h-e-r-e a-r-e y—*

Cold metal presses into the back of my skull.

I don't move.

I don't blink.

I don't breathe.

Even though I know who it is behind the barrel.

Jace's smooth voice breaks the silence. "Weren't we always destined to end this way?"

I will strength into my tone, satisfied when confidence seeps past my lips. "It's too late. Aurora's safe."

"For now... She'll never be far from my grasp. Don't you get that? Maybe tomorrow, I'll be her classmate. Or next month, her new online dating match. That would be fun, wouldn't it? A little wine and dine, before I—"

"I'm gonna fucking k—"

"Kill me?" His vicious laugh bounces off the walls—a reminder of the true maniac he really is—as he presses harder, digging the barrel into my scalp. "Even if the roles were reserved, if *your* finger was along the trigger, and you ended me. Right here, right now. It wouldn't change a thing. Didn't you hear? The society would replace me in a day's time. I'm disposable. *I'm no one.*"

No one...

I picture Nicholas Astor, wholly out of his mind, reduced to an obedient zombie, while under the tyranny of his own wife. It hadn't occurred to me that Jace could be the same, acting outside of his morals, every decision marked by the swift tug of a puppet master.

"You don't know what you're doing. You're—"

"Hypnotized?!" he barks, interrupting me once more, this time the barrel shaking on the waves of an even greater laughing fit. *"God!* Wow, Tristan. To tell you the truth, I'm hurt. I didn't think you took me for such a fool. No, I found a way around that *bitch* and her mind games a long time ago. Not that she knows, of course."

Hope blooms in my chest, just a sliver, that we may find some sort of common ground. "Then why listen to her?"

"Because I'm loyal to the cause."

I grit my teeth. "And that *cause* involves murdering an innocent girl?"

"Who said I'd actually go through with it?"

Shock pummels through me. "Wait, what—"

"I must confess, I've never truly taken much interest in ending your sister's life. Not when the real person who deserves to die is *Diana Astor.* If you ask me, The Oculi desperately needs new management, but that would involve cutting her out entirely, root and stem. Eradicating her entire line of succession. And I plan to do so."

My jaw drops, terror darting through my conscience, realizing who he means. Clenching my fists, I hiss, "Lauren has nothing to do with this."

He drives the metal harder, forcing my head down. "Don't be a lovesick clown. *Wake up!* It's in her blood. She'll end up exactly like Diana and her grandfather before her, drunk on power and veering the society off in all the wrong directions. And I don't plan on letting that happen—"

"You'll never lay a finger on my wife."

His snicker boils my blood. "Well, that'll be hard to prevent when you're slumped on the ground, won't it?" The pressure eases, before returning to the back of my head in brutal force, cutting my protests short.

And plunging me into the black void.

"TRISTAN?" a woman beckons, her sweet voice so familiar.

"Tristan."

There she is again. Close, yet far off on the horizon. More desperate this time. But... *why?* Haven't we been here before? Doesn't she know I'm only dreaming? A blissful dream, afforded only by the acute knowledge that, in reality, I'm right there in bed beside her, where nightmares can't possibly penetrate my mind.

Because everything's right in my world.

"Tristan!"

That is, *until I wake up...*

Eyes fluttering in a blurry haze, my surroundings sharpen. Confused, I cock my head, taking in the worry deepening every line on her beautiful face. "Lauren...?" I whisper, right as I register the pounding against the back of my skull.

"It's okay." She *shushes*, brushing a soothing hand through my hair. "Aurora's fine. We got to her in time. Bryson took her back to his place."

And then it all comes back in a flash.

Groaning, I stumble to my feet, wobbling, then catching myself against the wall. *"No,"* I croak out, the adrenaline infusing power into my veins, dulling the ache.

"Tristan, didn't you hear me? I said everything's going to be—"

A horrid cackle rattles down the empty hallway, unhinged and demented, standing every one of my hairs on end. I whip my head, catching Jace's shadow lurking around a bend, rounding to our corridor. Lauren's wide eyes catch mine, before I snatch her hand and book it down the opposite direction.

"What does he want?" Lauren huffs, fighting to keep up with my pace.

Way beyond the point of sheltering her from the truth, I practically scream, *"He wants to kill you!"*

Her features morph into terror, as we weave between ballerinas, some of whom wait by the curtain or touch up their makeup, but all shoot us looks of shock. *"Move, move!"* I shout at them, my ears picking up dreadful footfalls behind us.

Reaching the end of the maze, we burst through an exit door. My heart pounds like the clashing of symbols, and I swing my head left and right, pushing through the mental fog to decipher where we're at.

"This way!" Lauren dashes, hugging the building's perimeter. Close on her tail, we round a corner right before the door bursts open behind us, hopefully buying us some time. Reaching my bike parked off the sidewalk, we hop on, strap our helmets across our chins, and take off in record timing.

BANG! POP! POP!

Lauren's blood-curdling scream rattles my eardrums as bullets soar past our peripherals. Whipping my head for a split second, I catch Jace atop another motorcycle, right on our tail. Several more *pops* ring out, and I rev my engine, flying down the street.

I battle the terror flowing through my body, and lean in low over the handlebars, homing in on my years spent riding bikes. With skilled mastery, I thread between taxi cabs and bicycles and jaywalkers, with any and all destinations in mind, as long as they get us far away from him.

Still riding hard, I peek behind once more, catching no sight of him. When we're surely out of his range, I note Lauren's hands gripping my waist with vigor.

"Are you okay?"

"Yes." Her answer muffles through her helmet.

I loosen a weighted breath, only for his words to dominate my every thought.

The society would replace me in a day's time.

I'm disposable.

There's no denying the truth—and I didn't the moment he spoke the horrible notion. Because they *would* replace him. After seeing what we did today, discovering the vast number of members under Diana's thumb, there's no telling how many Jaces are out there. And most of them probably *are* under her spell, unwillingly willing to bend to her dubious commands—and that includes killing my sister, the only soul I have left on this earth to call family.

Except... *that's wrong.*

I have family right here, looping arms around my waist, who stuck her neck across the deadly line to save my sister. Who possesses the courage to crawl down low, to the deepest and darkest of unknown lairs, to help *her* family and society. And who trusts me, despite my many flaws.

But no matter what I choose, my family suffers.

As if he's riding right there beside me, Bryson's wisdom hits home, offering a solution. *The only solution.* That night in the bar, he told me I had one strike—and one strike only— against The Oculi. And he's right.

It has to be a knockout.

Tires screeching against the pavement, I make a sudden left and then another, heading back in the opposite direction. Revving the engine, one destination burns a hole through the back of my mind.

"Where are you going?!" Lauren muffles through her helmet.

"Pull out my phone!"

"What?!" she hollers over the wind.

"Pull out my phone and do exactly as I say!"

~

LAUREN CLUTCHES my smartphone in her grasp around my waist, readying to launch the script the moment we get into range, as we soar like lightning through the city streets.

9th Avenue...

57th Street...

Then Broadway.

POP! POP!

Fuck! More bullets dart past our heads, springing my heart into my throat. *How did he find us?!*

Swinging the handles, I squeeze between cars on a triple lane switch, narrowly avoiding a crash, as I reach the opposite bike lane on the one-way road. Lauren's scream pierces my ears again, as more *bangs* echo across New York City's night sky. Up ahead, a large crowd of pedestrians and tourists comes into view, who all gather on sidewalks and crane their heads, watching a powerful array of lights and pixels.

Almost there, almost there, almost—

Black steel comes up parallel to us, matching our speed, and when I look through the rider's dark helmet, it's like staring the angel of death in the face—who points a lethal barrel at my wife. With a choked scream, I watch his finger pull back the trigger.

Click.

Jace's eyebrows tighten through his visor.

Click-click-click.

No bullets. Air bursts through my lungs, right as those powerful lights dance across our helmets, drenching our world in a million different shades as we enter their space.

Maybe it's my need to win at everything in life—or maybe it's just the smug asshole in me, I don't know—that leads me to flip up my visor, and stare right through Jace's. But it's truly unfortunate that we're barreling down Broadway and not sitting inside some cozy coffee shop off Lafayette Street. Because, if we were, I'd have all the time to spell everything out for him, only so I could watch in glee as his face morphs into absolute horror. When he realizes the monumental back-door I possess.

And have always possessed.

But never had the evidence to use.

"NOW, LAUREN!"

The power play.

With one press of her finger, every screen in Times Square plummets into darkness...

Jace's eyes blow wide, flicking up to the buildings, before they dart back to me and uncoil with a sharp understanding, aware of the colossal hammer that's dropping atop his head, inches from crushing him and his *precious cause* into rubble.

...LIGHTS.

Lauren gasps, tightening her grip along my torso, as the screens play back our evidence. The data center. The workers. The hypnosis chambers. Her mother and father. Everything. Pedestrians stop in awe and turn their heads, some angling cameras up at the screens, as powerful audio blasts through the square, revealing Diana Astor for who she really is.

Rage marks Jace's features, and his arm juts out towards us, meaning to—

BAM!

I swerve, narrowly missing the backside of the vehicle he plowed into at full speed. Flying down Broadway, I blink, dumbfounded, questioning if the object of my terror for the past two years really just met his fate at the hands of a FedEx truck...

And then I'm laughing.

Shameless and all-consuming, the merry sounds burst out

in endless waves, shaking my entire body and stinging tears along my eyes. Lauren squeezes around me in response, and I know she's joined me in my hysteria. When we finally catch a grip, I slow and pull off on the sidewalk, right beside another crowd of gawkers.

Removing her helmet, Lauren hops off, noting people's heads pointing upwards and even the traffic that's now at a standstill.

She smirks my way. "Quite the light show."

"Oh, you know me..." Hanging my helmet off a handlebar, I sweep a hand through my hair. "Anything to impress my wife."

Her cheeks blush, before deep emotions turn her gaze glossy. Lip trembling, she springs forward, looping her arms around my middle. Sighing, my lids fall, and I melt into her touch, falling ever-so deeply in love.

"Tristan," she murmurs against my chest, "I... I..."

"I know, baby." I brush her hair, holding her tight. "I know." Breathing deep, I bury myself into her aura. Her light. And open on heavy lids to—

Oh, FUCK.

Acting only on instinct, I reach behind my back, fingers grazing the handle of my gun at the same moment Jace cocks his. With shredded clothes and a severe wobble to his walk, he raises his arm, an exact mirror to mine, and fires a terrible sound.

A sound that strikes fear into the soul.

The synchronized bang.

FORTY-ONE
LAUREN

BEEP...

Beep...

Beep...

And breathe.

"Oh my God—*oh my God, she's awake!*" a woman exclaims through the dense fog shrouding my brain, her voice muddled, as if I'm listening from the inside of a fishbowl.

"Shhh," another scolds. "Keep your voice down, Sofia."

I groan, feeling like a bus has run me over. Eyes fluttering, my vision unveils a hazy Sofia, whose face is an inch from mine. Confused, my eyebrows scrunch, shocked when my voice sounds like an old man who smokes two packs a day. "You guys shouldn't have let me drink so much."

She snickers, black hair tousling when she whips her head. "Hear that? She thinks we went out last night. I'd say she's just fine. All back to normal."

Back to normal?

Another face swings into view. When my eyesight adjusts, I catch Hannah's brown eyes full of concern. Then I hear the *beeps,* and everything comes trickling back to me, confirming that although yesterday was a nightmare, it wasn't a dream. But reality.

My mother leads The Oculi and has my father captive... She *funds* their twisted cause... They stole Astor Security's data... Aurora was in danger, being hunted by—

JACE.

Shooting up on a gasp, I take in my surroundings. Lying in bed, my feet poke out of fresh linens, clad in hospital socks with rubber grips splotched all over them. Flower bouquets stand neatly in glass vases by my bedside. And wires tread through the armholes of my white gown, attached to what feels like adhesive patches on my chest.

Hannah grabs my hand. "It's okay, it's okay—"

"Is it?!" I heave, agitating my heart monitor. *"Where's Tristan?!"*

"He's fine!" My blood pressure plummets back down to the floor, shoulders sagging in relief. "He just went out for a moment, probably to eat something. He's been by your side the whole time."

"Wow... And you guys, too...? Thank you."

"Of course, Lauren. We love you. You're like family." She offers a warm smile before her eyes blow wide. *"...But!* Family or not, you got some *major* explaining to do! When you're up to it, of course." She winks, earning a smirk from me. "I know you two had something to do with whatever catastrophe is all over World News right now. Astor Security and some secret society, and your mom's name being thrown around everywhere?! I mean, everyone in New York City is grabbing their pitchforks. What has Silicon Avenue come to —"

Her eyes flick over my shoulder, prompting me to whip

around and find Tristan standing in the doorway, still wearing his black zip-up and holding a bouquet of tulips. Motionless, he stares into my eyes, a surge of emotions cascading into his. Then he jerks his head out the doorway.

"NURSE!!! WE NEED A NURSE IN HERE!"

My friends laugh in unison, then Hannah squeezes my hand. "We're so thankful that you're okay, Lauren." She smirks at Tristan. "But we'll leave you to Mother Bear now."

On their exit, Tristan rushes over to me, tears filling his eyes. "Thank God. *Oh, thank God,*" he blubbers, cupping my jaw before pressing a gentle kiss to my forehead, then hugs me. "Lauren, I'm so sorry." His chest rumbles against my cheek. "I should've never dragged you into all of this. Should've never let you go after my sister..."

"Tristan," I mewl in his tight grasp.

"...I'm so relieved you're okay. You scared the shit out of me. Do you hurt? Are you feeling any pain?"

"Tristan..."

"...Oh, I'm sure you do. No need to talk. The nurse is coming soon. They'll take great care of you. Everything turned out fine, no big deal..."

"Tristan!"

He freezes—"Oops"—and loosens up.

I sigh, a giggle escaping me. "I'm okay, really," I say, though I question the notion immediately. *Am I okay?* Most definitely still under the aftereffects of anesthesia, I search my body, ripping off the blankets and pushing up my sleeves, discovering a thick bandage covering my right shoulder.

"The doctor said he could've pulled the bullet out without surgery, but I insisted."

Butterflies swarm in my stomach, as I weather the flush staining my cheeks. "So, I was lucky, then?"

"You could say that. Or that Jace has terrible aim."

My blood freezes over. "Is he...?"

Dead?

Dark circles form along his striking features. "Mine is much better."

The knot in my stomach loosens, only to tighten right back up. "What about my father?"

"Don't worry about him." He grabs my hand. "We did everything we could, and we succeeded. From my intel, the FBI is conducting major raids in the Down Under as we speak —using information I anonymously tipped. They'll find everything, no doubt, including the data center and your parents."

I nod, chewing on his words.

Despite my father's absence, I believe Tristan. Deep down, I know I'll see him again, and I'll do everything in my power to make sure he gets the help he needs and returns to the man he was. And as devastating as the discoveries were, just as I dealt with Oscar Bass, I'll handle Diana Astor. Because there's no denying who my mother really is and how her actions affect society.

When I'm silent, he nudges me playfully. "Come on now."

A smile tugs at my lips. "Come on, what?"

"Make some room." He lifts up the bed sheet. "I'm hopping in."

I giggle, shuffling over as his weight sinks the other side of the bed. Cozying in beside me, he wraps an arm around me and—

His body goes rigid.

"Tristan?" I study his shocked expression, then follow the path of his stare.

Standing in the doorway, Aurora dons a pleated skirt

paired with a sweater over a white-collared undershirt. Flicking her gaze between us, the vase of flowers she holds reveals a slight tremble.

"O-oh," she stammers, noting our intimacy, and swivels on her heel. "I'll come back later."

"Aurora, wait!" Tristan bounds out of bed.

Shoulders tensing, she turns back around, laughing nervously. "I-I just wanted to drop these off." She shoots me a shy smile, lifting the impressive array of wildflowers and pink peonies.

"They're beautiful." I say the first thing that comes to mind, before tension seals my lips back shut.

I haven't seen Aurora since our wedding, where we had a very brief introduction. But I know how important she is to Tristan and the weight this moment carries, given she's the only remaining member of his family who's tied to him by blood. And while, according to Tristan, their strained relationship that stemmed from childhood has since been mended, their hesitancy says there's still some lingering wounds.

"A-and to say how sorry I am, Lauren." She tucks a strand of hair behind her ear, eyes widening like a deer caught in headlights. Standing pencil-straight, her legs don't move an inch from the doorway. "I haven't the slightest clue who this Jace person is, or why he'd want to bring me any harm, but it seems you got caught in the crossfire, and Bryson won't tell me anything, and..." she trails off, meeting Tristan's stare.

Then the oddest thing happens.

Tristan folds his arms over his chest. "Don't play naive with us, Aurora." He calls her bluff in an authoritative yet somehow teasing tone. A dynamic known only to a brother and sister. "You know more than that."

Offended, her palm presses to her chest.

Tristan's eyebrow ticks upwards.

"Fine." Lips pursing, her hand juts to a now popped-out hip—a similar pose I often strike when I've had enough bull-shit. "I don't live under a rock, you know."

I catch Tristan's throat bobble.

Wow, I'll admit, that doe act had me fooled.

Tongue ticking, she breezes past Tristan, rounds my bed, and places the vase beside the others on the nightstand. "Look"—she offers me a frank expression—"I really am glad you're okay, but your family is all over the news." My mouth falls open, but I'm unable to get a word in. "And my gut tells me this Jace guy—who I truly have zero idea about—was involved." She whips her prying gaze back to Tristan. "Which means somehow you were involved, because you knew he was coming after me."

As she connects the dots, his face falls further and further.

"I'm close, aren't I?" she asks.

"Aurora..." He says her name with precious care, outstretching his palms. "I can—"

"Explain?" she finishes his thought. "That's all you ever want to do, Tristan." She takes a step towards him, splattering guilt straight across his features. "Growing up." And another. "In therapy." Until she's an inch from him. "Even now, years later."

With teary eyes, Tristan stares down at his sister. Sickness crawls up my throat, as I can hardly bear the tremor in his voice. "Isn't that what you really came here for? My explana-tion of all this?"

My heart thunders inside me, and I anticipate the drop of the hammer—Aurora tearing the heart from her brother's chest. The clock breaks through our silence, drawing out time on a slow wane.

Tick...

Tick...

Tick—

"No." Tristan perks up the same time I do, right as she jerks her chin towards me. "I thought I'd let someone else give it a shot for once."

Tristan cocks his head tentatively, observing the subtle smile she musters along her lips. "You mean..."

"I mean"—she jabs a finger into his chest—"I'm not here to demand an explanation from you, Tristan Walker. Or to show you that I'm okay..." She lets out a sigh, thick emotions wavering her next words. "I'm here to see if you're okay."

Then it's like his entire body melts. His shoulders relax. Eyes brighten. "Y-you are?"

"Yes, you big dummy." Fanning her eyes, she blinks away tears. "Now give me a hug."

Instantly, he snatches her in his grasp. Shiny long locks drape off her backside, scrunched between Tristan's arms looping around her frame. Resting his chin atop her shoulder, Tristan's face contorts with emotions, which riles a surge of my own.

"Gosh," Aurora sniffles. "You gotta make everything so emotional, don't you?"

"I know, I know," he mumbles into her hair. "I'm sorry."

"When are you going to get it through your head that I'm not mad at you? We're not kids anymore, Tristan. I know all you ever do—and always have done—is protect me. Okay? I love you. And it's going to stay that way, no matter what happens."

Oh my God. I clear my throat, blinking away my own tears as he reciprocates that love. *Keep it together, Lauren!*

Reaching for the tissue box, I stop midway, locking eyes

with Tristan. Then freeze, caught up in their depths. Because there's something different in them. A first of its kind.

That pesky guilt has thawed.

Revealing long-awaited hope.

"TRISTAN, I'm flattered, but you really didn't have to buy out the whole place for our date."

My stare sweeps across the *empty* restaurant. White tablecloths cover small, intimate tables, all flickering beneath burning candlelight, even though not a single soul sits in the chairs. On the far wall, a Michelin Star chef cooks in the see-through kitchen, presumably preparing our next course.

Floor-to-ceiling windows dominate the entire perimeter, allowing my eyes to soak in a breathtaking, one-eighty view of the city at night. Swinging my focus back in front of me, I study the most delectable sight here. And—*wink, wink*—it's *not* my perfectly cooked salmon filet.

Donning a Brioni suit, Tristan is the epitome of eye candy. Charcoal gray linen molds to his body like glue, bringing out the flecks of amber in his dark eyes. And candlelight flickers against his strong jaw and smooth lips as he takes a bite of his steak.

"I wanted you all to myself tonight." He cuts off another corner of his steak, beaming a smirk that has me thankful that I'm sitting down. "But don't worry, I only rented it out."

"Rented the most exclusive restaurant in the city?" I shake my head. "And how much did that cost you?"

He shrugs. "Not too bad."

"Oh, I'm sure," I tease, swiping a gentle touch across my collarbone. "Just like this necklace wasn't too bad?"

His gaze turns smoldering, running along every emerald looped around my neck, searing satisfaction down my middle.

Tristan's taken care of me for over a week, doting on my every need. He even kicked out his housing staff, ensuring our alone time together, and stubbornly insisted he'd do all the cooking, as I'm apparently not allowed to move an inch while healing. And, admittedly, his cooking attempts were, well, *attempts.* But I ate every overcooked chicken breast and slightly crunchy pasta with a smile, because I appreciate the genuine effort and am pleasantly surprised by this overprotective side of him. And now that I've made a full recovery, he surprised me with a dinner date, this time prepared by—in his words, not mine—"*a competent chef.*"

"Thank you for taking care of me," I say, for perhaps the twentieth time, emotions catching in my throat. "I've been doing everything on my own for so long now, it's hard for me to be vulnerable, to pass off some of that pressure."

His face softens, eyes brimming with passion, as he collects both my hands in his. "Lauren, I'd always take care of you..." Swallowing, he sweeps his thumbs across my skin, holding my eyes captive. "And always will, if you let me."

Sucking in a breath, my heart thumps more powerfully.

I note my wedding finger—his too—and the barrenness forming shadows around them. After we left the hospital, we stopped wearing our bands, agreeing that we didn't want any remaining traces of the society still between us. But that was that. We didn't lay any ground rules. We didn't ask the obvious question, the one I can't help but now ask myself.

What are we?

"Are you asking what I think you are?"

He smiles. "I'm asking whatever it is you want me to. You

don't have to agree to a real marriage. You don't have to stay moved in with me. You don't have to do anything you don't want. We can take it slow or fast or at any pace in between. But Lauren, please, if you feel the same. If you love me as I so desperately love you..." Fingers threading between mine, his voice thickens with longing.

"Just agree to be mine."

I laugh through an ugly sniffle, batting a tear seeping down my cheek. "I'm already yours." I blink furiously, holding his awestruck gaze. "I love you—and I've *been* in love with you, Tristan Walker, ever since I realized you're the only man I see in every room, even in the ones you're not."

His frame visibly melts at my words before he cranes across the table, pinches my chin between two fingers, then kisses me. And in his lips, I find perfect harmony, encased by a perfect dream. A dream where I'm certain of my future and the people who will be there.

And at the heart, is Tristan.

EPILOGUE

2 YEARS LATER

"Have I told you how ravishing you look in that dress yet?" Tristan asks from behind, his hands looping around my waist. Tugging me close, his tenor tickles my ear. "Because you do, and I got plans for you later."

A thrill shoots through me, and I drop the olive into the martini I'm making. Twisting on my six-inch heels, I face him, nearly squealing, when he places his hands on either side of the countertop, trapping me in his aura. Biting my lip, I hum, "Maybe only ten times tonight."

"Not enough, then." His fingertips trace down my back slowly, before squeezing my ass cheek, a playfulness to his tone. "At least twenty more times shall suffice."

Giggling, I lurch into his chest, the wool in his dark sweater tickling my cheek. After another round or two of teasing, he sets me free and moves to my side. Working on his own drink, he grants me a full view of my apartment—which is now triple-owned by myself, Hannah, and Sofia, and used solely for girls' nights and celebrations.

Like tonight.

Lounging on the sofas or taking pictures on the spiral staircase are the members of our small gathering. Hannah sits in Damien's lap on the third step, posing for a Polaroid, while Sterling, Damien's brother, snaps the photo with a wide grin. In the kitchen, Sofia whips a cocktail shaker with one hand, checking out one of my co-workers from across the room, who smirks back at her. All the while, Bryson and Aurora make eyes at each other on the couch, their hands intertwined.

Seeing all my friends here reminds me of how grateful I am to have such a full life. A fuller one than I could've ever imagined prior to meeting Tristan.

Wearing a content smile, I lock eyes with Hannah from across the room, and I'm suddenly taken back to the night I lay in a hospital bed, unsure of who it was I was waking up to.

The past two years have been a whirlwind—but a whirlwind of successes. Aside from the law dictating we're still legally married, Tristan and I agreed to be boyfriend and girlfriend—essentially starting over, on our own terms this time. But, although we decided to take things slow, I never moved out of his house. Initially, I thought I would, but I couldn't seem to get a suitcase out the front door without it feeling *wrong*. So, I followed my intuition and stayed, and have never once regretted the decision.

In terms of Tristan's little Times Square stunt, The Oculi have been the leading story of tech news for two years, unraveling the dark side of Silicon Avenue to the public eye. And nothing—and I mean *nothing*—has been left out...

Including the underground data center. Astor Security's investigation finding database tamperings being linked back to my mother. My mother's trial—which I stood as a witness upon the stands and was *not a part of* the prosecution team, by my own decision. Her recent imprisonment. Astor Security's found innocence. And, lastly, Tristan's more-than-willing transition of power back to my father, who regained all of his shares, his CEO title, and has made a full mental recovery from the horrid things done to him in the Down Under.

Which is the long way of saying...

Everything is perfect.

"Your *extra-dry* martini." Tristan offers me the glass, which I grab by the stem. Turning back around, I find Hannah. She snatches my wrist, eyeing Tristan.

"Mind if I steal your date?"

"Not at all." He gives me a wink, before sauntering over to Bryson and his sister, who shoots him a beaming smile.

I flick my head towards the staircase. "Have those polaroids developed?"

"Yes!" she squeals, the alcohol subtle on her breath, bringing out her bubbly side. "I'll show you." From her pocket, she reveals three films. Leaning in, I inspect the small photographs, discovering Sterling's excellent camera work, having put them dead in the center.

"Those turned out amazing." My eyes catch the glimmer shining off her finger. "Oh, wow, Hannah. I haven't had time to really look at your wedding ring from close up. It's beautiful!"

She twists the band encircled with diamonds. "Thank you. I love how it turned out."

"How does it feel to be newlyweds?"

"Amazing. I can't believe it's already been a month since the ceremony."

Sipping my martini, I squint, lacing mischief into my tone. "I bet you two have been busy."

Her mouth plops open. "Do you mean—"

"Yes." I nudge her shoulder. "Of course I mean sex." Her cheeks stain a dark red, and when she only offers a guilty grin, I ask, "So... how is it, then? How's sex now that you're married?"

"I mean..." A fit of giggles overtakes her. "It's fucking amazing!"

"It sure is..." I sigh, staring at Tristan through my lashes, over the top of my drink. While our sex life is possibly the only thing that hasn't been taking things slow between us, I want to know what it's like after a true wedding. A marriage where we have full control and can savor every moment that follows.

Eyebrows ticking, she follows the line of my gaze. "So, you'd say yes? To a real proposal?"

Now it's my turn to blush.

"Oh my God, you so would!" She bats me with her small purse. "Do you know when he's going to ask?"

"Hopefully soon," I admit.

"That'll be unbelievable." She sighs. "Then you'll be like us! Fake engaged or fake married or fake *whatever,* only to become the real deal in a few years... Maybe *every* girl needs a fake relationship."

I nearly spit out my drink.

"Anyway!" she laughs. "Enough with the soft stuff. Let's celebrate you! That *is* what tonight's all about, *Miss Youngest Senior Partner in Astor Associates HISTORY."*

"That's my girl," a male voice chimes behind us, over-hearing Hannah's excitement.

I gasp.

Whipping around, I find my father. And he's the Nicholas Astor I know him to be. Donning a meticulously tailored navy suit, his watch peeks out from his cuff, gleaming rays of refined gold. Gray streaks through his dark hair, which slicks straight back, not a single strand out of place. And his proud smirk feels like home.

"Dad!" I squeal. Like a kid again, I jump into his arms. "I didn't think you'd make it."

"Sorry I'm late, sweetie." He pats my back, and I breathe in his familiar scent. Cedarwood and subtle hints of tobacco. Pulling away, my eyes open to another surprising face.

Dressed in his signature checkered pants and polo combo, my brother winks at me. "I'm taking the blame on that one. We had to make a pit stop first." He lifts a gift bag with tissue paper craning out the top.

My heart overflows yet again. "You didn't have to." I bring him in for a warm hug, then accept the gift.

"Ohh, yes, we did. It pairs well with our congratulations." Felix grins, patting our father's shoulder like old pals, who returns his smile.

The jester is so small yet speaks profound volumes for their mended relationship. A few months ago, Felix found his way back home, bringing his new husband, Dimitri, with him, who's completely won over my father and received his wholehearted approval. Honestly, I'm unsure if that would've happened years ago. After everything went down, enduring the trials and the public scrutiny, we've had to lean on each other for support. And in a way we never imagined, we've strengthened our bond.

As a family.

"Open it," Felix urges.

I tug back the paper, earning Hannah's curious gaze. "Ohhh, you really shouldn't have."

I pull out the bottle of champagne. Which isn't just any

champagne, seeing as it's very hard to come by. Familiar gold foil encases the top, concealing the cork in an elegant wrap, all the way down to the bold label in the center. Veuve Clicquot.

"I know who will appreciate this." I laugh, nudging Hannah with my elbow. But I find her staring at the bottle with wide eyes, her mouth hanging low on its hinges. "Come on, Han. You can't be that surprised. It's my favorite."

She shoots my brother a narrow gaze. "Ahh," she teases. "I see what you're up to."

Felix chuckles, confused. "And what's that?"

"You're trying to steal my thunder!" Hannah parts us down the middle, tugging back the handle on the fridge. And out comes the exact same bottle, with a red bow tied neatly around the foil, clutched between her manicured nails as an offering.

Grabbing the second, I hold the hefty bottles, one in each hand. "Well, now I just look like an alcoholic."

Hannah rolls her lips between her teeth, eyes filled with mischief. "Only one way to fix that." She sucks in a deep breath...

Uh, oh. What's she up to now?

"EVERYONE OUT TO THE BALCONY! LAUREN'S POPPING CHAMPAGNE!"

Holy, party animal. Didn't she used to be shy?

Cheers erupt across the room, and in a flash, we all file out onto the balcony, letting the warm night air brush our skin on a slight breeze. From seventy stories up, the penthouse gives a jaw-dropping view of New York City's soaring skyscrapers and impressive lights.

Standing by the railing, while mindlessly peeling off the foil of one bottle, I take in the guests once more, who all wear grins and point cameras my way. But it's Tristan who leans against the doorframe, glowing with pride, as if he's utterly transfixed with unspeakable emotions.

Someone clears their throat. "Toast, anyone?"

Hannah immediately takes the initiative, jutting her glass high in the air. "To the baddest chick I know!"

Everyone *woos* and *dings* their glasses with excitement, especially Sofia, who practically screams at the top of her lungs. I roll my eyes on a laugh, and shake the bottle with vigor, before popping the cork and letting fizzy bubbles rain over the side of the railing. When nearly half the contents dissipate, I twist on my heel, and find Tristan a hair's breadth from me.

Looping his arms around my waist, his lips crash to mine in a passionate kiss. Applause and whistles dart across the balcony and grow in strength when he leans me backwards for a dip. Swinging up, our lips unclasp gently. My heart thrums to the softness in his features, the adoration evident in his stare. Brushing a hand down my arm, he murmurs, "I hope you forgive me for stealing your moment."

Breathless, my chest lifts and falls. "If stealing my moment involves that much tongue, feel free to do it more often."

He sweeps a loose bang from my forehead, his touch tender. "No, baby. Not that. It's just..." He sinks a hand into his pocket. "There's no place better to do this than surrounded by family."

"Do what?"

He drops to one knee, prompting my gasp.

"Ask you to marry me."

My whole world stills.

A hush falls over our friends and family, with many holding hands to their mouths. Swept away by wonder, I stare into Tristan's eyes, which are a canvas of emotions. Anticipation dances in them, reflecting a mixture of excitement and nervousness—a nervousness he shouldn't sweat. Because the moment I've waited two long years for is finally here, with the only man in my life I'd want to see down on one knee before me.

"Lauren Astor." My name on his lips is pure heaven. "Will you allow me the most incredible privilege of marrying you?"

Opening the small velvet box, Tristan steals my breath away, unveiling what's surely the largest wedding ring I've seen with my two eyes. A myriad of flawless diamonds encircle the platinum band, dancing with radiance in countless directions. Nestled at the center sits a stunning, pear-cut rock in timeless elegance. And yet, the true crowning jewel?

It glimmers with the promise of forever.

With tender care, I gently cup his jaw in both hands, reciprocating the adoration marking his features. Crouching, I bypass the ring for something even more enticing—his mouth. And the moment our lips make contact, his breath hitches, sensing my answer before I mumble it between our tongues.

"Yes."

"You know this isn't our honeymoon," I tease.

"No, but I couldn't possibly wait a whole year to see you in *that* bikini on *this* beach."

Hand-in-hand, Tristan and I walk down the sandy shores of Crete, Greece—the exact beach we supposedly came to on our honeymoon. Or, at least, that's what the powers of technology led ByteBuzz and every other gossip site to believe.

Pushing my sunglasses higher up the bridge of my nose, I let my eyes crawl across Tristan's body with zero shame. Clad in only board shorts, his muscles flex with each step. Intricate tattoos paint his arms and chest, leaving room for the star of the show—his tan washboard abs.

Toes curling in the white sand, I shoot him a playful look. "Such an impatient man, aren't you?"

"With you, I am."

His smoldering gaze meets mine through our lenses, before it drags down the length of my body, even more blatant than I did, leaving my skin hot beneath my scanty red bikini. Rounding the perimeter of a sea cliff, we discover a section of beach without a single soul.

"I must say..." He drapes his arm around my center, resting a possessive hand on my hip, right above my risqué thong bottoms. "Artificial intelligence didn't do you justice."

Pursing my lips, I roll my eyes, infusing sarcasm into my tone. "Wooowww, what an amazing compliment. Can't say I've received that one before."

He pinches my skin, earning a yelp.

I giggle with a squeal. "No, really! It's sooo unique!"

"You enjoy teasing me, do you?" he growls into my ear, pinching again.

When I only laugh, he sweeps me off my feet, bounding straight for the ocean. "Tristan!" I gasp, squirming in his grasp, as he clomps into the water. "My hair—*Tristan!*" He stops, the warm surface tickling the bottom of my ass, as he's halfway in himself. Sucking in a sharp breath, I anticipate his release.

"Say you're sorry."

My jaw unclasps...

"I'm all ears, baby." His grin is smug.

Stubbornness has my eyes narrowing. *"Tri—"*

He drops me in.

"Tristan!" I squeal, partially submerged, before standing back up on my tippy toes.

He laughs, and it's all it takes for me to smack the water his way, spraying him in the face, soaking his sunglasses in streaks. Gasping, he fights back, reaching the top of my hair, which is now totally drenched. Then he snatches my wrists, tugging me close into his chest.

"You're gonna get it later, Lauren."

His suggestive undertones send blood racing between my legs. Craning my head back to look up at him, I bite my lip, feeling my nipples pebble beneath the thin fabric. Wandering downward, his gaze darkens when he catches the evidence of my arousal.

Groaning, he says, "But these can't wait."

Pointing his back to the shore, shielding me from the beach that's already empty, he pinches both nipples. Rolling them between his digits, he frees a moan from my lips, then brushes the fabric aside, exposing both breasts. Excitement courses through my veins as I scan the beach from the corners of my eyes.

He grabs fistfuls of my ass cheeks, then lifts. "No one's going to see, baby." Suspended halfway out of the water, my legs naturally wrap around his strong waist, ankles locking at his lower back. His ravenous gaze flickers across my bare skin—"So fucking perfect"—before he sucks a nipple between his lips.

Pleasure ricochets through me, forcing a whispered cry from my lungs. His groan rumbles against my skin as he takes more of me into his mouth. When his teeth scrape against my sensitive bud, and he sucks harder, my hands shoot to the back of his scalp, fingers threading through his wet locks.

"Fuckkk," he growls, and switches to the other, grabbing the backside of my neck while supporting my entire weight onto his arm. When he flicks my nipple between his teeth, sparking an intense pleasure, need blooms between my legs. Stifling a moan, I rock my hips into him, eyes fluttering.

I gasp, peeking over his shoulder, catching a tourist rounding the cliffside.

"Someone's coming," I hiss.

He frees my nipple with a *pop* and instantly drops me back down, shielding my torso beneath the water. In a rush, I fix my bikini with an anxious giggle. But all those nerves fizzle into the water when I catch him staring down at me, his eyes filled with lust but also a burning passion.

Cupping his jaw, I kiss him deeply, uncaring of who might see, earning a satisfied groan from him. Sweeping my tongue, I lose myself between his lips, lose myself *in him,* until time expands and then wanes into a bead of sand off the shore. So slow, the moon might overtake the sun, and I wouldn't have known...

Until our lips pull apart.

And all I see is him.

"Is this why you proposed?" I tease. "So you can dump me in crystal-blue water and have your way with me in front of the locals?"

His smirk only brightens the fire in his eyes. "No, baby. I proposed because..."

He scores another timeless peck.

"I can't live, let alone breathe, without you."

THANK YOU!

If you enjoyed *Power Play*, I'd be grateful if you supported me by leaving a review on Amazon or Goodreads. As an indie author, every review, however short, helps tremendously.

❧

Need more Lauren & Tristan?
Read their FREE sexy bonus scene by typing the following URL into your browser:

https://BookHip.com/FLNLNSV

(Spoiler: It's titled "Just an Apron")

THE KNIGHTLY SHOP

Want a signed paperback for your shelf or book plate for the
book in your hands?

Go to alexisknightly.com/shop

KEEP IN TOUCH WITH ALEXIS

Readers' Group: facebook.com/groups/knightlyreaders
Newsletter: alexisknightly.com/newsletter
Website: alexisknightly.com
TikTok: tiktok.com/@authoralexisknightly
Instagram: instagram.com/authoralexisknightly
Goodreads: goodreads.com/alexisknightly
BookBub: bookbub.com/profile/alexis-knightly

Join my private Knightly Readers' Facebook Group for writing updates, exclusive giveaways and more by scanning the QR code below!

ABOUT THE AUTHOR

Alexis Knightly is an author who writes romance with angst, family drama and a heavy dose of spice. Heroes in her stories are possessive and obsessive, have filthy mouths and know exactly who they want. Happily-ever-afters are guaranteed, but not before banter ensues and flaws are conquered.

A true lover of rain, she resides in Washington State with her family, two spoiled cats and beloved boyfriend. When she's not writing, she can be found doing yoga, binging Grey's Anatomy, trying her hardest to become a runner, or painting with a glass (or three) of wine.

Printed in Great Britain
by Amazon

44981340R00219